Also by Rebecca Zanetti

The Dark Protector series
Fated
Claimed
Tempted
Hunted
Consumed
Provoked
Twisted
Shadowed
Tamed
Marked
Talen
Vampire's Faith
Demon's Mercy
Alpha's Promise
Hero's Haven
Guardian's Grace
Rebel's Karma
Immortal's Honor
Garrett's Destiny

The Realm Enforcers series
Wicked Ride
Wicked Edge
Wicked Burn
Wicked Kiss
Wicked Bite

The Scorpius Syndrome series
Scorpius Rising
Mercury Striking
Shadow Falling
Justice Ascending

The Deep Ops series

Hidden

Taken (e-novella)

Fallen

Shaken (e-novella)

Broken

Driven

Laurel Snow Thrillers

You Can Run

You Can Hide

UNFORGIVEN

Rebecca Zanetti

LYRICAL PRESS
Kensington Publishing Corp.
www.kensingtonbooks.com

LYRICAL PRESS BOOKS are published by

Kensington Publishing Corp.
119 West 40th Street
New York, NY 10018

All Kensington titles, imprints, and distributed lines are available at special quantity discounts for bulk purchases for sales promotion, premiums, fund-raising, educational, or institutional use.

Special book excerpts or customized printings can also be created to fit specific needs. For details, write or phone the office of the Kensington Sales Manager: Kensington Publishing Corp., 119 West 40th Street, New York, NY 10018. Attn. Sales Department. Phone: 1-800-221-2647.

First Electronic Edition: June 2022
ISBN: 978-1-5161-1125-1 (ebook)

First Print Edition: June 2022
ISBN: 978-1-5161-1126-8

Printed in the United States of America

This one is for Chicks with Sticks, my golfing team. For Debbie, Jessica, Desiree, and Marianne. We've been friends for many years, and I'm thankful for each one of you. Getting fourth place during last winter's league was awesome—and yes, there were four teams. Go Chicks!

Acknowledgments

Thank you to everyone who has been reading and liking the Deep Ops series because I get to keep on writing it! I have many people to thank for getting this book to readers, and I sincerely apologize to anyone I've forgotten. In addition, after 70 books, I've run out of nice adjectives to describe everyone I need to thank, so I've moved on to just thanking people. You're all awesome, hardworking, amazing, and wonderful.

A HUGE thank you to Tony Zanetti for being the best husband in the world, and thank yous to Gabe and Karlina for being such awesome kids. Being your mom is my biggest blessing.

Thank you to Jim Dorohovich, who came up with the perfect name for this series as well as how to improve on a Moscow Mule.

Thank you to my wonderful agent, Caitlin Blasdell, and to Liza Dawson and the entire Dawson group, who work so very hard for me.

Thank you to my hardworking editor, Alicia Condon.

Thank you to the rest of the Kensington gang: Alexandra Nicolajsen, Steven Zacharius, Adam Zacharius, Ross Plotkin, Arthur Maisel, Vida Engstrand, Jane Nutter, Lauren Vasallo, Lauren Jernigan, Kimberly Richardson, and Rebecca Cremonese.

Thank you to Anissa Beatty for the absolutely fantastic work as my virtual assistant and especially with my street team, Rebecca's Rebels.

Thanks also to my constant support system: Gail and Jim English, Debbie and Travis Smith, Stephanie and Don West, Jessica and Jonah Namson, Kathy and Herb Zanetti, Chelli and Jason Younker, Jillian and Benji Stein, and Liz and Steve Berry.

Chapter One

The desk light barely kept the darkness from pushing inside the windows, its shadows slinking to the edges of the office. Gemma Falls finished neatly filling in her calendar while chills skittered down her back. The chills were a part of her. She'd learned to accept them instead of fighting each cold finger. They always won.

Sitting at her maple desk, her gaze lifted from the computer screen to the closed office door, which was locked. Just one lock, though. Would it seem odd to her new colleagues if she added three more locks as well as a security chain? Probably.

She hunched closer to the screen and prevented herself from turning on the main light in the office. Her screen was good enough for now.

The winter storm grew stronger outside, scattering ice against the windows. She looked out, noting the icicles barely visible around her second-story window. Tree branches scraped the brick building, their tendrils making an eerie noise against the window. Rising, she stepped around the box of discarded holiday decorations her friend hadn't had time to put away and walked to the window, looking outside.

Her office faced an interior courtyard surrounded by brick buildings. Snow and ice covered the picnic tables and benches, and no footsteps were visible, because the university had been closed for the holiday season. The new semester started the next day, and the cold of January wasn't letting up any.

The darkness of night failed to offer any comfort, so she studied the small office. Serena had left her books and supplies on the shelves, although she'd taken her personal belongings. Gemma's things would take less than ten minutes to unpack. All stuff she'd picked up the last few years that looked personal but didn't give a clue as to her life. Souvenirs from places she'd only passed through, as well as a couple of photographs of her with people she didn't know. Pictures she'd snapped at public places that looked as if she was in a group having a great time.

She didn't even know the names of the people in those pictures.

It was all right. She was smart and she was careful. A mantra she'd learned to repeat to herself nearly every day, hoping the words dug deep and took root. There was too much to lose, and it was her job, her duty, to make sure she stayed smart and careful. Her stomach growled from missing dinner and probably lunch. For now, she had to get ready for this life. Her new one. She returned to the desk to finish the syllabi she'd need to hand out during her two Monday classes the next day.

She'd never taught before.

What if she failed at teaching a subject she barely remembered? She sat back and forced her shoulders to relax. This was just another persona, and she could do it. It helped to pretend she was somebody else, so she imagined she'd been teaching college for years and this was merely another semester. By the time she became accustomed to the schedule, she'd be gone. At least she'd have some money in her pocket when she left. Times had been tough the last six months, and the odd jobs she'd managed to pick up hadn't given her much comfort.

A sharp rap on the door had her biting back a scream. Her heart thundered into motion and her breath seized.

The tree branches scraped an ominous warning against the window as the wind increased in strength.

Slowly, she drew a snub-nosed .35 from the top drawer to set at the back of her waist beneath her blue cardigan. She'd obtained the gun illegally, so there was no record of her owning it. Swallowing, glancing uneasily beneath the desk, she rose and walked around it, past two student chairs and boxes she had yet to unpack. She reached the door. Asking who was there would seem weird because she wasn't at home.

So she unlocked the door and opened it, her body on full alert and ready to go for the gun.

"Hi. Saw your light." A man stood in the darkened hallway, only the night lights illuminating the long spans of faculty offices. He stood slightly back as if giving her room, his voice soft in the evening and his British accent unmistakable. "I'm Jethro." He held out a large hand.

She swallowed and accepted it, shaking quickly and releasing him. Good. He was a person who was supposed to be in the building, and that fact lowered her blood pressure immediately. He wore casual jeans and a

T-shirt beneath a battered, brown leather jacket. "Gemma. Gemma Falls." The name rolled easily from her tongue after a month of practice. "Jethro Hanson?" He was even better-looking than her friend had said.

"Yes." His smile would appear charming to most. He stood well over six feet tall, with dark blond hair, deep blue eyes, and a bone structure sharp enough to have been cut with a chisel. His accent was full-on British, his backpack professoresque, and his body muscled, no doubt from too much time in a gym. His shoulders were too wide for a professor's, and his torso tapered down to muscular legs in jeans. As he took her in, from head to toe, a lock of his thick hair fell over his brow to add a hint of boyish charm that almost softened the utterly male sexuality he wore so naturally.

"I see," she whispered, caught up in his scent for the briefest of moments.

If he noticed her confusion or reaction to him, he didn't let it show. The guy was probably accustomed to it. Instead, his smile deepened, showing a dimple in his left cheek. As if the rest of him wasn't enough, he had a freaking dimple. "Serena asked me to show you around DC University, but I didn't expect to see you until tomorrow morning. Not many people work Sunday nights around here."

She locked her knees in place and looked up, way up, to meet his gaze. So this was the guy who'd stolen Serena's office last year. They'd buried the hatchet and had become friends, according to her. Only friends, though. Perhaps he didn't steal the breath of every woman in his vicinity. Just Gemma's. Maybe her blood sugar was too low. "I wanted to get organized before class tomorrow."

One of his eyebrows rose. "This substitution is very last minute. Do you know where Serena is? Her email said she took a temporary research job and had already found somebody to take her classes. It's not like her to be rushed about things."

Gemma straightened her shoulders. Rushed? Not likely. She and Serena had arranged this a month ago, but to make their plan work, Serena had waited until the last second to tell DC University, so there was no choice but to hire Gemma. "It seemed like a good opportunity for her, and I'll only be here a semester, so everything will work out. Serena will be back in June, I believe." Gemma needed the money, but she could only afford to stay in one place for a few months. She barely kept from tugging on her blondish-white wig to make sure it remained in place.

"Serena isn't the impulsive type, so I'm concerned about her." Jethro took another step back, his gaze piercing. "Her email came from her university account, and I don't know how to reach her at the new place of employment. Do you have her contact information?"

"No," Gemma lied. "I'm sorry. She said she accepted a government contract with some sort of top-level clearance, and that's all the information she could divulge." It was close to the truth, and the explanation made sense, considering Serena was a genius in about every quantum field there was. "I'm sure she'll be in touch when she can be."

He just studied her. This close, he smelled like expensive cologne. The good kind that was outdoorsy and masculine. "Then I suppose it's fortunate you were available to substitute for her this semester, and on such late notice."

"Sometimes things work out. I was between jobs and more than happy to help out," Gemma said, trying not to squirm beneath his regard. She had the oddest feeling he didn't like what he saw. That was good. She didn't have time to make friends, and the more people who left her alone, the better. Safety was all that mattered.

"I see. How do you know Serena?" he asked, his body language casual and relaxed. Even so, a tension came from him, one that sped up her breath.

"How does anybody know anybody?" she asked. "Serena and I go way back." It was the truth. They'd met as undergraduates in college, and they'd gone their separate ways to earn their graduate degrees. Gemma had followed the wrong path, without question.

If he caught her avoidance of the question, he didn't let on. With a smooth motion, he shifted the heavy-looking pack from one muscled shoulder to the other. "That's good. We'll miss Serena this semester, but it's nice to have new blood around. How about I meet you early tomorrow, say around seven, and show you the campus?" he asked, his tone polite.

She forced a smile. "That's kind of you, but I've already explored and know my way around. Thank you, though." She kept her tone pleasant but dismissive.

His chin lifted slightly. Barely enough to be observed, but she'd learned the hard way to notice signs of irritation in a man. His intelligent gaze pinned her, and for a second, she felt trapped and breathless. Not scared. Then his gaze relented. "I see. Very well. If you require any assistance, please call on me, *Ms*. Falls."

Had he emphasized the title? Heat started to filter through her face, but she shoved down emotion. She barely kept from defending herself, pointing out she had earned a master's degree in statistics with an emphasis in game theory. She didn't have a doctorate. Most professors at the elite university held doctorates, and apparently this one was a snob about it. Fine. That was good. She didn't want to join their titled ranks. The real world would crush a guy like this—one who'd no doubt lived his life inside the cocoon of academia.

She glanced at her watch. Pointedly.

"It's fairly dark outside and the storm is getting worse. Would you like me to walk you to your car?" he asked, all warmth gone.

"No. I have another hour or so of work to do here," she said, taking a step back. She'd parked beneath a light pole as close to the building as possible, making sure she'd have a clear line of sight from the front door to her clunky car. "Good night." Without waiting for his response, she shut the door. Her head ringing, she placed her right hand on the heavy wood and then leaned in, ear to door, listening for his retreating footsteps. Once the sound dissipated, she quietly engaged the lock.

Deep breath. Take a deep breath. She did so several times before turning back to her work, quietly edging around the sharp corners to sit in the ergonomically correct chair, then pushing back to look beneath the desk.

Trudy remained curled up on the large pillow beneath her worn green blankie with the elephants on it, her three-year-old body lax in sleep, her face peaceful. Her curly brown hair had escaped its twin ponytails, and her pink lips were pursed as she dreamed, hopefully of ponies and kittens.

A burst of love pulsed around Gemma's heart a second before the edge of fear crept in. "We're safe, baby," she whispered.

For now.

Chapter Two

"You're lucky you're so cute," Jethro said to the mutt as they walked along the wide hallway through throngs of students, many of whom stopped to pet the dog.

Roscoe panted happily, butting up against a tall, leggy blonde.

The teenager dropped to her haunches and dug both hands through the dog's fur, scratching his ears. "He's so sweet. What's his name?"

"Roscoe," Jethro said. "I have to bring him to work with me on Mondays because it's my longest day, and I don't trust the bloke at my flat alone for that long." Somehow, no matter what Jethro did, the dog found any alcohol on the premises and created a disaster. He needed to store his wine collection somewhere else.

The young woman stood, shoving her backpack over her shoulder. "You must be Dr. Hanson."

"I must be," Jethro agreed, giving Roscoe a look. They only had an hour for lunch, and the dog had already wasted too much time trying to get attention from pretty ladies. They'd both spent the night over with a lady friend they'd met at the dog park, and Roscoe had gotten plenty of love that morning from the stunning brunette—one Jethro would probably never see again.

"I've heard about you and your accent." The student rocked back on thick snow boots. "I'm Laura Jenkins, and I'll see you tomorrow in your Intro to Philosophy class."

Ah. A freshman or sophomore. Jethro smiled and unobtrusively shoved his fingers beneath Roscoe's collar to tug him along. "I'll see you in class, Laura. It's nice to have met you." He kept his grip strong enough that

Roscoe finally moved into action next to him, winding through students trying to find their classes on the first day.

Roscoe barked and yanked free, skidding through a classroom door and right into Gemma Falls as she tried to exit.

The woman yelped and backed away, dropping several file folders. Papers slid out, cascading to the ground and landing on Jethro's boots.

He sighed and leaned down to clean up the mess. "I'm sorry, Ms. Falls. He's an idiot."

Roscoe sat, wagging his tail and displacing more papers.

She eyed the dog and gingerly reached out, patting him awkwardly on the head. "You bring your dog to work?"

"I'm just dog sitting for a friend and couldn't leave the mutt home alone all day." Jethro straightened and handed over the papers and file folders.

"Oh. Well." She accepted them and regained her composure quickly. In full daylight she was even more beautiful than she'd been the night before, but just as glacier-cold. White-blond hair bluntly cut at her shoulders, pale skin, and brown eyes that were almost flat. No emotion anywhere near her.

He backed up a step and wanted to tell Roscoe to forget it. There was no warmth in that woman. Unfortunately he was more than acquainted with her type. All she was missing was diamonds at her ears and strands of pearls at her throat, and she'd be a dead ringer for his late mum. May the devil have her.

The dog was too dumb to notice and edged toward Ms. Falls, lifting her hand with his nose.

"Sorry." Jethro pulled him back by the collar before she could freak out. Or freeze the animal with a death glare or something. He should be polite, considering Serena had asked him to look out for the ice queen. "How was your first class?"

"I believe it went well," Ms. Falls said, brushing past Roscoe. "I was headed for my second class, which lasts two hours. I guess my lunch will be at one."

"This is my lunch hour," Jethro said, glaring at the dog. He liked to eat early and always set his lunchtime for eleven in the morning.

As she turned, he noticed she was wearing a drab gray suit with green heels. It was a little too big for her frame, which was a trick his mother had often used as well. Neither woman needed to look smaller than she was—both were petite. Too petite and too thin. The shirt underneath Ms. Fall's jacket appeared to be a plain white shell.

No jewelry, though.

Maybe she hadn't unpacked it yet.

She glanced at the dog. "Serena didn't tell me what you teach. Just that you were here and I could call you if I needed help."

This was a woman who never needed help. Or if she did, she certainly wouldn't ask for it from him. That much he already knew. "I teach philosophy, with an emphasis on ethics, mortal theory, rational choice, game, and decision theories."

She blinked. Just one lift of those too-long eyelashes that were too dark for her coloring. They were probably fake. "Trying to figure out the meaning of life?"

"No," he said, tightening his hold on Roscoe as a group of happily chattering sophomores wandered by. "I'm trying to figure out why there is evil and what we can do about it, if anything."

Her surprisingly full lips twitched and she seemed to stare through him. Beyond him. "You believe in evil? That it's a force of its own?"

"Yes," he said, wondering what she'd look like with that hair all mussed and her skin flushed. "I believe evil is inside all of us, and I think it grows. Or can grow." He hadn't figured out how to end it, or even how to live with it. Not yet. "I take it you don't believe?"

Her gaze landed squarely on his. "I believe. Evil exists and it never stops coming, does it? No matter what we do." She seemed to shake herself and then tucked her file folders more securely beneath her arm. "Have a nice day, Dr. Hanson." She turned on a green heel, wobbled just slightly, and then continued down the hallway.

He watched her go, trying rather hard not to notice that her butt was cupped perfectly by the gray skirt. So only the top was too big.

Roscoe whined.

Jethro looked down at him. "Not for you, pal. She'd freeze your ears off." Hell. The woman was so cold and vain, she could barely walk in those shoes. They were probably three sizes too small for her.

He remembered his mother using a thick wedge to get her feet into shoes that pinched. He also remembered how fast she was with a backhand to the face. "Let's go, Roscoe. I need time with innocence now for sure."

* * * *

"There you are," Sofia Gomez said, throwing a stuffed cotton block at his head.

"Sorry I'm late. It's the dog's fault." Jethro caught the block and tossed it over his shoulder toward the reading corner, which was beyond the secured gate that kept the little people from wandering out. He leaned down and opened the gate, letting Roscoe inside the cheerful area with colorful mats on the floor and instructional signs on the walls, including a new one with bright A, B, and Cs. A wide window at the far end showed a swing set covered in snow outside.

Sofia sighed, the many lines in her cheerful face softening when she looked at Roscoe. For the first day of the semester, the head of the day care had worn a hand-knitted green sweater and dark jeans, along with what looked like new snow boots. “He is a cutie.”

“So are you,” Jethro said, inhaling the scent of cookies. “Why don’t you just give in and marry me?”

“Oh, you,” she said, waving her hand in the air, her arthritic fingers looking swollen. “Forgetting the fact that you’re thirty years too young for me, I’d hate to ruin all other women for you. Before I forget, swing by after work for the popcorn you ordered before the holidays. We made enough in that fundraiser to keep the women’s shelter running for half a year.” She turned and bustled her ample form past the hooks by the doorway to her office, her gray hair up in a tight bun. “I’ll just need ten minutes to eat my salad. Try not to get into trouble.”

A rustle of sound had Jethro turning just in time for a miniature attacking midfielder to smash into his legs, coming from the hallway to the east.

“Jet!” the boy said, wrapping both hands around Jethro’s legs. “You’re back! I’m back, too. We’re back!”

Jethro lifted the kid by the hips, spinning him over. His dad taught in the English department. “It’s good to see you, Pete. How was your Christmas?” He set the boy down on his feet so he could pet Roscoe.

“Awesome,” the four year old said, rubbing Roscoe’s ear. “I gots a train from Santa. A real one that lights up.” He looked up, showing a gap in his front teeth that hadn’t been there before. “And I gots five dollars from the tooth fairy.” He held out his small hand for a knuckle bump.

Jethro bumped knuckles and let the moment expand inside him, hopefully banishing some of the darkness that would never let go. “Where is everyone?” The day care, which was just for university staff and faculty, usually had twenty kids a day.

“Snack time,” Pete said simply. “I ate fast.”

“Pete. I told you not to leave the main group.” A fortysomething woman with glitter in her hair and paint on her jeans bustled down the hall, stopping when she caught sight of Jethro. “Oh, good. Hi, Jet. Glad you’re back for another semester.” Barb grinned at Roscoe. “You’re on dog duty again.”

"Yeah," he said, eyeing a new urchin tripping along behind her with a green blanket clutched in her small hands. "Angus and Nari are visiting her family and they flew, so I'm dog sitting." Part of him figured Nari had left Roscoe on purpose because she thought he was lonely, but he couldn't prove it. "Who's your little friend?"

Barb turned and drew the cutie forward. "This is Trudy. She's new."

Trudy tripped over the edge of the blanket, her blue eyes wide as she stared at the dog. "Doggy."

Roscoe immediately recognized a new ally, one who might have a cookie stuck in her other hand, and moved toward her in quiet dog mode, not making any sudden movements. Reaching the toddler, he sat and, swear to the saints, he smiled.

The girl dropped the blanket and reached for his face.

"Whoa." Jethro moved to crouch next to her, setting a hand on Roscoe's head. "I'm Jethro and this is Roscoe."

The girl grinned.

Man, she was adorable, with curly, very messy brown hair, clear blue eyes, and delicate bone structure. "Cute doggy."

"He is cute and he is nice, but you want to always be careful not to put your face right in a dog's face. Okay? Big teeth," Jethro said.

As if on cue, Roscoe yawned, showing his sharp canines.

Trudy's eyes widened. "Big teeth." Then she smiled again and patted Roscoe's nose.

Movement sounded behind Barb and she stepped out of the way. "Incoming."

Jethro partially turned to take the hit of several toddlers ramming him head-on with happy cries of his name. He fell over and then rolled around, gently wrestling and letting the kids use him as a jungle gym. Little Trudy, the only new addition for the semester, seemed content to pet Roscoe while the rest of the kids ganged up on him.

Barb let them play for about five minutes before declaring it was story time and everyone should head for the corner. The kids reluctantly wandered away, and Jet stood, brushing glue from his jeans. His phone rang, and he tugged it from his pocket, his body going still when he saw the private number. He waved to Barb and the kids, motioning for Roscoe to follow him as he headed for the door. He answered once outside in the falling snow. "This is a surprise." Usually his former commander called on Sunday if he wanted to chat.

"We have a problem," Cecil said without preamble.

Jethro looked up at the swollen clouds that had become relentless in their release of fat snowflakes. The brutally cold air burned his face and he tucked his free hand in his pocket to ward off the cold. "Define problem." He turned down the shoveled sidewalk to make his way back to his office, letting the snow melt on his head and face while the devastating wind tried to kill him.

"Belmarsh prisoner number 2342352 escaped from a transport taking him for questioning three days ago," Cecil said.

Jethro stopped moving and Roscoe bumped into the back of his leg. "You're jesting."

"No."

"Why the bloody hell didn't you call me the second he escaped?" Jethro snapped, turning to look at the wide parking lot next to him where the cars were already covered in white powder. The wind blew more snow around, shooting a chill through his entire body.

Cecil cleared his throat. "You're not with MI6 any longer, friend."

"Bullshit," Jethro said. "Where is he now? Have you tracked him?" It had taken Jethro six months to hunt down the bastard and put him away, and now he'd gotten loose four years later. Jethro was going to hell for that mission alone.

"We've partially tracked him, and he's across the pond, Jet. He's in your neck of the woods. Which means..."

Jethro sought threats in the surrounding trees, seeing only clumps of ice. He'd known. From day one of putting Fletcher away, Jet had known they'd meet up again. "He's coming for me."

Chapter Three

Gemma finished tucking her file folders into her borrowed black leather satchel and then reached for her thick, borrowed coat as a knock sounded on her open door. She looked up and smiled. "Mrs. Franks. Hello." The administrative assistant had been more than helpful in getting Gemma squared away for the semester under short notice.

"Hi, and I told you to call me Louise." In her mid-fifties, Louise wore cherry-red cat's-eye glasses. "How was your first day?"

"Enjoyable," Gemma said, pulling on the heavy coat she'd found in the back of Serena's closet. "The students are a smart bunch."

Louise nodded. "That's good. I wanted to catch you before you left because the selfie picture you sent for the faculty website was too blurry." She drew a phone from the pocket of her thick green skirt. "Let me take another one."

Panic spasmed down Gemma's esophagus, but she remained in place and forced a smile. "Oh, not now. I look terrible after a long day."

"You're lovely," Louise argued, lifting the phone and squinting at the face. "I'm good at this. Trust me."

"Wait." Gemma set down her bag and pulled out a set of wire-rimmed glasses. "Let me at least look like a professor." She zipped the coat to add bulk and then pulled on the glasses, which were clear glass because her eyesight was 20/20. Then she moved to the window, which would light her from behind and partially shroud her features.

Louise shook her head. "The light is wrong there. At least move in front of the bookshelf."

Was there anything on the bookshelf that would identify her? "Sure," Gemma said easily, moving toward the shelf and staying at the edge, where the light coming in from the snowy day would still cast a shadow.

Louise clicked several shots. "Those glasses are way too big for your face."

"I like them," Gemma said. Of course they were too big for her face—that was the best way to disguise her features short of wearing a mask. "I'd prefer not to have my picture on the Internet."

"Sorry." Louise put the phone in her pocket. "It's university policy—we like for the students to see their professors." She winked. "Besides, you're so pretty, I figured you'd want your picture out there. We like to link to social media pages, but I can't find any for you. Am I looking in the wrong places?"

Gemma forced a laugh. "No. I think social media has destroyed our society and refuse to take part."

"You're not wrong, and it's smart not to have things out there that can damage your reputation. I totally agree." Louise nodded. "Also, your bio hasn't updated on your faculty page yet. You have your degrees listed but no institutions or work experience."

"That's odd. I updated those. I'll take a look tomorrow." How long could she hold off on that? Gemma clasped her bag, needing to see her baby. She'd spent her late lunch with Trudy and met the other kids, and now she wanted to go home—to Serena's home anyway—and snuggle down and read a story. She'd worry about the picture on the Internet later. Hopefully Louise wasn't a very good photographer. "I'll see you tomorrow."

"You bet." Louise hustled away.

Gemma locked her door and scrunched her feet in Serena's old boots, wishing they were a size bigger. But she'd been lucky to find them in the back of a closet, and her friend had told her she could borrow anything she wanted while staying in Serena's eclectic home. Gemma pulled a yellow knit hat out of the satchel and plunked it on her head, making sure not to dislodge her wig. She needed to find gloves. Steeling her shoulders, she walked down the long hallway to the exit, taking one last breath of heated air before opening it.

Her steps quickened as she strode outside and down the salt-covered but still icy steps. Cold instantly assaulted her bare skin. Perhaps Serena had a couple of scarves somewhere. Gemma hunched her shoulders, tucked her hands in her pockets, and walked around several brick buildings to the day care, noting that the snow had increased in force. January in DC seemed colder than she'd expected.

She hurried inside the day care and warmth welcomed her chilly body. Trudy looked up from her seat on a bright orange pillow in the reading corner, her trusty blanket over her lap.

A myriad of kids occupied different areas of the large room with a couple of girls playing dress-up by the window.

"Mama!" Trudy gurgled, happily standing and yanking up her blanket.

Warmth and love flooded through Gemma. "Hi, baby."

Barb, a lovely woman with glitter in her hair, stood and set down the book she'd been reading out loud. "We had a good day." She brought Trudy to the door and reached for a clipboard from a set of shelves. "You just need to sign her out."

Gemma did so, and then Barb opened the gate, allowing the toddler to barrel out.

"We ate fish," Trudy said happily, her blue eyes dancing.

"Fish? Yum!" Gemma bent down and gathered her daughter in a hug, inhaling her scent of baby powder, glitter, and crayons. "Those are my favorite crackers, too."

Her daughter chattered on about her day as Gemma carried her outside into the cold, rushing over to her car, which she'd parked as close to the day care as possible. She wanted to keep Trudy out of the cold, so parking at the day care and walking across campus had been the best move. Snow covered the ancient Subaru she'd purchased with cash, and she carefully secured Trudy in her car seat, tucking her knit hat down over her ears and ensuring her little hands remained beneath the extra blankets kept in the car. "Keep those blankets on you until the car finishes warming up," she said. Then she shut the door, jumped into the driver's seat, and ignited the engine.

Trudy continued talking about a doggy named Rot-co.

Gemma smiled, feeling lighter than she had all day. She fetched the scraper from the floor, jumped back out into the frigid air and went to work on the windows while smoke puffed out the rear exhaust.

She'd almost finished when she noticed the back right tire. It was flat. Not just a little flat, but down to the rims. She swallowed and bent to look closer. The tires were all-weather but worn. Very worn down. A flat was not unexpected. She ran the scraper across the icy rubber but couldn't see any evidence of a puncture.

This was normal. People got flat tires—especially when their tires were old and the temps were freezing.

She could handle this.

Okay. She moved to open the trunk and stared at the stained carpet. Reaching for the little handle at the edge, she said a quick prayer that there'd be a spare tire where there should be. She should've already checked. Her sigh of relief wafted visibly through the cold air.

A tire—a smaller one than the others—lay in the well. She pulled it out, biting her lip. It was a temporary tire. Where was she going to get the money to buy a new tire before she was paid? Payday was two weeks away. The wind ripped against her skin and she set the tire on the ground, reaching for the jack. One thing at a time.

A car pulled up next to her. A big, black, shiny SUV with what looked like brand-new snow tires. She turned to see Dr. Jethro Hanson jump out of the driver's side with his dog right behind him. The dog was a German shepherd with gorgeous black markings, and it moved fast.

"Need help?" he asked politely, already reaching for the tire.

"I don't think so," she said, rolling the spare tire toward the flat one. Sure, she'd never changed a tire before, but how hard could it be? "That's kind of you, though."

The dog whined near her rear door, and even with the engine running, Trudy's happy yip of "Rot-co!" emerged loud and clear.

Gemma paused and tried not to notice how solid and strong the British professor looked in the dismally gray day. "Rot-co?"

"Roscoe," Jethro said, opening the back door and allowing the dog to jump inside.

"Hey," Gemma protested, releasing the tire to dash for the door, where the dog had already flattened himself across the back seat, his head on the blankets in Trudy's lap, her little hands already petting him. "Is he, I mean, is..."

Jethro chuckled, eyeing the dog. "He's great with kids."

Gemma looked up at him, her mind spinning. "How has he already met my daughter?"

"We often drop by the day care during my lunch hour. The kids love dogs." Jethro smoothly rolled the tire to the side and crouched, reaching for the jack. "You need new tires."

No kidding. "I've been busy," she said, trying to keep the defensiveness out of her tone. Shouldn't the hottie professor be off finding one of his notorious one-night stands? Serena had been more than free with her gossip about the handsome man.

"I'm sure you've been very busy," he said, his voice too level and even. "Yet you have a child in the back seat, and you need better tires. Her safety should come first."

Heat exploded through her body, making her cold hands shake. "When I require parenting advice from you, Dr. Hanson, I'll ask." What a jerk. Of course he was right. Trudy came first, but Gemma needed money to buy tires. She could probably qualify for a credit card, but that would be just one more way to track her, so she'd avoided taking the risk so far.

Maybe she didn't have a choice now.

Jethro looked up, snow falling on his too-long eyelashes. They were beautiful, and he didn't deserve them. "I apologize. Didn't mean to overstep." His deep blue eyes had flecks of gold throughout, and if they'd held an ounce of warmth in them, they'd be stunning. Right now, they were veiled.

"Well, you did," Gemma said, pulling a bag as well as the silver thingy that loosened the lug nuts from the car and heading toward the jack. "Please take your dog out of my car and leave. I neither require nor want your assistance." Even if she looked like a crappy parent right now, she was doing her best, and it was really pissing her off that she felt an urge to cry at his judgment. "Go away, Dr. Hanson. Go steal someone's office or something."

His chuckle was a hint of warmth in a freezing day. "I didn't steal Serena's office, and I finally got the stubborn genius to admit it over coffee. It was a misunderstanding, and I offered her the corner office, but she said she liked her view better. But it's nice to know she's still giving me a hard time over it."

Gemma leaned back. "You miss her."

He nodded easily. "Yes, I miss her. She's a good friend, and she can argue game theory and philosophy better than anyone I've ever met. We're good mates."

So just friends. Gemma had wondered, although Serena was too smart to be anybody's one-night stand. Not that it mattered. "I see. Well, she'll be back for the summer session, so how about you go judge somebody else's parenting skills while I change this tire and take care of my daughter? You can take care of your…dog." Gemma pushed the jack beneath the car and dismissed him as coldly as she could.

"Fine." The Brit stood, opened the door, and whistled for his dog.

Roscoe reluctantly shimmied out of the car the way a human would, not jumping up or turning around. He hit the ground and turned, running toward the entrance to the day care building.

"Have a lovely day, Ms. Falls," Jethro said, gracefully following his dog.

She waited until he'd entered the day care before scrabbling in the bag for the lever to use in jacking up the car. "'Have a lovely day,'" she mimicked, rolling her eyes.

What a complete ass.

Chapter Four

Jethro carried the three large tins of popcorn back into the storm, wondering how he'd been talked into buying three. He didn't even like popcorn. Irritation clamped onto his neck as he saw the snow pelting the blonde struggling furiously with the lug nuts on her too-worn tire. Damn stubborn woman. He'd been inside the day care for at least fifteen minutes, and instead of asking for assistance, she'd left her toddler in the car while fighting the wheel.

"I can't believe it," he muttered beneath his breath, opening his passenger side door and dumping two of the containers. "*Now* can I help?"

She looked up, her eyes a brown matte color that showed no emotion in her pale face. Too pale. She glanced toward the back seat and her shoulders sagged just enough to be noticed. "The lug nuts are on tight."

That was as good an invitation as he was likely to get. He opened the back door and slid a popcorn tin inside. "You good, Trude?"

Trudy looked up from munching on a cracker and eyed the tin. Her eyes were a happy blue and her chubby cheeks flushed with healthy color. "Yep. What's that?"

"Popcorn for you." He let Roscoe jump inside to entertain the kid and then shut the door.

"No—" Gemma started to protest.

"Yes," he said, taking the lug wrench from her uncovered hand. If she was going to give him baloney about flavored popcorn having too many calories, he was going to lose it. Hopefully she didn't already put pressure on her kid to be as rail thin as she was. His mother had done that to several of his female cousins when they'd visited for summer breaks.

They'd soon stopped visiting the massive mansion in the country.

He dropped and made quick work of the lug nuts, loosening and then removing them. Without giving her a chance to object, he yanked out the offending tire and pressed the temporary into place, not explaining anything to her. The car surprised him. She was a woman all about image and the vehicle was a heap.

He finished tightening the last lug nut. "This car does not suit you."

For the first time a hint of color rose from her neck up to her high cheekbones. "I'm between luxury vehicles at the moment."

It took him a second to catch the thread of irony in her frosty tone. Had she just made a joke? He stood and rolled the tire to the back of her car, placing it, the jack, and the bag in the trunk. His mother would've chosen cosmetic surgery and designer shoes over a vehicle, without question. He shut the trunk and studied the new professor. Her clothing was not designer.

Not even close.

The boots were scuffed, the wool coat raggedy at the edges, and the earrings simple gold hoops. In fact, hadn't he seen Serena wear those? "You're not adding up, Ms. Falls," he said, moving around to Trudy's door, his mind clicking facts into lines that didn't work.

"Not everyone is a math problem," Ms. Falls retorted, stretching her back and ignoring the snowflakes bombarding her smooth face.

He grinned. "Not even remotely true." He opened the door to let Roscoe out. The dog had been rooting around the floor for discarded cracker pieces and lifted his head, a Goldfish on his nose. "Out."

The dog bounded gracefully out, hitting the icy parking lot and skidding several feet.

Jethro ducked. "Trudy, it was nice to meet you." While the mother's clothing was worn, the kid's looked new and warm. A quick look at the car seat showed it was top-of-the-line, with every safety feature, and a juice cup had been placed neatly in the round hole next to the child.

Interesting.

He gently shut the door and looked at the mother over the top of the snowy vehicle. "People usually fall into easy equations."

"Aren't you a philosophy professor?" she returned, shivering and shoving her bare, reddened hands into her pockets.

"Yes," he agreed. "The philosophy of statistics is a hobby of mine." Figuring out the how and why was usually more interesting than the what. He had a feeling that he hadn't nailed any of those with this woman, which was rare for him. "There's a Bobbo's Tires about three miles west of here. I'll follow you there so you can buy new tires." The spare might not even make it there, and the other three didn't look much better.

Her chin lifted. "That is not necessary. I appreciate your assistance, and the popcorn gift to Trudy was kind, but we have taken up enough of your time." Her tone had returned to distant and dismissive.

He missed the subtle joke and glimpse of humanity she'd shown earlier. Before he could argue with her, his phone tinkled "American Rebel" from his pocket. The tune had his attention sharpening as he lifted it to answer. "Hanson," he said, still watching the woman.

"We have a problem," Clarence Wolfe said without preamble. "I'm holding down the fort and took the call. There's a body in DC."

Jethro sighed. "I'm out of the business, Wolfe. I helped your team track down Lassiter because you needed a philosopher, but that life is over for me. No more." Of course, Wolfe had saved his life while on a mission, so if he requested help, Jethro would give it. But maybe Wolfe didn't need assistance. Plus, Jethro was on another case right now, whether he wanted that or not.

"The body has a message directed just to you, Professor," Wolfe drawled before rattling off an address in the Shaw area of DC. "See you in a few." He clicked off.

Jethro slowly slid the phone back into his pocket. A message? "I have to go. Please take care of that tire." He looked around the quiet parking area, which was still half full of vehicles with folks working late or taking night classes.

A message for him on a dead body?

* * * *

The wind blew through the darkened alley that smelled like rotting garbage and fresh death. His head protected by a crime-scene tent, Jethro looked down at the body of a fortysomething blond female who'd been disemboweled. Her Chanel suit, probably a size two, had been cut right down the middle, and one matching Chanel shoe hung off her foot while the other remained in place. Genuine pearls decorated her ears and neck, while several rings covered her pale hands.

He crouched, studying the barely visible scars at her neck, evidence of a face-lift in the last few years. "Who is she?"

Wolfe stood next to him, flanking him as only the ex-soldier could. "Tate is getting an ID."

Jethro looked up at his friend.

Wolfe was six and a half feet of badass killing machine with a heart of pure marshmallow. Usually. Right now, the rugged structure of his face was set in rocky lines, his eyes hard in the lights set up around the perimeter. "Do you recognize her?"

"No." Jethro stood, his stomach rolling over three times. This could not be happening. Not now. Not ever again. He'd left death behind to make a new life.

"She doesn't look like a lady who'd be in this alley," Wolfe mused, shoving his hands in the pockets of his leather jacket.

That's because she probably wasn't. She'd been brought here on purpose to send a message. He'd met enough killers in his life to realize that sad fact. What he didn't understand was the woman's connection to him. A metallic taste filled Jethro's mouth and he swallowed it down.

MPD Homicide Detective Tate Bianchi finished speaking with a couple of uniformed officers near the mouth of the alley and turned, heading their way. "Dr. Hanson."

"Detective," Jethro said quietly. They'd worked a serial killer job together during the summer, and Tate had seemed like a decent guy. A little cranky to be working with the ragtag HDD, a DHS offshoot group that Jethro consulted for, but he'd gotten the job done. "You called Wolfe for this?"

"No. I called Angus Force for this, considering he's one of the best profilers in the country. Apparently he's out of town until tomorrow and Wolfe is covering things," Tate said easily, snow covering his black wool jacket. The homicide detective stood about six four and was built like a vegetarian linebacker—all smooth muscle and no fat. His eyes were a dark brown, his skin a smooth black, and his stance dangerous. He looked down at the victim, her platinum-blond hair smashed into slushy, dirty snow. "Do you recognize her?"

"No," Jethro said shortly. "I don't know this woman. Who was she?"

Tate flipped open his small notebook. "We've identified her as sixty-year-old Liping Julian. She's the owner of the Julian Art Gallery in downtown DC. Does that ring a bell with you?"

Jethro flipped back through his memories, already knowing he'd never met her. "No. I don't believe I've ever been to her gallery." He moved aside as a crime scene photographer edged in to continue taking pictures. "Maybe she taught a class or two for the university?" Art wasn't his thing, no matter how badly his mother had wanted him to study the subject.

"I'll find out," Tate said, motioning toward a tech scouring the area by the closest building, which seemed to be a series of apartments on the second floor and small businesses at street level. All windows in the area were protected by solid iron bars. Sirens trilled in the distance, heading, no doubt, to another crime scene. "Her residence is listed as being in the Great Falls area."

Wolfe nodded. "She looks like she has money. Are those pearls real?"

"Yes," Jethro said. "Wolfe mentioned that I'm involved somehow. Care to expand on that?" None of this was making a lick of sense.

"You tell me," Tate said quietly, studying him.

Wolfe looked from Tate to Jethro. "Stop playing games."

Yes, and Tate wasn't going to show his hand until Jethro gave something up. The homicide cop was smart. Jethro shrugged his shoulders. "Couldn't tell you." Or rather, he wasn't going to say a word until he knew more, even if he had an idea what this was about, which he did not.

Tate partially turned to face him more squarely. "You know, Professor, I don't think we've ever really chatted. All I know is that you're some expert in philosophy and you consulted with Wolfe's team about a serial killer who left philosophical notes on his victims. Yet here we are, with another victim in a crappy alley, and she has a connection to *you.* Is it just me or is this a surprising coincidence?"

"I find it to be neither surprising nor a coincidence," Jethro admitted, having learned neither truly existed. "Please define 'connection.'"

Tate handed over his phone and brought up a picture. "The woman had a note addressed to you pinned to her body."

Jethro accepted the phone to read the letter.

"What does it say?" Wolfe asked, angling his body closer.

Jethro dug deep into his training to remain calm as he began to read.

Dear Jethro,

I've had years to consider your betrayal. How about you? Have you thought of me? Of us? Of what we could've been? It's odd to leave a silly little note for you, but I've followed your so-called career since you abandoned your duty. Your country. Your family. I take it you like chasing killers who leave notes, so here you go. This is to keep you comfortable. It's just the start, as no doubt you know. Consider her a present...a substitute, if you will. I did. As such, I enjoyed her last scream more than I'd hoped. Was it as much as you enjoyed Isla's last breaths? Did she, like this one, try to force out tears from those eyes that had experienced the touch of a scalpel? Apparently plastic surgery can harm tear ducts. Who knew? Unlike your Lassiter case, unlike that crazy bastard, I do not consider this a game. Oh no, Professor. You want to know about good and evil? You want to ignore the evil inside you? I won't let you. This is just the beginning.

Philosophical and cool professor, knuckle bump right to you.

Fletcher

Jethro handed the phone back to Tate, the sound of the blood rushing through his head nearly drowning out ambient noise.

Tate accepted it, his face rock hard. "Who's Fletcher?"

Jethro steeled his shoulders, the cold of the night no match for the ice gathering inside him. "I have no idea."

"You're lying," Tate snapped.

"Prove it," Jethro said, turning and striding into the darkness of the alley, Wolfe at his side.

Wolfe waited until they were long out of earshot before speaking. "Who's Fletcher?"

Jethro thought about lying to him, but Angus Force had allies on both sides of the pond and would find the truth soon enough. Pissing off Wolfe wouldn't help anything. "Fletcher is my brother."

Chapter Five

Gemma stood in Serena's closet with a glass of white wine in her hand, trying to figure out what to borrow for school the next day. Trudy was sound asleep in the office that had been turned into her room, the kitchen was clean, and Gemma's body was tired. She touched a navy-blue pantsuit that wouldn't fit right now. She'd lost too much weight. Plus, she was several inches shorter than Serena, so pants were a problem.

The light gray skirt would have to do, perhaps paired with one of Serena's thick sweaters.

Yawning, Gemma looked around the master bedroom, which was decorated in a mismatch of bright colors that somehow worked. Knowing her genius friend, Gemma thought she'd probably used some mathematical formula to create the seemingly accidental effect.

Gemma reached out and ran her fingers along the three good—very good—wigs she'd blown her meager savings on. One a thick red, one a short black, and the other the blunt blond bob she'd wear for the next several months. She rubbed her scalp, enjoying the feeling of her own brunette hair falling to her shoulders. It was easier to use wigs than constantly dye her hair.

She turned and moved to the love seat, sitting and staring out at the blustering snow. Serena was just renting the cute bungalow while she finished building a house in Virginia, and she'd already packed many of her items, leaving the boxes in the garage, next to where Gemma now parked. Gemma could take over the rent payments on the first, and there would be no need to tell the landlord.

For now, how was Gemma going to drive on that crappy tire until payday?

Sighing, she sipped the wine Serena had left and watched the storm. How had she ended up here? Her mind grew hazy as she allowed memories to trickle in.

She was twenty-two years old again, graduating with honors from Washington Tech with her master's degree in statistics. One of the youngest in the program and one of the few graduates not married.

Nobody sat in the outdoor bleachers for her. Her friends were either graduating with her or had done so and moved on to doctoral programs elsewhere. That was all right. She'd known it was a long shot for her mother to attend the ceremony, so she held her head high as she crossed the stage and accepted her diploma, the breeze keeping her cool beneath the heavy black robe. Then she met the families of several of her friends, kindly refused their offers to attend parties or dinners, and hurried outside in the warm spring evening to her car.

"Bet you think you're better than me," her mother slurred, sitting on the hood of Gemma's leased convertible.

Gemma sighed and set her diploma carefully in the back seat. "Why didn't you come inside?"

"And embarrass you?" Fran swept her hand down the bright red tank top that exposed a black bra, tight jean shorts, and flip-flops. "What would your fancy friends think?" She slid off the car, wobbling slightly. "You think you're better than me."

"Well, I'm more sober anyway," Gemma said, catching a whiff of . . . gin? Something strong. Her stomach hurt, but she could handle that. She always did. "It was nice of you to come. Would you like to have dinner with me at my apartment? I could make us spaghetti." She'd been fending for them both since she'd turned eight years old and had figured out how to make money by weeding gardens for neighbors.

Fran's startling blue eyes narrowed. "Not good enough to go to one of your parties, am I?"

Gemma opened the passenger side door. Hadn't Fran said she was going to stop drinking last year when they'd run into each other in a bar in Seattle? Right. "I wasn't going to a party."

"You're such a bitch," Fran said, swinging out.

Gemma hadn't expected to incur violence so early and wasn't prepared to duck. Even so, her mother's palm didn't land. Instead, a strong hand caught it in midair, yanking her to the side. Gemma's mouth dropped open as she turned to see the handsomest man she'd ever imagined. "Whoa."

He grinned, his eyes crinkling. "Couldn't let a graduate get hit on graduation day." He was about six feet tall, with thick brown hair and eyes as blue as a sea beneath a perfectly sunny day.

A surprised chuckle escaped her. Had he just made a joke? Who was this guy?

"Hey." Fran jerked her arm free. "What's, I mean, who's..." She slipped out of one flip-flop and looked him up and down.

Gemma knew what she saw. Not his stunning and obviously intelligent eyes nor his wide chest. Fran saw money. High-end jeans, long-sleeved, expensive shirt, Italian loafers.

Fran smiled. "That was a mistake. We were just goofin' off." She fluttered her dark eyelashes and stepped closer to him.

He angled toward Gemma and pointedly ignored Fran. "My mom wasn't a hitter, but my stepdad threw a good punch until I became taller than him." He held out a hand. "Monty Cameron."

"Gemma Salsbury." She slipped her hand into his, noting how much warmer and bigger his palm was. "It's nice to meet you." He looked to be maybe in his late twenties. "Are you here for a graduate?"

"No. I guest lectured earlier today for a biology class and just hung around for a while," he said, his gaze not leaving her face. "I'm a doctor. Well, I'm in my residency."

Fran gasped. "A doctor?"

Gemma ignored her drunk mother. "A doctor who prevents injuries. You should specialize in that."

He smiled, and his eyes twinkled. In a word, he was perfect.

The wind whistled loudly outside and a clump of snow fell off the roof to the frozen grass, jerking Gemma back to the present. She shook off the past and tipped back her glass, finishing off the wine. The liquid splashed into her stomach, swirling around.

Turned out perfection was deadly. Who knew?

* * * *

Jethro's neck prickled as he walked toward his SUV after classes had concluded. His second day of the semester had involved spirited debates with several intelligent students, and he had high hopes for his classes, providing his brother didn't shoot him. He looked around at the motionless cars and softly falling snow, noting several decent vantage points in the surrounding trees.

His phone buzzed and he absently answered it. "Hanson."

"Hi Jethro, it's Alison. We met at Blarney's Bar?" a smooth voice said.

Yes. Pretty blonde who worked as a nurse practitioner in the middle of the city. "Hi," he said, pausing. "What can I do for you?"

"I thought we could meet up," she said, a smile in her voice.

He winced. His track record with women wasn't good, most likely because he was a killer trying to be a professor to find redemption, which wasn't truly possible. Plus, now his sociopathic brother was on the loose. It was rare he'd spend more than one night with any woman, no matter how wonderful she might be. "Sorry. I can't make it." He kept his voice kind but ended the call, figuring it was easier that way. For both of them.

Roscoe paused by his side, lifted his head, and sniffed the air.

Jethro looked down at the dangerous German shepherd and tucked his phone back in his pocket. "What is it?" He stared back at the large oak and pine trees. "What do you smell?"

Roscoe barked, bunched his muscles, and took off at a dead run through the lot.

"Hey," Jethro yelled, angling his backpack over his shoulder and lunging into pursuit. "Roscoe, stop. Knock it off."

The dog changed direction, still in the massive parking lot that took up the west and north sides of the campus, his legs sliding out from under him. He yipped several times, regained his balance, and ran full-on between parked vehicles toward the trees.

Jethro slipped on the ice but kept going. "You're going to get hit," he snapped as a truck swerved out of the way.

Roscoe barked and ran onto the sidewalk near the day care. Then he rammed full force into a wool coat. A scream echoed and a box of candy flew up into the air.

Jethro recognized the voice immediately, even before he looked up into Ms. Falls's startled face. Trudy held her hand and peered around her coat to watch Roscoe plowing through the candy. "Bad doggy," she murmured, tilting her head.

"Damn it." Jethro grasped Roscoe's collar and yanked him away from the round chocolates. "Don't tell me. Rum balls?"

Ms. Falls nodded and pushed her daughter behind her, watching the crazy mutt.

Jethro sighed. "I'm sorry. He has a slight alcohol problem and must have smelled the rum all the way around the far building."

She blinked. "Alcohol? Not chocolate?"

Roscoe whined and pawed at the mangled mess on the ice.

"Yes," Jethro said, pulling the dog away and then smashing the balls into the icy snow with his boot.

Roscoe whimpered.

Ms. Falls's face softened and she crouched down. "You poor baby. Come here."

Hanging his head, Roscoe went into full-on pathetic mode, slinking toward her to bury his nose in her neck. She wrapped both arms around him and crooned into his snowy fur, telling him it was okay.

Jethro's mouth almost dropped open. Who was this woman? Where was the ice queen with the flat eyes? "He's working you," he managed to get out.

She looked up, a smile of pure delight on her face. Her suddenly lovely face. "I know." Leaning back, she scrubbed both hands behind the dog's ears. "Even so, I can tell he's sorry."

That smile hit him right in the chest. Square on and hard.

Trudy toddled up and patted the dog's head. "Yeah. Him's sorry." She looked up at Jethro, her eyes wide. "Don't be mad at him. Him's a good boy."

Jethro blew out air. How could he say no to that cute face? "Okay. I won't be mad."

She blew hair out of her little eyes. "Promise?"

"I promise." He held out a hand. "Let me help you up, Ms. Falls."

She paused and then took his hand, standing and regaining her balance on the icy sidewalk. "Considering your dog just assaulted me, how about you call me Gemma?"

Was that another joke? He cocked his head. She was full of surprises, wasn't she? "Fair enough, if you call me Jethro."

"Jet-ro," Trudy said happily. "Jet-ro and Rot-co."

"Okay," Gemma said, releasing his hand and looking around as she stepped back. "So, well. I guess we shouldn't tell Barb that her famous rum balls were smashed into the ground?"

Jethro looked her over. Barb was very particular about sharing her rum balls, so she must really like Gemma. "Er, no."

"Rot-co," Trudy gurgled, petting his back. "I likes him."

"Me too," her mother said gently.

Jethro was liking the dog more than he had a moment ago, and he really liked that Gemma hadn't corrected her daughter. Maybe he'd misjudged her. Then he caught sight of her car by the entrance. "You didn't get a new tire?"

"Um, no." She reached down for her daughter's hand. "It's on my list to do. We have to go, baby." She turned toward the car.

Trudy reluctantly released Roscoe's fur. "Can doggy come?"

"Not today," Gemma said, stepping gingerly over a clump of dirty ice.

"You have to get a new tire," Jethro said, following them. "It's dangerous to ride around with the spare." What the hell was going on? The woman obviously cared about her daughter, so why would she put the child in danger?

"I know." Gemma reached the car and lifted Trudy, carrying her around to the passenger side and her car seat.

It hit him. Slowly but smack-dab in the head. The woman didn't have the money to get a new tire. In fact, she was wearing one of Serena's skirts beneath her coat. Why didn't she have money? She was a college professor. "Do you have a gambling problem?" he asked mildly before he could stop himself.

She shut the rear door and glared at him over the roof of the car. "What is *wrong* with you?"

"I'm not certain. There's probably a long list of things," he admitted, enjoying the color bursting into her cheeks.

She rolled her eyes. Actually rolled them. "No, I don't gamble. Why do you jump to the worst conclusions about me? About my mothering skills?"

Yes, he had done so twice. He rubbed a hand over his chest. "You look like my mother and she was…unkind."

"Oh." Gemma drew back, her eyebrows rising. "Well, okay, then. My mother was unkind and drunk, so I get it. No worries."

He smiled. "Ah. We're in the bad mother club. I see."

"No club." She looked down and then hurried around to the driver's side.

He beat her to the door and opened it for her. "Come on. We're bonding over our crappy childhoods."

She sat quickly, tossing her bag to the other seat. "No. No bonding here. None." She looked straight ahead, her entire body stiff.

He frowned. "Okay. Well, drive carefully." He gently shut the door, stepping away when she immediately started the engine and began backing out of the spot.

That was odd. Unfortunately for both of them, he'd never been able to ignore a puzzle.

Chapter Six

"You called?" Jethro escaped the rickety elevator, surprised once again it hadn't dropped him to certain death as he rode it down to the basement office space currently utilized by the Deep Ops Team. Roscoe bounded out at his side, happily running toward the dangerous men who occupied the room.

Wolfe looked up from his seat, three extra-large pizzas spread over the desks that formed a hub in the middle of the room. "Yeah."

Angus Force munched on a piece of pepperoni at the adjacent desk, his boots up on the side. While Wolfe could be considered the muscle of the group, Angus was a strategic genius and the leader. His hair was black, his eyes green, and his jaw unshaven. "Just got home and it sounds like we have a case concerning one of us."

"I'm not one of you." Nonetheless, Jethro strode out of the vestibule into the depressing space and reached for a piece of plain cheese. The last thing he wanted to do was get the team into a fight with his brother. Life was too short.

"Humph," Wolfe said, scratching Roscoe's ears.

Jethro drew out an empty chair and sat. "Listen. I appreciate your interest, but half the team is out of town." While Mal and Pippa were relaxing in a cabin somewhere on a mountain, Raider and Brigid, their most buttoned-down agent and their computer expert, were up north visiting her father. The group had worked through the holidays on a case, and once the office had closed, they'd taken off for some late vacation time. "I can handle this."

Wolfe shrugged. "No."

There wasn't time or energy to deal with the stubborn ass. Jethro kept his stoic expression in place. The cheap, seventies-style overhead lights buzzed loudly, crackling through the air. He looked at the peeling walls beneath wildlife photographs before glancing at the concrete floor. "I thought you all were moving to a better building within HDD."

"Haven't had time," Wolfe said.

Angus snorted. "I like the autonomy we have in this place, you know?"

Jethro could understand that. Angus Force operated under his own rules, and that'd be tough at one of the main HDD centers. Even so, a body had once been found in the office, so Jethro had thought Force would move everyone. Guess not. "Where are your women?" It was rare to see the two men after hours without the women they loved.

"At my place," Angus said. "It's poker night, and while Millie is back in town, they're still missing a few of their friends. Have you heard from Serena?"

"No," Jethro said. "I've only received one email, but I am going to track her down. I don't like how abruptly she left." Plus, he wanted more information on her intriguing replacement. "Where has Millie been?"

Millicent was their Q in a world of intrigue. She could make a battery out of anything, but the woman had more secrets in her eyes than Jethro did.

"On walkabout was all she'd say," Wolfe supplied, his tone casual but his eyes sharp. "Right now, we're not pushing her."

That was certainly not Wolfe's style, so Millie must not have given him a choice. Jethro absently rubbed the healed bullet wounds in his thigh. Wounds he wouldn't have survived if Wolfe hadn't carried him over his shoulder across a mountain while being fired upon. That was enough saving for one lifetime, and Jethro wouldn't put his friend in more danger. Especially when he was soon to be a father. "How is Dana feeling?"

"She finally stopped puking and is happier now that she's twenty weeks along," Wolfe said, snatching another piece of pizza. "Although she got bored working for Deep Ops and started taking on freelance assignments again." His brows drew down. "She was safer here than she is as an investigative journalist."

Jethro finished his pizza. "Writers write, chap. Like it or not." He'd never thought Dana would want to change careers, but it had been nice for Wolfe to dream for a month or so.

"I'd ask about your girlfriends, but we'd have to go alphabetically, and we don't have that much time," Wolfe drawled.

Jethro rolled his eyes. "I do not have a love interest."

"You should get one and stop tomcatting around," Wolfe advised wisely. "It's a lot more fun. Love's cool, man."

Jethro couldn't help but grin. Wolfe did have a way of putting things. "I'm not a long-term type of guy, but it's nice you two are, and I'm happy for you." No woman deserved to be stuck with his screwed-up head. Plus, his gene pool resulted in more sociopaths than good people, so there was that to consider.

"Tell us about your brother," Angus said, tipping back his beer bottle.

Roscoe whined.

"No," Angus said mildly, keeping the bottle out of the dog's reach. "Your drinking career is over."

Jethro shook his head. "No. The matter is personal, and I don't require your assistance."

Wolfe reached for his beer. "A dead body turned up in DC, which makes this matter *not* personal."

"True," Jethro acknowledged, reminding himself that Wolfe was about to be a father and Angus would probably soon be planning his own wedding. He couldn't put them in his brother's crosshairs. "Yet, as you pointed out, the body showed up in *DC*, and that's the locals' jurisdiction, not the feds'. In other words, you all don't have any involvement in investigating this murder." It was fairly clean-cut really.

"The locals have called me for a consult, thinking this killing might turn serial," Angus said reasonably. "You're a part of this team, and thus we are involved."

Jethro exhaled slowly, tamping down any twinge of anger. He didn't have a temper, so it should've been easier than it felt. "I appreciate your application of the transitive property there, but no jurisdiction means no jurisdiction, regardless of an attempt to pick your impressive brain."

Irritation crossed Wolfe's face, which was a clear indication that he might punch next.

Angus set down his beer rather forcefully. "We're not going to let you swing out there alone on this."

Jethro's chest heated at the offer of acceptance. Yet he'd always been alone. While he'd been happy to offer his thoughts to Angus about a couple of cases, he had never worked with a team. Never been a part of a team. Now wasn't the time to start, even if he'd had the inclination or the first clue how to go about it. "I appreciate it, but this is a family matter." He stood. "You all have a nice night."

Wolfe's chair scraped back and he stood. "You are family, asshole."

Jethro's bark of laughter escaped before he could stop it. "Definitely not, mate. We've never tried to kill each other." With that, he turned and headed toward the elevator. "Thanks for letting me have the dog for a while—we had fun. Have a nice evening."

He was going hunting.

* * * *

After a full day of classes, Gemma's temples ached. She'd received another email from IT asking why her biography hadn't been updated online. She couldn't create a false bio because it'd be too easy to disprove. Her genuine one was probably safe, but who knew what kind of Google searches Monty had in place—in addition to any private detectives he might've hired.

She strode down the sidewalk, hugging the building where more of the ice had melted away. The sun had finally beaten away the clouds, shining bright in the sky and making the snow sparkle on the ground and in the trees. The sky was a dark, cold blue, deep and fathomless.

She saw the man by her car and stopped short. Panic seized her, and it took a few precious seconds before she recognized him. Then she hurried toward him instead of running full-on into the day care to protect her baby. "Dr. Hanson?" She stomped down the sidewalk to the spot she'd chosen that day. "What in the world are you doing?"

He finished tightening the lug nuts on a brand-new and very strong-looking snow tire and then stood, turning to face her. "Someone left you new tires. Santa must've come late this year."

Her mouth dropped open as she looked at the tires. Brand-new and no doubt expensive. "You had no right," she whispered, her voice shaking.

He tossed the wrench into the back of his open SUV and wiped off his gloved hands on each other, not looking surprised at her outburst. The highlights in his hair shone in the sunlight, and his eyes appeared an even deeper brown than before. A shadow covered his jaw, several hues darker than his hair. "I merely gave Santa a hand. We're mates." His British accent emerged, sounding educated and unemotional.

What would it take to get this guy to show emotion?

She swallowed. "How much do I owe you?" Where was she going to get enough extra money for four high-end snow tires?

He shut the back hatch and moved as gracefully as any cat toward her. "I put the old tires into the boot of the car."

She shoved her chilled hands into her pockets to keep from smacking him. Not that she hit people. Even so, her fingers clenched into fists, warming her palms. "How did you get into my trunk?"

He paused, just looking at her.

She would not blush. There was no way she'd meant that sexually, and they both knew it. "*Dr.* Hanson?" God spare her from academics who thought they were helping.

"Every lock is just a physics problem," he said easily, reaching her and blocking out the sun.

It was surprising how broad his chest was, considering he lived his life within the walls of academia. That must be some gym he attended. He'd broken into her trunk, and that was illegal. Not that she'd ever expose herself by filing a police report, even under her newest name. "I did not ask for your assistance," she said through gritted teeth.

"I wasn't assisting you." His gaze flicked past her to the day care entrance before returning to her face. "Trudy and I are blokes. I helped her."

Right. Before meeting Monty, she would've been charmed by what appeared to be a kind gesture. Now she knew such gestures led to more danger than she'd ever thought possible. She'd made a mistake in trusting the wrong man once, and now she had more to lose. Much more. If she ever trusted another man, which was doubtful, he wouldn't be brilliant. He wouldn't be charming. He'd be real and honest and raw. Not like this man. "I will repay you, but it'll have to wait until payday," she finally admitted, keeping her tone business crisp. "I expect you to charge the appropriate interest."

"How about we make an even exchange?" he asked mildly. "I'm in the middle of a time-consuming project and I could use someone to cover my game theory class for the semester. It's on Tuesdays, Wednesdays, and Thursdays from ten to eleven, which is a time you have free."

She didn't ask how he knew her schedule. It also wasn't surprising that a professional academic had an important project that took time away from teaching. She looked for the trap and couldn't find it. "All right."

His expression didn't change. "Excellent. Tomorrow I'll drop off the class materials, in addition to PowerPoints for each of my lectures, including the assignments, quizzes, and tests I'd planned to give this semester." He waved a hand in the air before she could object, striding around the front of his SUV, his broad back to her. "You can use them or not. I change them every semester and never reuse the same quizzes or tests, but it's up to you."

She swallowed, feeling ungrateful. Even so, she had not asked for new tires. But teaching game theory would be fun, and if he had all the work already done, she could just enjoy the experience without too much stress. "Where's your dog?"

He paused and turned to face her, looking for a moment like a predator rather than a harmless professor. "He's back with his family."

She cocked her head, unwilling curiosity rippling through her. He was a good-looking man and shadows haunted his intelligent eyes. Deeper shadows than she would've expected, and for some asinine reason, they drew her. "Not with your family?"

A veil dropped over those eyes faster than any vault closing against a threat. "I don't have a family."

Even though the sun was out and the wind had disappeared, a chill clacked down her spine.

She shivered and forced her feet to move toward the entrance to the day care. But she couldn't help it. At the door, she turned to find him still standing in place, watching her. "Thank you for the tires, Jethro." Without waiting for his response, she opened the door and fled inside to safety.

Chapter Seven

Jethro sat back in the cold metal chair in the interrogation room, eyeing the steaming cup of truly horrendous coffee on the worn wooden table. He'd been waiting for nearly ten minutes and the crap still steamed. Finally the door opened and Detective Tate Bianchi walked inside, file folders beneath one arm and a matching coffee cup in his hand.

"Sorry about the wait," Tate said, drawing out a chair and sitting across from him. "Where were you the night of the murder?"

Amusement tickled Jethro's lips into an unwilling smile. "Seriously? If that's your angle, you can sod off, Detective."

Tate rolled his eyes. "It's not my angle, but I do need to look at all avenues here. Help me out, Dr. Hanson."

"I was home with the dog, working on assignments for this semester," Jethro said easily. "I'm sure Roscoe will provide backup, but you'd have to bribe him with a beer for him to speak." There were cameras all around Jethro's home, but he wasn't going to reveal that fact unless absolutely necessary.

Tate sighed and opened a file folder, flipping through it. "You're a professor who teaches a bunch of shit dealing with games and theories and good versus evil, and for some reason, you sometimes work with our Homeland Defense Department. Let's start there. How did a Brit end up consulting with Angus Force, who isn't known to play well with anybody, much less an academic from another country?"

That was a fairly perfect description of Angus Force.

Jethro reached for the coffee, willing to take another stab at it. He'd come directly to the requested interview with the detective and hadn't had a chance to fetch supper as of yet. "The first time Angus Force hunted down the serial killer known as the Surgeon, when Force was still with the FBI, he sought me out to decipher the more cryptic notes left at murder scenes." The Surgeon had dug deep into philosophy as well as early works of obscure writers and poets. "I helped him, and when it came time to catch the Surgeon a second time, when it became apparent the psychopath wasn't deceased as believed, I assisted again." Jethro sipped and the truly shitty coffee hit his stomach. Grimacing, he gave up and set the cup back in place.

"I know. It sucks." Tate glared at his coffee cup. "How did Force find you?"

"He never said and I didn't care," Jethro admitted. "I was teaching at Cambridge at the time, and somehow he discovered me."

Tate sat back. "Why make the move from Cambridge to DC University?"

Jethro had buried his mother and put his brother behind bars, and it was time for a new start. "DC made me a good offer, and I was ready to try something new. Sometimes it's that simple." Nothing was ever that simple.

"Huh," Tate said, his dark gaze piercing. "Tell me about Fletcher."

Well, now. They didn't have that kind of time. "I don't know who this Fletcher is, although he does seem to know me."

Tate lifted his chin, his gaze communicating that he'd like to knock Jethro upside the head. Hard. "Don't lie to me."

It wasn't a crime to lie to a local detective. So long as Jethro wasn't telling a material falsehood to harm the case, he wasn't interfering with the investigation. Holding back the truth might, but he'd always have the umbrella of his MI6 clearance upon which to fall back. "I'm sorry, but I can't give you any more information than that." It was true that he hadn't been cleared to reveal anything about Fletcher to anybody.

"What about Isla? The woman mentioned in the note?" Tate asked.

"Again, I have nothing to add to the note," Jethro said.

Tate flattened a large hand on the table. "You're interfering with an investigation, and you're rapidly moving into the territory of being a possible suspect."

Jethro flashed a smile. "You think I wrote a note to myself?"

"If you're batshit crazy and still fucking brilliant, then why the hell not?" Tate asked, letting his tone go quiet at the end. "Work with me, Jethro. I know you're smart, and the sight of that dead body didn't have you doubling over to puke, so I can tell you've been around. Probably with Force and his team, and that's decent training. But you have no idea what we could be dealing with here, and I need your help."

Oh, Jethro understood exactly what they were dealing with, and the DC cops were out of their league on this one.

The door opened and a tall woman built like a model walked inside. Her suit was light green, her hair and eyes dark brown, and her chin stubborn. “Sorry I’m late.” She took the seat next to Tate and studied Jethro as if he were a bug on a slide.

Tate gestured toward her. “This is my partner, Detective Buckle. Buckle, meet Dr. Jethro Hanson, who’s an expert in philosophy, game theory, a bunch of other crap, and also seems to have decided to hinder our murder investigation for some unfathomable reason.”

“Hello,” Jethro said smoothly.

Buckle smiled, revealing a very slightly crooked front tooth that was more adorable than out of place. “I’ve been trying to find a man named Fletcher in the serial killer world without much luck.”

“That’s unfortunate,” Jethro said. “I wish I could help you.”

Her smile slid away. “I had a friend at the State Department contact a buddy over in the UK, and you know what I discovered?”

Tate eyed her sideways. “Oh, this is getting good, now isn’t it?”

Buckle leaned forward, smelling slightly of lilacs. “Yes. I figured it wouldn’t hurt to run a background on the good professor. Guess what I found out, Tate?”

“Do tell,” Tate drawled.

She tapped unpainted nails on the table. “Turns out Dr. Jethro Hanson was raised by a single mother, a duchess no less, named Isla Hanson.”

“Well, isn’t that interesting?” Tate said, his jaw hardening.

Buckle stopped tapping. “There’s more. Isla had another son, one a mere year older than Jethro, named…Fletcher.”

The detective was good. Very good.

Tate’s eyebrows rose toward his gleaming and badass bald head. “Now that teases the senses, doesn’t it? Tell me more about this Fletcher.”

“It’s a mystery,” Buckle said quietly. “The records show that Fletcher Hanson became a barrister, was good at it, then one day just closed up shop and disappeared.”

Tate turned to look at her. “Seriously?”

“Yep. In addition, mere weeks before that time, Duchess Isla died. So sad. The death certificate listed cause of death as a heart attack. Is it just me, or does that not feel right?” Buckle tilted her head.

Tate’s nostrils flared. “That doesn’t feel right.” He frowned. “Tell me about your brother.”

“There’s not much to say,” Jethro said. “I’m sorry.”

“I will arrest you,” Tate snapped.

The door opened, and a tall man with intense blue eyes, sandy blond hair, and muscled forearms strode into the room. At this after-dinner hour, he wore black slacks and a pressed, white, button-down shirt with the sleeves rolled up. "I'm sorry to be late."

Tate sighed. "Scott? What the hell are you doing here?"

Scott came around the desk and drew out the remaining chair, the one next to Jethro. "It's good to see you again, Tate." He poured the full force of his charming smile onto Buckle. "Detective Buckle, it's even better to see you again. Although it's sad to see you two still harassing innocent people."

Jethro turned toward the guy. "Who are you?"

The man held out a hand. "My apologies. I'm Scott Terentson from Terentson Law Offices, formerly Terentson and Terentson."

"I didn't call for a barrister." Jethro shook the man's hand before turning back to the detectives.

"Your team called me." Scott faced Tate.

Tate shook his head. "Last time you worked with those folks, you were shot and in the hospital for six weeks. You sure you want this?"

Jethro glanced at the man. "That was you?"

"Yeah. That was me," Scott said, not losing his interested smile.

Jethro pursed his lips and nodded. Fair enough. Scott had been shot while representing Angus Force, and Force couldn't say enough good things about the guy. Considering Force disliked most people, that meant something. "While I appreciate the backup, I don't have a team and don't require the services of an attorney. Should that occasion arise, I will call you."

Buckle kicked back in her chair, looking like a fashion model on vacation in her perfectly cut suit. "What happened to your partner, Terentson?"

Scott shrugged. "My uncle chose to retire after I recuperated from my injuries. Said he wanted to live life on his boat and not look back. Can't blame him."

"Neither can I," Buckle said, her eyes darkening. "Tell your client he might want to cooperate with us so we don't have to kick this up to the federal level. Apparently we have a foreign national on our soil, one who seems to have disappeared from the UK and may have been involved in the killing of a citizen of the United States. Unless your client wants the HDD, FBI, CIA, DHS, and so on involved?"

Jethro's gut turned over at the thought. "Unless you have proof that there's a foreign national involved in a crime, there's no reason to bring in the big guns. This is a murder in your jurisdiction, and the only clue you have is that someone signed the name Fletcher to a note? Give me a break. Unless your department can't manage the investigation, I mean. If you need assistance, you should ask for help."

Buckle coughed out a laugh. "You can't tick me off, Professor."

"She is rather unflappable," Tate said easily.

They worked well together, and Jethro took in their easy rapport. He'd never had a partner. These two were relaxed and professional, and together they were very striking. He didn't get the sense of anything more than a professional relationship, though. "I don't mean to anger you, but I'm finished with this interview. If you discover who left the note, please inform me if I'm in any danger." He pushed back his chair and stood.

Scott did the same.

Tate jumped to his feet, making the table wobble. "That's it? We have a dead woman, one who certainly didn't deserve to be disemboweled, and you won't help? Did your brother kill her?"

"I have no knowledge that my brother is on US soil," Jethro said honestly. Of course his brother had killed the woman. "So, I would tackle this case like any other. Who wanted the woman dead? Find out who had the motive and opportunity and go from there." He strode toward the door and opened it for Scott to walk through first. "You're good at your job. Ferret out who wanted her dead."

Tate grabbed his arm in a strong grip. "Are you trying to tell us something?"

Jethro pivoted to face him directly, breaking his hold. "Yes. Do your job and you'll find the killer."

"Is your brother a serial killer?" Detective Buckle asked from behind Tate.

"No." Jethro glanced to the side and watched the woman get to her feet. Her legs really did go on forever. "He is not Lassiter and he has no game to play. This woman was killed for a reason that has nothing to do with Fletcher or with me. Do your job and find out why she's dead." That was all he could give them. Hopefully it was enough.

He followed Scott through the door, down the hallway, and outside into the night. The snow had stopped falling, the temperature had risen, and thick clouds rolled above. Streetlamps illuminated his SUV waiting by the curb as thunder rolled an ominous threat in the distance.

"Want to get a drink and talk about this case?" Scott asked.

Jethro shook his head and kept walking. "Thank you for your assistance, but I don't need a lawyer."

"Too bad. I already have the retainer," Scott said, loping easily by his side. "You told the detectives much more than you needed to in there. Want to explain why?"

Jethro pressed the fob button and his engine started. “I want them to find the killer of that woman. Why wouldn’t I?”

“Even if the killer is your brother?” Scott asked.

Jethro kept walking around the front of his SUV. “Especially if the killer is my brother,” he said, opening his door and jumping inside. There was no doubt Fletcher had just gotten started.

It was up to Jethro to hunt him down like the sociopathic animal he’d always been.

Again.

Chapter Eight

A light pop woke Gemma out of pleasant dreams. She sat up, her senses on full alert and her heart pounding. Holding her breath, she fumbled for the switch on the light next to the bed.

Nothing. The power was out.

Thunder crashed outside, and then lightning zapped the earth.

"Mama?" Trudy stumbled into the room, her blanket trailing behind her.

"Here, baby." Gemma jumped from the bed and shut the bedroom door, quickly engaging the lock. Then she settled the little girl in the bed. "It's just a storm. You go back to sleep."

Trudy turned over, curled up, and mumbled something.

Gemma's hands shook as she covered her daughter with the blankets up to her vulnerable neck. The power outage was just because of the storm. It had to be. She dug in the bed table for the flashlight she'd put there and quickly spun it around the room. Nothing. Okay. She looked at Serena's heavy dresser, which was to the right of the door.

"You're being ridiculous," she muttered, even as she moved to the far edge of the dresser. She turned, scooted down, and used her butt and hips to slide the furniture in front of the door. If there was a fire, she could get Trudy out the window.

Lightning struck again, and she jumped.

Trudy didn't so much as move. When her girl slept, she really slept.

What would that be like? It was too late for Gemma ever to relax completely like that, but she thanked God Trudy felt that safe. Gemma swallowed down the metallic taste in her mouth and then moved to the window, keeping the flashlight off so nobody could see inside. The world was dark outside and the rain ominous.

The street was vacant, and it didn't appear that there were lights on in any of the older houses on the other side.

Okay. She could handle this. A sound came from the basement. She paused, not moving. Her ears strained for any more sounds. Nothing. She forced herself to breathe easily so she didn't hyperventilate.

Thunder grumbled above, sounding as if the storm might be moving away.

She moved back to the bed table and removed the gun from the top drawer, setting it on top. She glanced guiltily at the small, fragile form of her daughter. It probably wasn't safe to have a loaded gun so close to innocence.

But it was more dangerous for Gemma to let down her guard. She needed that gun. She couldn't get back into bed and relax. So she took the gun and sat on the love seat, watching the storm outside. Watching shadows that didn't move and weren't a threat to her. If anything moved besides the tree branches, she'd see.

For hours, she watched the storm, her eyelids growing heavy. She rested her head back on a row of books and let her body relax.

It was the end of the best summer of her life. She was in love and had never felt so strong. So solid. But she knew what was coming. Monty was going to Seaville, Oregon, to join his brother's medical practice, and she was headed to Yale to earn her doctorate. She sat across from him in the restaurant, her hand safe in his, her heart already breaking at the thought of their being apart.

He paid the check, as he always did, and sighed. Then he took her other hand, his touch gentle. "I can't live without you." His normal smile was gone.

"I know. Me too." She would not cry. Well, she'd try not to cry. They'd pretty much been living together for the last two months, and the idea of not having him around was killing her. He made her feel as if she was the most important person in the entire world. The only person in the world.

"Come with me." He tightened his hold. "You're everything to me. I need you."

She wanted to go with him, she really did. But she needed to get her doctorate. "We can make it work."

"No." He released her hands. "I can't do it, Gemma. My mother left us all—she deserted us. I feel the same way right now and I can't take it. I can't do this." He moved to the side of the table and dropped to one knee. "Let's do all of this together. You and me. I know it's fast, but I know that we're perfect together." A ring box appeared in his hand and he flipped it open. "Marry me."

She gasped. Marry? "Monty."

"Do you love me?" he asked, looking both strong and vulnerable.

"Yes," she whispered, reaching out to touch the sparkling diamond. Was this what real love felt like? Was this what family felt like?

He slipped the ring on her finger. "Come to Oregon. You're so young. We can get my practice established and then we'll figure out how you can get your doctorate. Make a house for us. Make a family for us. You're the only one who can." He leaned back. "Unless you don't want a future with me?"

"I do want that," she hastened to say, touching his face. The hurt there was too much for her. "I say yes."

"Yes." His smile lit his entire face. He picked her up and twirled her around, oblivious to the many tables around them. He paused, looking at everyone. "She said yes."

The diners erupted in applause.

Thunder ripped her from the past into the present, and she looked outside, still seeing only darkness and shadows. The electricity hadn't turned back on in her house, but the porch light on the house right across the street was now glowing. She gulped. Maybe hers would come on soon. She looked over to make sure Trudy was still sleeping and then forced her body to relax.

Her electricity would return any minute. She waited nearly an hour and let her head rest against the books again, allowing the memories in.

It was the first day in their new house, the one way outside of town in the woods. The only one Monty said he could afford and had purchased without consulting her.

"What do you think?" he asked.

Peeling wallpaper from the seventies covered all four walls in the tiny living room. They'd turned in her leased car before driving across the country in his truck, and he'd brought her right here, saying he had a surprise. They hadn't even looked at the town yet. "I'm not sure," she murmured. "Why didn't you ask me before buying it?"

"Because I'm in charge of finances, considering I'm the only one bringing in money." His expression changed to one she hadn't seen before. "This isn't good enough for you?"

"Of course it is," she murmured. But it was way outside of town and she didn't have a car. "I just expected—"

"What? A fucking palace right off the bat?" he exploded. "You're as bad as my mother."

What? "No, Monty," she hurried to say. "I'm not—"

The back of his hand to her face took her by surprise and knocked her down. Shock smashed through her before she even registered the pain. She looked up at him, her mouth opened in surprise. "Monty."

"What is wrong with you?" he yelled.

"Nothing." She scrambled back as he lifted his leg to kick her.

He paused, his face going slack. "Shit, Gemma. I'm so sorry." He moved toward her, wincing when she backed away. "I just love you so much, and you know how my mother treated us. The move has been stressful, being responsible for us both." He gingerly reached out to touch her aching cheekbone. "I'm so sorry. It'll never happen again. I love you." Tears filled his eyes. "Please forgive me."

She snuggled into his chest, her mind fuzzing. It was an accident. She loved him. Nobody had ever loved him, and she could prove to him that he was worthy. That they were safe. This was nothing. Just their first fight, and he'd never do it again. Nobody had ever loved her before either. She could be strong enough for them both.

The sound of an engine rippled through the air, and she slowly opened her eyes. A Jeep Cherokee emerged from the garage across the way, backing up and taking off down the street. The electric garage door closed.

She moved off the bench and stretched her neck, grateful that light was coming in through the window. Gulping, she checked on Trudy and tried the lights again. No electricity. Taking a deep breath, she fetched her cell phone from the bedside table and searched for the electrical company.

"Vonn's Electricity, this is Sally," a woman answered.

"Um, hi. This is Serena Johnson and my electricity is out," Gemma said, giving the address. "It looks like other homes in the neighborhood have regained power, but my house hasn't."

The sound of typing came over the line. "You should have power," Sally said. "It was a pretty bad storm, and your breaker might've kicked off your power. Have you checked the box?"

"No," Gemma said, glancing at the sleeping child.

"Do you know how to find it?" Sally asked, her voice businesslike and still kind.

Gemma cleared her throat. "Yes, thank you. I'll call back if I can't fix it." She ended the call and bit her lip. What should she do? She didn't want to leave Trudy alone in the bedroom, but if she carried the little girl downstairs holding the gun in her hand, she'd frighten her child. That was crazy. Chances were the breaker switches had been flipped because of the storm.

She padded barefoot to unlock the bedroom door and gingerly open it, swinging out the gun the way she'd seen on television. The living room and kitchen were empty, lit by the now sunny morning outside. She gently shut the door behind her and tiptoed to Trudy's room, swinging inside and clearing it before taking on the powder room, near the kitchen.

The house was empty.

She was starting to feel silly, but at least Trudy was safe. The gun felt cold in her hand, so she tightened her grip, crossing to the basement door by the fridge. If there was danger, it was down there, away from her daughter.

That was all that mattered.

She opened the door and swung the flashlight down with one hand, keeping the other strong on the gun. Nausea rippled through her stomach, but she didn't have anybody to call for help. She fleetingly thought of Jethro and how he'd fixed her tires, but what would she say? That she was afraid to go down into the basement to see if the breaker had blown?

He'd want to know why.

Gathering her courage, she tiptoed down the rough wooden steps to the bottom, turning to point both the gun and the flashlight into the small room that held storage on shelves on one side and a washer and dryer on the other.

Relief swamped her so quickly she became dizzy. Lowering the gun, she hustled to the big metal box set into the wall by the shelves, quickly snapping the buttons back where they should be. The heat instantly engaged. She shut the fuse box door and shook her head, feeling like a moron.

She was totally losing it. As she backed away, something chilled her toes. Looking down, she noticed a small puddle of water. Then she glanced up at the one window in the room, which she kept shut and locked. Rising on her toes, she double-checked the lock, which was in place. Frowning, she looked down at the small puddle.

It didn't make sense, but perhaps the washer had leaked and she hadn't noticed? So long as the window was locked, she was fine.

She looked up and out at the bright daylight. Crap. She and Trudy had to hurry.

Chapter Nine

Jethro found Gemma Falls sitting at a window table by herself in the cafeteria at lunchtime. She was staring out at the snow with her food untouched on the plate in front of her. He wound through students and their tables to reach her. "You okay?" Without waiting for an invitation, he dropped into the seat across from her and slid his tray onto the table.

She jumped and then swiveled to face him, her eyes wide. "Um, yes. I was lost in thought."

The woman was too pale, and a thin blue vein glowed beneath her jaw; there were dark circles beneath her eyes. She'd apparently tried to brighten her skin with makeup, but the darkness was still present. "Another storm is coming in." She looked down at her uneaten salad.

Jethro took a drink of his tea, watching her carefully. Her hands were shaking and her eyes were bloodshot. "Is the extra class too demanding? I can take it back, if you'd like. It's only your first semester—I shouldn't have overburdened you." He fought the urge to pick her up and cuddle her right against his chest. If anybody needed a snuggle, it was Ms. Gemma Falls. Of course she'd probably pop him right on the nose, and he'd deserve it. Even so, everything inside him wanted to shield her from whatever was causing the fine trembling in her shoulders. "Gemma?"

"No. I'm fine." Her smile barely moved her lips as she reached for a cup of what looked like hot chocolate. "Just lonely because the day care had an early lunch of pizza, so I couldn't eat with Trudy. Now it's nap time." She took a sip and sighed. "Why can't we have nap time?"

He grinned. "Go sit in one of Dr. Potter's history classes. I promise you'll fall right asleep."

"I'll keep that in mind." Her smile looked natural now. Worn down, she appeared vulnerable and much more approachable than usual. For the first time, the weariness on her face actually softened the hard cut of her ice-blond hair.

"What's wrong?" he asked. "You can tell me." Then he could fix her problem before taking off to fix his.

Her long lashes swept up, and for just a second she looked at him as if she wanted to confide. Then her face fell into polite lines, betrayed by the tired tilt of her head. "There's nothing wrong. I'm just busy, like everyone else." She shifted uneasily in the chair as he continued to study her.

Yeah, he'd used that look to break a terrorist once. He might have every fault in the book, but patience was his weapon. Well, one of them.

She sighed. "Fine. The storm woke me up last night, and then the power was out and Trudy was scared. For some reason I couldn't get back to sleep. It's silly." She pressed the heel of her palm against her forehead. "So silly. Really."

The woman in front of him was anything but silly. "Did the power return?" he asked.

"Yes." She rolled her eyes. "The breaker had flipped, so I went downstairs and had to move the switches back into place."

His heart warmed. Man, she was cute when she let down that guard. More than cute. Beautiful. "If you ever need help, call me." He dug into his pack for a pen and wrote his cell phone number on a napkin before pushing it across the table.

It was telling that she accepted it. "Thanks." She twirled it around, watching the numbers move.

"Yours?" he asked, wondering if she'd give it.

She blushed a light peach and then rattled off her number, which he memorized instantly.

"Dr. Hanson?" A tall grad student in a very tight blue sweater rocked back on her heels near the table.

"Hi, Sharon," Jethro said, keeping his gaze above her chin.

"I was hoping you'd have extra office hours this week. I'm really struggling with the Kierkegaard assignment and could use some help." She smiled and wiggled her hips.

Jethro kept his smile in place. "No extra hours, and I'd suggest you work with your assigned study group. Dora Jefferty is in your group, and she has an excellent grasp of Kierkegaard. Have a nice day."

Pouting, Sharon flounced away.

Gemma snorted. "What are you? Indiana Jones?"

Now she was downright appealing. “Something like that.” He shook his head.

“Well, you handled that very nicely, especially for an orange throat.” She finally picked up her fork and stabbed at her boring-looking salad.

He chuckled. “Orange throat? Forgetting the fact that you just called me a lizard, I’m a blue throat all the way.” In game theory, the side-blotched lizard was a favorite example of a cyclical game, which meant it might not ever end, where the orange-throat lizard was represented as an alpha with many females, the yellow throat a beta sneaking among the females, and the blue throat a true alpha with only one female.

She chewed thoughtfully. “A one-female lizard type of guy, huh? Wouldn’t have thought that of you.”

He eased into the joking, enjoying the chance to exchange game theory quips with an intelligent and rather sexy woman. “You’re violating the Nash equilibrium, Professor.”

She coughed and took a drink of her hot chocolate. “How am I deviating from my present strategy? Wait a minute. What’s my present strategy?”

“Freezing me out and keeping me at a distance,” he said easily. “If you’re going to deviate, so am I.”

She paused, as if thinking about it. “I’m just being cordial.”

“You being cordial makes me friendly.” He was actually flirting with her. Well, a little bit. “Don’t dart off like a dove, now.”

She shook her head, amusement dancing across her features. “That would make you the hawk?” She blew out air. “Figures you’d like the hawk-dove model.”

He could do this all day with her. “Actually, game theory is a secondary interest to me. You in to philosophy?”

“Enough to know that your friend Sharon should just let it be.” She grinned at her own joke.

He laughed out loud.

“All right.” She sipped her drink. “Here’s a mathematical puzzle for you. Take a closed room in a basement with a locked window and a washer and dryer against the wall. A small puddle is on the floor, away from the washer and dryer, with no connection to the window. How did it get there?”

He scratched at the whiskers on his jaw. “Any chance there was a trail from either the window or the washing machine that evaporated, leaving just the puddle?”

She finished the drink. “Maybe.”

“The only way to tell is to wait for the next puddle,” he said.

She exhaled. “Yeah. That’s what I figured, too.”

* * * *

His healed leg aching from the oncoming storm, Jethro returned to his office after lunch, unable to get the professor's pale face out of his mind. He'd always been a sucker for a damsel in distress. However, this damsel had made it more than clear that she didn't want to be rescued by him.

Not that he had any illusions he could rescue anyone. Still, one thing he'd learned early on in his career was the importance of knowing exactly what he was dealing with in any situation. So he shut his door and dialed a phone number, telling himself he'd just feel out the terrain. The phone rang several times and he was about to end the call when Brigid answered.

"Hi, Jethro," she said, her voice light. "It's so good to hear from you. It's Thursday afternoon. Why aren't you in class?"

It wasn't a surprise that the Deep Ops computer expert knew his schedule. "Afternoon classes were canceled so students could attend a career fair." He had no right to bother her on her vacation. "I'm just checking in. How's your dad, and how's Raider doing at the farm?" Raider was more of a plan-an-op-to-the-last-detail type of guy than a relax-at-the-farm man.

Brigid laughed. "Oh, you know Raider. He's going nuts. But it's nice to see him getting along with my dad. They're out repairing the roof of one of the barns right now. He's surprisingly handy around here, although I don't think I'll ever be able to get him to retire to a farm." Her voice lowered and softened. "Guess what?"

"What?" Jethro asked, settling back in his chair.

"We got engaged last night. I haven't told the rest of the team yet because I wanted to do it in person, but I can't keep the secret with you on the phone. I'm so freaking excited." Happiness all but bubbled from her.

He smiled and turned to see the snow had started falling again outside. "That's lovely, Bridge. I'm pleased for you."

"Good. Now how about you tell me why you really called?" A very slight Irish brogue emerged with her brisk question.

He shook his head. "I was just checking in."

"Bollocks," she returned. "You don't just check in. Come on, Jethro. You've called because you need a favor, and honestly, I'm going a little nutty here without something to hack. Please tell me why you called."

Well, she did ask, and she was one of the best computer hackers in the world. He cleared his throat. "If you have time, and only then, I was hoping you'd do a deep dive on my new colleague. Her name is Gemma Falls, and she's teaching game theory and statistics here at the university."

Brigid was quiet for a moment. "Why?"

He stilled. "What do you mean, why?" Brigid wasn't a woman who asked that question.

She sighed. "If you're interested in Gemma Falls and this is personal, the last thing you should do is dig into her personal life without an invitation. If this is business, I want to know what I'm dealing with before I dive."

That was fair. More than fair. He ran a hand through his thick hair. "You're right. Forget it."

"Oh no you don't," she said. "You wouldn't ask unless you had a reason. Spill it, Professor."

He wasn't accustomed to sharing his thinking with anyone, but he had called her, so he didn't have much of a choice. "It's just a gut feeling," he said honestly. "She's interesting, but there are shadows in her eyes that I can't read." Rather, those eyes were usually turned away, so he couldn't read her at all. "I don't know. She's intriguing, so perhaps it is personal. In which case, you're correct. I shouldn't invade her privacy." In truth, he didn't have a valid reason for wanting to conduct a background check. "For now, let's forget it."

"Jethro, you're one of our team, and if you want help, I'm your gal," Brigid said. "But I also don't want you to screw up a possible romance because you're being a dumbass."

Jethro grinned. "That isn't nice, Brigid."

"Nobody has called me nice in a while," she mused. "Although I am. I'm a freaking peach, if you ask me. Sometimes it's difficult keeping you guys in line. I swear. Wolfe almost blew things up with Dana several times, but now they're solid. I'd love to see you happy, too."

God save him from happy couples who thought everyone else should be as googly in love. "That's kind of you, but I'm regretting the fact that I made this call."

"Too late," she said, her voice sounding too pleased. "Do you need us at home? I talked to Wolfe yesterday and he told me about the dead woman who was found in an alley. It's almost as if this Fletcher character is trying to copy the Surgeon, but he's targeting you instead of Angus Force. What's up with that?"

So Brigid didn't know that Fletcher was Jethro's brother. Wolfe must've kept that close to his vest for now, and apparently Brigid hadn't felt the need to do a deep dive on either Fletcher or Jethro, so that was a good thing. "I don't know, but I'm not worrying about it," he lied. "The DC police seem to have the case in hand, and it's not a federal one, so your team won't be called in. Just let Tate and Buckle handle it." He paused. "Have you searched for her first name, by the way? It's something none of us know."

"Nope," Brigid said. "Your curiosity isn't a good enough reason for me to violate Detective Buckle's privacy."

Yeah, fair enough. "Enjoy your vacation. Sorry I bothered you."

"Jethro," she said quietly. "Whether you like it or not, you are a member of our team. If you need help, you're going to get help. So put yourself in front of this right now and tell me if you require my assistance."

"When you get ticked, your Irish brogue is stronger," he mused.

"When you're hiding something, your British accent clips every word at the end," she returned.

He shut his lips. Bollocks.

Chapter Ten

Gemma finished lunch—a too-enjoyable lunch with the handsome Dr. Hanson—and hustled out to her car by the day care. A quick glance inside confirmed that it was still nap time. Man, she could use a nap. Instead, she needed to take advantage of the fact that her afternoon class had been canceled.

Her engine took a few moments to turn over in the cold. Though it hadn't started snowing again, the clouds were dark and swollen above her. Finally the engine caught and the car roared to life. Well, sputtered to life. It was doubtful the heap would last through the winter.

A worry for another day.

She drove away from DC University, choosing a random direction. If she picked Trudy up at five, she had ninety minutes to drive one way, do what she needed to do for an hour, and then drive the ninety minutes back. To be safe, she only needed thirty minutes once she stopped.

Exactly ninety minutes later she sat in a coffee shop outside Sharpsburg, Maryland. The place had weathered wood walls, a mellow vibe, and no security cameras.

Sitting at a table in the far corner, she booted up the laptop she rarely used. The one with the IP address scrambler. Then she dug into her pack for a burner phone and turned it on, waiting for the screen to clear. She drank several gulps of her honey oat latte and then dialed the number, trying to keep her voice from sounding panicky.

"Cameron Medical Practice, Julie speaking," a chipper young voice answered.

Gemma's shoulders slowly relaxed. This was a new voice. "Yes, hello. My name is April and I'm new in town. A friend of mine recommended Dr. Monty Cameron to me, and I was hoping I could make an appointment."

"Sure. What's going on?" Julie asked, the sound of typing coming over the line.

"I injured my shoulder, I think. Or maybe it's my back. I'm not sure, but I'm in a lot of pain and need to get in as soon as I can." Gemma's hand trembled as she reached for her latte.

More typing. "Okay. Well, the soonest I can get you in to see Dr. Cameron would be the end of next week. We do have a nurse practitioner you could see tomorrow."

"No, I really need to see Dr. Cameron," Gemma said as calmly as she could. "It's so painful. Does he have anything open before that?"

"No, I'm sorry," Julie said.

Gemma sighed loudly, letting the sound echo into the handset. "Okay. Well, I'll take that appointment, but could you also put me on any cancellation list you might have? I'd really appreciate it." Was Monty really that busy, or was he out of town? If he was out of town, what did that mean? Had he found her? That puddle by the washing machine just wouldn't leave her mind. Plus, what about the flat tire? Sure, her tires were worn, but…what if?

"Oh, I normally would, but Dr. Cameron is on vacation right now. He'll return on Monday."

The world narrowed from outside in, muffling all sound. Gemma swallowed. "Vacation?"

"Yes," Julie said cheerfully. "He's in the tropics somewhere, not stuck in snow like the rest of us. I'm a little jealous."

Gemma couldn't breathe. "Oh. Okay. Well, my pain is pretty intense. Maybe I'll head down to the emergency room and then schedule a follow-up with the doctor once I know what's going on." Her head spun. The entire coffee shop spun around her.

"Sounds good. Call back any time." Julie clicked off.

Gemma sat frozen for a minute. Monty could be on vacation. Or he could have found her. It'd be just like him to play games and mess with her head. But she'd been so careful. Counting her breaths in and then out, she tried to calm her body while tearing apart the phone. It'd go in the garbage when she left.

Then she punched up a video call on the special laptop, hoping her friend was available.

Serena's stunning face came into view.

Hope leaped into Gemma's chest as she shoved in her earphones. "It is so good to see you."

Serena smiled. "You too." Her kinky black hair had grown out, and a fine smattering of freckles spread across her nose and cheeks, darker than her russet-brown skin. She wore a red shirt depicting a dancing Yoda, along with a white lab coat. "Are you safe?"

"I think so," Gemma said. "Thanks to you."

Serene shook her head. "I wish I had known what was going on and could've helped you sooner."

Gemma had called Serena when she'd been broke with nowhere to stay, and Serena had instantly created this situation for her. Safety and an income for a brief time. "I owe you, but I'm not entirely sure where Monty is. What about you? Are you safe?" she teased, forcing lightness into her voice.

Instead of smiling, Serena frowned. "In the same boat as you. I'm not certain."

Gemma stilled. "What are you talking about?"

Serene looked over her shoulder and then leaned closer to the computer. "I don't know. It's probably nothing, and I can handle it. For now, how's my girl?"

"She's good." Trudy was more than good, in fact. "Feeling safe, which is what matters."

"I wish you felt safe," Serena said quietly, her dark eyes sympathetic.

Gemma nodded. "Me too. But there's nothing I can do that I'm not already doing." Going to the authorities without proof of Monty's violent temper wouldn't get her anywhere, and all that mattered was protecting Trudy. If Monty ever discovered he had a daughter, God only knew what he'd do. Without question, he'd kill Gemma, and then where would Trudy be? With him. With no criminal record, with no proof that he was a monster, he'd be granted partial custody at the very least. It was the law, and there was no way around it. "I've met your Dr. Hanson."

Serena finally grinned. "He's not mine, but he's a great guy."

Gemma had no reason for asking, but she couldn't help herself. "Is there anything between you?"

Serena laughed now. "No. I mean, he's attractive and all, but after that mix-up with our offices was straightened out, we ended up just friends. Too much alike, I think. Plus, he likes to get around, and that's not my thing." Her expression turned dreamy. "I want to meet somebody totally different from me. Someone more…rugged." She shrugged. "Maybe I have. I actually have a date tomorrow night. What about you?"

Gemma shook her head. "Being on the run doesn't give one much chance to date."

Serena sobered. "You can't run forever."

A chill spread through Gemma's chest. "That's what I'm afraid of." They chatted for a few minutes and then Serena said she had to go. Gemma ended the call and shut the laptop, her awareness pricking as several people walked into the coffee shop as if a concert had been let out or something. Soon all the tables were filled.

A man approached her table, a cup of coffee in his hand and his light brown eyes sparkling. "I'm sorry to bother you, but do you mind if I take this seat?" He looked over his shoulder at all the occupied tables. "We're having a symposium in the warehouse down the street and we're on a thirty-minute break."

She paused. The guy didn't look like a private detective, and all of the tables were full. "Sure." She'd need to be getting on her way soon.

"Thank you." He pulled out the chair and dropped gracefully into it, setting his coffee on the table. "You're very kind. I didn't see you at the symposium?" His hair was a thick, dark brown, and his smile revealed a dimple in his left cheek. What was up with handsome men and dimples these days?

"No. I'm just passing through," she said, reclaiming her cup. "What's the symposium about?"

"Wood," he said, nodding. "I represent a couple of lumber companies up in Pennsylvania, and the symposium is one dealing with better lasers for more exact cuts. It's pretty interesting, actually." He drank his coffee.

"What does that mean? How do you represent the lumber companies?"

"I work for a PAC that protects their interests politically. Learning about lasers is just part of what I need to know." He leaned toward her, his eyes sparkling. "Plus, lasers are cool. So I said I'd attend the two-day demonstrations."

She smiled. How long had it been since she'd been able to sit and have a normal conversation with a handsome man? Sure, Jethro Hanson was sexy, but she couldn't get close to anybody at the university. This guy was here for less than half an hour, and she was going to enjoy herself. "It's nice of you to take one for the team."

His chuckle was deep. "So true. What do you do anyway?"

"I'm a struggling author," she lied, keeping her smile in place. "My father created one of those dot.com companies and sold it twenty years ago, so I have the freedom to keep trying. Maybe someday I'll get a real job."

"Writing is a real job," he said, all charm. "What do you write?"

"Thrillers," she said. "You know. Serial killers, good guys, bad guys, lots of danger?" Based on her life, she'd probably qualify to do so.

His strong throat moved as he swallowed more of the cinnamon-scented brew. "That sounds like fun. Do you have any life experience or do you just make it all up?"

She finished her drink. "I've never worked as a serial killer, but I guess I'm still young."

His laugh was deep and rich. Oddly familiar. The guy looked like he could be in movies or something; maybe he'd had a former life, just as she had? "Well, don't start your new career with me. I like my heart beating in my chest." He looked around the now-bustling coffee shop, sobering. "I also like my freedom."

"Ditto," she said softly, slipping the now-silent laptop into her bag, where she'd already placed the remains of the burner phone. She'd have to find a place to dump it on the way back home.

"I hope I haven't scared you off," he said, putting his cup back on the table.

"No." She smiled, ignoring the fact that her head was itching beneath the stupid wig. Sometimes it drove her nuts. "I have an appointment I need to get to, but it was nice meeting you."

He twirled his cup in large hands. "I don't suppose you live anywhere near DC and would like to meet up for something more substantial than coffee? Say dinner and drinks? Or just drinks? Or maybe more coffee, if that's your thing?" His dimple appeared again. "I like coffee. It could become our thing."

The girl she'd been at twenty-two would've jumped at the offer. The woman she'd become couldn't afford the risk. He was handsome and seemed kind, but his brand of charm led to pain. Or it could lead to pain. Either way, she had a daughter to protect, and going for dinner and drinks with a nice guy wasn't going to happen. Not for a long time, if ever. "Thank you for the offer, but I'm seeing someone." It was the easiest way to refuse his invitation. "And I don't live anywhere near DC. I'm just here to do some research for a book."

His expression dropped, but his smile remained in place. "Fair enough. Tell your boyfriend he's a lucky man." He patted her hand and quickly withdrew. "Would you at least give me your name? So I can tell my buddies all about the gorgeous blonde I met in the middle of nowhere who turned me down?"

She chuckled. "Sure. I'm Sylvia."

"Sylvia." He rolled the name over his tongue. "It suits you. Very pretty."

"Thank you. My mother liked it." It was too easy to lie these days. "And you? First name only. Let's keep this intrigue going." She took one last minute to enjoy flirting with a man as if she had nothing to lose.

He held out a hand, waiting until she'd placed hers in it to shake. "I like intrigue. Sylvia, I wish I'd met you before you'd met this other very lucky guy. Remember me fondly. My name is Fletcher."

Chapter Eleven

The call woke Jethro out of a nightmare in which his mother died in his arms. Again. He reached for the phone. "Hanson."

"We have another body," Detective Tate Bianchi said. "Along with another note for you."

Jethro shoved himself from the bed. "Give me the address. I'll be right there."

Tate rattled off the address and then ended the call.

Thirty minutes later Jethro found himself on the fifth hole tee box at the Blue Ridge Golf Course, just over the DC and Virginia border. An officer was waiting to lift the crime tape and escort him over to Tate.

Yet another white tent had been erected to protect the body from the elements.

"Evening," Tate said, his dark coat wet and his boots muddy. "Though it's not, is it?"

"No." Jethro ignored the crime scene techs buzzing around and crouched for a better view of the deceased man. The guy appeared to be in his late sixties or so, with thick gray hair and a paunch. He was dressed in silk pajamas and his feet were bare, while a bloody hole in his forehead showed a bullet's path through his brain. There was also a mess of evidence that he'd been disemboweled. "Who is he?"

Detective Buckle drew up alongside Tate, a notebook in her gloved hands.

"Name was John Randolf, and he was a securities officer in the Miltonery and Masterson Investment firm. No record. His prints were on file because of his job; otherwise he doesn't pop in the system." The wind whipped her curly hair around and snow hung in the thick tendrils. "Any idea how he and the first victim might be connected?"

"My best guess is that they aren't connected," Jethro said, standing and sliding his hands into his wool coat pockets. "What did the note say?"

Tate lifted his phone to his face, illuminated from behind because of the powerful lights set around the perimeter. "Let me read it to you, Professor." His tone was pissed.

Dear Jethro,

How are you, brother? It's nice to be on the same continent with you again. Feels right. Feels like we can pick up where we left off, but we both know that's not true. Isla is dead, and that's your fault. I'm away from home, and that, too, is your fault. Most of all, everyone you care about is in danger, and that is...you've got it. Your fault.

Until next time,

Fletcher

Tate shoved the phone into his pocket. "Tell me about your connection to this victim."

"I don't have one," Jethro said, hunching his shoulders against the cold. Ice was crusting over the dead man's eyes, and Jethro's stomach lurched.

Buckle stepped toward him. "The note clearly says that everyone you care about is in danger, thus you must care about this victim. Stop messing around with us and tell us what is going on with your brother. Who is he, where has he been, and why is he killing on US soil now?"

Jethro could and had withstood torture by brutal enemies, and an angry brunette who looked like a model didn't faze him. Even so, he understood her frustration. "We don't even know this is really my brother, Detective. It could be someone who read about the Surgeon killings and is copying them, but targeting me instead of Angus." It was most certainly Fletcher, and how he'd reached US soil without being detected would need to be investigated. His brother had always been brilliant, so his ability to elude the authorities wasn't a shock. Unfortunately Jethro didn't have the clearance to share what he knew about Fletcher with the DC detectives, no matter how much he might want to clue them in. "So I'd approach this like any homicide and look to see who'd want this particular person dead."

Buckle stepped up into his face. "You study good and evil, right?"

"In a matter of speaking," he said mildly, noting her lilac scent again.

"According to Dante, isn't there a special place in hell for people who can make a difference but don't?" Her brown eyes blazed.

"Not exactly, but possibly close. Virgil showed Dante a place for those who neither committed good nor evil. Both Heaven and Hell denied them entry, so they reside in the Ante-Inferno, chasing a blank banner and being attacked by insects. Neutral angels suffer eternally and painfully with them."

If anything, her glare grew darker. "Aren't you afraid of going there?"

He subtly angled his body to protect her better from the wind. "Detective, there are far more certain and excruciating rings of hell for me, I assure you." He turned toward Tate, who was watching them impassively. "I've told you all I can for now. If you attempt to take me in, I'll immediately call my attorney, who will immediately get me out. For now, I have finished with this discussion."

Tate glared at him. "You know, you're an interesting guy, Professor."

"Do tell," Jethro said, knowing what was coming.

"Yeah. We can trace your teaching career about four years back, but before that, nothing. I mean, we have your birth records and family statistics, and a record of you attending college, but then…nothing. It's like you just fell off the face of the planet for years. Years and years," Tate said, his voice low.

Detective Buckle nodded. "It's so odd, especially considering the fact that your brother also disappeared after working so hard to become a lawyer. Excuse me. Barrister."

Tate smiled, and the sight looked like a warning. "*There are more things in heaven and Earth, Horatio, than are dreamt of in your philosophy.*"

Jethro gave his own smile of warning right back. "Your Shakespearean quote fails to apply to this situation, Detective. While I appreciate the attempt, I'd go a mite deeper with your research into philosophy if you want to uncover the true evil we have here in front of us."

"Isn't it within us?" Buckle asked smoothly.

He turned to look down at the woman, his leg aching from healed bullet holes and his back from several knife wounds. "That it is, Detective."

* * * *

Thank goodness it was Friday. Gemma needed some time to gather her thoughts and figure out whether she was safe here. As she hurried toward the day care at the end of the day, she stopped cold at the sight of the shattered left rear window of her car. Her breath heated and she froze in place.

Jethro emerged from the front door of the day care with a box in his hands. "Gemma. Hey." He paused and studied her, following her gaze to the back driver's side window. "Bloody hell." Quickly he moved toward her and shoved the box into her hands. "I heard there was a snowball fight earlier in the parking lot but didn't catch wind of any damage. Morons."

He gently took the sleeve of her jacket to draw her toward the day care. "Go inside with Trudy and I'll cover it the best I can."

Snowball fight? Gemma numbly looked around the parking lot but just saw ice chunks and a couple of rocks. Was she losing her mind? Or was this another odd coincidence? Jethro thought it was and even had a reasonable explanation, but he was a nice professor who had no clue what it felt like to be hunted. "Um."

He turned toward her.

She reacted instantly, flinching away from him.

He released her and stepped off the sidewalk to the parking lot. Even so, he was still taller than she. He shoved his hands in his pockets, his gaze measured. "Did I drop a clanger, sweetheart?"

Heat flashed into her cheeks and she straightened, her brain late to the party. "What's a clanger?"

The intensity of his gaze didn't relent. "It's a British expression. I feel like I scared you, and I don't know how. What did I do?"

"Nothing." She looked beyond him to the trees, searching for any sign that Monty was near. Wouldn't she sense it if he was in the vicinity? Or was she letting her fear of him haunt her even now? When she was safe and many states away from him. "I need to fetch Trudy." She looked down at the square box. "What is this?"

"Rum balls," he said quietly, that knowing gaze sliding beneath her defenses. "Should we talk about your reaction to my sudden movement?"

"There's nothing to talk about." Ignoring his stare, she turned and hurried to open the door and move inside, her gaze seeking her daughter. When she spotted Trudy playing with blocks with another girl in the far corner, her heart finally started beating again. Trudy was safe.

Barb looked up from her task of tidying up the reading area. "Hi, Gemma. How are things?"

Freaking not great. "Wonderful." Gemma plastered a smile into place. "But the back window of my car is broken. Was there a snowball fight in the parking lot earlier?"

Barb pushed books into place in the short bookshelf and stood, wincing as she stretched her back. "Yes. It was a loud one, too. Several hit the building, but the kids thought it was funny." She ambled closer, wiping at red marker lines on her left hand. "When they were finished, I looked outside to check for damage, but I must've missed seeing your car window. I'm so sorry. What should we do?"

"I'll get a new window," Gemma said, biting her lip. She wouldn't get paid for another week, so how the heck was she going to afford a window?

But it wasn't as if she could let Trudy sit in the back seat with an open window during January. Especially this January, when it seemed that Mother Nature was making a statement about her power—and moods. "At least they only hit one window."

"You look tired, honey." Barb patted her arm. "The first week of school is always an adjustment. You'll get the hang of it."

Gemma bent down to hug Trudy when she ran up. "I know." She smoothed her daughter's curly brown hair away from her face. No doubt the braids that had tamed the mass that morning had disappeared before lunchtime.

Trudy grinned, showing cookie crumbs at the side of her mouth. "We pretended we were animals today and I was Rot-co. A big doggy. Bark. Bark." She snorted and butted her head against Gemma's leg.

Joy filled Gemma and she laughed, hugging her baby. They were safe. She was on the lookout for threats as she should be, but she didn't need to create terrors out of nothing. Well, not nothing, but coincidence maybe.

Barb chuckled. "Don't forget we have the science party and dinner for the kids Monday around suppertime. Maybe you could go get some rest or just have some 'me time' during the party?"

Gemma appreciated that the day care had such events, but she didn't like being away from Trudy so long. Still, she had to give her daughter some freedom and a chance to grow. "Thanks, Barb." She took Trudy's hand and led her through the gate, pausing to sign her out before heading for the door. "We have a broken window in the car and it'll be cold on the way home, but we'll figure out what to do together," she said, opening the door and drawing Trudy out.

Jethro straightened near the car and turned to face her, his gaze veiled. "I put Trudy's car seat in the back of my rig. We can go grab a treat while Phil's Glass Company comes and takes care of the vehicle. I already called and they're on the way." He crossed his arms.

Gemma's neck straightened. "That's kind of you, but I can—"

He cut her off. "Trudy? How about a milkshake? There's a place just around the corner where they mix chocolate and strawberry. Into the same milkshake. Can you believe it?"

Gemma gasped.

Trudy jumped up and down. "Yes. Oh, yes. Mama, can we? Can we go?"

She gave him the look of death, and he nodded. Oh, he knew exactly what he'd just done.

He lifted one shoulder. "I'm sorry, but it's unsafe right now, and Phil will fix it. You've done me a great service in taking on that class, so I figure I still owe you. This will make us even."

"Yay!" Trudy yelled.

Gemma's nostrils flared, and she could feel heated air leaving her lungs. The man needed a kick to the shin.

Then he smiled. Damn men and dimples.

Chapter Twelve

Jethro couldn't get the image of Gemma flinching away from him out of his mind. He'd taken mother and daughter to get milkshakes, and Trudy had been a delight as she described her day. Gemma, on the other hand, had singed him with venomous glares. Yes, he deserved it for taking charge like that, so he hadn't taken umbrage.

Even so, she could have relaxed for a minute.

Well, at least the window was fixed and Trudy was warm. It appeared Jethro would have to be content with that outcome because the fledgling friendship he and Gemma had begun was now gone. Completely.

Why had she flinched?

He wasn't that scary. Sure, he was much bigger than she was, but he was charming, damn it. So if she hadn't flinched from him, who had hurt her? The idea that somebody out there had harmed the petite blonde shot fire right through his torso, hitting each healed wound on the way. His mind was still flipping the problem over while he mounted the stairs to his apartment and unlocked the door.

It took him a precious second to realize that all was not well.

He stiffened and then nudged the door open with one knuckle. The German shepherd hit him square in the chest, licking his neck before dropping back down to all fours. "Bloody hell," he muttered, wiping slobber off his cheek and walking inside, where the scent of steak enchiladas wafted around, making his stomach growl. He slammed the door and stalked through his industrial-chic apartment to the utilitarian kitchen.

"Jethro. Hello." Dana finished tossing a salad. The pretty blonde had a dish towel over her slim shoulder as she worked, and her belly looked just a little rounder than the last time he'd seen her. That baby was probably growing fast.

"Hey," Wolfe said, sitting on a red barstool at the raised counter, next to Dana. He tipped back a beer. "Nari is down in your wine cellar, by the way. If there's a bottle you want to protect, you'd better get to it."

Jethro focused on him. "Why are you all in my apartment?"

"We're here to work the case," Wolfe drawled. "Right now we're leaving Bridge and Raider, as well as Mal and Pippa on vacation, but I can call them home if necessary."

"No." Jethro remained in place, his stance set. "How the hell did you all break into my apartment?" He kept his voice calm so he wouldn't spook the baby inside Dana, but it took effort.

Angus emerged from Jethro's bedroom. "I had a key, remember? And you didn't change any of the security codes. As a profiler, I find that interesting." Angus Force was a battered and wounded ex-FBI agent with black hair, green eyes, and an aura of pure danger. Yet when Nari emerged from the cellar, his eyes softened to barely deadly. "Did you find a good bottle?"

"Several." Nari Zhang was a shrink who loved to dig into people's heads. She wore white jeans and a black sweater that matched her long hair. "Jethro, it's good to see you. I wish you had called when trouble came knocking." She put the three bottles on the counter. "I chose midpriced and didn't go for the good stuff in the northern corner, so don't worry."

Roscoe whined from near Wolfe's feet.

"No," Nari said firmly. "We brought you food and water, but you do not get wine. Don't even think about it."

The dog lay down and put his nose on his paws, looking truly pathetic.

Jethro lasered in on Angus. "Why were you in my bedroom?"

Angus rolled his eyes. "I wasn't going through your panty drawer or anything. Dana was in the powder room earlier, and sometimes she throws up for a long time, so I just had to use your bathroom. Give me a break."

A break? Give him a break? "You weren't invited," Jethro said, his voice hoarse. "None of you were invited."

Wolfe shrugged one monstrous shoulder. "We're family. I've learned that family doesn't need an invitation."

Dana chuckled and grasped his good pot holders to open the oven and bring out first one and then another dish of what definitely smelled like steak enchiladas.

Nari opened the nearest drawer. "Where's the—here it is." She pulled out a wine opener.

Jethro cleared his throat. "Listen. I appreciate the fact that you all are here, but I don't want help."

Dana took a notepad out of his junk drawer and made a couple of scribbles. "We can loop in everyone via computer if necessary. Then the whole team will be involved, except for Serena, and we should talk about her next. I don't like that she just took off."

Jethro twisted his neck to keep from yelling. They weren't listening to him.

Angus nodded. "We've obtained—and don't ask how—the recording of the last interview you had with your brother when he was in custody. Do you want to watch it while we eat dinner or afterward?"

Jethro saw red.

Roscoe instantly was by his side, nudging his furry head beneath Jethro's hand.

Jethro petted him, forcing his body back to calmness.

"Huh," Wolfe said mildly. "Really thought we were finally going to see the professor lose his temper. Bummer."

* * * *

There were many things Angus Force disliked in this life, and walking in blind to any situation was top of the list. He sat on Jethro's surprisingly comfortable, industrial-styled sofa with Nari next to him. His arm was around her slender shoulders, and he played with her long hair, letting the soft strands soothe him. The rest of the team had sprawled around on furniture or on the floor while Nari tinkered with a laptop, pointing a projector at the brick wall above the modern fireplace.

Jethro sat in a chair to the right, and his gaze kept straying to the painting Wolfe had kindly removed from said wall to lean against the far window.

"It's a fucking painting, Jethro," Angus snapped.

Jethro swung his irritated gaze to Angus. "That is an original Angela Wakefield."

Didn't mean a thing to Angus, but Nari seemed suitably impressed. Angus knew his friend wouldn't blow up with the ladies present, even though the ladies could fight. Well, Nari could fight. The Brit was too well-mannered, and that could easily be used against him. Although he was deadlier than anybody in the room realized—with the exception of Angus. He'd read Jethro's file. One of them anyway. No doubt countries all over the world had a file on Dr. Jethro Hanson. "Why didn't you call?"

"I don't require assistance," the Brit said stubbornly, his hand over the side of the chair petting Roscoe.

Angus kept his temper in check, looking beyond the painting to the floor-to-ceiling windows gridded with heavy metal. His gaze returned to the blue hue of the double-sided gas fireplace, through which he could see a rec room with a pool table and another bar. With its cement floors and stark furnishings, the place should feel cold but didn't. "The Homeland Defense Department has taken over the case, and we've reached out to MI6 and Scotland Yard. You've been assigned as a witness as well as a consultant, so you're all clear to talk to us, Jet. Nari, do you believe Jethro requires assistance?"

Nari cleared her throat. "Yes and no. He's good at his job, but his brother is insane, and everyone needs backup." She snorted. "Let me rephrase that. Jethro was good at his former job. When he worked for MI6."

Jethro knocked his head back on the metal chair. "Everyone knows?"

"Yep," Angus said easily. "We're a team and we know one another's pasts. Or at least part of them. We can't cover you if we don't understand everything."

Jethro looked toward a pregnant Dana in the chair across from him with Wolfe sitting on the floor, his back against her chair, his legs extended. "None of you are going to cover me. Period."

"Might need an intervention," Wolfe said calmly.

Angus remained stoic. Wolfe's intervention style usually involved a broken nose. "That's not necessary. Boot up the interview."

Nari typed and an interrogation room took form on the brick wall. Jethro sat on one side and a man with similar features sat across from him. Jet's hair was lighter and his shoulders broader, but there was no question they were brothers.

"What gave me away?" Fletcher asked, smiling.

Before Jethro could answer, the screen fizzled and went dark.

"Hey," Nari said, typing rapidly.

Jethro sighed. "We're not a backwoods corporation. You're dealing with MI6 there. Even if you had Brigid hack them, which apparently you did, they wouldn't just let it go."

Angus looked at Jethro. "Well, I guess you start talking, then. Here's what I know so far. Your brother was a serial killer who apparently liked to disembowel people, and he's somehow circling around you right now. So what's your connection to the two victims?"

"No connection," Jethro said, sliding off his glasses and tossing them onto the glass coffee table.

Angus searched his face for any sign of deception. "You're trained to lie?"

"Yep," Jethro said. "But I'm not lying. Also, my brother wasn't a serial killer." He paused. "Let me rephrase that. He fits the description because he killed many more than three people, but he doesn't fit the psychopathy that you're accustomed to with serials."

"Go on," Angus suggested, keeping his tone light when Nari put her hand on his thigh in warning.

Jethro caught the action and his eyes flared. "Fine. Fletcher is older than me by a year, and there was always something off about the chap." Jethro fetched his wineglass from the shelf by his elbow and then swirled the thick liquid around. "You know. Charming and brilliant, but with odd proclivities. Let's just say that the animals in the vicinity of our childhood home often disappeared."

"Sounds like the childhood of a serial killer to me," Dana said thoughtfully.

Jethro shrugged. "Maybe. He attended university to be a barrister, and he created an admirable practice. Well, until it became apparent that he was also killing people." Of course, he'd also worked for MI6, but Jethro couldn't admit that unless he personally received clearance.

Nari took a notebook from the bottom of the pile and began to scribble in it. "Don't tell me. Society blondes and then older men started dying."

"No," Jethro scoffed. "Again, my brother is not a serial killer."

Angus looked up. "How about you explain that?"

Jethro cocked his head. "My brother was a contract killer. One of the best, actually."

Dana gasped. "Your brother killed people for money?"

"Yes," Jethro said.

"Was it a game between the two of you?" Angus asked.

Jethro looked at him, his brows drawn. "I really don't know, Force. I believe he enjoyed killing before I was brought in on his case, but once I was, it felt…"

"Personal?" Angus asked.

"Yes. MI6 brought me in because the deaths kept occurring in places familiar to me, and a pattern emerged. Oh, I didn't know the victims, but I knew the places. It was as if he was doing a job and then taunting me." For the first time there was a fine edge to Jethro's words. He shrugged. "I chased him, he made a fortune, I figured out his pattern, and I went after him full time."

"You caught him," Wolfe said.

"Yes." Jethro finished his wine. "He stabbed our mother right before I got to her and she died in my arms. Neither one of us was close to her, but he knew I'd blame myself for not getting there in time. I did."

Angus would unpack that later. "How'd your brother get free?"

"I'm waiting for the report to learn the details, but he's brilliant, so I'm not surprised." Jethro held out his glass when Nari motioned with the bottle, and she leaned over to refill it. "Now he's here, and no doubt he's been hired to kill these victims."

"But he's leaving them for you again," Angus said softly.

Nari cleared her throat. "Should you quit your job or work remotely? Maybe make it more difficult for him to find you?"

Jethro shook his head. "No. I won't run or hide from my brother. Besides, it would just tick him off, and he'd do something to make sure I came out into the light. We're doing this my way, which means I keep teaching and living my life." His jaw set in a stubborn tilt.

Fair enough. Angus took a drink of his wine. "Is it odd that he's communicating with you through notes?" The action seemed beneath Fletcher.

Jethro nodded. "It's odd but I think I get it. He's being an ass."

That about summed it up. "I figured," Angus murmured. "He's making fun of our last case and the fact that you're working with us. The notes are just him having a little fun." No doubt Fletcher believed that the ragtag group within the HDD was nothing compared to MI6.

"Exactly," Jet said, his gaze on his wine.

Angus lifted a shoulder. "I have no problem being underestimated. You need to understand that even though he seems methodical, there is emotion involved here. You caught him and turned him in to the authorities. In other words, you beat him." It wasn't difficult to profile the jackass.

"Yes." Jethro sat back. "Fletcher was always a jealous little shite, and now he wants revenge, although he'd argue he's above that. He is not. The farther away all of you stay, the better."

That wasn't going to happen. Not now and not ever.

Angus smiled.

Chapter Thirteen

Gemma spent all of Saturday making sure the house was safe. She installed another lock on the basement window. Though the window was small, a man could twist his body in such a way to make it through. So she also put sharp tacks and broken glass across the sill. Then she installed a lock on the outside of the door that led downstairs.

The windows and main doors had good locks, so she just purchased thin wooden rods to ensure that neither the windows nor the sliding glass door by the breakfast nook could be opened. She'd also purchased more bullets.

Finally she and Trudy had eaten dinner, had a bubble bath, and then gotten into bed. Well, Trudy was in bed. "Okay. That was three books," she whispered, leaning over to kiss Trudy on the head. Her hair fell forward onto her daughter's face. Her real hair.

Trudy giggled and grabbed a strand. "Mama's hair. Just like mine."

"Yeah," Gemma said softly. "Just like yours."

Trudy looked up into her eyes. "Blue eyes like mine. Yours and mine."

Gemma nodded. "Yes. But we keep a secret, right? Just you and me."

Trudy's little face scrunched up. "Why?"

Gemma smoothed back her daughter's hair, helplessness choking her. Then she swallowed. "It's a grown-up reason, and someday you'll understand, but right now you have to promise. It's our secret."

Trudy grinned. "Okay. Secret."

Hopefully the little girl would understand. Gemma had a good reason—several really—for keeping the child's biological father away from her. But what if he could've been a decent father, even though he was a crappy fiancé? Every instinct in Gemma's body screamed that Monty was dangerous not only to her but to Trudy. "Night, sweetie."

Trudy closed her eyes and snuggled down, falling asleep almost immediately.

Gemma listened to her breathe for several long moments, taking comfort in the fact that they appeared to be safe. For now.

She forced herself to stand and return to the living room, where she was folding laundry when her phone buzzed from the credenza. "Hello?" she answered, keeping her voice low to camouflage it.

"You sound odd. Are you ill?" Jethro asked over the line.

Relief had her straightening and moving into the living room to sit on the comfy gray sofa. "I was whispering because I just put Trudy to bed." Her heart rate picked up. The sexy professor had called her, and she could take one moment to enjoy that fact. "I'm still mad at you," she said, not having the energy to put any heat into the words.

"About that." He cleared his throat. "I owe you an apology for being overbearing about the tires. Not a half-assed one where I justify myself by saying I was doing the right thing. I'm sorry."

She looked around the quiet room with the curtains hiding the darkness and her heart warmed whether she wanted it to or not. "What brought this on?"

He sighed, and fabric rustled as if he'd sat down. "Let's just say I was on the other end of that type of situation last night. My friends mean well, but they were interfering, and they didn't listen when I told them nicely to sod off. It was a good lesson."

It sounded like he meant it. "You're forgiven."

"Thank you." He rustled again and then settled. "Shouldn't you be out on a date?"

She chuckled and reached for a plush throw to settle over her legs. "Right. I'm a single mom in a new town. There's no dating." She lay down on her side, enjoying feeling her body actually relax. "What about you, Dr. Charm? Surely you could find a grad student or someone to take out."

His chuckle was deep. Sexy. Strong. "Grad students aren't my type."

She could continue flirting and ask him about his type, but she knew better. This couldn't go anywhere, no matter how safe he seemed or how freaking good-looking he was—just like a young Indiana Jones. Indiana Jones had never settled down either.

Not that she could settle down in one place herself. "I need to go, Jethro. Have a nice night." She ended the call and turned to stare at the ceiling. She'd made a choice, and now she had to live with it. The memories rolled in faster than the snow outside.

It was a week out from her wedding, and she sat on an examination table at Cameron Medical Practice, after hours.

Tears streamed down her face, burning the bruises and cuts across her jaw. "Where is he?" Her voice trembled.

Dr. Jack Cameron, Monty's older brother, snipped off the end of the suture above her left eye. "I told him if he didn't stay in the waiting room and calm down that I was going to call the police on him myself." He stepped back, his kind face set in harsh lines of worry. "You can't keep on like this."

Her entire body hurt. This time after Monty beat her, he'd held a gun to her head. "He's going to kill me if I leave. If I don't go through with the wedding next week," she whispered, her split lip protesting and her voice hoarse from being choked. She believed Monty. There was no doubt he'd hunt her down and kill her.

Jack sighed, sounding weary. Beaten. He lived alone and would probably always only have Monty as family. His brother meant everything to him. "What was it about this time?"

She hung her head. "He said I was faking it last week when I fainted. That I manipulated him to bring me here and wasted your time on all the tests. That I just wanted attention." The last thing she wanted was attention.

Jack leaned against the salmon-colored counter by the sink. His temples had already gone gray and he had a slight paunch, but he seemed like a kind man. He was ten years older than Monty, and right now he looked much older than that. "I should never have left him with our mother and stepfather when he was just a kid. So young." Tears gathered in his eyes, and his face had gone ashen. "It's my fault. I just left him and went to medical school, not looking back. They used him like a punching bag."

"I know how that feels now." Gemma reached for the bag of ice on the counter and pressed it to her aching wrist. For a moment she'd thought Monty had broken it.

Jack watched her. "You've lived with him for six months and it's only getting worse. You can't fix him, Gemma. He's going to kill you."

Gemma was so tired. Monty was right when he said she'd never be able to make it on her own. She'd been raised by an alcoholic mother and she didn't understand life. She'd been so stupid to believe that she could do anything, and she was lucky Monty wanted to take care of her.

His voice came in loud and clear in her head.

Plus, he'd given Fran money, and she loved him. If Gemma ran, her mother would actually help him find her. Gemma was on her own.

"When he's nice he's so nice," she whispered. But just when she'd start to feel safe, the other Monty would appear. It was like a switch flipped and he became somebody else. "I thought I could love him enough."

Jack shook his head. "I have a duty to report this, but I can't. I've failed you as badly as Monty has, and I'm so very sorry." He looked toward the closed door. "Gemma? If you are ever going to run, it's now. We're leaving tomorrow for his bachelor weekend, and it's the last chance you'll get." He opened a drawer and took out a thick envelope. "I have five thousand dollars here. It's all I could get on short notice, but it's yours." He handed her the envelope.

She looked down at the money. "I don't understand."

He exhaled loudly. "Your tests came back and I destroyed them."

She blinked, looking up at him, although her eyesight hadn't returned in her left eye yet. Monty had nailed her right in the temple. Everything hurt. "Why? Am I dying?"

"No. You're pregnant."

The words came from very far away. A universe away. "Wh–what?" she asked.

Jack nodded.

Terror strangled her, stronger than Monty's grip. "Maybe..."

Jack shook his head.

No. This wouldn't change Monty. Nausea welled up her throat and she nearly puked. If Monty hit her again, he could kill the baby. Was he even capable of love? Was this her fault? She just didn't know anything any longer. Her hands went automatically to her abdomen. A baby.

Determination mingled with fear inside her. "He can never know." Maybe Monty would forget her or move on without her if she got away. Oh, he'd be furious and embarrassed that she would take off right before the wedding, and he'd look for her. Possibly he'd give up after a year or two. But if he discovered they had a child, he'd never stop hunting her. She knew that with every ounce of her soul.

"Agreed," Jack whispered.

She handed him the envelope. "Leave this at the reception desk for me and I'll pick it up tomorrow after you guys leave town." They were headed to Las Vegas for the weekend and wouldn't return until Sunday night. That gave her three days to flee. She'd take a bus to a bigger city and then pay cash for a car sold by a private person. Could she use Facebook to find cars for sale?

"Where are you going?" Jack asked.

She didn't have anywhere to go. So she'd travel to a state other than Oregon, wait however many weeks were required to establish residency, and then she'd legally change her last name. She could do that as many times as necessary, and she would. Also, she'd have to dye her hair and buy colored contacts. She was curvy, and Monty had always been on her to lose weight.

So she'd either gain a lot of weight or lose every curve to change her body shape.

The door opened.

She stiffened, sitting upright in her flannel pajama set with only one sock on. Jack unobtrusively slipped the envelope back into the drawer.

Monty walked inside the room, the knuckles on his right hand bloody and bruised. "I'm so sorry." Tears filled his too-blue eyes and his broad shoulders hunched. "I don't know why you make me so angry. What is it?"

"I don't know," she whispered.

He scrubbed a hand through his thick hair. "Things will get better when we're married." He looked at his older brother. "Thank you for stitching her up. I thought she was wrong to call you, but I'm glad she did."

Hopefully he meant that and wouldn't make her pay for the phone call when they returned to the cabin. Right now he seemed to be calm, and that look—the one that told her pain was coming—was gone from his eyes.

Monty moved to her, and she gathered every ounce of her control not to flinch. He wrapped his arms around her, pulling her against his strong chest. "I'm so very sorry." He released her and leaned back, looking deep into her eyes. "You know things will be better when we're married, and I know you're committed only to me. I need that."

She swallowed. "I need that, too."

His smile was the same one he'd given her that first day. "You're going to be a beautiful bride. The most beautiful bride in the world."

One who would need tons of makeup to cover her bruises. Instead of saying so, she smiled, barely holding back a wince as her bottom lip cracked open again. "I can't wait for our wedding."

"Me either." He looked over at his brother. "I don't want to go to Vegas and leave her. She needs me."

Jack laughed, but the sound was strained. "That's too bad, younger brother. I wasn't there for you growing up, but I'm here now, and I'm your best man. Everything is paid for and all set, and we are going to celebrate your last few days as a bachelor in royal style. I'm sure Gemma has tons to do while we're gone."

"I do," she said quietly. More than Monty could ever know.

Monty kissed the bruise on her nose. "It'll be lonely and quiet for you out at the cabin. I need to have the car serviced while we're gone."

So she'd be trapped. "All right. I'll enjoy the quiet," she said. If she had to walk the twenty-five miles to town, she would. Heck, she'd hitchhike. There were a lot of nice people who lived in the country who would give her a ride. "Don't worry, Monty. Everything is going to be perfect."

She awoke with a start, instantly knowing where she was and where her daughter slept. Safe in Serena's house. A home that couldn't be traced to Gemma, no matter what. She was Gemma Falls now. Turned out it cost money and was a pain to legally change a name, so she'd only done so officially three times. Unofficially she'd used several names while taking jobs that paid under the table. Her waitressing skills were top-notch, and she'd no doubt return to that profession after the semester ended.

Years after fleeing Oregon, she could feel Monty's hands wrapped around her neck. He was still coming. She'd outrun a private detective only four months ago in Orlando, barely getting free and losing almost all their possessions that time. Even so, she'd kept her daughter safe while having learned one thing without a doubt.

Monty would never stop coming.

Chapter Fourteen

Early Monday evening, Jethro spotted the light on in Gemma's office as he headed toward the exit. The woman had made it more than clear on the phone that weekend that she wasn't interested, so he should keep on moving. Plus, he didn't date long term, so it wasn't right to keep charming her, if that's what he'd been doing. Something told him she wasn't fooled by charm. Yet he paused at her doorway, surprised to see her staring sightlessly out the window at the quiet night.

When he'd been young, very young, he'd thought his mother beautiful. Blond hair, brown eyes, graceful movements. A lovely face to be studied. As he'd grown, he'd learned very quickly that warmth was more important than beauty—a lesson he carried with him to this day.

Gemma had more warmth in her than he'd initially thought, and in profile she truly was lovely. A sense of loneliness hung around her, heavy and sad.

He cleared his throat.

She jumped in the chair and turned to face him, her cheeks losing color.

Shite. "Sorry." He hadn't meant to scare her, for goodness' sake. "You okay?"

"Um, yes." She gathered papers into a pile, busying her hands. "Sorry. I was thinking."

"Obviously." He slung his pack over his other shoulder, wanting to give his healed scars a break. "Are you walking to the day care? I could accompany you." Why did she look so sad, and what could he do to fix that? Nothing, if she didn't give him the chance.

Even her smile didn't reach her eyes. "The day care is having a special science party and the kids were excited. I won't pick Trudy up until seven, so I thought I'd get some extra work completed."

Ah. He was never a chap to let an opportunity go, and if nothing else, the woman truly needed to get out of the office. "How about we grab dinner just around the corner?" He held up one hand before she could refuse. "My pantry is empty and I was just going to hit a drive-through, but I'd rather have Italian food and debate game theory." Then he waited, surprised by how badly he wanted her to accept his invitation. "It's on me. I could use a relaxing dinner." Which was the truth. He still didn't have a line on his brother and hated the thought that it would take another dead body to give him a lead.

She stared at him, obviously thinking it over. "Just as colleagues?"

Well, that was a mite insulting. "Of course," he said smoothly.

"Okay," she said, a hint of suspicion in her tone. "I guess that would be all right."

He grinned. "If I'd had an ego, you just destroyed it completely."

Her laugh came more naturally than had her smile as she stood and reached for the ugly wool coat. "I have no doubt your ego is still nicely sized and in a healthy state."

He stepped back to allow her to precede him into the hallway and out the door, into the chilly night. "I'm parked over here," he said, somewhat surprised she'd accepted his invitation.

They didn't speak on the way to the restaurant or as they were seated in a secluded corner.

She looked around at the intimate interior. In the candlelight her features appeared even more delicate than usual. "This seems romantic." Based on her frown she didn't like that.

"They have great food," Jethro said. "Although I usually pop over for lunch and it isn't so dark, to be honest."

The words seemed to relax her. They ordered and each had a glass of wine. By the end of dinner, he'd learned that she was more than qualified to teach the upper division game theory classes if she wanted. It was one of the most relaxing and enjoyable meals he'd had in years, and as he paid the check, he wished he had the right to ask her about her fears. About the way she stiffened when anybody came too close and then had to make an obvious attempt to relax herself.

Somebody had scared her and somebody had hurt her.

So he ignored his urge to place his hand at the base of her spine as they left and instead kept his hands to himself. The more he was around her, the more he wanted to touch her.

They strode out into the night, where it had started to snow again.

She sighed and looked up, blinking away moisture. “Any idea when the weather will get nicer?”

He barked out a laugh and escorted her to his vehicle, down the lot. “Yes. A few months from now.”

Her laughter was a warm sound that dug into his chest and took root. He let the sound fill him, so in tune to her that he let his constant vigilance slip, just for a second.

It was a second too long.

“Hey. Wallet.” The guy came out from behind a tree, gun extended, a dark blue ski mask over his face.

Gemma gasped.

Jethro pivoted and concealed her with his body. “Sure. There’s no need for a weapon.” He reached into his front pocket to hand over his wallet, his peripheral vision already taking in the scene. Two other guys, one wearing a red ski mask and the other a purple one, jumped up from behind an adjacent car. Purple held a knife and Red held nothing, both twitching. Had they been waiting specifically for him?

His vehicle was the nicest in the lot, so perhaps they had been.

He catalogued them. All around six feet and in their early twenties. One white, one black, and one he couldn’t quite tell through the mask. The masks did a good job of shrouding their features.

He pressed back until he could feel Gemma behind him. “We don’t want any problems on this fine night. I have nearly a thousand dollars in my wallet and it’s all yours.”

“A thousand?” Red burst out, his gloved hands sweeping. “Awesome.”

Purple nudged him. “We’re supposed to, um, take the woman.”

Gemma stepped up to Jethro’s side, a snub nose in her hand that she pointed at Blue, who gasped and tightened his hold on his gun.

Shock took Jethro for a second and then he moved. The woman had a bloody gun? “Whoa. Wait a sec. Everyone chill.” He placed a hand on Gemma’s gun and gently pushed down, ready to leap in front of her if Blue squeezed the trigger of his gun. The moment her weapon was pointed down, he edged her behind him again.

Apparently he had no choice here. He held out the wallet to Blue, and when the idiot tried to take it, Jethro struck.

* * * *

Gemma's hand shook around the cold metal as Jethro put her behind him again, his solid body forming a bulwark between her body and the threat. Maybe gun to gun wasn't a good idea, but now he wasn't covered.

Then he moved.

Fast.

One second he was in front of her and the next he had the other guy's gun in his hand, striking fast and hard. The guy with the blue mask fought back wildly, and Jethro countered each punch almost methodically, striking painful-looking blows, often with the butt of the attacker's own gun. Finally Jethro punched the man in the neck, and he went down to the ground, out cold.

Jethro turned toward the other two, who'd frozen in place. He cocked his head and stuck the gun in his pocket. Snow fell onto his dark blond hair, and his usually warm eyes held cold warning. He rolled his shoulder and just watched the other two men as if he had all the time in the world. His chest was wide, his stance set, and his body deadly.

"Jethro?" Gemma whispered. Why had he put the gun away? Where had he learned to fight like that? *Who* fought like that? How did he seem so...*calm*?

The guy with the knife smiled and charged.

Gemma screamed.

Jethro turned at the last second, grasped the man's wrist, and twisted. The knife clattered harmlessly across the ice. Then Jethro pulled, and something snapped. Loudly. The guy cried out and tried to pull away, but Jethro held him by the broken arm, staring impassively at the wounded attacker.

The guy sniffed and then punched out with his other hand.

Jethro caught the guy's fist in his palm and twisted again.

The wrist broke. Gemma gagged, backing away. How could such violence be so calm?

The man fell to the ground, shrieking and clutching his broken arm. Jethro kicked him right in the face, and his head bounced twice before settling, his eyes closed.

The last man standing, the one with the red mask, shook out his hands. He looked at his unconscious buddies and then lowered his head and charged, ramming Jethro with a strong tackle right in the gut. They smashed onto the ice, skidding to the center of the parking lot, Jethro beneath him. They came to a stop, and for a second nobody moved.

The attacker levered himself up, fist raised.

Jethro almost causally threw out his arm, blocking the punch. Then he wrapped both legs around the man, scooted him down, and pressed his legs hard against his neck. “Go limp,” he suggested.

The other man flopped like a fish, struggling and grunting with the effort. Jethro kept him in place.

His air gone, the other man had no choice but to go lax.

Jethro loosened the hold of his legs and pushed the man off him before gracefully rolling up to his feet. He walked toward her and straightened his clothing, brushing ice off his jacket. He looked like he’d just gone for a peaceful stroll through a park. There wasn’t a bruise on him.

Gemma’s mouth gaped open and she looked at the three unconscious men on the ground. She was too stunned to move. Her brain wouldn’t process the intense and yet oddly peaceful violence. How could violence be peaceful? The saliva in her mouth dried up and her throat ached.

“Are you all right?” Jethro asked, halting several feet away from her.

She had the strongest urge to point her gun at him. “What just happened?” she croaked.

His brow furrowed. “I’m not certain. Please go back inside the restaurant while I call the authorities.”

How could he act so normal after he’d just kicked the crap out of three armed men without breaking a sweat? There was no doubt he could’ve killed all three had he so chosen. Who was this man? She stepped back, her hand shaking so wildly on the gun that she had no choice but to drop the weapon back into her purse. She glanced at her watch. “I–I have to get Trudy.” She couldn’t be late to pick up her daughter. Trudy should never be scared.

Jethro sighed and looked around, as if not quite sure what to do. “All right.” He reached in his pocket and drew out his car keys. “Take my vehicle and drive directly to the day care—it’s just around the corner. Please park my car right next to yours and leave my keys under the seat. Also, be very careful driving home. I take it you’re staying at Serena’s?”

Numbly, she nodded.

He handed her the keys. “The roads are icy and the crews haven’t had time to clear them.”

Her brain reeled. The man was asking her to be careful and giving her his SUV?

The attacker closest to him, the one with the blue mask, started to stir. Jethro, almost casually, kicked back and nailed the man beneath the chin. The man’s head flew back and thunked loudly on the icy sidewalk. His body went slack, blood dripping from his bottom lip.

She felt as if she was in a daze. Her stomach cramped. Hard.

Stumbling, she backed away from Jethro and turned, barely keeping herself from running for his rig.

"Wait a moment." Jethro strode to the center of the parking lot and partially lifted the guy with the red mask to drag him closer to the sidewalk, dropping the limp body carelessly. "There you go. The lot is clear now."

Gemma gagged. "Thanks." She opened the driver's door and jumped inside, slamming it shut and locking it. Her hand convulsed around the keys and she dropped them to the rubber mat. Crap. A quick glance confirmed that she could start the SUV by stepping on the brake and pressing the button on the console. She did so and then drove sedately out of the lot, her mind still reeling.

He'd been so violent. So freaking casual about it.

Should she run again?

Chapter Fifteen

Irritation clawed Jethro's back as he shoved the third man next to the other two and then kicked the guy wearing the purple mask in the ankle. "Wake up, jackass," he muttered, kicking him again.

The guy stirred. Barely.

Jethro sighed and tugged his phone out of his pocket, making a quick call.

"Bianchi," Detective Tate Bianchi answered.

"Hi, Detective," Jethro said. "I'm at Louivanni's near DC University and have three men here who might be able to assist with your homicides."

Tate was quiet for two beats. "You're just sitting there with them?"

"They attacked me and now they're waiting patiently to speak with you. I don't know for sure they can help, but either way they need to be arrested." Though Tate was a homicide detective, surely he could assist. "If this doesn't interest you, please send officers to arrest these morons." He ended the call.

Looking around, he spotted the knife half-wedged into a chunk of ice. "There we go." He fetched it and returned, grasping Purple by the sweatshirt and dragging him into a seated position. "Wake up, blighter. Time to chat." Jethro yanked off the ski mask, taking some blond hair with it. "I don't have a lot of time here." He slapped the guy several times.

"What?" The guy woke up and his eyes widened. He gasped and tried to edge away.

"No." Jethro flipped the knife around in his hand and pressed it to the man's jugular. "I don't have time to be nice. Talk to me or I'll slice your throat and move on to your buddy. What's your name?"

The guy's blue eyes widened. "Steven Gammonal. Don't kill me." A snot bubble popped out of his nose. He had to be in his early twenties and still had a spray of acne across his face that was rapidly turning a bruised purple.

Jethro let the moment draw out. "That depends. You said that you were supposed to take the woman. What does that mean?"

Steve gulped. "I don't know."

Jethro winced. "See, I don't have time for lies." He cut into Steve's neck.

"Wait. Okay. Wait," Steve cried, going pale. "All right. This guy hired us to follow you from the university and then beat you up. Said there probably wouldn't be anybody with you, but if there was a chick, he'd give us a hundred grand extra if we brought her to him. I'm sorry." He sniffed. "We just needed the money. We wouldn't have really kidnapped any woman. He said probably nobody would be with you and that you were a loner."

Sirens sounded in the distance.

Relief flashed across Steve's face.

"Not so fast, Steve," Jethro said, his voice low. "I can still kill you and claim self-defense."

Steve looked frantically at his prone buddies, but neither moved. "I'm sorry. We wouldn't have hurt her. I promise."

Yes, that promise meant quite a lot. Not. "Who hired you?"

Steve shrugged and then winced at what was probably a torn rotator cuff. "I don't know. He kind of looked like you and had an Irish accent like you."

For Christ's sake. "That's British, you moron." Jethro cut a little deeper, stopping when Steve cried out. "How did he find you? How did he know to hire you?"

Steve's eyes widened. "I don't know. We were all recently arraigned for a B and E, so maybe our reputation is out there?"

More likely Fletcher just looked at recent crimes and tracked down the morons.

A squad car careened into the parking lot. "Did the guy who hired you say anything specific about the woman who was with me tonight?"

Steve sniffed, his gaze landing on the police car with a look of hope. "No. He just said that if anybody was with you, especially a woman, he wanted to meet her. Like it was no big deal."

So Fletcher wasn't aware of Gemma. Good. But what was this lame attack all about? Fletcher had sent three idiots for Jethro to fight. Was he just messing with him? Or had he wanted to make a statement in front of anybody Jethro might be hanging around? Start hurting his reputation at the college? Damn Fletcher and his need to draw things out.

Jethro released Steve and stood as two female officers rushed his way.

"Dr. Hanson?" The closest officer was a tightly packed African American woman who looked at the three prone men impassively. "Detective Bianchi said to tell you he's on the way and to hold tight."

"Sure." Jethro turned away from the men and didn't miss Steve's sigh of relief. "I need to make a quick phone call." He walked to the entrance of the restaurant and leaned against the wall, dialing quickly.

"Force," Angus answered absently.

Jethro straightened. "Hi. I have an issue and need Millicent Frost. Could you have her meet me in the parking lot of DC University in about thirty minutes?" An unmarked black car skidded into the lot and parked. Detective Bianchi jumped out, took in the scene, and then shot Jethro a look of pure irritation. "Make that an hour."

"What's going on?" It sounded like Angus was already on the move.

"I'm not certain. Tell her to bring all her fancy devices for finding bugs. Thank you." Jethro clicked off and waited for the detective to reach him. "Good evening, Detective."

Tate turned and surveyed the prone men. "Is this your doing?"

"I believe they all slipped on the ice," Jethro said helpfully. "However, I also think they've been in contact with your recent killer, and perhaps they have clues for you."

Tate turned toward him. "I think I'll arrest you."

Jethro smiled and shoved his hands in his pockets. "You don't have probable cause. These blokes attacked me and I defended myself."

"How are they connected to the homicides?" Tate asked.

Jethro kept his mild expression in place while all he wanted to do was check on Gemma and ensure she was all right. He must've scared the hell out of her. "I don't believe they're connected to the homicides, but I think the man who hired them is your killer. That's all I can tell you right now."

Tate stared at the man in the blue mask, who was just starting to awaken.

"Oh." Jethro drew out the bloke's gun and handed it over. "He had this." Then he handed over the bloody knife. "The petty criminal in the purple mask brought this to the evening."

"A weapon makes it more than petty." Tate motioned for an officer to hand over evidence bags. "You fought a guy with a knife and one with a gun?"

Jethro shrugged. "They weren't very good."

Tate bagged the weapons, looked at the three attackers, and then turned to face Jethro. "Something tells me there's more to your background than being a philosophy professor."

Perhaps this had been Fletcher's intention. So much for Jethro continuing to fly under the radar. "Things are rarely what they seem, Detective."

* * * *

"You were on a date?" Angus Force asked, holding on to his patience, as Millie ran all her doodads across Jethro's car.

Jethro lifted the collar of his jacket to shield his neck from the now-billowing snow. "No. I wasn't on a date. I just grabbed an early supper with a colleague." He lounged against the stark brick building and watched as Millie worked with Roscoe bouncing around her feet.

Angus scanned the vacant parking area, quiet building, and surrounding trees. "Huh. Too bad. I know Nari thinks you should start living your life instead of busying yourself in pursuit of more knowledge." Actually Nari said Jethro needed to get a girlfriend and start living, but close enough. She was an excellent shrink and was probably correct about Jet. "Who was the woman?"

"Nobody with whom you need to concern yourself," the Brit said, angling his head to watch Millie. "Anything?"

"Not done," Millie called back, shimmying beneath the SUV with a long metal pole.

Angus whistled for Roscoe to leave her alone.

It was nice having the woman back in the fold, and he hadn't yet grilled her on where she'd gone. Millie was in her mid-twenties but sometimes seemed younger to him, even though she was a genius with all electrical devices and weapons. Her blond hair was streaked with blue dye, giving her the look of a college coed. Her small form disappeared beneath the large vehicle. "Should you be on a blanket instead of the ice?" he yelled.

"No," she yelled back.

Jethro sighed. "I don't want her to fall ill."

Angus rolled his shoulders in his heavy leather jacket. "Listen, Jethro. I've already scanned the preliminary police report and saw that you took out three guys." Tate had texted him what he'd known so far, so that could count as a prelim report. Probably. "Why would your brother play games like this?"

Jethro shrugged. "I don't know. He's been imprisoned for several years, so perhaps he wants to draw this out. Putting a bullet between my eyes might be temporarily satisfying, but he's had a lot of time to plan this."

"He's a lawyer?"

Jethro nodded. "Yes."

"When you caught him and he went to prison, why wasn't there a trial? Or at the very least a newspaper report?" Angus had never looked into

Jethro's previous life, but now he had no choice. "I had Brigid scour the archives, and there was no word of a trial. His colleagues believed he'd left the country to learn to paint and find a new life."

Jethro remained silent.

Angus kept his cool. Hitting Jethro wouldn't help and Millie hated violence, so he'd just tick her off. "You know that Wolfe considers you his best friend."

Jethro twitched. Finally. A reaction.

Angus barely kept from smiling. "Yep. Clarence Wolfe thinks you're brothers, man. So it's time you let us in completely, or things are going to get messy."

Jethro finally looked at Angus, his eyes veiled as usual. "We had one op together."

"Apparently that's all it takes with Wolfe," Angus said easily. "He's been occupied with Dana's pregnancy, but she's feeling better now, and he's going to turn his attention to you. I learned the hard way that it's better to keep Wolfe involved than to try to push him away. There's no dissuading that guy, and he's all in with family. Like it or not, you're family."

Jethro's nostrils flared. "I don't have family."

"Stop being an ass," Angus snapped. "Seriously. I'm going to let Wolfe loose if you don't knock this off. From what I can tell, your blood brother is here taking hit jobs, making money, and involving you each time. Does he always disembowel his targets?"

"No," Jethro said. "That's his preferred method of killing, but he only uses that if it's up to his discretion. He's more than capable of making a murder look like an accident." Jethro straightened. "In fact, you should investigate other deaths in the area for the last month. Or have Tate do it."

"Already on it," Angus said. It wasn't like he was a novice either.

His phone buzzed and he lifted it to his ear. "Force."

"Hi. It's Nari." The sweet sound of her voice calmed him like nothing else in the world. "I've been pulling strings with my dad and he finally got back to me." Her father was the head of an elite force at the Homeland Defense Department and now their boss. "From what I can tell, Jethro wasn't just MI6. He was in The Increment."

Angus stiffened. "That unit really exists?"

"Unconfirmed rumors," Nari admitted. "But there's more. His brother wasn't a barrister. Well, he was, but that was a cover."

Angus lifted his chin, looking directly at Jethro. "Jet's brother was in The Increment as well?"

No reaction. None. Jethro didn't even tilt his head. Fuck, he was good.

"Maybe," Nari said quietly. "That would explain a lot, don't you think?"

Unfortunately yes. The Increment was only a rumor. An SIS-run unit that was a secret cadre within MI6, working under the radar in so-termed deniable operations. "Thanks, sweetheart," he said, ending the call. "That's interesting."

Jethro remained silent.

Well, that could certainly explain the search for good and evil and the nearly pathological need to right the scales. Even if it meant hunting down his own brother and putting him away for life. Angus slipped his phone back into his pocket while the wind tried to freeze his hand off. "Sounds like we have much to discuss."

Millie shoved her way out from under the vehicle, a small button held triumphantly in her hand. "Whoever set this is good. Really good. I'm better." Rolling, she came up on her feet and plopped the silver device into Angus's hand. "It's a tracker. Very well placed."

Angus flipped it up in the air and then caught it. "Jethro?"

Nothing. Not even a blink.

Damn it.

Chapter Sixteen

Gemma paced by her window, listening to the house quiet around her as Trudy slept. They'd had bath time, playtime, and reading time. Now Trudy was out, and Gemma couldn't stop thinking about Jethro and his handling of the three attackers. He hadn't lost his temper once. How was that possible? How was he possible? Maybe he was a professor trained in martial arts? Even so, the attacker had mentioned taking out whoever was with Jethro. So he was targeted? None of it made sense.

Usually when something troubled her, she packed up her daughter and left town.

But the danger had been aimed at Jethro, not at her. Obviously they couldn't spend any more time together. She had enough problems of her own.

The knock on the door didn't surprise her. She'd kept the colored contacts in her eyes and the blond wig on her head, just in case. A quick look through the peephole confirmed that Jethro was on the other side, snow on his dark blond hair.

She took a deep breath and opened the door.

"I brought ice cream." He held up a gallon of vanilla and then drew a bottle of B&B from behind his back. "And B&B. We can make B-52 bombers."

She blinked. That was not what she'd expected. Taken off guard, she slid to the side, allowing him entrance.

"Thank you." He moved beyond her, heading straight for the kitchen, which was visible from the entry.

She shut and locked the door. With Jethro in the house, the place felt different. His energy, calm and strong, smoothed out the edges of the place. "Are you all right?" she asked.

He stood on the other side of the tall counter, at the sink. "That's supposed to be my question." In the darkened kitchen, his eyes looked more amber than brown topaz.

She studied him. While she'd noticed his height and the breadth of his chest before, she hadn't considered him truly dangerous. Now she knew better. He was a brilliant man who was an expert at fighting. If what had happened could even be considered a fight. He'd basically reduced three other men, two of them armed, to unconsciousness. With little effort.

He started opening cupboards. "Blender?"

"Left of the sink," she said, staying across the living room. What was she thinking, allowing him inside?

"I won't hurt you," he said, finding the blender and plugging it in.

She'd heard those words before and she'd believed them. Even if she thought Jethro would be true to his word, she wasn't staying in town for long. Whatever this was between them—and it was something—had to end. Right now.

He looked around and unerringly chose the utensil drawer, pulling out an ice cream scoop. "Apparently I have some issues with which to deal, so we can't spend time together any longer." He finished scooping the ice cream into the blender and then looked up, his gaze piercing across the distance. "But I thought one last drink might be nice."

She opened her mouth but didn't have any words.

He poured alcohol into the blender and pressed the button, mixing the concoction with a grinding noise that made it impossible to speak. He fetched two glasses from a cupboard, stopped the blender, and poured the thick white liquid into the glasses. Then he brought them around the counter and moved toward the thick chair by the sofa, holding out one glass.

She accepted the cup and sat on the sofa, tucking one leg beneath her. This was all surreal. "Who were those men and why did they have different-colored ski masks on?"

"They wore different ski masks because they're morons. As to their identities, I neither know nor care." He took a drink of the grown-up milkshake and didn't even get any on his upper lip.

She sipped, allowing the cold sugar to fill her. "It's good."

"Yes." He put the cup on a coaster on the coffee table and shrugged out of his jacket, dropping it to the floor. "Are you all right?"

She held both hands around the mug. "Not really. Why were those men looking for you, why did they want to kidnap me, and where did you learn to fight like that?" The questions burst out of her, and if she didn't get answers, her heart was going to do the same. She would not notice how big and strong and solid…and sexy he looked. No. A badass Indiana Jones with a British accent wasn't her type. But she had been looking for raw, and maybe raw was calmly deadly. She shook her head.

He retrieved his cup and drank, his lips full and firm on the glass. Well, what she assumed to be firm. What the heck was going on in her head? She hated violence. The man in front of her had transitioned from calm to violent in a heartbeat. Yet he'd been in control the entire time. Was that it? Was that why she wasn't terrified right now? Because he'd not only controlled the violence but himself and everyone around him?

Memories of Monty's flushed and furious face, of his uncontrollable temper, had her shivering.

Jethro was different. He'd just proven it to her.

He cleared his throat. "I worked for MI6 before becoming a professor and learned to fight there. The men after me tonight were mere puppets, if you will, geared to tick me off. Or expose me to the local authorities perhaps."

Who, what? "MI6? Like the MI6 with James Bond and Q and everyone? Seriously?" Her brain misfired as she tried to grasp this crazy reality.

He sighed. "Yes to MI6, and I don't want to go into the rest of that sentence."

Holy crap. All right. She tried to make sense of his remaining words. "These terrifying men were just puppets? For whom?"

He finished his drink and put down the glass again. "I assisted a local HDD unit with a couple of cases, just using my knowledge of philosophy, and that might've made me a target."

What? So much for the hallowed halls of academia. "Didn't 007 work for MI6?" Of course she'd heard of the organization, but she didn't really know much about it.

One of his eyebrows rose. "Er, well, yes. While Bond has given us some notoriety, he wouldn't make it as an actual agent. We try to follow the law."

Wow. A real former MI6 operative. She looked at him with new eyes and he seemed like the same guy. Calm and intelligent—and sexy. Had he killed people? Been injured? "Why are you in the US?" she asked.

"I needed a change and wanted to teach at DC University. I'm not undercover—I've left the service." His smile was patient. "If I hadn't, I wouldn't be able to tell you that I formerly was an agent. That's how you really know." He ran both broad hands down his black slacks. With his green button-down shirt, he looked tough but approachable. "I'd appreciate it if you'd keep this knowledge under your hat, so to speak. I left that life behind and don't want to revisit it."

"Why?" She couldn't help but ask the question. "Why did you leave?"

He looked over her shoulder at the wall behind her for a moment and then refocused on her face, his gaze inscrutable. “It was time. There was an op, and it was a lot, and I was done when I closed the case file. My expiration date had passed as far as I was concerned.” He rubbed a hand over his five o’clock shadow, which was darker than his blond hair. “I needed something new and left my undercover post teaching in the UK for a real job teaching here. Maybe trying to figure out if my soul could be redeemed.”

She sipped her drink, letting the alcohol cool her throat and relax her muscles. This was all teetering on being absolutely insane. “Have you decided? About your soul?” How tortured was he?

“Regrettably, no.” His cheek creased, flashing that one dimple. “I haven’t found the path to redemption.”

“Perhaps helping the local HDD team is your path,” she said softly. His eyes had warmed when he’d talked about that unit.

He shook his head. “I think not. However, right now I seem to be stuck in the middle of a bit of a mess, which touched you tonight. I apologize for that sad fact. Also, this means you and I can’t spend time together. But I wanted to make sure you were all right, and I wanted to say that I enjoyed our friendship, or whatever it was becoming.”

Becoming? The guy didn’t even know her true eye color. The urge to confide in him, to make him a part of her life, was shockingly strong. Must be the adrenaline of the earlier fight and the alcohol now. Everything inside her wanted to soothe him, but that wasn’t her job. Never would be. “I understand.” She didn’t need more danger in Trudy’s life.

“Good. You’re safer away from me,” he said.

Maybe. The guy could seriously fight, and if they had more time, she’d ask him to teach her. But she was the dove…and he the hawk. “You said that your, um, talents were revealed to the authorities. Did you have to make a police statement?” If so, she’d be asked to make a witness statement, and she couldn’t do that. She could pack after he left and be on the road at dawn in true dove style. Trudy would be so disappointed to leave the day care, and it’d be terrible to abandon her students, but Gemma didn’t have a choice.

“I did make a police report but didn’t mention you. I told the authorities that I’d eaten alone and didn’t recognize the blonde in the parking lot.” He shrugged. “The attackers were all a little fuzzy and probably aren’t sure of anything, so you won’t be bothered.”

She barely hid her sigh of relief. Okay. Even if the attackers told the police there had been a blond woman in the parking lot, there were a million blondes in DC. She hadn’t noticed any security cameras at the restaurant, and she'd driven Jethro's vehicle to the school, not her own. She was safe and could remain in town and keep teaching.

He leaned forward, his powerful forearms on his thighs. "Are you in trouble, Gemma?"

For the briefest of seconds, maybe just one, she considered telling him the truth. Maybe he could take care of Monty for good. Immediately she banished the thought and felt shame in that hope. She couldn't ask that of Jethro, and she couldn't live with murder on her soul. Oh, if Monty ever came after her, she'd defend her baby. But planning his demise was wrong. "No. I'm not in trouble."

"Who hurt you?" Jethro asked softly.

"Nobody," she lied.

He watched her, his patience obvious. "The snub nose gun was a surprise to me. I have no doubt it's unregistered, and it's illegal to have a weapon like that on campus. You're not someone who'd break the law unless you had a very good reason."

"I'm a woman living alone outside of Washington DC. That's a good reason to be armed." She reached for another coaster and slid her cup onto it, standing. "Thank you for dinner and for dessert."

He took the hint and stood, snagging his coat from the ground in one smooth motion. "You're welcome."

She preceded him to the door and opened it. "Good luck with, well, everything."

He pulled on his jacket, a leather one this time, and wrapped his hand over the opened door. "You too." Then he looked at her, his gaze dropping to her mouth.

She should step back. Definitely. Yet her breath sped up and her body flushed. She swallowed. "Jethro."

"Yeah." He leaned in, brushing her mouth with his.

Warmth exploded down her. Her eyelashes fluttered shut and she leaned up, kissing him.

He took over, his mouth strong, his lips firm. Only his mouth touched her, and when he swept his tongue past her lips she moaned. Her body sprang alive, as if she'd been sleeping for years.

All too soon he leaned back, his eyes darker than any amber. "Goodbye, Gemma." He shut the door and was gone.

She touched her mouth, leaning against the wall, her mind blank and her body on fire. "Goodbye," she whispered.

Chapter Seventeen

Jethro drove past the many warehouses in his neighborhood, parking in his spacious garage and jogging his way up the interior stairs to his apartment. The only one in the steel structure. He'd left a couple of nasty surprises on the exterior steps should Angus try to break in again. Oh, they weren't deadly, but his friend would find himself covered in glitter glue and then feathers.

It was nice to rely on old training once in a while.

Plus, he liked to check on his other two vehicles, one a rugged old truck in case he needed to go undercover and the other a Bentley Continental Flying Spur. A gorgeous car. His baby really.

He reached the top of the stairs and paused, his senses going on full alert. A bloody handprint, big and fresh, marred the wall by the metal door, which was open. He dropped his pack and nudged the door all the way open.

"Jethro? Need some assistance here," called a male voice.

Jethro jerked and then grabbed his pack, striding through the entryway to his kitchen. "What the bloody hell are you two doing here?"

His old friends Ian and Oliver Villan had taken over the kitchen, with Oliver on his back on the counter and Ian bending over him, sewing up a gash in the man's arm. Oliver's shirt lay in tatters on the floor, and more bruises and stitches bloomed across his massive chest.

"We heard you were in trouble and headed over here the second we finished a mission," Ian said, leaning closer to inspect the wound. "To be more exact, we heard that fucking Fletcher had escaped and figured he was coming for you."

They were both beat to hell. Leaving blood drops all over Jethro's floor. Damn, it was good to see them alive and fairly well. He'd missed them. "You should've sought medical help."

"We did," Oliver groaned, his muscled body sprawled over the hard cement block. "Both got stitched up on the transport here, but my stitches popped open. We jumped on board with some old pals after finishing our mission, and they were kind enough to drop us off in DC on their way home."

Ian tied off the sutures, obviously having found one of Jethro's surgical kits. Then he tugged his twin into a sitting position, finally turning and leaning against the counter. His face was battered and stitches punctuated the side of his neck.

"I thought you two went into private security," Jethro said, his body settling as he realized they were both all right. Bruised and cut, but nothing worse.

"Yeah." Oliver picked at a scab on his wrist. "We did, and that includes extraction. Went into Afghanistan to get out folks who'd been deserted there and came across some American vets doing the same thing. We combined forces and were on the way home when we caught wind of your problem. So here we are."

Jethro exhaled. Then he leaned in and hugged first Ian and then Oliver. "Glad you're still breathing."

"Ditto," Oliver said, his face ashen beneath the bruises.

Jethro shook his head. "You're out of the agency, I'm out, and yet somebody gave you a heads up about an ongoing mission? That doesn't make sense."

Ian grinned. "We still have friends at MI6, Brother. We helped you take Fletcher down once and we'll do it again."

Jethro looked at the two men who had become closer to him than his own blood brother. They looked good beneath the injuries. Black hair, hazel eyes, strong-as-hell bodies. Ian had more blue in his eyes and Oliver more green; otherwise they looked nearly identical. Their different scars helped him to tell them apart, though. "Have you eaten?"

"No," Ian said. "I'm starving. First, how about you tell us why your front entrance is half-assed booby trapped?"

Figured they'd seen the signs. Jethro shrugged. "Apparently I have busybody friends on both sides of the pond." It was good to see them, but anybody near him was just another target for Fletcher. They didn't have the agency backing them now, so they were swinging out there on their own. He couldn't let Fletcher hurt anybody else. The man had killed his own mother, for goodness' sake.

"No," Oliver touched the stitches across his bare chest and gritted his teeth. "We're in this with you."

Why did everyone suddenly want to work with him? Jethro shook his head.

Ian moved to the fridge and opened it, leaning down. "You don't have any food."

"I wasn't expecting company," Jethro said mildly. "I'll order something in, and my wine cellar is stocked. If I recall, you like a good red."

Oliver still sat on the counter and leaned to peer around his brother. "Is there any Guinness in there?"

"Of course." Ian grabbed several bottles and turned to plunk them on the counter next to Oliver. "I wouldn't let my little brother go without, would I? Or rather, Jethro wouldn't."

Oliver rolled his eyes. "I'm younger by three minutes. Give me a break." He took a bottle and smashed off the top with his fist.

Jethro looked them over. He'd trained them and he'd led them. "You need to listen to me and get back home. You've only been out two years and your business needs your attention." They'd created a private company dedicated to security and all that it entailed.

"You should come on board as a partner," Ian said. "We've been asking for years."

"No," Jethro said. "I'm out of that world. All of it." Well, except for getting shot at and nearly blown up with Wolfe the previous summer. His leg still felt buggered up sometimes.

Ian opened his beer and drank several swallows, studying Jethro carefully. "Is that lipstick on your chin?"

"No." Jethro wiped off his chin, still feeling Gemma's soft lips beneath his. He'd relived that kiss every second of the drive home, and it was nearly impossible not to turn around and head right back to her home. Well, to Serena's home. He wanted more than one kiss, but that could not happen right now.

Not while Fletcher was seeking vengeance.

"So." Ian grinned. "I call dibs on the guest bedroom."

* * * *

After her last Tuesday class Gemma fetched Trudy from the day care early and headed out in the opposite direction from her last trip, going into Virginia for an hour and reaching a cute little restaurant outside of

Kopp. There was another winter storm heading in, so she wanted to get this over with as soon as possible.

"Dinner?" Trudy asked sleepily from her car seat in the back. She'd snoozed the entire time.

"Yes. At a restaurant," Gemma said. "We're going to be big girls at a restaurant." She had about forty dollars to her name, so she'd just order a salad. She needed the rest of the money to last them until payday. Although she'd already taken ibuprofen, her neck hurt all the way up to her head in what had to be a tension headache. She'd been up all night replaying that kiss from the unpredictable professor. The bookish badass who used to work for MI6. The more she thought about it, the crazier it seemed.

When he'd kissed her, she'd lost her mind. Never in her life had she been kissed like that, and a day later, her body was still awake. Needy. How would it feel to actually be with a man like Jethro?

Would she even survive? The thought finally had her smiling. The man could kiss.

She tossed her satchel over her arm and lifted Trudy from the car, casting a look at the tumultuous clouds. The breeze tossed her hair around, chilling her face, and she hustled inside the warm diner. The cute waiter, who had to be all of eighteen, flirted with her and led them to a booth in the back. Excellent. She could keep her back to the wall and see the doorway, even though no way had anybody followed her.

Trudy sat up like a big girl in her booster chair across the table, her eyes sparkling and her cheeks rosy. Giving a happy yip, she reached for crayons and a printout of ponies, instantly starting to color.

Gemma ordered and then pulled out her phone. "Baby? Mama needs to make a call. You be quiet, okay?"

Trudy ignored her and scrambled for a purple crayon for a pony's tail.

Gemma swallowed, trying to calm her nerves. Monty should be back at the office if that Julie had been telling the truth. She had to know, and she was far enough from home to use another burner. Her last one. She'd have to wait until she was paid to buy more, if she could find a place close to the school that sold them.

It was five o'clock in Virginia, so it'd be two in the afternoon in Oregon. She called the medical practice.

"Cameron Medical Practice, Laina speaking," an older voice said.

Shoot. Too bad it wasn't the new and chipper Julie. Gemma had met Laina several times, so she adopted a southern accent. "Hiya there. My name is Florence and I'm new in town. Jennie down at the vet's office recommended Dr. Monty Cameron to me."

"Sure thing," Laina said. "What do you need to be seen for?" She loudly popped her gum.

"I have a sore throat," Gemma said. "My cousin just called me and said she has strep throat, and we were together this weekend, so I figure I might have it. Maybe I don't have to see the doctor and can just get an antibiotic?" She knew there was no way she could, but she didn't want to seem too eager to see Monty.

The sound of typing came over the line. "You have to see the doctor to make sure it is strep. So, you're a new patient?"

Gemma nodded. "Yes. New in town." She'd tried to space out her calls, but it had been several years of her impersonating a new patient who never showed.

Something rustled, and then settled. "Gemma? Is this you?" Monty asked.

Her body went ice-cold.

He sighed. "Would you knock it off? I know you call once in a while pretending to be a new patient. Give it up. We're over and I want nothing to do with you."

Yeah, that's why he'd sicced a private detective on her a few months ago. At least that guy hadn't discovered she had a child.

Monty chuckled, and the sound sent chills right to her toes, keeping her trapped in place. "I'm engaged to a wonderful woman—she'll make a much better wife than you could've ever been. Go live your life without me. You lose, I win. Go to hell."

She ended the call, her hands shaking, and dropped the phone to the table. It clattered and jumped before stopping. She stared at the device as if it could come to life and bite her.

"Mama?" Trudy asked, pausing in her coloring.

Gemma exhaled loudly. Oh. She grabbed the phone and pulled it under the table to tear it apart. "Oops," she said, making her lips curve in a smile. "Mama is clumsy." She pulled out the SIM card and set the parts to the side. All right. Monty was in Oregon, not here. Was he really engaged? Was she free? She drew her laptop from the bag and set it to the side on the table, facing her. A quick search of the *Seaville Press* brought up recent engagements.

There he was. Her heart leaped.

Dr. Monty Cameron and Ms. Jennifer Pottsam announce their engagement to be married on June 1.

Gemma sat back, her head reeling. Was it true? Monty appeared happy with his arm around the waist of a petite brunette, who looked as if she had blue eyes. She was smiling, leaning against his chest. In fact, she looked a little like Gemma.

Had Monty changed? Or had he just moved on to another victim?

Gemma turned back to study him, seeing her daughter's dimple and the shape of her eyes.

Slowly, she shut the laptop and turned to Trudy. Were they really safe?

For the first time since she'd fled the small Oregon town she let hope start to flicker inside her.

Trudy dropped the crayon and pushed the paper across the table. "Horsie."

So much love burst through Gemma that she could barely breathe. "Trudy, it's beautiful. And so are you."

Trudy grinned. "Mama bootiful. Jet-ro bootiful, too." She scrunched up her face. "Wish Jet-ro and Rot-co were here."

"Me too," Gemma said. She wasn't ready to take that kind of chance, though.

Probably.

An older man with a cane returned from the restroom and paused by her table. "What a cutie," he said, his voice hoarse, his gaze on Trudy.

Gemma smiled. "Thank you."

He nodded, smiling. "Looks like my granddaughter did when she was young." He dug in his old man pants and drew out a postcard advertising a local craft show. "She designed this and I'm giving them to everyone. I'm so proud of her." A dimple appeared in his left cheek and he moved on, his movements slow.

Gemma looked down at the colorful note card. The old guy had a damn dimple. It was as if the universe was trying to tell her something.

Chapter Eighteen

Jethro sat in his parked truck, in his safe garage, and set his head back on the seat. No doubt the twins were still occupying his apartment, and he needed a few minutes to breathe. After the kiss the previous night, after tasting sweet Gemma's mouth, the day had been torture for him. He'd spent time in his classes and his office, studiously avoiding her.

He could *feel* her in the building all day. Before this semester began he would've bet his entire savings—even his hidden accounts—on the fact that he'd never be interested in a cold-looking blonde. Without question, he would've lost that bet.

His dreams had been filled with her, but he'd turned her into a brunette by the ocean. Not only was he losing his mind, he was being a sodding ass about it. Her hair was fine.

It just reminded him too much of his mother's perfect hairstyle.

He concentrated on relaxing his body, one muscle at a time. Then he closed his eyes and let the memory take him away. The last one he had of her.

For six months Jethro had been chasing the serial killer known as the Expert. For one month he'd known he was actually chasing his brother. Fletcher was the killer, and Jethro finally had proof. His phone rang as he zipped through the countryside in the borrowed police car, knowing his brother was headed home. It was the only place left for him since Jethro had successfully tightened the net. "Hanson," he answered.

"Hello, Brother," Fletcher said cheerfully. "I have to say, I'm rather proud of you right now."

Jethro tightened his hold on the wheel, having taken the car after finding the last body in the pub. There was only one way for Fletcher to flee. "I'm sickened by you," he returned, taking a corner too fast and quickly correcting his course.

Fletcher sighed. "You're no better than am I. Let's see how good you really are."

"Jethro?" Isla's voice came over the line, low and shaky. "I don't understand. What is happening?"

Jethro drove faster. "Fletcher is a killer, Mum."

"I'm sure you're mistaken," she said, her tone strengthening. "I can take care of it. As a family, we will handle the situation."

Jethro slammed his fist on the steering wheel. "No, Mum. We will not hide this and we will not sweep this under the rug. For years you've covered for him. The dead animals and the frightened girls. Then his problems with authority." As a duchess, and an extremely wealthy one, Isla could make a lot of problems disappear. "We're facing this and putting Fletcher where he belongs."

"I'm sorry to hear that, Brother," Fletcher said quietly, the tone in his voice a new one. "I do not believe you'll get here in time. Don't forget. You want her dead as badly as do I."

Isla's scream ripped over the line, and then it went dead.

Jethro turned onto the family estate, speeding down the long driveway and pitching to a rough stop in front of the grand stone steps up to the mansion. He took them four at a time, rushing into the drawing room to find his mother on the antique carpet, blood staining her white cashmere sweater, her hand over her wound.

Even so, her hair was perfectly in place.

She looked up at him, her eyes wide in shock. "Jethro."

"Mum." He dropped to his knees and skidded to her, placing one hand over hers while calling the authorities. The police were already on the way, but he barked for them to bring medical personnel.

"He just stabbed me," she said, her voice hoarse. "I don't understand. He said you'd be blamed. That you deserve to be blamed."

Figured his brother would set him up. "I know. Don't talk. Help will be here soon." He kept his pressure firm and cradled her head in his lap. "Just hold on."

A tear leaked down her flawless face. "We're family, Jethro."

"I know," he said softly, wanting to smooth back her hair but knowing she wouldn't want him to disturb the perfect strands.

"Help him," she whispered. "Don't let our name be tarnished. No matter what, please keep this a secret."

The betrayal slashed through him more painfully than the knife that had harmed her. "Fletcher needs to pay, Mum."

"Please, Jethro," she whispered, her body going lax and her eyelids closing. "Protect our family name. Promise me."

He leaned over her, attacked by too many feelings to identify just one. "I promise. I do."

With a sigh, she went completely limp.

He lifted his head in shock. "Mum?"

Her clear eyes had lost their sparkle as she stared sightlessly at the van Gogh on the far wall. Anger shook his hand, but he gently closed her eyelids, holding her briefly in a way that she'd never held him.

She was gone, and now he had to capture Fletcher while keeping the matter private. SIS would work with him, no doubt wanting to keep the matter quiet, too. She'd mentioned Fletcher setting him up, so Jethro looked for any proof. Ah. No doubt his prints were on the knife. He gingerly wiped down the handle and had just enough time to erase the security tapes for the entire property. If he was going to hunt his brother, he didn't have time to also clear himself.

It was almost too much.

* * * *

The smell of stew surprised Jethro as he stepped into his flat after the flashback in the truck. "Honey, I'm home," he muttered, shutting the door and dropping his pack to the floor.

Oliver peered around the corner from the modern kitchen. "Ian is on the phone with contacts trying to track Fletcher's path from prison to US soil, and I went to the store and purchased goods for dinner. You're welcome." He disappeared.

Jethro sighed and strode across the cement floor, turning into the kitchen. The entire purpose of his open-designed, high-end loft was safety, and now he had two ex-operatives in the place making themselves at home. "While I appreciate you trying to help me, we've been over this and I'm done discussing it." Even so, the stew smelled good.

Oliver's bluish-green eyes twinkled. "It's nice when you put up a fight, Jet. Even so, how was your day, sweetheart?"

What a smart-ass. "If I were looking to get domesticated, it wouldn't be with you, jackass." Jethro tugged a stool away from the counter and sat, stretching his neck. The image of Gemma flashed through his brain.

A woman like that could certainly tempt him into taking a chance on forever. And the cute little one needed protection from the world. He could provide that. Easily.

But a family wasn't for him.

Fletcher's newest appearance slammed that fact right home.

He studied his friend. "Are those my clothes?"

Oliver looked down at the ripped jeans and black T-shirt covering his muscled and bruised body. "Yeah. I was surprised to find something so casual in your repertoire. Great jeans." His feet were bare.

Jethro exhaled. "I suppose your brother also raided my closet?"

Oliver grinned. "I tried to talk him into the blue sweater-vest, but he wouldn't go for it. What are you even doing with a sweater-vest? Don't you think you're trying a little too hard with this professor bit?"

Jethro rolled his eyes. "The vest was a present from a nice lady who runs a day care, and it's hand-knitted."

Oliver turned to check on the stew, stirring once. "A lady who knits? Is there a romance alive, Brother?"

"Yeah. I've asked her to marry me about five times and she's refused," Jethro drawled.

Oliver ducked into the fridge and brought out a bottle of Guinness, which he slid across the counter. "Smart woman. You shouldn't let her get away."

Jethro popped the top off the rich brew and took a deep drink. Maybe having Oliver around wasn't so bad after all. "I've tried, but she seems to want to retire without me." He grinned.

Ian strode out of the office wearing a pair of Jethro's dark jeans and a green sweater. The bruises on his cheekbone had started to yellow already. "You're not going to believe this, but nobody can get a line on how Fletcher made it across the pond."

"I believe it," Jethro said grimly. "He was one of MI6's best, and no doubt he had contingency plans in place. Several of them." His phone dinged and he drew it from his pocket, glancing at the screen. It was an email from an account he didn't recognize, and his body chilled. He stood and grasped his beer in one hand. "It's the school and I have to take this." He angled his head toward the stew. "How much longer?"

"Ten minutes," Oliver said, reaching for a salad bowl.

Jethro nodded and walked past Ian, heading to his office and shutting the door. This was probably nothing. He moved to his desk and sat, looking out the steel-gridded windows at the snow blowing in every direction.

He booted up his laptop, opened the email, and clicked the link in the body.

His brother's face took shape on the screen. "You answered my call?"

"Figured it was you," Jethro said, setting the beer next to the computer as invisible knives slashed through his insides. Yet he kept his expression neutral. Fletcher looked healthy. His brown hair was swept back from his angled face, and his eyes, a light brown, were clear. "What's your game, Fletcher?"

"I was hoping you'd share our mother's last moments with me," Fletcher said, his tone smooth. "We never had a chance to speak about it, not really. What did she say?"

Jethro tilted his head. "I'm not playing this game with you." He moved to shut the laptop. His brother was too good to be traced, so he didn't worry about trying. No doubt Fletcher was using a scrambler and would probably toss the computer the second they finished, and Jethro didn't want to chase windmills. The only way to catch the bastard was by getting into his head, and playing hard to get was the first step.

"Oh, I wouldn't," Fletcher said, kicking back in his chair. A black sheet covered the wall behind him, and there were no ambient sounds coming through.

Jethro sighed. "Why not, Fletch?"

Fletcher studied him. "Do you remember when we were kids? When those Donnely brothers picked on you and I taught them a lesson?"

"Yes," Jethro said softly. He'd been eight years old and the Donnely kids nine and ten. Fletcher had been nine years old, and he'd gone after them with no anger…just purpose. "You put the oldest one in the hospital." Fletcher had managed to convince not only their mother but the authorities that Johnny's fall down the ravine had been an accident. Fletcher had pushed the kid.

Fletcher smiled. "We're brothers. I protected you and you didn't turn me in."

He should have. Jethro might've been able to prevent all of this if he'd told the truth that day. Although their mother would've intervened, wanting to protect her reputation above her children. "You know you're a sick fuck, right?"

Fletcher snorted. "You've committed as many atrocities as have I, Brother. In fact, I wasn't even a member of The Increment. You were."

"Any action I took was under orders and for Queen and country," Jethro said, forcing a yawn. "You killed for money. You're no better than an average hit man."

"Oh, I'm much better than average," Fletcher said, stretching his neck as if they were just catching up with each other. "As you know. Still. Mum was stronger than I believed. She lasted just a few seconds longer than I'd planned."

The words pierced to Jethro's soul, so he smiled. "You cut Mum in the kidney and liver, but she held on long enough to try to protect you. You're not as good at timing as you'd hoped."

Fletcher lost the smile and his eyes started to glitter. "Well, at least that frigid bitch served one decent purpose in her life. She did get a deathbed promise from you to keep our name out of the press. Just think how much easier that made escape for me." He drummed his fingers on the desk the way he'd done as a child.

Jethro's throat went dry. "You know there's a special place in hell for someone who kills for money, as well as one for a degenerate who kills his own mother."

"Oh, Brother. You'll be there before I will," Fletcher said.

Jethro eyed him. "Is that a new scar by your temple?"

"Yes. Prison isn't the vacation one might imagine," Fletcher said easily. "The other bloke is dead."

"I have no doubt."

Fletcher leaned over and typed into his keyboard. "I must run, Brother. But here's a present for you." He disappeared.

Jethro shook off his anger and opened the email that had just arrived, clicking on another link.

Then his blood stopped completely.

A video of Gemma facing someone across a table in a diner came up. She was smiling and seemed at ease.

Jethro was on his feet in a second, the phone in his hand. "Wolfe? I need help."

Chapter Nineteen

Gemma tiptoed out of Trudy's room and partially shut the door. The girl was exhausted after their big-girl restaurant time; they'd have to take baths in the morning.

She sighed and stretched her arms over her head, still musing over the phone call with Monty. Her pajama bottoms pulled tight on her body, along with her tank top. Could she trust that Monty had moved on? The woman in the picture did seem to be his type, and if the brunette had truly caught Monty's eye, he'd be fully focused on her. He didn't know about Trudy, so maybe there actually was a chance for freedom?

What would that feel like?

Perhaps she could stay and earn her doctorate while teaching. She'd talk to Serena and see if there were any openings at the university. How much fun would it be to work with her?

How possible might it be to see Jethro Hanson? Did she want that? Although his emotions had been in control, he'd been deadly the other night. If he ever turned on her, he could kill her in a second. She wished she didn't have to take such thoughts into account, but there wasn't a choice.

She rubbed her freed hair, grateful she'd been able to ditch the wig. Her eyes felt scratchy even though she'd removed the dark brown contacts. It was nice to be herself for a brief moment.

The storm howled outside and the wind screamed.

She shivered and moved to the kitchen to pour herself a glass of Prosecco. Just one would help her relax and get some sleep. A movement sounded at the front door and she paused.

Simultaneously, the sliding glass door at the back of the house opened smoothly and a man's large black boot became visible beneath the blinds.

Panic manacled her. She jumped and dropped her glass, turning to run toward Trudy's room.

Both locks on the front door disengaged at once and the heavy oak swung open.

She skidded across the wooden floor, her arms flailing, her mind trying to process what was happening.

"Gemma." Jethro stepped inside, snow blowing around his legs and his hair ruffled by the wind. He stopped cold, his head rearing back. His eyes darkened as his gaze careened over her natural hair to land at her eyes. Her very blue eyes.

She gaped, her breath panting out. Almost in slow motion, she turned to see a mammoth of a man kick past the blinds and calmly shut the sliding glass door by the breakfast nook.

His dark hair was windblown too, and his chest was wide enough to count as a mountain. He wore jeans and a leather jacket, a gun strapped to his muscled thigh. He cocked his head. "Thought you said she was blond."

Terror seized her vocal chords. She leaped for Trudy's door.

Jethro caught her around the waist, lifting and turning rapidly to set her butt on the back of the sofa. "Don't scream. You'll scare Trudy."

Tears filled Gemma's eyes and she kicked out, the coils of energy inside her so sharp they caused pain.

"It's okay." Jethro's voice remained low and soothing as he reached over to shut the front door, one hand still flattened across her abdomen. "We're covered at every angle outside. Listen to me."

She shook her head, trying to jump off the sofa and run to grab Trudy.

He flexed his hand, easily holding her in place. The whimper that escaped her sounded wounded.

Jethro straightened and removed his hand, taking a step back and putting himself against the wall. "Listen. I'm sorry about this, but you're in danger. A lot of danger, and we're here to help." He held both hands up in a move that should have made him appear harmless.

It didn't.

She couldn't think. This was too much. She turned to view the killer by her back door.

He smiled and looked like he was going to eat her.

The blood rushed from her head and she swayed.

"Stop smiling, Wolfe. You're scaring her," Jethro snapped.

The man stopped smiling. "Sorry. Dana says I have a charming smile, but she does love me, so maybe rose-colored glasses and all that?" He frowned and rubbed snow from his hair. "I don't want to scare you, lady.

It's hard to believe, I'm sure, but we're the good guys." One monstrous shoulder lifted and then fell back down. "Usually. Not always. But today—"

"Shut. Up. Wolfe." Jethro remained eerily still, as if he didn't want to scare her any more than he already had.

Wolfe shut up.

Gemma's shoulders trembled so hard her chest hurt.

Jethro lowered his chin, catching her gaze. "Look at me."

She did so, gulping down pure terror.

"There you go," he crooned. "Remember my past? Where I used to work?"

She nodded.

"Brilliant. It turns out the trouble has found me and now found you, too. Did you meet a man called Fletcher recently?" Jethro asked, leaning back against the wall as if they had plenty of time for a discussion.

She frowned, her brain finally focusing on something. "Fletcher?" She shook her head. "Yeah. I met him the other day at a coffee shop a couple of hours away from here. He works for some lumber companies. Why?"

Jethro grimaced. "He's my brother, he's a killer, and he followed you."

Her breath heated her already aching throat as she flashed back to the man's dimple. The same one Jethro had. "He seemed so nice."

"Yeah. That's a gift of his." Jethro remained in her sight and Wolfe didn't move from his spot by the door. "He also apparently gave you something the other day? Some sort of postcard."

"No. That's not right." The image of the old man with the postcard bloomed bright in her mind's eye. "An elderly man with a cane gave me the card." She stilled. "How do you know about that? About either time?"

"Fletcher told me," Jethro said. "He was the old man in disguise. Now you need to listen to me. Okay?"

Slowly, she nodded. This was way out of her experience.

"Good," he said. "Pack everything you and Trudy will need for a month—we have to go." His gaze took in her curly hair. "Don't forget your wigs." The tone suggested that was a topic they'd be discussing soon.

"Oh," Wolfe said, nodding. "Guess that's how she was a blonde."

"Guess so," Jethro agreed, his tone mild. Too mild?

* * * *

Jethro could barely think. As a blonde with brown eyes, Gemma was beautiful. As a brunette with red highlights and warm blue eyes? She was fucking gorgeous.

He'd deal with the fact that she held more secrets than he did at a later date. Right now he had to get her to safety. He lifted his phone. "Angus, we're clear in here."

A minute later Nari Zhang came through the door, her aim right for Gemma. "Hi. I'm Nari." She held out a glove-covered hand. When Gemma took it, she pulled her from the sofa. "I'll help you pack, and we need to hurry."

"Are you an agent?" Gemma whispered, sounding so bewildered that Jethro wanted to hug her.

"Yes," Nari said, steering Gemma toward Serena's bedroom. "I'm the shrink for the unit, but I'm also the best fighter. Do you have a lot to pack?" They disappeared into the room.

Wolfe finally gave up his impression of a statue and walked toward Jethro, his big, black boots leaving spots of water. "Your woman has some issues."

"I noticed," Jethro agreed. He'd never seen a woman more terrified than when he'd broken her locks and walked inside.

"Her hair is pretty," Wolfe said casually.

Jethro nodded. "I don't know about the why of the wig. Let's worry about that another day." His phone dinged and he lifted it to his ear. "Millie? What did you find?"

It was nearly impossible to hear her over the wind. "The outside of the house is clear," she yelled. "No cameras and no bombs. I'll do the inside once you get everyone out."

"All right. If you see anything, get out," he said. Bombs weren't Fletcher's style, so he wasn't worried about that. But there very well could be cameras or bugs in the house, and Millie would find them. He leaned back against the wall just as Trudy's door opened and the little girl toddled out, her blanket in one hand and her thumb in her mouth. Pajamas with unicorns on them covered her tiny body. She looked at Wolfe sleepily and then caught sight of Jethro. "Daddy!" She ran for him.

Shocked, he dropped and caught her.

She snuggled right into his neck with a happy sigh.

He stood, keeping her against his chest, and found Wolfe's eyebrows raised.

"Got something to tell us?" Wolfe asked.

Jethro didn't have a reply. He held the little girl aloft, and she went lax against him, already back to sleep. His chest warmed and his instincts went primal with the need to protect her. Just in case they were attacked, he kept one hand free, although Wolfe looked at the ready.

Gemma and Nari returned with suitcases and boxes, Gemma's eyes widening when she saw her daughter. "Trudy? Come help me pack your things."

"No," the little girl said sleepily against Jethro's jugular. "I wanna stay with Daddy."

If a woman's jaw could actually drop, Gemma's did. "Wh–what?"

Nari nudged her into Trudy's room. "It's normal. She probably sees other daddies at the day care, has spent a little time with Jethro, and just adopted his cute British butt."

"Cute?" Wolfe mouthed.

Jethro shrugged, careful not to dislodge the child. Maybe Nari was just trying to ease Gemma's mind. "I am cute," he whispered.

"Huh," Wolfe said, eyeing the little girl with no small amount of wariness. "You know what you're doing with her?"

"No," Jethro whispered, feeling as if he might break her if he moved.

Wolfe backed away. "Don't look at me."

Jethro frowned. "You're having one of these in a few more months."

Wolfe shook his head. "I'm having a boy who will be solid. Not little. He'll be like a cement block."

"You're having a boy?" Jethro asked.

"I think so," Wolfe said, his gaze still on the sleeping child. "Dana wants the gender to be a surprise, but I wouldn't know what to do with one of those, so it has to be a boy. Right?"

Jethro nodded. "Right." It made as much sense as anything else did right then. His neck prickled with the need to get moving, just in case Fletcher was near. But Nari knew what she was doing, so he wouldn't push.

The front door opened and Ian and Oliver walked in, looking battered and bruised. They'd ridden with him to Gemma's neighborhood and then had searched the immediate vicinity for any threats. If they both were present, there were no threats anywhere near this house. Angus had the place covered, but they still needed to move fast.

Wolfe cocked his head. "No threats?"

"No threats," Ian said, adopting a Midwestern accent. "Saw you when we jumped out of Jet's truck. I'm Fred and this is Ethel." He jerked his head toward Oliver.

Oliver sighed.

"Wolfe," Wolfe said. "I'm Jet's best friend."

Jethro paused and then just let the moment unfold.

Oliver's dark eyebrow rose as he also adopted a flat Iowaesque accent. "Jet doesn't usually have friends."

“I’m special,” Wolfe drawled, no doubt meaning it. “Want to tell me why you and Fred are faking American accents?”

Ian studied him and Oliver grinned.

Yeah, Wolfe was no dummy. Oh, he was batshit crazy sometimes, but he was solid, and he was smarter than he let on. Even so, Jethro wasn’t giving out names if his former teammates wanted to remain under the radar.

“I’m Oliver and he’s Ian,” Oliver said in his British accent. “We used to work with Jethro back in the day.” He looked at the little girl. “Before he carried toddlers around. Do you know what you’re doing with that cutie?”

“No,” Jethro gritted out.

Wolfe scrubbed a hand through his hair again. “It’s nice you headed over the pond to help out my friend.”

“Of course,” Oliver said. “He was our friend first.”

“Fair enough,” Wolfe said generously. He ducked to pick up a box. “Why don’t you two make yourselves handy?” He tossed the box to Oliver, who caught it easily, not letting on that he’d probably just pulled his stitches.

Jethro sighed.

Chapter Twenty

Gemma sat against the window in the back of Jethro's SUV with Trudy's car seat in the middle and one of the two British twins on the other side. He had stitches down his neck, and she thought that meant he was Ian. Oliver sat in the front and Jethro drove.

Who the heck were these massive men?

Trudy kicked out her feet, wide awake now. "Jet-ro?"

"Yeah, honey?" Jethro asked, his hands capable on the steering wheel as he drove through the blizzard.

"You hafta keep the secret," Trudy chirped.

The tension in the vehicle rose.

Gemma patted the blanket into place around her daughter, her vision narrowing. This entire night was crazy. "Go to sleep, Trudy."

"What secret?" Jethro asked, his tone still gentle.

"About Mama's hair and eyes," Trudy said, kicking happily. "It's a grown-up secret. Only we know." She angled her head to look at Ian. "And you know, too."

Ian looked at her, his eyes softening. "We're good with secrets, little Trudy. You can trust us."

She grinned. "I like your talk."

"Most women do," he agreed, turning to look back out at the dark night.

Gemma swallowed. Jethro had mentioned he used to work with the twins. Did this mean she was in a vehicle with three ex-MI6 operatives? Former spies? When had her world gone down the rabbit hole? How was this even possible? And that Nari was with the local team Jethro had helped? Gemma had so many questions she could barely contain them, but she needed to speak with Jethro alone. She couldn't talk in front of

Trudy, and maybe she wasn't even supposed to know that these guys were MI6; she didn't want to get him in trouble.

Maybe the twins still worked for the mysterious agency.

The SUV skidded on the ice and Jethro easily corrected, keeping them on the road.

"Where are we going?" she finally asked.

"Somewhere safe," he murmured. Finally he pulled into the parking lot of a grocery store. "We need to switch vehicles here. I had this one checked for bugs, but I'm taking no chances." He looked at Oliver. "You two okay staying at the apartment?"

"We're fine, Mom," Oliver said easily. "I hope he comes after us and not you."

Jethro looked back at Gemma. "Angus and Nari are picking us up, and we're taking you to a safe house." Had he not mentioned the location on purpose? These spy guys were over the top.

She could only nod. Once she got her feet under her, she'd decide if it was time to run or not. Right now having trained agents around gave her a sense of safety she'd lacked for years. Yet the promise in Jethro's eyes that they weren't done talking made her stomach turn over. She'd lied to him from their first meeting and she was fine with that fact.

If he had a problem with her secrets, it was too bad.

A black truck drew up beside them, looking fairly new. A tall man who must be Angus jumped out of the driver's seat and opened his back door before opening Gemma's. He held out a hand to assist her and she jumped down, turning to release Trudy's seat.

"I've got her," Angus said. He was just as big as Jethro, with a quiet aura about him. While he wasn't as obviously scary as that Wolfe person, he emanated a tension that hinted he might be even scarier underneath.

Gemma jumped into the back seat and scooted over, assisting with the car seat when Angus placed Trudy inside.

The little girl giggled, holding tight to her blankie. "This is fun."

Gemma's head hurt. "It is fun, isn't it?" She made sure the car seat was secure and then double-checked Trudy's seat belt. If her head got any worse, it would be a full-on migraine. She didn't want to throw up in Angus's spotless truck.

Jethro hauled himself inside and shut the door.

Nari turned from her position in the passenger seat and smiled. "Hi, Trudy. You're awake now. I'm Nari and this is Angus. You already know Jethro."

Trudy stared at the woman. "You're pretty."

"You're pretty, too," Nari said, her brown eyes sparkling in the dim light. "That is a very nice blanket. Green is my favorite color."

Trudy plucked at the blanket. "I love my blankie. Pink is my favoritest color."

"That is a lovely color," Nari agreed, turning back around as Angus jumped in and drove away. "We're clear?"

Angus nodded. "Wolfe followed us here to make sure nobody else did. We're clear."

Gemma had been on the run for years, but she'd never coordinated a move this smoothly. Maybe she could learn a thing or two from these folks. "Now can I know where we're going?"

Angus and Jethro were focused outside the truck.

Nari turned again as much as her seat belt would allow. "We live in a small subdivision in Virginia, and Serena just finished building a house in our neighborhood. She doesn't mind sharing with you, so we thought you could stay there until we figure out what's going on with Jethro and his brother. He hasn't told us all he needs to, but I'm not angry about that."

"I am," Angus said quietly as he drove.

Gemma could almost feel Jethro roll his eyes.

He reached over and covered Trudy's pajama-clad legs with her blanket. "I agree with this decision, but Serena hasn't even purchased furniture yet, if I recall."

Nari nodded. "Dana is on it right now. By the time we get there, there will be beds and bedding at least. Knowing Dana, we'll have dishes as well." She looked at Gemma. "Dana is Wolfe's fiancée, and they live across the street from the house Serena just built."

"Sounds cozy," Gemma said, the lights of a migraine bursting behind her eyes.

Nari coughed out a laugh. "Well, it feels cozy and is safe. It's the safety that lets Angus sleep at night."

That was sweet. "It's kind of you to help us." Gemma swayed. "I don't suppose you have an aspirin?"

* * * *

Jethro looked over the toddler at her mother, who'd gone pale. "Are you all right?"

"There's a migraine about to hit," she said, holding a hand to her left temple.

"I have aspirin." Nari leaned forward and dug in her purse, pulling out a small packet and handing it back. "Do you have migraine medication? I didn't see any when we packed up the bathroom."

Gemma took out four pills and swallowed them dry. "No. I used to, but…"

But she'd obviously been on the run and had probably avoided medical offices. Jethro wanted to be angry with her, but she didn't owe him a bloody thing.

Angus slowed down and pressed a button to open a gate to a private drive.

Even through the furious storm, Jethro could make out cameras as the gate connected to fences that disappeared into the snowy abyss. "Private drive?"

"Yes," Nari answered, tugging on her shoulder strap as it choked her. "We have about a hundred acres and have turned this into a private, gated subdivision."

Jethro had never been out this way and didn't know what type of security they had in place. Hopefully Wolfe hadn't planted anything that could detonate. Considering that Angus's dog was known to explore, the surrounding area was probably free of explosives. He had no doubt it was mined with cameras, floodlights, and sensors in every direction. "How many homes?"

Nari smiled. "It started with two in a cul-de-sac. One is owned by Mal and Pippa, while the one next to it is now Wolfe and Dana's. They added on this summer while Serena and Raider and Brigid built across from them. Angus and I built a house at the same time, and there are more lots available if we add on to the team."

"We're halfway through building a clubhouse but had to halt because of supply chain issues," Angus said, passing through the gate and driving at least five miles to another gate. "It's next to our house at the very end of the cul-de-sac."

Clubhouse? Jethro cocked his head. What was Angus up to?

The second gate opened and Angus drove through.

Gemma turned to watch it shut behind them. She rubbed her arms as if suddenly cold, although she wore the ugly wool coat.

Jethro glanced in the back at most of her possessions. About 90 percent of everything they'd brought was Trudy's. Books, toys, bedding, and clothing for the little girl filled most of the boxes. Gemma only had a duffel of wigs and a borrowed outfit of Serena's that she said she could combine and alter for the week. Whatever that meant. She also had her gun.

He'd misjudged her from the beginning. She gave everything to her daughter and seemed to exist on very little. Was she so thin because she lacked money, or had that been another way to alter her appearance? He had no right to her, but he couldn't let her be in harm's way now. He would take care of whatever was haunting her.

Maybe she didn't even need to know what he was doing.

They pulled to the right to the first house, which had lights blazing.

"Here we go." Angus pressed a button on his dash and the garage door opened. "I had to let the contractors in while Serena worked, so I have access. We'll unload from inside so we don't get everything wet." He pulled in and cut the engine.

Gemma nodded and reached to unhook Trudy.

"I want Jet-ro." Trudy pouted, her face scrunching up.

"Sure thing," Jethro said, reaching for the little girl.

Gemma started.

"If it's okay?" he asked, having no clue what he was doing.

The girl plastered herself to him and wrapped both arms around his neck, holding tight.

"It's okay," Gemma said, turning and exiting the vehicle.

Jethro stretched out and hurried into the house, where it was warm. The interior door led to a combo mudroom and laundry room, and he continued on through a modern kitchen with white marble countertops and cupboards to the living room, which only had a fireplace and no furniture. Same with the breakfast nook.

Dana appeared out of a bedroom, discarded bedding bags in her hands. "Oh. Hello." She smiled as her gaze caught on Trudy, who was still snuggled against Jethro's throat but turned her head to stare at Dana.

"Hi," Trudy said.

Gemma emerged behind them with a box in her hand. "Hi."

Jethro introduced them.

Dana nodded. "We managed to get beds for the three bedrooms as well as bedding. I figure one of the bedrooms is supposed to be an office, but we made it Trudy's bedroom for now."

Gemma looked around. "Three bedrooms?"

Angus and Nari brought in the remainder of the boxes.

"Thanks, Dana," Jethro said.

"Sure." She nodded at Nari. "I'll see you tomorrow?"

Angus shook his head. "Hop in the truck, Dana. I know you only live across the cul-de-sac, but this storm is brutal, and Wolfe is at least fifteen minutes behind us. We'll drop you at your front door." He cut a look at Jethro. "How about we meet at my place in thirty?"

Jethro nodded.

Nari patted his arm before following Angus and Dana back into the garage.

Jethro looked down at the little girl. “How about we check out your new room?” He carried her down the hallway, where he spotted a master bedroom, a guest bedroom, and a smaller room with an adorable Cinderella-themed bed, complete with gauzy drapes.

Trudy gasped and struggled to get down. He let her and she ran toward the bed, leaping onto it.

Gemma sagged against the doorframe, her face too pale.

“Bad migraine?” Jethro asked.

She nodded, looking as if it hurt to move.

“Okay.” He took her hand and drew her toward the master bedroom. “You’re in here. I’ll take the guest bedroom.”

She blinked. “You shouldn’t stay in the house.”

He didn’t have time to argue with her. “How about I stay here tonight and we talk tomorrow when I have a plan for Fletcher and you’re feeling better?”

She looked toward her daughter’s room. “That’s fair.” In the soft light she looked delicate and breakable.

“Who are you running from, Gemma?” he asked. They’d come too far not to be honest with each other. He’d told her he worked for MI6, for goodness’ sake.

She pulled away. “Nobody. I just like my privacy.”

So much for trust. “I’ll be just a couple of houses away and should return in a couple of hours. Call me if you need me.” Without waiting for an answer, he strode out the front door and let the cold take away his anger as it shut behind him. Grasping his phone before he stepped off the front porch into the blistering wind, he called Brigid.

“Hey. What’s up?” she answered.

“I need you to do a deep dive on Gemma Falls right now,” he said without preamble.

Brigid was quiet for a moment. “How deep?”

“Light her up,” he said, striding into the night.

Chapter Twenty-One

Jethro kicked off his boots and jacket at the entryway to Angus and Nari's new home. Smooth lines and modern angles formed the exterior of the house, while comfort and elegance reigned inside. The place had definitely been designed by Nari, but touches of Angus and his love for the outdoors were everywhere. A couple of antique fly-fishing poles were crossed above a bookshelf near the window.

"Come on in, Jethro," Nari called from the kitchen, which was to the left beyond the great room, with its thick sofa, chairs, and other furnishings, which all faced a white stone fireplace. A flat-screen was above it.

Angus strolled out of an adjacent home office. "Hi. I thought we could have a smaller briefing as the team regrouped." He handed over a beer and Jethro took it, ready to down the entire thing.

Nari strode from the kitchen with a tray of snacks she placed on the coffee table, her dark hair up in a ponytail and a glass of wine in her free hand.

A knock sounded on the door and it opened. Wolfe stomped inside and toed off his boots, placing his coat on a hook next to Jethro's.

Nari paused in arranging little napkins by the tray. "Hi, Wolfe."

Angus frowned. "I told the team to take the night off and we'd interview Jethro so we could brief everyone tomorrow. No offense, but what are you doing here?"

Wolfe's eyes were sharp. "I'm Jethro's best friend. Figured I should be here."

Angus's eyebrows rose. "You were serious about that?"

"Yeah." Wolfe moved past them as if he had been there many a time and headed right into the kitchen, returning with a beer. "Let's do this."

Jethro's head reeled. Best friend? Had he ever had a best friend? "Huh." He looked around. "Where's Roscoe?"

"He's with Dana right now," Wolfe said. "I'll bring him over to your place after we meet tonight."

Nari nodded. "That's a good idea. A dog will help Trudy to feel more comfortable in the new situation. Never underestimate the power of an animal," she murmured.

"Plus, there's no alcohol there," Wolfe said, loping around to drop into a plush gray chair. He frowned, shifted his weight, and yanked a baby-blue throw pillow out from his back and set it on the floor.

Nari picked up a notepad from the sofa and sat.

Sighing, Jethro followed suit, taking the chair across from Wolfe, while Angus sat next to his love. Great. Two shrinks and a Wolfe. That summed up Jethro's life right now.

"Spill it," Angus suggested when they were all in place.

So Jethro did. He started with the childhood he'd shared with his brother and told all about their mother and her problems. Then he described how Fletcher joined the agency and created a cover as a barrister, and Jethro did the same, not creating his cover as a professor until much later. An identity he now truly inhabited. Finally he wound down.

Wolfe was on his third beer, but his eyes remained clear. "That's fucked up, man."

Jethro coughed out a laugh. "Aptly put."

Nari tapped one red fingernail against her lips. "The question is, why is Fletcher here now?"

Jethro had been thinking of little else. "We managed to freeze most of his bank accounts, but I always figured he had one or two we couldn't find. He must've accessed those after sneaking into the US, and now he's taking contracts to kill as a way to rebuild his coffers, so to speak."

Angus reached for an olive from the tray. "It's not a coincidence that he's taken up work in your area of the world, Jet."

"I'm aware," Jethro agreed. "Don't make the mistake of thinking he's some type of game player like Lassiter was. Fletcher is only leaving notes as a nod to you and your team."

Nari sipped her wine. "In other words he's letting you know that he can get to anybody in your life. That he not only knows about the team but is well versed on our last big case." She set down the glass. "He's also kind of making fun of you. That you're working with Yanks who've corresponded with note-making serial killers in the past. It's funny to him."

Jethro nodded. "Yes. I think it's more that he's showing off and trying to make me feel vulnerable, but I don't know why."

"It's revenge," Angus said easily. "You put him away. You betrayed him and he's going to make you pay."

"There's more to his motivation than just that." Jethro sat back, his mind oddly calm. "Fletcher doesn't like to waste energy. I think he enjoys killing, but not just for the sake of killing, you know? Not like a normal serial killer. He does it for money; the enjoyment is on the side. He no doubt hates me, but if he wanted to put a bullet in my head, he could've already done it. His main goal here in town is to make money so he can disappear again."

"No," Angus said, his profiler look stamped hard on his face. "He could've done that anywhere, but he's here. He's your brother, and while he might feel hatred for you, there's probably love in there somewhere, too. Or if he isn't capable of that, there's still a family tie. You hurt him and he wants to hurt you, Jet."

They didn't understand Fletcher, but Jethro didn't quite get him either. "He already killed our mother and I failed to save her. That means he's already won."

"Yet you put him in prison," Nari said gently.

"Not for long enough," Jethro pointed out. Yet they were correct that Fletcher had chosen to mess with him on purpose. "I need to keep my distance from the team. While taking out people without a reason isn't his thing, I don't want to put any of you in danger."

"No," Wolfe said, stretching his long legs to cross at the ankles.

Nari munched on a piece of celery. "I agree. We're already on Fletcher's radar, so taking a leave of absence from us wouldn't fool him. He knows you're part of the team, and at this point it appears he has learned our identities. The question is, what's his next move?"

Wolfe tipped back his beer. "It sounds like his next move is to kill people and make more money."

"Agreed," Jethro said. "While leaving me notes like Lassiter did you." Frustration crawled like ants beneath his skin; he forced his body to relax and then reached for a cracker.

Angus slipped his arm around Nari. "I'm having trouble on the international front getting his records from his time in prison. I'd love to see who communicated with him and if he had any dustups."

"Nobody communicated with him and there were no recorded dustups," Jethro said. "Fletcher would've at least looked the perfect prisoner to the authorities. He only escaped because of a routine transfer that he shouldn't have known about. He was going from one prison to another as a result of planned remodeling, and he was to be questioned again. Which meant that Fletcher had somehow known of that in enough time to plan an escape."

"He killed two guards while escaping," Angus said. "That's all the information I could get."

"The kills were necessary for him to escape," Jethro said. "No emotion and no regret for my brother. In addition, whoever helped him, somebody to whom he no doubt paid a substantial sum, is also certainly dead. Either in the UK or here. Doesn't matter. Those bodies won't be found because they weren't contract killings." Was it a testament to the damnation of his soul that he could speak so strategically and objectively about his murderous brother? Most likely.

His phone buzzed, and upon seeing Brigid's pretty face on the screen, he answered the call. "Hi, Brigid. You're on speakerphone and I'm at Angus and Nari's house."

"Perfect," she said. "You can use their flat-screen to watch this. The deep dive didn't take me long. Your woman is smart, Jet."

"She's not my woman and I already know that she's intelligent," Jethro said, certain there was no way he could talk Brigid into giving him the report confidentially. He sighed. "What did you find out?"

"Nari? I'm connecting my laptop to your flat-screen remotely. Let me know when I'm up." She waited patiently.

Nari turned on the flat-screen, clicked several buttons, and Brigid's laptop screen took shape. Wow. That was cool. "We're up and can see your screen," she said.

"Excellent," Brigid said, and several file folders clicked across the screen until one opened. "Meet Gemma Salsbury, born in Los Angeles to Fran Salsbury, father unknown." A picture of Gemma from a high school yearbook came up on the screen. Her brunette hair was long and curly and her blue eyes were crystal clear. She looked young and full of life. "There are several arrest warrants for Fran, mainly for public intoxication." Brigid clicked a button and a woman with Gemma's facial features took shape. In the mugshot, Fran looked worn down and her blue eyes were cloudy.

Jethro set down his beer. "Keep going."

Brigid remotely brought up a picture of Gemma with several other students in front of a brick building. A college? "Gemma earned a full ride to Washington Tech outside of Seattle and graduated with her master's degree by the time she was twenty-two. I found this picture on social media." She clicked through several shots. "There are several pictures of Gemma with this man, but neither of them now have social media accounts." A young man came into view: dark brown hair, intense eyes, broad shoulders.

"Who is he?" Jethro asked, noting the similarity to Trudy's eye shape. He was trained to spot similarities like that.

"Dr. Monty Cameron," Brigid said, clicking through several photographs of the doctor at his clinic and in the town of Seaville. "Here's their engagement announcement." A photograph of the doctor and a young Gemma came up. Both were smiling in front of a copse of trees.

Jethro took a hit to the chest, not bothering to examine why the image bothered him so much. "They were married?"

"No. Not that I can see." Brigid clicked through several different state documents, her voice distant over the line. "There's nothing more on Gemma Salsbury until about three or so months after this photo was taken, when she legally changed her name to Gemma Peterson in Texas." A new driver's license, this one with Gemma as a redhead, came into focus.

"I take it there's a medical record of Gemma Peterson giving birth?" Jethro asked, thrumming his fingers on his thigh.

Brigid cleared her throat. "No. She changed her name again to Frances Mitchell about five months later, while living in South Dakota." She brought up a birth certificate from the state of Maine. "Frances Mitchell gave birth to a baby girl, naming the father as a Douglas Mitchell. I haven't found a record of any Douglas Mitchell who could've been the father."

"She made up the name," Nari said softly. "If anybody not as good as Brigid searched for births for unwed mothers, this one would not have popped up because she named a father."

Brigid sighed. "Exactly. She's really smart. She named the baby Beatrix Mitchell. Then she moved to Iowa and changed both of their names to Gemma and Trudy Falls. From what I can tell, most of her employment has been under the table."

Jethro sat back, his mind on the good doctor. "Any medical reports from her time with Monty Cameron?"

"No," Brigid said, her tone darkening. "But he is a doctor." She clicked through several more documents. "He has hired a total of five private detectives to find Gemma, paying quite a lot to each. One nearly found her in Florida at the beginning of the spring, but she got away. His report doesn't specify that she had a child." Brigid paused for a moment. "I don't think he knows."

Wolfe looked at the screen. "Is there any record for this guy?"

"Just one from high school," Brigid said, bringing up an arrest record. "He beat the hell out of his girlfriend." A picture came up of a young brunette with bruises across her face and a cast on her arm. "It was a first offense, and he pleaded it out. The girl and her family didn't pursue the issue, so I can't find the details online."

"I don't need the details," Jethro said grimly. The picture was more than complete. "Where is the doctor now?"

Brigid turned off the picture and her screen saver of swimming fish covered the flat-screen. "He's still in Oregon, and it looks like he might've just gotten engaged. So there's a chance he's forgotten about Gemma."

Wolfe cast a look Jethro's way. "You believe that?"

"No," Jethro said, his fingers curling into a fist. Gemma wasn't a woman who could be forgotten. "What else can you find out, Brigid?"

"Nothing via the web, but we can go deep on this guy. We'll need to track his life in real time, though," Brigid said.

Jethro ran through the options.

"We're a team," Wolfe reminded him, his jaw set hard.

Jethro let his body relax. "Fair enough. Let's do it." No doubt Gemma wouldn't appreciate their interference, but Trudy's life could be at stake as well. "I'll face the repercussions." In for a pound and all of that. "Nari, I also need a favor."

Chapter Twenty-Two

Gemma sat on the hard wood of Serena's living room floor, her back to the wall, her legs extended, and her laptop on her thighs. The gas fireplace burned merrily, while the storm blustered outside. Somebody at the door knocked in a familiar pattern, *dunt dunt a dunt dunt...dunt dunt*. She set the laptop to the side and stood, groaning as her butt protested. The floor really was hard.

She moved to open the door, stepping back at seeing the giant on the other side.

Roscoe leaped inside and danced around, chasing his tail.

Wolfe remained outside, his head and coat also covered in white powder. "We thought Roscoe should stay here tonight to make you and Trudy more comfortable." The wind gusted behind him, and he blocked it from her, but his hair ruffled.

"Oh. Sorry." She stood frozen at his intimidating size. Or maybe it was the scar on his neck, or the ones on his hands. "Would you like to come inside?"

His upper lip curled, just on the left side. "That's sweet, but I need to get home to Dana. It's about the time she sends me to the store for ice cream." He glanced back at his own house. "I have some stashed in the garage freezer. She'll be so happy." He angled his head to see the dog. "Sit."

Roscoe sat, panting happily.

"Be good, Roscoe," Wolfe ordered.

Roscoe snorted.

Wolfe shifted his attention back to Gemma. "Jethro is a good guy, just so you know."

"I know," she said softly, her fingers relaxing on the doorknob.

"I mean, he could kill us all within a minute, but he'd never do that," Wolfe continued, his gaze mellow. "Well, probably. We're all trained. It's more likely it'd be a bloodbath if we ever tried to end one another." He scratched the shadow on his rugged jaw. "I'm not sure who all would be left standing." He straightened. "Except Nari. Yeah, my bet would be on Nari." Then he frowned. "And Dana. I guess I'd make sure Dana was safe no matter what. So Dana and Nari for sure. Well, Pippa too." He nodded slowly, as if thinking about it. "And Brigid. Couldn't let Brigid get hurt."

Gemma took a step back. "So all the women?"

Wolfe dusted snow off his cheek. "Yeah. Well, Jethro too. He is my best friend."

"How about everyone survives?" Gemma suggested, charmed even though she didn't want to be.

He full-on grinned, transforming his face from killer to handsome. "That's a better scenario. Sorry about the rabbit hole there—I've been hit in the head a few times. I was just trying to say that even though Jethro is dangerous, he'd never hurt you or any innocent. Plus, isn't it better to have a dangerous dog in your corner than a pussycat?"

"Probably," she agreed. "But Jethro and I are just colleagues. Maybe becoming friends."

Wolfe's gaze ran over her face. "I guess I read you two wrong." He shrugged, and more snow fell onto his boots. "It seems like you could use a good guy, a deadly guy, in your corner. Jethro needs somebody to be on his side to support him, maybe teach him he can let down his guard and be himself. That he doesn't have to be so perfect."

Gemma blinked. Apparently Wolfe was more insightful than she would've imagined.

Wolfe looked over her shoulder toward the hallway. "You're doing a great job with that little girl—you don't need help there."

Gemma started. "You're not going to say she needs a father?" This conversation had gotten way too deep way too fast.

"The wrong father is worse than no father," Wolfe said quietly. "I like that if you go for my friend, it'll be because you want him and not some type of perfect life. That's cool."

Had the behemoth soldier just given her his blessing? "I'm not going to date your friend," she said gently, even as her imagination began to spin a fantasy with Jethro in the middle of it. The man could kiss.

It had been far too long since she'd been kissed. Until he'd touched her, she hadn't even realized that fact. Now she couldn't stop thinking about him, his talented mouth, and his wicked-hard body.

"Huh," Wolfe said. "Okay. 'Night." Without another word he turned on his heel and disappeared into the blizzard.

Gemma slowly shut the door and locked it. That was one interesting man. Shaking off her unease as well as the unrealistic notion of seeing where her attraction to Jethro could lead, she returned to her position on the floor and set her laptop back in place. Okay. It was a cheap laptop with a very expensive scrambling program, and it didn't look like she'd be heading off in a new direction for a little while, so she might as well make the call.

Perhaps Fran wouldn't be home.

Her mother's form took shape on the screen. "I wondered if you'd call." Fran hiccupped. Her hair was a brassy red and her eye shadow a clumpy blue. Thick gunks of mascara clung to her lashes, and a cigarette moved on her cracked red lips when she spoke.

"Happy Birthday, Fran," Gemma said, catching sight of the telltale signs of her mother's alcohol problem. "How are you?"

"Alone," Fran snorted. "Completely alone because of you." She squinted into the camera. "When are you coming home?"

Gemma studied the area around Fran. The view was sharp, showing worn wallpaper with a framed photograph of running horses. "Where are you?"

"Motel," Fran said, shrugging and dislodging her white top from her shoulder. "It's temporary."

It usually was. Gemma sighed. "You must've gotten a new phone. The picture is so clear."

"Yup," Fran said, taking a deep drag on the cigarette. "Why won't you at least tell me where you are? Maybe I could come visit you?" Her eyes were bloodshot and new wrinkles extended from the corners. She'd also spent the last year in the sun, based on the numerous brown spots dotting her chin. "Haven't you been away long enough? You'll never get Monty back now."

So her mother was still in Oregon. Good to know. Monty had helped her move to an apartment in town but had stopped paying the rent the second Gemma fled. Her mother had let her know it during one of their yearly talks. Sometimes Gemma called at Christmas, but she had to make sure Trudy was asleep and invisible. "I don't want Monty," Gemma said honestly. "Ever."

Fran rolled her eyes. "He's a doctor. How can a doctor not be good enough for you?"

"That doctor likes to hit women," Gemma said without heat.

"Right. So you two fought a few times. That doesn't mean you should desert him or your own mother. He was heartbroken and so am I." Fran hiccupped and reached for a glass of clear liquid to drink, somehow keeping the burning cigarette in her mouth. "You're so selfish."

It was surprising that the words didn't hurt any longer. Was it because of Trudy? That now Gemma truly knew unconditional love because she felt it for her daughter? If anybody hurt Trudy the way Monty had harmed Gemma, she would not rest until it ended. Until he ended. "Well, I hope you had a nice birthday. I should get going," Gemma said, letting go of all her emotion. Perhaps she wouldn't even call next year. Maybe it was time to make a complete break.

"I never shoulda had you," Fran slurred, taking out the cigarette and waving it around. "I knew better. You ruined my life."

Gemma looked at the woman and wondered where she'd gone wrong. "Sorry about that," she said.

Fran leaned closer to her camera. "You're a flippant bitch, you know? Your father didn't want you, and neither did I. Now there was a man who'd throw a punch hard enough to crack a jaw."

Gemma started. "You've never said he hurt you." In fact, Fran would usually clam right up about whoever Gemma's father had been. For years Gemma had doubted Fran even knew.

Fran shrugged. "Doesn't matter. I had you, and look how you've forgotten that. Selfish. Now you've lost Monty."

"Good," Gemma said.

Fran hissed. "Good? He's moved on. I saw it in the paper. But if you come back, I'm sure he'll give you a second chance."

Gemma softened her voice. "I am never coming back, Fran. I think this is goodbye. The final one." Her mother was never going to change, and Gemma couldn't risk Trudy with her. She was a woman Trudy never needed to know. Life was good with just the two of them. Even as the thought settled inside her, she couldn't help but think of Wolfe and his Dana. The love and strong protection of everyone on his team who would protect their baby.

Gemma's baby deserved protection, too.

Most importantly, Trudy deserved safety, and Gemma could give her that. They'd need to get on the road again as soon as possible. She wasn't going to stick around for more danger with Jethro. He could handle his own problems. She'd had enough for a lifetime.

"You can't just abandon me," Fran snapped, tossing the cigarette out of range.

The camera shifted and blurred. Monty's face came into view with that calm and calculating glitter in his intelligent eyes. The look he got right before he struck. "Hello, Gemma."

She swallowed and forced herself to face the monster. Never again would she cower in front of him. "What a shock. You two are keeping in touch, huh? Good." It shouldn't surprise her that Fran had told Monty about the yearly calls. The only shock was that it had taken this long. Fran had probably needed money for cigarettes and booze, not thinking a thing about betraying her daughter. Thank goodness for the IP scrambler.

Monty looked past her, no doubt just seeing the plain, beige-colored wall. There was nothing to identify Gemma's location anywhere around her. "Where are you?" he asked.

"Doesn't matter," Gemma said, her stomach cramping and her migraine flaring back to life. She'd had them since he'd thrown her down the stairs one time, but they had become more sporadic as time passed. "Give it up. You're engaged now, right? Go have a nice life and forget about me, Monty."

His nostrils flared and crimson crossed his cheekbones. He looked like such a monster. Why hadn't she seen that in the beginning? He hissed out an angry breath. "You know what? I really did want to move on. Wanted to forget what a complete and selfish bitch you are and forget all about you. I've been *trying*."

"Good." She reached for the lid of the laptop. Hopefully his new love would get out in time, but Gemma couldn't worry about her. Maybe Jack would help her as well.

"Not so fast, Gemma," Monty snapped. "Something has interrupted my plans, and you know how much I hate that."

Oh no. Was he going to hurt Fran? Gemma stopped closing the laptop. "Leave her alone, Monty. She hasn't done anything and she has no clue where I am. She will never know."

"But somebody knows." Monty slid something across the table on which the phone sat. "Apparently I have friends I didn't even know about."

Gemma stilled. "I don't know what that means."

"I think you do." Monty lifted up a photograph to place it in view of the camera. "Want to explain this?" He held the picture too close to make anything out.

Even so, Gemma's chest compressed. "I can't see anything."

"Oh. My apologies." Monty moved the photograph back, revealing a picture of Gemma and Trudy. One taken at the restaurant in Virginia just the other night with the two of them sitting across the table from each other, both laughing. "She looks like me, you worthless bitch."

Gemma slammed the laptop shut and jumped up, bumping her elbow on the wall. Fletcher had found out all about her and sent the picture to Monty?

God. They had to run.

Now.

Just before she made it to Trudy's room, reality smacked her in the face. She didn't have her car. Halting, she planted one hand on the doorframe, sucking back a sob. Okay. It was time to stop existing on instinct and panic. There were options she'd never had before right now. She could wait out the night and go to work, make an escape from there. While she hated leaving Trudy's toys, they'd buy more. Or, she could trust the team around her, the people who were trained and dangerous, to work with her to protect Trudy. Trust was difficult for her, and telling her entire story would be painful, but she was a smart woman, and keeping her daughter safe was the only thing that mattered right now.

She released her breath. No matter what, they were safe in the sheltered subdivision for the night.

So there was time to make a good plan.

Chapter Twenty-Three

Jethro returned to Serena's house after midnight and found it silent. He put the bottle of wine in the fridge. So much for having a drink with Gemma and discussing her past. He peeked in on Trudy and then on Gemma; both were sound asleep. Though he'd need to speak with Gemma the next day, he appreciated the reprieve, even as he felt oddly bereft that she was asleep. He had to get a grip on this attraction for her; there was too much going on right now to pursue it.

Roscoe looked up from the edge of Trudy's Cinderella bed, eyed him, and went back to sleep.

Jethro turned and dug his fingers into the nape of his neck, trying to dispel the headache that kept trying to claim him. After making sure the entire house was secure he headed for what apparently had become his bedroom. He shucked his shirt and jeans, yanking on sweats just in case, and sliding right between the soft sheets. Then he stared into the darkness at the ceiling, much the way he had as a child. An odd memory took him, and he followed it into dreams.

He was ten years old, in the dark, watching the shadows dance across the ceiling.

Fletcher climbed in his window, out late again.

Jethro turned and flipped on the light. "Why don't you come in your own window?"

Fletcher fell to the floor and then stood, wiping dirt and leaves off his shirt. "Mine has brambles too close. Yours is easier." He cracked his knuckles.

"What were you doing now?" Jethro asked, almost afraid to ask.

Fletcher pulled a leaf from his hair. "Just watching the Donnely house."

Jethro sighed. "You got them back for picking on me. You have to stop beating Barry up—it's enough. You nearly broke his nose yesterday." They fought almost every day.

"I don't have it right yet," Fletcher said, shutting the window. "I keep imagining the exact right way to make him hurt, and it's not right yet. I punched him too low in the gut yesterday. There's no way to stop until I get it right." He turned off the light. "Just be happy I don't want to hurt you."

Jethro's eyelids flew open and he sat up, turning on the bed. Something had awakened him. He stood and strode out of his room into the hallway, his footsteps silent.

Gemma cried out.

He pivoted toward her room just as the front door was crashed in. Instantly he slid into the entryway and caught sight of a hulking form. Without a sound he ducked his head and charged, hitting the interloper in his gut and lifting him. They crashed into the wall and plaster flew. The guy kneed Jethro in the rib cage, and pain exploded through his torso.

Countering, he sent a series of hits and kicks that had the attacker grunting. The room was too dark to make anything out. The guy clapped him on the head and Jethro caught his wrist, yanking him down and rolling on top of him, his fist pulled back for a strike to the neck.

The light flipped on and he stopped cold.

Wolfe grinned beneath him and turned only his head toward Gemma, who stood wide-eyed at the end of the hallway near the light switch. "I told you he could fight."

"Bloody hell." Jethro rolled off Wolfe, stood, and held out a hand to help him up. "What are you doing?"

Wolfe stood and shook out his neck. "I couldn't sleep so I scouted the perimeter."

"In this storm?" Gemma asked, her hair curling to her pink tank top, which revealed high, firm breasts. The top had matching shorts that showed toned legs and bare feet.

Jethro's body flew wide awake.

"Yeah," Wolfe said. "I heard you cry out and came in through the front door."

Jethro sighed and forced improper thoughts about the brunette to outer space. "Sorry I hit you."

Wolfe clapped him on the shoulder. "No problem. A guy comes in your front door, you don't stop to chat. You take him down, and hard. That was some great fighting, Brit."

Jethro clenched his teeth. "I could've hurt you."

"Probably," Wolfe said agreeably. "But when I barely fought back, you transitioned to hurt rather than kill. So we're all good."

Jethro rubbed his aching rib cage. "You could've broken one of my ribs with that knee shot."

"But I didn't," Wolfe said. He looked over his shoulder at the broken door. "Serena is going to be pissed."

Rosco wandered down the hallway, looked at them both, then turned back around. His tail wagged and, swear to the saints, he looked like he shook his head.

"That is one intriguing dog," Gemma murmured, turning to watch him go.

"Jet-ro?" Trudy toddled past Gemma, dragging her blanket, her eyes sleepy. She looked at Wolfe and then at the door. Her little brow drew down and she increased her pace until she reached Jethro. "Up."

Well, all right. He obediently lifted her against his chest. She wrapped one arm around his neck and pouted her lips, looking at Wolfe. "Who's him?"

"That's Wolfe," Jethro said, hoping she didn't kick his aching rib cage. "He helped us move your stuff here, remember?"

She studied Wolfe. "Him's your best friend?"

Bloody hell. Jethro sighed. "He's my best friend."

"That's right," Wolfe said, his grin wide.

"Oh." Trudy's body relaxed against him. "Okay. I don't have a best friend."

Wolfe shrugged. "I didn't have one until this summer and I'm old. You have tons of time."

She laid her head on Jethro's shoulder and pretty much ripped out his heart. "Rot-co is my friend. Maybe my best friend?"

"Sure," Wolfe said easily. "That's a good dog and a great friend. He has another friend named Kat that maybe you could meet tomorrow. Do you like cats?"

"Yeah," she said, yawning widely.

Gemma walked toward them, holding out her arms. "Let's go back to sleep, baby."

"M'kay." Trudy kissed Jethro's neck and then turned for her mother's arms.

Jethro took the hit to his heart and remained stoic.

The two disappeared down the hallway, and Wolfe stood there, grinning like a lunatic.

"What?" Jethro snapped.

"You've got it bad, dude." Wolfe turned and tried to set the door back into place. "Um, don't tell Dana about this, okay?"

Jethro just rubbed his aching ribs.

* * * *

Gemma had just finished settling Trudy back into bed when her phone dinged. She hustled back into her room to read the text and then grabbed a sweatshirt she'd borrowed from Serena and pulled it over her head before walking back out to the living room. "Jethro?"

He stood at the door, trying to settle it back into place. The muscles in his back tightened with his movements.

Her mouth went dry.

His broad shoulders tapered to his waist, showing twin dimples above his low-hanging sweats. She'd only seen those in pictures on the Internet and had never imagined they weren't added in later. Then he turned, and his muscular chest caught her eye before her gaze traveled down. Holy crap, he had a clearly defined inguinal crease—that amazing V-shape that showed off his amazing abs. She'd thought only Mark Walberg had those.

Not to mention a six-pack. A clearly defined six-pack.

She couldn't breathe. Her head spun. "Um."

Jethro pushed his thick hair away from his face. "It's the best I can do with the door tonight, but I'll fix it tomorrow with more locks. We're more than safe here, though." He frowned, his face sharply angled and all male. "Did your phone buzz?"

"Phone?" She looked down at her hand. "Oh. Yeah. Phone." She shook her head, glad she'd thrown on the sweatshirt. Her nipples were betraying her, and her body felt flushed. Head to toe. "It was an automated message. School is closed tomorrow due to weather."

Which meant no flight for her. Any other options that staying were now gone.

"That's good. Since Fletcher found you, I was going to suggest you work remotely anyway." He crossed his arms, and damn if more muscles didn't flex all over. "You look disappointed."

She blew out air. "One of my options was to make a run for it again." Might as well tell him the truth.

"Interesting." He loped toward the kitchen, all dangerous, muscled grace. His expression hadn't altered one iota with her proclamation.

She gulped. "Aren't you mad?"

He stopped, turned, and faced her. "Mad?" Those sparkling eyes glittered.

She almost took a step back. "Yes," she whispered.

He tilted his head. "Yeah. I'm mad." He looked at the broken door. "I have no clue at this point if I have a right to be angry or not, but I am. Nobody I know will hurt you. I have you in a safe place." He held up a hand.

She cringed.

"Shite," he muttered. Then he dropped to his knees before sitting flat on his butt, crossing his legs.

She blinked. Heat flared into her face. "What are you doing?"

"Looking harmless," he said.

Amusement bubbled through her. "You don't look harmless." A bruise was forming on his chin from his fight with Wolfe, making him appear even more dangerous.

"Oh." He looked at the hardwood floor. "I could lie down on my stomach, but that will make it difficult to talk."

She couldn't keep her smile from emerging. He really was cute in a sexy, deadly, 007 way. "What about on your knees like you were before? That's how they get the bad guys off balance on television." Now she was teasing him? When was the last time she'd just goofed off?

"That actually is easier to move from than this position," he said, his tone serious but his eyes filled with amusement.

She put her hands on her hips. "Prove it."

One of his dark blond eyebrows rose. "You're certain?"

"Yes." Her breath caught in her chest.

He moved to his knees. "All right. This is the position you see on television, when the police subdue somebody before arrest, and they have to get it exactly correct." Then he crossed his ankles, or it looked like he did, and intertwined his fingers at the back of his head.

Wow. Just plain and simply wow. So much hard muscle and so many sharp angles. "What now?" she whispered.

"Don't be frightened." He looked like he could stay there all night.

She could watch him sit like that all night. "I'm no—"

Quicker than a heartbeat, he rocked back and shot to his feet, dropping into a fighting stance.

Her chin fell to her chest. "That was incredible."

He grinned and straightened to his full height. "Aw, shucks." The Southern accent was dead-on. "Nari sent me home with a bottle of wine and said there were wineglasses somewhere in the kitchen. You game?"

She wanted that wine with him more than anything in the world. "Yes." It was after midnight, this was crazy, and they were half-dressed. "I'd love a glass of wine."

"Well, we don't have school tomorrow." Winking, he turned that spectacular body toward the kitchen and fetched the wine, searching through the cupboards until he found the glasses. He quickly poured the rich, red liquid into them and returned, handing one over. "Guess we sit on the floor?"

She gingerly sat, putting her back to the wall and extending her legs.

He followed suit, right next to her, both of them looking at the damaged door. "I put it in place as best as I could."

She chuckled and took a sip, letting the taste warm her mouth. "This is good."

He nodded. "So. You were having a nightmare?"

"I get them sometimes." There was no reason to lie, considering he'd heard her cry out.

He turned his head to look at her. "I prefer your natural hair and eye color. Much warmer, and they suit you."

"Thank you," she said, suddenly shy. "Are you no longer mad?"

"I am not angry, and even if I were, I'd never harm you." He swirled the wine in his glass. "But I know that you've been hurt before, and you've been on the run."

She sighed. It was fairly obvious, considering the disguise. "Yes."

He looked back at the door. "I've put you in danger because of Fletcher, and you were already in danger, so I'm not going to tell you what to do." He glanced back at her, his eyes brilliant in the soft light. "Running isn't a good idea, but if that's what you need, I can get you safely into the UK with new identifications. I promise that Monty Cameron will never find you."

Monty? Her hand shook. "You investigated me?"

"Yes," Jethro said, taking her wineglass before she could spill it. "From what I could discern, he beat you, and you ran once you discovered you were pregnant. You were very smart and changed your name a couple of times. He doesn't know about Trudy."

Gemma plucked at a string at the bottom of the sweatshirt. She had to make a decision here. Either she trusted Jethro and his team or she didn't. She went with her gut. "He does know about Trudy. I think Fletcher took our picture at the restaurant and sent it to him." She exhaled, trying to rid herself of the panic. "He's coming for us. Now."

Chapter Twenty-Four

Jethro went cold. “Fletcher unearthed your true identity and history?”

She nodded. “He must’ve been the one who sent the picture to Monty. I didn’t see him take the shot, but that was the night he acted like an old man and gave me the postcard at the diner.”

Jethro had already checked out the postcard, which the restaurant had been giving away at the entrance. It didn’t mean anything. He cleared his throat, anger burning harshly through his veins. Now Fletcher was just messing with him. But why? Why bring Gemma into it? “I’m sorry.” He put his wineglass next to hers and reached for her hand. “I’m used to getting things done.”

She looked down at their entwined hands and held on. “What does that mean?”

How could he explain this to her without sounding like an ass? “I see a problem and I fix that problem.”

To his utter surprise, she grinned. “We have tons of problems. How would you fix them?”

He liked that she held on to his hand, considering how hard it must be for her to trust him. He tamped down the urge to protect her. For now. “I’d call a lawyer tomorrow and see what your options are, while continuing to hunt for my brother. Then I’d make a decision from there. One of the options is relocating you through unofficial channels.” Now that he knew Fletcher had found her, had figured out her true identity, he couldn’t go through official channels. It was possible Fletcher still had connections.

She bit her lip. “Talk to a lawyer?”

“Sure. Just to figure out your options. Then go from there.” He’d call Scott in the morning if she wanted.

She looked up at him, her eyes a deeper blue in the darkened house. "And if I decide to run?"

He studied her lovely face. Every instinct he had told him to lock her down safely, yet he knew that doing so would destroy the freedom she'd fought so hard for, and he couldn't do that to her. "Then you run." Although he'd have Wolfe track her. Or maybe the twins because Wolfe was expecting a baby soon.

A light peach tint slid over her cheekbones. "You're all right, Jethro." Then she leaned over and kissed him, her hair falling on his bare shoulder.

Lust jolted through his system. Slowly, not wanting to spook her, he partially turned and slid his hand into that thick hair as he'd wanted to for the last few hours. She made a small sound of surrender, and it was all the invitation he needed.

He lifted her easily, sitting her on his lap and taking over the kiss. She tasted sweet and felt hot, and he slanted his mouth over hers, coaxing her response. She stiffened and pressed her hands against his bare chest. He was just about to release her when she tentatively slid her tongue along his, as if just remembering how to kiss. How to let go.

Her palms scorched his skin as she slid her hands up to curl her fingers over his shoulders.

This was what he'd needed from the first time she'd hugged Roscoe and showed her soft side. This passionate, trusting, and so damn sweet energy between them. He knew her secrets and she knew some of his. The ones he could share.

She tangled her fingers in his hair and her body gyrated on him. He went rock hard at feeling her soft thighs on his. Fire roared through him with the need to go deeper. To take her and make her his. The thoughts zinged around his head, escaping his attempt to grab them and shut them down.

Twisting his wrist, he tangled his fingers in her silky hair and slowly pulled her away from his mouth.

They were both panting, and her lips were a swollen ruby red.

He groaned. "Gemma."

"What?" she asked, her voice throaty.

His blood pounded through his veins, rough and wild, urging him to stop talking. "Think for a moment." Hell to the no. There should be no thinking. He grimaced and forced his body to stop acting like he was still eighteen. "I've been honest with you."

"Me too." Her gaze dropped to his lips.

He nearly bit through one to keep from kissing her again. "Listen to me."

Her gaze jerked up, and her stunning eyes were slightly dilated. "I am listening."

Her butt was so sweet on his thighs he almost surrendered, but this was too important. "What I said before, about us, about you—that's what I'd do assuming we're colleagues. Friends."

She blinked, her cheeks rosy now. "Friends?"

"Yes." He was having trouble finding words. "Do you understand?"

"No." She arched an eyebrow, and it was the sexiest thing he'd ever seen. "What are you saying?"

He allowed his free hand to settle at her waist and curve over her hip. She was a woman who'd fought hard for her independence, and she deserved to do whatever she wanted. "If we're together, I protect you." When she straightened he forged on. "I'd never hurt you, but I can't allow anybody else to hurt you either. You want to be with me, I'm in charge until I take out Fletcher." And quite possibly Monty Cameron. He wouldn't murder the guy, but he might cause him enough trouble that he'd crawl back under the rock where he belonged. "Get it?"

"In charge?" Her eyes were still sleepy, but her tone had quickly sharpened.

"Yes. You can run, little dove, but I can fight. The hawk always fights."

She leaned back and yet remained on his legs. "I'm not sure this is a time for game theory."

He let her distance herself. "It's always time for game theory, luv."

She patted his shoulders and caressed his pecs, lowering her chin to follow her path. "You use that accent to your advantage."

"Whatever works," he said, nearly holding his breath.

She breathed out and dropped her hands. "I need to think."

Ah, damn it. "I understand." He released her hair and helped her off his legs. Her instincts were good. There had been too much violence in her life already, and it was always part of his. Sometimes he thought violence flowed right through his veins. "For now, how about I make an appointment with my attorney tomorrow?" It appeared she'd be looking at her options on every front.

"You guys done kissing?" Wolfe bellowed from the other side of the front door.

Jethro jolted. He hadn't heard the man approach in the storm. "What are you doing here?"

"I brought plastic to finish covering the door until we can get a new one tomorrow," he bellowed.

Gemma giggled. "He's your friend."

"Best friend," Wolfe called back.

* * * *

The door was already fixed when Gemma emerged from her bedroom dressed in a pair of Serena's leggings and an oversize sweater, her hair up in a ponytail. It felt good to ditch the wig. She looked at the door and then at the three men gathered in the kitchen. "Morning."

"Morning," Jethro said, his gaze warm on her face.

Wolfe nudged a holder of whipped-cream-topped lattes with candy cane sprinkles. "I brought you a single, and there's a hot chocolate for your girl."

That looked like a lot of sugar. Gemma strode toward the treats, noting that Jethro had already drunk some of his. "This is kind of you."

Jethro nodded to the other man, who was blond and tall. "This is Scott Terentson, my attorney. We've been telling him about your case."

Scott stared at the sugary latte in his hand, put it down, and held the same hand out to her. "It's nice to meet you."

She shook and then took a tentative sip of the drink. Sugar and love. She smiled and took more of a sip, even though she'd have to work out extra hard later in the day.

Scott cleared his throat. "How about we chat here in the kitchen while Wolfe and Jethro go do something else?" He looked at the two men, who appeared to be ready to argue. "If you stay here, Gemma waives client confidentiality, and I'm not allowing that to happen."

Gemma stilled. Wow. The guy had some guts talking to the other two like that. She studied him more closely.

"Fair enough." Jethro clasped Wolfe around the neck. "We'll go shovel the drive. Again."

It didn't look like the blustering snow had lessened any. Jethro winked at her and then headed into the mudroom with Wolfe, where they suited up. If they'd been together the night before, if she hadn't decided she had to think, would he have kissed her before leaving?

She shook her head. Now was not the time for dreaming.

Scott's hands were large around the disposable cup. "So, here's what I know. Correct me if I'm wrong." He laid out her activities the last several years with surprising detail, also noting that he believed Monty had beaten her. Finally he wound down.

"That's all correct," she said, sipping her drink. "From the research I've conducted online, because there's no record of Monty harming me, it's his word against mine. He's a doctor in a small town."

"That's true." Scott leaned both elbows on the counter. "Is there anybody who could corroborate your side?"

She told him about Jack, Monty's older brother. "He helped me to get free, but I don't think he'd testify against Monty. In addition, I can see him wanting a niece and foolishly thinking that maybe having a daughter would help Monty turn into a decent human being. I disagree." She understood the law, and she knew that it'd be too risky to submit Trudy to a custody dispute. "I don't think I have a good chance of winning if he sues me for partial custody."

Scott tipped back more of his sugary brew. "I agree."

"So I need to keep running," she said, her stomach hurting. "Also, I forgot to tell you that my mother would probably testify for Monty as well. I don't have anybody on my side."

"That's not true," Scott said. "You have some very smart people on your side."

She twirled her drink around on the counter, her fingers nimble. "Smart doesn't beat the law and you know it."

The two men returned through the door, along with Dana, whose baby bump looked a little bigger than it had just the other night. Wolfe kept his hand on Dana's shoulder.

"Hi." Dana had startling green eyes and an infectious smile this early. "It's coffee time."

Wolfe fetched one of the many remaining lattes and handed it to her, standing behind her and settling the cup in her hand. "It's decaf with almond milk." He pressed a kiss to her head, and the sight was sweet. Surprisingly sweet.

Jethro removed snow gloves to toss into the sink. "What did we decide?"

"The law won't help me," Gemma said sadly, already missing this group of people who'd created a family. For the briefest of moments she'd allowed herself to dream she could be a part of it. Be friends with them, and maybe have an extended group of people to look over Trudy. But Monty would always win this fight, and he'd draw out any battle. Plus, she wasn't certain he wouldn't figure out a way to kill her, although she was feeling much safer with these people around her. With Jethro next to her. Yeah, he was definitely part of the pull.

Wolfe flattened his hand across Dana's entire stomach, pulling her back to rest against him. "Then we take him out."

Scott held up a hand. "Whoa. I'm your lawyer. Don't say things like that in front of me."

Wolfe rolled his eyes. "I don't mean we kill him." He paused and looked at Jethro. "Right?"

"Right," Jethro said. "We just make his life miserable enough that he decides to leave you alone."

Wait a minute. "How?" Gemma asked, a slight flicker of hope igniting inside her.

Jethro shrugged. "We find out everything about him and then start taking it all away without harming anybody. It's really not that difficult, and because he's a coward who harms women, it'll be a pleasure for every person on the team."

"Yoo-hoo," a chipper voice said, pushing open the front door. "Wolfe? There had better be a latte here for me." A pretty, very petite woman all but hopped into the room. She had streaked blond hair and looked like a pixie—and was probably in her mid-twenties. "I have security equipment in my rig that you boys need to dig out so I can get to installing it all." She paused. "Hi." Her gaze was square on Scott.

He looked as if he'd been hit with a bat. "Hi."

Jethro's lips twitched. "Millicent Frost, please meet Scott Terentson." He drew Gemma forward. "And Gemma Falls."

"Hi," Gemma said.

Millicent grinned. "Hello. Call me Millie."

"Um, hi," Scott said, his tone throaty. "Millicent Frost? That's the coolest name I've ever heard."

She rocked back on her heels. "Thanks. How do you know the gang?"

"I think I'm their lawyer," Scott said, sounding bewildered about that fact.

Millie lost the smile. "Oh."

Scott sighed. "Don't like lawyers?"

"God no." She turned to Jethro. "Let's get this place locked up, shall we? I brought the good stuff."

Wolfe grinned at Scott. "At least you're an ex-Marine, according to Force."

"There's never an *ex* to the Marine part," Scott said easily. "Once a Marine…"

Wolfe nodded. "I get that. You ever think of going into another line of work?"

"Every day," Scott said, taking a full drink of the sugary latte.

Chapter Twenty-Five

After a lunch of sandwiches, Jethro finished helping Millie install the security system by the front door while Gemma and Dana cooked something delicious-smelling in the kitchen, chatting like they were old friends. It was something to see Gemma relax and be herself, not only in looks but in personality. She was a sweetheart when she wasn't running from a batterer.

Millie twisted the sensor into place.

"Good job," Jethro said. The woman was freaking brilliant and deserved the nickname of Q from the ragtag group. "Not for nothing, but Scott is a good guy, lawyer or not. He did get shot for Angus last summer."

Millie rolled to her feet. "That was him?"

"Yes," Jethro said, still on his knees as he double-checked the secondary sensor.

"All I need in my disastrous life right now is a lawyer," she said, stretching her arms above her head and rolling her neck. "My personal life is off-limits."

Jethro started and looked up at her. "That's an option in this unit?"

She grinned. "Yeah, but I'm not Wolfe's best friend."

Wolfe looked up from where he was playing with LEGOs on the floor with Trudy, his long body stretched out on the wooden floor. "No, but you're my little sister. I think that might be worse."

Millie paled. "When did I become your little sister?"

Jethro planted a hand on the wall and gracefully stood.

Wolfe placed a pink LEGO in place on the attack tank they were making, waiting until Trudy nodded in approval before reaching for another piece. "Last summer. Didn't I tell you?"

"No," Millie whispered.

Jethro could almost feel sorry for her. It was probably a good thing that Scott had taken off to do some research into Gemma's case. Jethro glanced at his watch. "Gemma? I need to run to the university for a couple of books and files to prepare for class next week." Because it was possible the weather would keep school closed for several days, he'd need to make adjustments in his overall class schedule. "Do you want to come or just have me pick up whatever you need?"

Wolfe handed Trudy a green Lego. "We can stay here and watch Trudy, if you want."

Trudy smacked him on the shoulder, her back resting against the snoring dog. "Maybe I watch you."

The soldier grinned. "That's probably a good idea. Sometimes I get into trouble."

Gemma faltered, her hand around a wooden spoon.

"I'm fine fetching your materials for you," Jethro said gently. He could understand her not wanting to leave her daughter, with all the uncertainty in her life right now.

She steeled her shoulders. "Are you sure you don't mind, Dana?"

Dana grinned. "No. We might as well get practice now, and Wolfe is having fun. I'll finish up here, and by the time you guys return, dinner will be ready."

Gemma handed her the spoon. "Let me go throw on a wig and get my coat."

Jethro caught the keys Wolfe lazily threw toward him after yanking them from his pocket. "Thanks."

"Yep." Wolfe leaned in to study the realistic-looking tank. "I think we need more blue."

"I'll go warm up the truck," Jethro said, tugging his jacket from the floor and heading out into the white world. The snow still pummeled the ground, and the wind pierced his clothing and froze his bones. January was a rough one this year.

Gemma ran out behind him, and they jumped into Wolfe's truck, heading toward the university.

They were quick and efficient at the too-silent school and, if anything, the snow increased while they fetched their belongings.

Soon they were back on the road and darkness was starting to descend.

Jethro kept both hands on the steering wheel of Wolfe's truck while keeping an eye on the silent woman in the passenger seat, who didn't look right beneath the blond wig. Now that he'd seen the real her, he wanted more of that woman. She'd been quiet and introspective during the afternoon. At the moment she sat stiffly, her hands clenched together in her lap. "Now that we have our class materials, I can take you back to the house and then go fetch my things from my apartment," he said for the third time.

She exhaled, her chest moving. The very impressive chest he'd felt against him the night before for too brief of a moment. "No. Trudy is safe with Dana, Wolfe, and Roscoe. I know that's true, and I have to stop hovering." She rubbed her temple. "Do you think all parents go through this?"

"Just the good ones," he said. "I promise I'll be quick." It didn't make sense to go all the way back to the house and then to his apartment, but he didn't want to cause her any more stress.

His phone dinged and he pressed a button on the dash, his phone already connected to Wolfe's system. "Hanson."

"Hey. It's Tate."

Jethro's gut clenched. "Please tell me you're just calling to check in."

"Nope. We have another body, and we need you on scene," Tate said evenly, rattling off an address. "Like right now."

Jethro glanced at his watch. "I have a stop to make first." In fact, he needed to go in the opposite direction, which would take him an extra thirty minutes at the very least.

"No. Right now, Hanson. Trust me," Tate said.

Gemma patted his arm. "It's okay."

Nothing felt okay. "Fine. I'm on my way," Jethro said, slowing down to make a U-turn and pressing a button on the navigation screen to end the call. "I'm sorry about this."

"Who's Tate and why is he calling you about bodies?" Gemma asked, turning to face him more fully.

He winced. "It's a long story, but here it is." While she knew about Fletcher, Jethro hadn't given her the entire story, or even as much of it as he was cleared to share with the team. By the time he pulled into the parking lot of a strip mall comprised of a massage parlor, a pet store, and a bondsman, she was staring at him with shock in her pretty eyes.

"That's a lot," she murmured.

He parked the truck outside of the yellow crime scene tape. Red and blue lights from the emergency vehicles cut through the falling snow, and he could almost make out Tate beneath the building's overhang. "Stay here." He jumped out of the truck, leaving it running. Then he nodded at a uniformed officer, who lifted the tape for him so he could continue striding toward Tate. The wind and snow attacked him, and he hunched his shoulders. "Where's the body?"

"Was just taken away," Tate said, slipping his notebook in his pocket. "I'm really sorry about this."

Jethro stiffened.

Two men in overcoats moved out of the shadows, and one flipped open an HDD badge. "Jethro Hanson, you're under arrest for the murder of Liping Julian and John Randolf," the younger guy said, motioning with his finger. "Turn around." He pulled out cuffs.

Jethro shot Tate a hard look. "You could've just asked for me to be interviewed."

Tate shrugged. "The HDD thought you were a flight risk and didn't give me the chance. If you ever get out of this, I'll make it up to you."

* * * *

Gemma's heart pounded in the warm truck as two men handcuffed Jethro and started to lead him through the snow to a dark blue sedan. One caught sight of her and turned, headed her way. Her hand trembled, but she scrolled through the contact form on the navigation screen and pressed Wolfe's number.

"Howdy. We're fine here," Wolfe said.

"Wolfe? I think Jethro was just arrested by two guys in overcoats and suits," she said, her voice shaking.

Wolfe was quiet for two beats. "Where are you?"

She rattled off the address. "There's a man coming to the truck."

The front door opened and the guy jumped up into the driver's seat. He wore a heavy trench coat and his blue tie showed above the buttons. "Hi."

She blinked. "Who are you?"

"I'm Special Agent Tom Rutherford with the Homeland Defense Department."

The word "motherfucker" came clearly through the speakers.

Rutherford's head jerked and he looked at the navigation system. "Who's there?"

"This is Agent Wolfe," Wolfe snapped. "What the hell are you doing now, Tommy?"

"I can't comment on an investigation," the agent said, his tone sly. "Gotta go, Wolfe." He shut the door and put the truck in reverse.

Gemma grabbed the dash. "What are you doing?"

He looked her way, snow falling off his ear. "You're a possible witness right now. You can either come with me voluntarily or I can take you into custody as a material witness." His voice softened. "I just need to interview you briefly. It shouldn't take long."

Her mind froze. Completely. She couldn't be interviewed because she couldn't lie to a federal agent. Martha Stewart had done that and ended up in prison. She looked out the window, feeling helpless for the first time in months—since that private detective had found her in Orlando. Interesting. Until that second she hadn't realized how secure she'd been feeling with Jethro in her world.

The same Jethro who'd just been handcuffed.

She leaned an elbow on the windowsill and set her chin on her hand, staring out at the dangerous weather. Her breath fogged the window. "Why did you arrest Jethro?"

"I can't discuss that," Agent Rutherford said, his driving capable despite the storm. "What's your name?"

Instinctively, she almost gave him a false one. "Gemma Falls," she said. The guy no doubt already knew her name because she worked with Jethro. "I'm a visiting professor at DC University."

"What do you teach?"

"Statistics and game theory," she said, watching a Toyota slide on the icy road and then correct, staying at the same speed. "Why do you want to speak with me?"

He turned toward downtown DC. "I believe you might have information material to an investigation. In addition, you very well could be in danger."

"I'm not," she said. Well, she was, but not from Jethro. "There was a body at that scene?"

"Yes," Rutherford said.

She sucked in air. "Jethro wouldn't kill anybody."

Rutherford scoffed loudly. "We believe but can't get substantiated the fact that Dr. Hanson was a key operative for the most dangerous unit ever created by MI6. There are only rumors of its existence, but we have decent intel on this. He's killed more people than you can imagine."

She didn't believe that. Even if he had, it had been part of his job and duty, and she knew without a doubt he'd never discuss it with her. With anyone. He probably couldn't by law and vow. "You must be afraid of him to trick him like that. Why not just call him and ask him to come speak with you instead of all the drama?"

"Because he could flee the country in a heartbeat and we'd never find him." Rutherford pulled into a parking garage beneath a tall, sleek office building. "He's a very dangerous man, Ms. Falls."

She already knew that.

Once they'd parked she jumped out of the truck and casually double-checked that her wig had remained in place. The colored contacts were bugging her eyes, but maybe that'd make them bloodshot and more difficult to read. Places like this probably had cameras and facial scanners everywhere. Taking a deep breath, she followed Rutherford to the elevator and then to the seventh floor.

They stepped out onto an opulent landing where Scott Terentson leaned against the wall, waiting.

Her heart leaped. "Scott?"

He straightened and smiled, still wearing his casual T-shirt and dark jeans. "Hi. They have Jethro in an interrogation room, and he won't say a word until he knows you're okay. You all good?"

Tears tried to attack the back of her eyes, but she kept them at bay. "Yes."

"Excellent." His gaze ran toward Rutherford and then back to her. "Then I can prevent him from tearing this place apart, which is a very likely possibility." Scott winked and grasped her arm, pulling her to the side. "Give us a minute, Rutherford." Then he drew her partially down a hallway so they were out of hearing. "I just spoke with Wolfe and he's remaining in place for now, so all is safe."

Gemma let out a breath she hadn't realized she'd been holding. Trudy would be more than sheltered with Wolfe, Dana, and Roscoe. "Thank you," she whispered.

"No problem." He patted her arm. "Someone is going to escort you to a room and hopefully give you coffee. You're not to say a word until I get there after handling Jethro's interrogation. Understand?"

Numbly, she nodded. That was a plan she could follow. "Tell him..." What should she say? What was there to say?

"I will," Scott said. "Promise."

Chapter Twenty-Six

Jethro's nonexistent temper was trying to explode, so he sat back in the chair and counted the tiles in the ceiling. Then he rearranged them in his mind. The interrogation room was chilly and the metal chair cold beneath his ass. The idea that Gemma was frightened somewhere in the building had him about to take out a couple of HDD agents and go find her, caring little for the repercussions.

The door opened and Scott walked inside, his expression carefully blank. He pulled out the chair next to Jethro and sat, his hands folded neatly on the surprisingly attractive maple table. "Gemma is fine. She's getting coffee now and I'll represent her at her interview, which will take place after this one. Your team is on this, full out, and Wolfe has remained in place."

Jethro nodded. He figured Wolfe would stay to cover Trudy, knowing she was the priority. There was no one better to protect the girl if Jethro couldn't be there right now.

Two men walked through the door. Agents Rutherford and Fields who were an odd combo. Fields was a grizzled man, close to retirement age, with sharp brown eyes. Rutherford was model perfect, with blond hair, broad shoulders, and an aura of pure ambition.

They sat and Rutherford took the lead. "Extra consideration is being utilized in your case because of your strong ties to HDD and the fact that Angus Force has sworn up and down that you are innocent. I have to tell you that I think you're guilty as hell. Do you think he looks innocent, Agent Fields?"

"Nope," Fields said, observing them all, no doubt not missing a thing.

"Dr. Hanson, are you crazy or sane?" Rutherford asked, setting a thin file folder in front of him on the table and a laptop bag on the floor.

Interesting lead.

Scott tilted his head. "Do you have any relevant questions?"

Rutherford smiled, showing perfect teeth. Jethro could help him with that problem easily. "Run me through where you were the night Ms. Julian was killed."

"I was home, got the call, and met Detective Tate Bianchi where the body had been found because there was a note taped to the victim's jacket addressed to me," Jethro said.

"Right. From your brother, Fletcher Hanson," Rutherford drawled. "Bianchi has said that your claim is that he escaped prison and is now stalking you."

Apparently the HDD had a full file at the moment. "No. He escaped prison and is taking on contract killings here to make money. I'm a side benefit." Jethro couldn't figure out Fletcher's end game yet. Even if he could, he wasn't telling these guys.

"Ah," Rutherford said. "So you don't have an alibi but are involved in the case. Isn't that interesting, Kurt?"

"It really is," Fields said, his suit and tie brown and well worn.

Jethro almost kept from rolling his eyes.

"Have you been arrested before?" Rutherford asked. "This seems boring to you."

Jethro nodded. "It does feel rather tedious, now that you mention it." He'd been arrested in more countries than he could count, but he couldn't reveal any of his missions. "Why did you arrest me?"

"Where were you when Mr. Randolf was killed?"

"No alibi," Jethro said. "If I were killing people, I'd have a rock-solid alibi, chaps. My background in game theory and philosophy should have given you that clue."

Rutherford planted his hand on the file folder. "Or perhaps your search for good vs. evil and for understanding has driven you crazy. Maybe you're killing people and pretending to be your incarcerated brother. That's just bananas, isn't it, Kurt?"

"Sounds batshit crazy to me," Kurt said, his jaw shadowed by more gray than brown.

Scott sighed. "Start making sense or we're shutting down this interview."

"Okay." Rutherford dug a laptop out of his bag. "Here's the deal. We have proof you committed these murders, and as soon as we obtain a warrant to search your residence, we'll have more proof." He booted up the computer, and the alley where Liping Julian was found came up. A man strode between the ramshackle businesses, his head covered by a knit hat and his frame around the same size as Jethro's. Over his shoulder, he carried Liping's body. Halting at the dumping site, he tossed her on the ground. Then he briefly looked up.

Rutherford hit a button and Jethro's face came into view.

Jethro didn't react and was pleasantly surprised when Scott didn't either. "Looks like you got a doctored video." Fucking Fletcher. "I have to tell you, if you knew anything about my brother, this wouldn't surprise you." But what was the damn point?

"All right." Rutherford brought up another scene—this one at the golf course. Once again, Jethro could be seen dumping the body. This time, the murder occurred right on camera, with the killer slicing through the victim's body. "Is this doctored as well?"

"Yes," Jethro said, irritated. "Get the recordings to Brigid Banaghan and she'll figure out what happened." Apparently Fletcher still had some decent connections in the world, because those recordings looked authentic. "Sometimes you can't believe your own eyes, gentlemen." It was a lesson he'd learned early with the agency.

"True," Fields said, reaching for the file folder. He took out a piece of paper. "We found your fingerprints on Julian's belt and Randolf's shoes. Apparently you drank some coffee when speaking with Detectives Bianchi and Buckle the other day, and they were nice enough to confirm your prints from the cup. Just in case you were wondering."

Huh. When this was finished he'd have his agency—or former agency—scrub his prints from the records. It wasn't like they hadn't accomplished that before. "My prints must've been planted."

"How about your DNA?" Rutherford asked. "Found it on both victims, and something tells me we'll find it on the newest one, too. His name was John Jordan. Want to tell us how you knew him?"

"His name doesn't ring a bell," Jethro admitted. "Who is he?"

"We're not sharing today," Fields said quietly. "Let us help you. Tell us the truth."

Jethro leaned back in his chair. "I've told you everything you need to know. My brother is a contract killer who is here in town. Find out who wanted those people dead and trace their movements and money. Fletcher won't stop on his own." It was shocking the guy was still working in town, but he apparently had a plan that included Jethro.

Rutherford sighed. "Well, now, there's the problem." He leaned over and typed several keys into the laptop, bringing up a twelve-by-twelve cell. "Your brother is back in custody right here in our country."

Fletcher looked up at the camera.

And smiled.

* * * *

Gemma settled in the truck, letting the heat warm her freezing toes. When she finally was paid she could buy new boots.

Jethro drove, his hands relaxed on the steering wheel. "Are you sure you're all right?"

"Yes," she said, an invisible knife stabbing behind her left eye. "My interview was pretty short. Scott came in, said you and I were university colleagues, and that I didn't know anything else about this case. I just kind of nodded." She shrugged. "I mean, I told them that your brother was in town killing people, but they didn't ask about my past, so I didn't volunteer anything." There was no law against her wearing a wig and colored contacts. "Scott said they'd probably call me back in when they had more information on me." She sighed.

Jethro flattened his heated hand over hers on her thigh. "We'll handle Monty together. At the very least I'll get you and Trudy to another country with new identifications. Once we make sure Fletcher isn't on your trail."

"Did the agents believe you at all about Fletcher?" Scott hadn't told her anything about Jethro's interview, and the good professor had been surprisingly silent about the entire situation. In fact, he seemed to be in his own world right now, but energy came off him in waves. "Jethro? Did they believe you?"

"No," Jethro said, taking a left turn toward what appeared to be an industrial area. "They have footage of Fletcher in a jail somewhere, but they wouldn't say where. My guess is some small town at the other end of the country, and now they'll send agents to the middle of nowhere, and none of the local police officers will know what they're talking about, creating even more confusion." Harsh lights cut through the murk outside the truck, and the windshield wipers worked overtime. "Fletcher is most certainly not in a cell in some small town."

She bit her lip. "Where are we going?"

"To my flat," he said, angling his head to look up at the dark clouds in an even darker sky. "I'd take you home first but time is of the essence, and there are a couple of items I need."

"What items?"

He didn't answer.

Well, then. "I thought we trusted each other?" The man knew everything about her, or mostly anyway. He knew her most frightening secrets.

"We do trust each other." He turned down a road flanked by looming industrial buildings. "There are some issues I can never discuss. I took vows and truly hate the idea of committing treason." His teeth flashed in a quick smile. "I have no secrets from you but those that can never be shared."

She turned and watched the snow attack the truck. It had been too many hours since she'd held her child and her hands felt empty.

"I'll be quick," he said, as if reading her thoughts.

Now she didn't answer.

He turned the vehicle through an open gate and drove by metal buildings until he reached the one at the end.

She looked up at the imposing structure. "You live here?"

"Apartment on the top floor, garage space on the bottom," he said. "I'll pull in, and you can wait in the truck. I'll just be a minute." He pressed a button, and one of the two wide garage doors started to open.

The earth rumbled.

For a breath everything stilled.

"Jethro?" she asked.

He grabbed her and covered her with his body. An explosion rocked the earth, and the truck flew back through the air to smash against another metal building.

They dropped, and the vehicle bounced.

Pain flared through Gemma's chest from the seat belt and an airbag slowly deflated. Powder hung in the air. She blinked several times. When had the airbag deployed?

Jethro turned toward her, his hands on her biceps. Blood flowed from a cut beneath his right eye. "Are you okay?"

She conducted a quick check of her body. "I think so." Her ears were ringing. She turned to see smoke and fire spiraling out of his building. "What just happened?"

"Bomb." He reached under the seat and brought out a matte black gun. "Shoot anybody you don't know and call this in. Call for an ambulance and then call Wolfe. Keep the doors locked."

"Wait." She clutched his wrist. "What are you doing?"

He jumped out of the truck. "Making sure my friends aren't dead. Lock this." He slammed the door shut and ducked into the storm, running across the now-cracked ice to the building and taking the exterior stairs three at a time.

Gemma called 9-1-1 and then called Wolfe, watching the fire blowing out of what must've been the front door.

"Wolfe," he answered.

"There's been an explosion at Jethro's and he just went inside," she said in a rush, panic heating her entire body. "I don't know what to do. I called 9-1-1."

Movement sounded as Wolfe reacted. "Are you armed?"

"Yes," she gulped. "Inside the locked truck."

"Okay. I'll send people there now. Dana and I will cover Trudy, so don't worry about her. I'll call you back." The line went dead.

Jethro emerged with flames behind him, carrying a bulky form over one shoulder.

Crap. Gemma jumped out of the vehicle and ran through the snow, slipping several times, to reach him.

"Get back in the truck." He moved fast, shoving the guy into the back seat. "See what you can do for him." Jethro turned and rushed back to the stairs, his shoulders smoldering.

Gemma coughed from the smoke. "Hello?" She nudged either Ian or Oliver. Bruises and cuts covered what she could see of his body, and smoke wafted from his tattered and burned shirt. He was out cold. She didn't want to move him too much in case he had a neck or spine injury. Holding her breath, she felt for a pulse.

Slow but steady.

Another explosion ripped the world behind her, and she partially leaned over him, protecting his head.

Sirens trilled miles away. "They're coming," she whispered. "Hold on. Help will be here soon." She brushed his thick hair away from his face, noting a deep purple bruise on his temple. "Just hold on." Turning, she looked frantically for Jethro.

He jumped out the front door and leaped down the stairs, the other twin over his shoulder. Fire bloomed behind them and another explosion ripped through the night. Glass blew out and half of the building started to collapse.

"Jethro!" she screamed.

The blast blew him forward and he fell, landing hard and rolling with the wounded man. In one impossibly smooth motion, he was back on his feet and readjusting the man over his shoulder, dodging through debris to reach the truck.

He placed the other man in the back seat. "Get in the truck," he ordered. "Now."

She hurried to comply, jumping into the driver's seat. Almost in slow motion, she turned, her brain mush. "Jethro? Your shirt is on fire."

Chapter Twenty-Seven

Gemma moved stiffly out of the examination room after getting the all clear from the doctor. She had contusions and a possible mild concussion, but she was thankful to be alive. If the bomb had detonated just a few seconds later, once they were inside the building, she'd be dead.

Then where would Trudy be?

She limped down the hallway to find Jethro leaning against the wall, his head back, his body wounded. Bruises marred the side of his rugged jaw and burn marks covered his arms. Most of his shirt had been burned away, revealing red skin and old scars on his chest.

His eyes opened and he laser focused on her. "Are you all right?"

"Yes," she said, pushing her wet hair out of her eyes. "I already gave my statement to Agent Rutherford while the doctor checked me out. How are you?" She looked down at his torn jeans. "Have you seen a doctor yet?"

"No," Nari answered for him, coming around the corner. "The stubborn ass won't see a doctor until his friends are checked out."

Angus was on her heels, two cups of coffee in his hands. He handed one to Jethro. "How are they?"

"Don't know yet," Jethro said, taking the cup. "I need you to drive Gemma home. Now."

Angus studied him, his eyes sharp. "Nari?"

"Sure." Nari moved toward Gemma. "We're parked right outside. I'll get you home to your daughter."

Jethro looked at Angus. "Where is everyone? We need somebody on them."

Nari paused. "I'm on us." She looked at Angus and shook her head. "Seriously."

Agnus grinned. "Where is everyone? Let's see. I've cut short vacations for the team and sent them to Oregon to investigate Monty Cameron. Wolfe and Dana are watching Trudy, Roscoe, and Kat." He winked at Gemma. "The animals will occupy Trudy. Don't worry."

Gemma couldn't finish a complete thought. "How are Ian and Oliver?"

Jethro rolled his neck. "They're both tough and were breathing, so I'm sure they'll be okay. I'd just like to know the extent of the damage."

Agent Rutherford emerged from the nearest room. "As would I. Is it just me, or is it quite the coincidence your apartment blew up right before I obtained a warrant to search it?"

Jethro stiffened.

Angus pushed away from the wall. "This isn't a good time, Rutherford."

"It never is," the agent said, his blond hair perfectly in place. "Who are the two men who almost died in your apartment?"

Jethro set his jaw and didn't speak.

"Is there a reason you'd want them dead?" Rutherford prodded.

Jethro looked down at Gemma, his eyes glittering. "Go with Nari, please. Now."

Nari grasped her arm. "Yeah, let's get going. If these boys are going to fight, it's better to get out of the way." She patted Jethro's arm. "Call us with updates on your friends." Then she went up on her toes and kissed Angus on his jaw. "I'll see you in a couple." Launching herself into motion, she pulled Gemma down the hallway and out into the blustery night. "The truck is right there."

The gray truck was waiting and already idling from remote start.

Gemma ducked her head against the cold and hustled behind Nari, jumping in the passenger seat and sighing as the heat filtered over her frosty skin. Then she put her head back, closed her eyes, and let her body finally relax and deal with the trauma of the bomb. She might've drifted off because it felt as if only minutes had passed when she opened her eyes to find they'd parked inside Serena's garage. "Oh," she mumbled, releasing her seat belt and all but stumbling from the truck.

Nari was there to steady her. "You okay?" Her dark eyes glowed with concern.

No. Not at all. "Yes, thank you." Gemma straightened and walked toward the door, anxious to see Trudy. She moved through the laundry room to the kitchen, which smelled like casserole. Then she stopped short. Wolfe and Dana played cards at an oak table—the one that had been in Serena's apartment. Her sofa and chairs were in the living room, and paintings were leaning against walls but hadn't been hung yet.

"Hey," Wolfe said, standing and stretching his back. "Trudy and Roscoe are asleep in her room."

"Thank you," she said, unable to stay and chat. She had to see Trudy. Her shoulders trembling, she hurried down the hallway into her daughter's room.

Trudy snuggled in the middle of her Cinderella bed and Roscoe had flopped at her feet. He opened one eye, looked her over, then shut it again.

The door from the kitchen closed, no doubt as Nari headed home to get some much-needed sleep. They all were running ragged and emotions were high.

Gemma reached her daughter and settled the blankets more securely around her. Trudy's curly brown hair spread all over the pillow, and her little pink lips were slightly open in sleep. Her breathing was deep and steady and she seemed peaceful.

Every bone in Gemma's body ached. She inhaled the smell of baby powder and crayons. Okay. So long as Trudy was safe, everything would be all right. She leaned over and petted Roscoe's head. He snuffled and started snoring.

Gemma bit back a sob. The night had proven without a doubt that the world was dangerous and she was alone. But she didn't have to be. Without asking for a single thing in return, an entire group of people she barely knew had made sure her daughter was safe. Wearily, she stood and walked out of the room and into hers, needing to check a bruise on her back. She wandered by the master bathroom and stopped short at seeing a rack of clothing hanging up in the closet. All new, with the tags still on.

Reaching out, she gingerly touched a silk suit. A gorgeous, blue, just-her-size suit.

"Jethro asked us to find clothing for you," Dana said from the doorway, her hand on her slightly protruding belly. "The clothes you borrowed from Serena weren't working for you." She smiled, her eyes dancing.

"No, they weren't," Gemma agreed, her gaze caught on another blue sweater. "There's a lot of blue."

Dana chuckled. "Jethro's orders. Apparently, he likes your genuine eye color." She pointed to a dresser in the corner. "That's new and it's full of items for you."

Gemma backed away from the enticing silk.

Dana rubbed her elbow. "Was Jethro okay? I won't feel better until I can see him, and Wolfe is going nuts even though they talked on the phone."

Tears gathered in Gemma's eyes. The couple had stayed behind in order to protect Trudy. "Thank you for everything you've done here. Jethro said he's okay, and he looked fine when I left. Well, beat up and burned, but still standing." She looked over at Dana. "The way he ran into that burning building was amazing, and he knew more explosions were going to happen. He carried out both of those hulking men."

Dana's eyes softened. "That's our Jethro. He's a hero, whether he believes it or not."

Gemma nodded. "It was the bravest thing I've ever seen." The man had been incredible and even now was calmly waiting to make sure everyone was safe. Not asking for anything, just being his controlled and deadly self.

"He's a keeper for sure," Dana agreed.

Gemma couldn't answer that. She most likely wasn't staying and wouldn't be the one to keep him. Not that he'd truly offered anything but perhaps one night. She turned her focus back to the beautiful clothes hanging in the closet. "I can't afford all this."

"Jethro can," Dana said. "You might as well let him help you. Right now his world is spinning out of control and it makes him feel good to help others, so why not just say thank you?"

"Would you have? I mean, before you and Wolfe decided to start a family?" Gemma asked, truly curious.

Dana scrunched her nose. "That's a good question. Wolfe and I were friends, then both of us were undercover at a BDSM club, and then we got pregnant. I do like clothes. I think I would've accepted them. Plus, when we were undercover, he was all dom to the max, so I wouldn't have said no. Well, probably."

Gemma's head ached as she tried to track that sentence. Perhaps Dana was a little nutty, too. She and Wolfe might make the perfect couple. "Wait a minute. What was that about a BDSM club?"

Dana chuckled. "Yeah. Wolfe was working on a case and I was working on a story as a journalist, and we ran into each other when it appeared our cases were connected. That night was a little explosive, and then we had to work together." She looked down at her belly, her face softening. "He's a lot to handle sometimes, but I can't believe we found each other. He keeps trying to get us married, but I want to wait until the baby is born and then have a huge blowout wedding with my family. Both of my families. This unit is definitely a family."

"I don't blame you," Gemma said softly. The stunning journalist would make a lovely bride. "Do you know if you're having a boy or a girl?"

"No." Dana's smile widened. "I want it to be a surprise, but Wolfe wants to know, so we'll probably find out next month just to ease his mind. For some reason he can't plan unless he knows. Plus, I would like to know how to decorate the nursery."

Gemma hadn't had a nursery. As soon as she and Trudy had been healthy enough, she'd moved to a new state. "That does sound like fun," she murmured, feeling a twinge in her heart that she might never be able to give her daughter a normal life.

Wolfe appeared behind Dana. It seemed he was never very far from her. "Jethro just pulled up. Let's get you to bed, Dana." He smiled at Gemma over Dana's head. "Jethro won't let anything happen to you. Also, I'll engage the security system before I go, and Roscoe will stay here with you two. He acts like a dork but is a phenomenal guard dog. You're safe here, Gemma. I promise."

"Thanks," she said, meaning it. Being safe, even temporarily, allowed her to let down her guard. "'Night, you two."

"'Night." Wolfe took Dana's hand and they left, saying something to Jethro before heading outside.

Gemma moved into the living room to see him lock the door and engage the new security system by using the keypad on the wall. "How are the twins doing?"

He partially turned, his clothing still in tatters and somehow making him look even more dangerous than he had before. "They'll live." He kicked off his boots and stalked toward her, all male intent. "How are you?"

Suddenly breathless. "I'm fine," she said.

He reached her and ran a gentle knuckle down her face. "I keep putting you at risk when all I want to do is guarantee your safety." His voice was hoarse and his accent strong.

"Safety is an illusion," she said, leaning into his touch.

"True." He didn't smile as she'd hoped. Instead, he let his hand fall and stepped away. "We can talk more tomorrow. Let's get some sleep tonight."

She was so tired of being vigilant. So exhausted from running and being alone. She was sick of telling herself she was just a mother trying to survive. There was more to her; she was just figuring out that she was a woman, too. Until she'd met him and his friends she hadn't realized how lonely she'd been. "I don't want to sleep."

His eyes flared. "Your defenses are down. I'm a violent man, sweetheart. You can't forget that."

"You're in control of any violence you create," she said softly. "That's what matters. You'd never hurt me."

"You're right. I'd never hurt you." He drew in a ragged breath. "But what are you saying?"

She wasn't a woman who took risks if she could help it. Just surviving was risky enough. Yet she stepped closer to him, filling her senses with his familiar scent along with the smoke. Too much smoke. She gently rubbed her hands up his torn and burned shirt, gingerly touching the skin above. He was warm and whole. Real. “I want you.” She stretched to her tiptoes and kissed him, slanting her mouth over his, wanting what they’d almost had the other day.

He stilled for a couple of seconds and then, with a groan, he took over the kiss.

Completely.

Chapter Twenty-Eight

Jethro's head thrummed and his gut hurt, but the second Gemma pressed her sweet lips to his, all pain flew away. He mumbled something, trying to keep control. Then she slid her tongue inside his mouth and he lost his mind.

Turning fully into her, he angled her head and kissed her the way he'd wanted to ever since he'd gotten a glimpse of the real woman beneath the disguise. The sweet, kind one with the intelligent eyes and adorable ass. Finally he let himself take her, showing her the side of himself that only the enemy had ever seen. The primal being with a ferocious need and dangerous fire.

She moaned and pressed even harder against him, both hands going up to grab his hair and hold on. The erotic pull nearly dropped him to his knees.

He wrapped an arm around her waist and lifted her, turning to plant her sweet butt against the wall. Having her close, tasting her...something cracked open inside him.

Just for her.

The more he was around her, the more he knew of her, the more he realized he wouldn't let her go. If she wanted to run, he'd provide protection.

Her legs lifted until her knees rested on either side of his hips. Trusting him.

The woman had dug her way into him, into his blood, and there was no way to stop that. He kissed her harder, knowing he should go slow but unable to stop.

She nipped at the corner of his lip and then his mouth crashed down on hers, finally taking what she was offering. Her nails dug into his nape, spurring him on, and he kissed her like he'd been starving for her.

He had been.

Now he had her, and he should be responsible and tell her to go to bed.

Fuck that.

The hunger hit him with a powerful stroke, and he slid both hands under her butt and turned, walking them both into his room. His mouth never stopped working hers, and if he had his way, this was just the beginning.

It was too late to think, even if he wanted to be reasonable. He'd held back from day one, but she'd kissed him. He was done holding back and thrust his tongue past her lips, pulling away to nip at her jaw and over to her delicate ear. Then he set her down on the bed, cupping her face. "Tell me this is what you want." His accent was so thick, he could barely understand himself.

She looked up at him, trust and need in her blue eyes. "This is exactly what I want." Her hands went to release his belt buckle.

He sucked in a breath, suddenly rock-hard. Slowly, he drew his shirt over his head, letting it fall carelessly to the floor. She hummed and released the belt, pulling it free.

Her hands hesitated before she unsnapped his destroyed jeans. "I, um, I haven't done this in a long while."

He cupped the side of her face and then moved his hand, tangling his fingers in her brunette curls. "I've got you." Then he leaned down and kissed her, continuing until he was on his knees before her, still taller than she was on the bed. She tore her mouth away, sucking in air. Who needed to breathe? He kissed her jaw and down her neck, each inch of her skin. A freckle here, a small mole there. A little scar was beneath her ear—he'd ask about it later.

She explored his chest while he kissed her, each finger light on his bruises.

He reached the pulse point in her throat and kissed her, pleased it was fluttering wildly. God, he wanted her. On his bed, naked, fully spread out for pleasure. Not just for this stormy night either. He wanted to sink into her and forget the entire world.

He forced his hands to remain gentle as he slid both of them up her torso and took her T-shirt with them. Dropping it on the bed, he flicked the clasp of her plain white bra, tugging it free. So beautiful. He hummed in appreciation and leaned down, flicking one pink nipple with his tongue.

She gasped.

He reached for her, surprised by how full her breasts were even though she was still so thin. He'd have to do something about that soon because she no longer needed to camouflage herself and hide. She filled his palms, and her breath grew ragged as her nails dug into his shoulders. "I could do this all night." He leaned down and lashed the other nipple.

She stiffened. "I think you'd kill me if it was all night."

Lust raged through him, and even so, amusement filtered in. He grinned and pressed her down, gently pulling the jeans off her small hips. "I'll try not to kill you." Although her plain white panties might kill him.

He had them off her in a second and then his mouth was right where he wanted it to be.

She gasped and wriggled her butt.

He shoved her legs apart with his shoulders and licked her, now truly humming in appreciation.

"Jethro," she moaned.

There was nothing like hearing his name on her lips. He nipped her hipbone and then went to work, using his tongue, teeth, and fingers to drive her crazy. The woman had been driving him crazy since the first time he'd seen her, so he prolonged her release as long as he could. She tasted of something pure with a hint of spice, and he was definitely going to do this again.

She whimpered, and there was a hint of pain in the sound.

He pushed her over, lashing her clit with his tongue.

She cried out and grabbed a pillow to smash it over her face, muffling the sound.

He chuckled against her, making her spasm more.

Finally she came down and set the pillow aside, her hair billowing all around her face. Her natural, gorgeous, honey-brown hair. Her smile was lazy. "That was amazing."

He stood and shucked his boxers, crawling up her body. "It's about to get a lot better," he promised, pressing against her core.

She blinked, her eyes blurry. "Do you, um, have something?"

Something? Holy shit. He hadn't even thought of protection. Gulping, he swallowed down pain. Then he noticed items on the dresser by the bed. Things Wolfe had brought for him when they'd gotten the furniture.

"We're about to see just how good a buddy my best friend really is." Jethro groaned, reaching up and opening the drawer.

* * * *

Gemma held her breath and nearly laughed out loud at Jethro's triumphant grunt. "Now, that's a good friend."

"Thank the gods," Jethro said, ripping the condom open with his teeth and spitting the wrapper somewhere else. He leaned to the side and quickly set the condom in place. "I owe him for sure."

"We both do." Even though she'd just had a spectacular orgasm, she wanted more. She wanted to be completely with him, completely taken over by him. She ran her hands down the hard contours of his arms, careful when she encountered slightly burned skin. Even without the recent burns and bruises, his body testified to his life as a warrior.

Healed bullet holes marred the hard perfection of his body along with several knife wounds and many other scars. She'd explore each one later. Right now she needed him. She grasped his hips and tried to pull him closer.

"Hold on," he whispered, kissing her and going deep.

She couldn't wait. He was right there, hard and full, so close to where she needed him. "Jethro, now," she moaned against his mouth.

He lifted up on an elbow, grasped her hip, and thrust into her with one strong stroke.

She cried out, pleasure and pain swamping her. After her orgasm she'd been ready, but he was still a lot. Her body pulsed around him, sending shocks through her entire being. Nothing in her whole life had ever felt this wild. This shockingly good. Pleasure rippled through her, and she clung to his arms, trying to ground herself and not fly away.

He ducked his head and lightly rasped down her neck to nip her collarbone. "I knew. The first time you smiled at me, really smiled, I knew you'd be perfect."

The words dug deep into her heart and took root.

"I imagined this," he admitted, pulling out and powering back inside her, firing nerves both ways. So many nerves and so much pleasure. His words in that accent nearly threw her into another orgasm. "It's better than I fantasized," he said, plunging hard.

So fucking hard.

Her body coiled tight and she lifted her legs to lock around his waist.

"There you go." He partially lifted her hip again, hammering inside her, taking complete control.

All she could do was hold on to his arms and let the ecstasy take her from head to toe. He was so much. There was so much. Her body was wound tight and relief was so close, but she never wanted this to end.

She arched up against him, her nails digging into his skin. Was he hurt there? She couldn't tell, but she couldn't let go either.

He moved faster, and the new headboard rocked against the wall. The world slowed down until there were only the two of them and the unbelievable pleasure washing between them. His hand moved between their bodies and he stroked her clit.

"Oh God," she whispered, taking even more of him. This wasn't gentle or calm. It was intense. Fiery. Primal. She shut her eyes and let her body take over.

He stroked her clit one more time and then grabbed her hair, twisting and bringing his mouth down on hers. Hard.

The kiss was everything, even as he continued to pound inside her, the hard planes of his chest warm against her breasts. She panted and reached out, her entire body going stiff.

The climax hit her out of nowhere, throwing her under. Sparks flashed behind her eyes and she cried out. He swallowed the sound with his mouth, kissing her again, his firm lips unrelenting and his tongue passionate. Her body shook with the force of her orgasm and she stopped breathing as she rode out the sharp waves.

He tensed against her, his grip tightening on her hip. Then he shuddered against her, sliding his head down so his mouth could latch onto her shoulder.

She went limp, her lungs panting, her eyes wide. "Wow."

He jolted and then chuckled, his body moving against her. More electrical shocks zipped through her and she moaned.

He lifted up and kissed her gently on her nose, both cheeks, her chin, and then her mouth. Pleasure darkened his eyes. His heart beat against hers, and she could swear they were in perfect time. The sharp angles of his face softened just a little. "Are you all right?"

She was completely overcome. "Yes," she whispered.

"Good." He pulled out and grinned at her whimper. "I'll be right back." He rolled from the bed and disappeared into the bathroom.

What had she just done? She scrambled up and crawled beneath the covers, her body sore and way too relaxed. Naked and vulnerable. Oh, she'd definitely wanted him, but that was more than sex. Never in her life had she felt overcome like that, and it was all Jethro Hanson. The college professor who was so much more than he'd appeared.

He returned and lifted one eyebrow when he saw her beneath the covers. "Feeling shy, are we?" He pulled back the bedspread and slid in next to her, reaching for her. "What shall we do about that?"

She snuggled her butt into his groin, letting him spoon his strong, scarred body around her. The feeling of warmth and safety nearly brought tears to her eyes. "That was a lot."

"Yes." He kissed the top of her head, his broad hand flattened over her abdomen. With his other hand, he played with her hair.

She could stay like this forever, but that kind of thinking would get her heart smashed in two. Even though he thought they could take care of Monty, he didn't know him. He'd never stop. Even if he lost everything, he would still keep coming for her because he couldn't lose to her. Never to her. She shivered.

Jethro pulled the covers up over her shoulders. "What are you thinking?"

That she was going to have to run again, even if they did manage to hurt Monty first. The guy was obsessed and would give up everything to find her and hurt her. She'd been fooling herself to think otherwise. Somebody like Jethro, a hero who understood good and evil, would never understand that reality. "I was just thinking that I had no clue uptight philosophy professors could be so good in bed."

He chuckled, his breath stirring her hair. "Same with frigidly cold statistics professors."

"Hey." She smiled, wiggling her butt and enjoying his groan in response. "I was polite. Not frigidly cold."

"Humph. We'll have to agree to disagree," he said, running his hand down her arm to take her hand. "I meant it when I said taking this step would change things between us."

She kept her breathing even. "What? Now you want me to meet you at the door in high heels with a seductive wrap around my body and a martini in my hand?"

He hardened behind her. "Is that something you Yanks do?"

She chuckled. "No."

"Tease." He tugged on her ear. "No. I was just making sure you understand that you're not running away now. At least not without saying goodbye and with a good plan in your head."

She had the oddest sense that he'd just added the last for her comfort and had no intention of letting her run. Even odder, that didn't scare her. Jethro would never hurt her, and that idea had her eyelids closing and her body relaxing.

Roscoe's bark had her sitting upright in the bed.

"Incoming," Jethro said, rolling from the bed and yanking on his sweats.

"Mama?" Trudy murmured, toddling right by the room on her way to the master bedroom.

Gemma covered her mouth to stop a chuckle and slipped from the bed, yanking a blanket around her naked body. "I'm coming, honey."

Trudy returned and looked into the room. "Oh. Are you guys playing?"

Jethro threw back his head and laughed, the sound deep and comforting. Now that was a sound she didn't want to leave.

It was too bad she understood the danger—this time—better than he did. The man was right.

Evil really did exist.

Chapter Twenty-Nine

Thursday morning Jethro finished his second cup of coffee as both Gemma and Trudy slept. He leaned back against the counter and relived the night before. While he should probably regret having slept with Gemma, he didn't.

Not in the slightest.

He wiped a hand across his brow and rolled his shoulders. Then he picked up his phone and called his former boss.

"Cecil Jones," he answered. Jones was so not his last name.

"It's Jethro. The US feds have a video of Fletcher in a cell somewhere. What do you know about it?" Jethro turned and poured his third coffee into the mug.

Cecil was quiet for a moment. "Not a bloody thing. Is the video authentic?"

Jethro prodded a fresh bruise across his hipbone. "I don't know. My guess is no because apparently Fletcher is leaving doctored videos all over the place. He has my face, DNA, and prints associated with two, most likely three, homicide victims." Jethro took another drink of the thick coffee, watching the storm through the back window. "Do you have any idea what he's up to?"

"No. Your brother is cattail crazy, and I can't read him any better than you," Cecil said. He'd managed both Hanson brothers, and he took the failure of Fletcher as hard as Jethro. "I want to bring you home."

"Can't leave," Jethro said. "Besides, I like Fletcher on foreign soil better than at home. He has connections and funds here, but nothing like he'd have at home." Plus, there was Gemma. Jethro hadn't taken care of her problem yet. Both she and Trudy were in danger, and he wouldn't move an inch if they needed cover. "Can you get the video?"

"I can try, but the Yanks don't love to share. I'll be in touch." Cecil clicked off.

Jethro dialed Brigid.

"Hi, Jet," the chipper woman said. "What's up?"

"Did you have any luck requesting the videos of me from HDD?" Jethro asked. While most of the team worked for HDD, they weren't exactly on the inside of the agency, even with Nari's connections.

Brigid sighed. "Not yet. Because we're in Oregon, I'm trying to go through official channels, but Rutherford is blocking me. I could just hack into the system, but I kinda promised I wouldn't do that anymore. I don't want to get fired. But if you want me to do it, I will."

His chest settled. "Let's hold off on breaking federal laws for now, but I appreciate the offer. How is it going in Oregon?"

Even her chuckle had an Irish brogue. "I'm not certain yet. We've gone through Monty Cameron's life, and we've tracked down two ex-girlfriends. We just need to interview them. If he's battered one woman, he's hit several. Then I'll seek out his current fiancée and feel her out."

Jethro shook his head. "I really appreciate this."

"No problem. We need a good written case to use against Monty, and then we'll attack from another side. I'm also looking into the medical practice for any complaints. So far nothing, but I just started digging." She coughed. "It's not as cold here as DC, but it's wet. Really wet."

Jethro put his cup on the counter. "I owe you one. Say hi to Raider for me, and please give me a call when you do obtain the videos." He clicked off.

His phone buzzed. "Hanson."

"Hey, it's Angus. I'm trying to back up Brigid with the request for those videos, but we might need Scott to get all lawyerly with Rutherford. I tried to go over his head to Nari's dad, and the stickler wants me to stay with official channels. Sometimes he's such a dick."

Jethro barked out a laugh. "Thanks for trying."

Angus snorted. "I'd like to meet up tonight after work and profile your brother. To do that, I need to dig into your head."

"It's all yours, but I haven't had any luck figuring him out or determining exactly what he's up to besides making money and messing with me," Jethro said. "But come over for dinner and we can talk afterward." Had he just invited Force for dinner like they were double dating? Did they even have any food in the house?

"Sure."

Jethro moved to the keypad by the garage door to make sure it was still active. "Are you at the office?"

"Yeah. We don't get snow days like college professors," Angus drawled. "Dana wasn't feeling well, so she and Wolfe stayed home."

More likely Wolfe wanted to provide backup should Jethro need it. "Thanks, Angus. I'll see you around suppertime." He put down the phone. Could he just order in? That would work.

Those stupid videos were driving him nuts. They were obviously doctored, and if anybody could figure out how, it was Brigid. She was the best computer expert in the entire DHS, but she refused to work for any unit but Deep Ops in the HDD. She could write her own ticket at this point and she loved the team. As well as Raider. Jethro needed to find the time to purchase them an engagement present. Pippa would help him.

His phone buzzed and he snatched it off the counter. "Hanson."

"Where are your two nameless friends who got caught in the explosion?" Agent Rutherford yelled.

Jethro winced and pulled the phone away from his ear. "Must you yell? Learn to control yourself, Agent," he said calmly, his mind flipping through the strategic venues the twins might've sought.

"I am going to arrest you for obstruction, you asshole," Rutherford snapped.

Jethro finally began to enjoy the snow day. "That might be a good time, considering my attorney would then sue you for false arrest, or whatever it is you Yanks call it." He scrubbed a hand through his hair. The twins wouldn't use his phone in case the government had it tapped, which was more than likely. That was fine. He didn't mind the authorities knowing he thought Fletcher was setting him up. "I haven't seen my friends since last night at the hospital."

"How about you tell me their names?" Rutherford said.

"I can't hear you," Jethro said, tapping his finger on the phone. "I think it's the storm." He ended the call and immediately called Wolfe.

Wolfe answered on the third ring. "What's up?"

"Can you cover Gemma and Trudy for me? I have to run an errand."

* * * *

The smell of coffee had Gemma wandering out of the master bedroom in yoga pants and a sweatshirt after brushing her teeth and pulling her thick hair into a ponytail. She stopped short at seeing Dana sitting in the breakfast nook, typing away on her laptop. "Morning."

Dana looked over her shoulder and her eyes focused. "Hi there. Coffee's on."

Gemma gratefully moved for the coffeepot and poured herself a large cup, immediately taking a gulp. "Bless you."

"You're welcome," Dana said, her blond hair around her shoulders and her face a little pale. "I actually made a second pot because I figured you couldn't drink the slop Jethro made. It was thick as mud." She shook her head. "Aren't Brits supposed to like tea with milk and really weak coffee?"

"I'm not sure." Gemma pivoted and sat at the table, her hands warming around the mug. "So, where *is* Jethro?" Heat filled her face, burning her skin.

Dana pressed her lips together as if she was trying not to laugh, but her pretty green eyes danced. "He's running an errand. Wolfe is shoveling your walkway and drive. So it's just us girls if you want to have some girl talk." She lost the fight and her face lit up with a smile. "You look so guilty."

"I'm not guilty." Gemma blew on her coffee. When was the last time she'd had a friend? The last time she had girl talk? She couldn't even remember.

Dana shut her laptop and reached for a glass of water. "You don't have to tell me, but if you want to talk, I'm here."

Gemma took another swallow. "Fine. Jethro and I, well, last night…"

Dana snorted. "You put that so succinctly."

Gemma chuckled.

Dana leaned toward her. "I have to ask. Is 007 as good in the sack as he seems?"

Gemma coughed out coffee and wiped her mouth. "He's better. There is no way 007 could touch the gifts possessed by Jethro Hanson," she confided. "Like unreal and out of this world."

Dana drank her water and put down her glass. "I'm so glad to hear that."

Gemma pursed her lips, thinking about it. "You know, I figured with the whole Brit thing, he'd be all gentle and ask questions."

"Not so gentle?" Dana asked.

"Thank goodness no," Gemma admitted. "And that man didn't need to ask one question. It was like we'd been together forever. Better than that. Like it was exciting and the first time, but he had a manual to my body that I didn't even know existed."

Dana winced and put her hand to her belly.

"You okay?" Gemma asked.

"Yes. Just the little one moving around, and I already feel a bit nauseated this morning." Dana exhaled. "Isn't morning sickness supposed to end after the first trimester? I keep getting sick."

"Everyone is different," Gemma said, remembering the first time Trudy had moved in her body. "I was sick a lot, too. But I was also scared and running, so I never knew what caused my nausea, you know?" It felt so good to be able to talk about her real life to someone she trusted.

Dana reached out and took her hand. "I'm sorry you had to go through that. Do you think you'll ever have more kids?"

Gemma's smile felt sad. "No. I understand you all think you have a chance against Monty, but he won't stop coming for me or for Trudy, now that he knows about her. The law is on his side, and even if he loses everything, he won't give up. I'll be running until she's eighteen, and then maybe I can relax." Even so, Monty would probably keep coming.

It was impossible to think she could outrun him that long.

The front door opened and Wolfe stepped inside the small vestibule, ditching his jacket and boots, snow on his black hair. "This storm isn't abating in the slightest," he complained, stalking toward them like a wild animal and kissing Dana on the head. "How are you feeling?"

"Better," Dana said, looking up and smiling at him. "Gemma doesn't think we can get her ex to leave her alone."

Wolfe grinned. "I guess we'll have to prove it to her."

Gemma shook her head. "If we stay within the law, we don't have a leg to stand on. I can't prove his abuse." She held up her hand before Wolfe could argue. "I won't go outside the law and hurt him. I can't do that."

Wolfe strode to the kitchen and poured himself a cup of coffee. "Jethro Hanson's physical prowess is trumped only by his strategic genius. If he wants Monty out of your life in a legal way, he'll do it. Don't underestimate him."

"I won't," Gemma said quietly. "I don't understand the plan, though."

"There isn't one yet," Wolfe said easily. "Brigid and Raider need to gather all the relevant information, and then we'll come up with a plan. Don't worry. It's what we do." He shrugged. "It's what we do sometimes. Other times we take down the mob, stop bombings, solve murders…" He took another deep gulp of the coffee and then sighed. "We need whipped cream and sprinkles."

Dana pushed her hair over her shoulder. "We have some at our house."

Trudy toddled out from the hallway with Roscoe on her heels. Her hair was a wild mess and crayon marker covered her right hand. She grinned. "Wuf."

"Hey, Sugar Plum," Wolfe said. "How was your night?"

She ran toward him, expecting to be lifted.

He obliged. "You hungry?"

She nodded and patted his cheeks. "Wuf, where's Jet-ro?"

Gemma tried not to be insulted that her daughter had become attached to the men in their lives and seemed to be forgetting her. She smiled. It was good for Trudy to see strong and good men.

"Jethro is running an errand, sweetling. Hopefully he'll be back soon," Wolfe said.

Gemma frowned. "What kind of errand?"

"He didn't say." Wolfe almost succeeded in hiding his own frown.

What the heck did that mean?

Chapter Thirty

Jethro drove exactly one hundred miles east of his former apartment, finding four motels within a block radius. He scrutinized the names of the places, having to squint through the nor'easter. He drove by each, checking out the names, and discovered Blue Motel, Robin Motel, Motel Seven, and Jackson's Motel.

Fair enough. Motels with an animal name or a female name were always where his team would regroup when they couldn't text each other.

His gun beneath his seat, he returned to Robin Motel, which had a light blue exterior with pale yellow metal doors. The L-shaped building held two stories, and a light in the office blinked through the storm. The parking lot was half-full, and many of the vehicles were buried in snow. He parked and counted four from the left, finding room number eight on the first floor.

He dodged out of the truck he'd borrowed from Raider because his friend was out of town and tucked the gun at the back of his waist beneath his battered brown leather jacket. Then he ran through the storm, reaching the door and knocking rapidly. "Open up."

A gun cocked inside.

"It's me, you morons." He didn't have time for this crap. His ears were freezing.

The door slowly opened and a greenish-blue gaze pierced him. Then Oliver moved to the side, wearing hospital scrubs and worn white tennis shoes. "Come on in."

Jethro moved inside and shut the door, looking at his friends. "You look like shit." Both men were covered in stitches and bruises, and Ian looked as if he'd been punched in the temple. "I'm assuming broken hurts worse than bruised, or is it the other way around?"

"Forget hurt." Ian groaned. "What matters is what slows us down."

"My wrist and his left ankle," Oliver said, his wrist in a black cast.

Jethro shook his head, looking around the empty room. "You have no provisions, but you managed to get your hands on a gun?"

Ian nodded, sitting on the one bed with his ankle in a blue cast. "Priorities, mate."

Jethro could appreciate that. "Well, pack up. You're coming home with me." He should probably check with Gemma first, but he couldn't leave his mates in this crappy dump with no food or clothing.

"No," Ian said, his rugged face set in lines of pain. "We don't know that bomb was meant for you. There are plenty of enemies out there who'd love to see us run the dirt red, so we're not going anywhere until we make sure."

"I'm sure," Jethro said, grabbing a plastic bag from the hospital from the floor. "I believe with every instinct I have that Fletcher blew up my apartment. The only question is whether he wanted me to be inside or not. We have a team going through the rubble right now and we'll know about the bomb soon."

"Fucking Fletcher," Oliver said, looking down at the stolen tennis shoes. "We might have to put him down for good this time."

Jethro nodded, his gut churning. "I know. For now let's go." He didn't like being away from Gemma this long with Fletcher on the loose, but at least Raider and Brigid were keeping an eye on the good doctor in Oregon, so there was one less enemy to contend with right this second. "Do you ever feel like we have too many enemies out there?"

Ian shoved to his one good foot, holding the cast aloft. "Every damn day."

Jethro glared at him. "Why didn't you just call me to pick you up from the hospital? You had to have known this was Fletcher's doing."

Ian shrugged. "You have a new life here, and we didn't want to muck it up. Plus, it's easier for us to work back channels if we're not on hospital CCTV leaving with you."

Oliver tucked the gun in the back of his scrubs. "It's not like you had difficulty finding us."

That was a true. He looked at two of his oldest friends. "We're still family, you know." After Fletcher's betrayal he'd left everyone behind. "I needed time to remember that." Now he had more family with the Deep Ops unit, and Gemma had helped him to see that.

"No problem," Oliver said, opening the door. "You're not the smartest bulb, but we figured you'd pull your head out of your arse at some point."

Jethro shoved his shoulder beneath Ian's arm. "We'll have to get you some crutches."

Ian leaned against him, his face ashen. "Fuck the crutches. Get me some pain pills."

"I can do that," Jethro said, helping him to the door and out into the storm. "I have a safe place for you both to recuperate." If he was family, so were they. Hopefully Gemma wouldn't mind houseguests. He was certainly taking advantage of Serena's good nature, he mused. "Before we go, is there anybody else after the two of you?" He didn't want to put the Deep Ops team into any more danger than he already had.

"No more than usual," Ian said, his face ashen beneath his bronze skin and his rough tone.

Then Serena's house was the best place to protect them while they healed.

They moved out into the wintery day and Jethro helped Ian to the truck. "So. How do you two blokes feel about kids and dogs?"

* * * *

After lunch Gemma continued working on lesson plans while Trudy took a nap. The dishwasher hummed happily and the storm pummeled the windows, giving her a sense of comfort. Of security. She let herself relax for the moment. New studies showed that it was good for the cardiovascular system to accept stress instead of panic about it, so she'd learned to stay in the moment.

Roscoe lay across her feet, warming them while he snored softly. He'd played in the snow earlier and was just now drying out, and he seemed to be more than content to do so on her. She smiled and looked down at his very handsome head. His markings were sharp and defined, and while he looked dangerous, he had been so sweet with everyone. It was difficult to imagine him attacking anyone.

A knock sounded on the door and Dana poked her head in. "Do you have a second?"

"Definitely." Gemma smiled at the quiet woman. They hadn't gotten a chance to talk much, but she had a gentle and calm presence that made her nice to be around. "Come on in."

Dana stepped inside and then carried three dishes into the kitchen. "Pippa, our resident amazing chef, is out of town, so I made you a chicken casserole and a cannellini bake, both with directions on the tinfoil. I'll put them in the freezer."

Gemma partially stood. How incredibly kind. "Can I get you anything?"

Dana slid the dishes into the bottom freezer and opened the fridge, taking out a 7UP. "I had these added to your grocery list since I figured I'd visit." She placed the third dish on the counter. "These are sugar cookies with peanut butter cups broken up inside them. They're Jethro's favorite, and it's Pippa's recipe, so they're good." Then she removed her coat, hung it neatly in the mudroom, and moved gracefully toward the table with her soda. For her visit, she wore a pink sweater, black jeans, and stunning black leather boots.

"Those are amazing boots," Gemma said, angling her head to view them better.

Dana smiled and sat. "I have a thing for boots." She leaned forward, her eyes dancing. "One of my sisters is a buyer for luxury brands now and always gets us great deals. It's awesome." She opened the soda.

Gemma would love boots like those. "It's kind of you to cook for us, but I don't want to impose."

Dana sipped her soda. "Pippa has gotten us all so spoiled with her cooking that when she's gone, one of us gives it a try. Right now I don't feel like writing anything, so I figured I'd bake."

Gemma took a drink from her water bottle. "We really appreciate it."

Dana nodded and smoothly unraveled a plush-looking green scarf from around her neck. "Anything to keep my mind off this baby constantly kicking me."

The front door opened and Jethro shoved his way inside, half carrying an injured Ian. Oliver, just as tall, broad, and dangerous-looking a man as Gemma remembered, followed behind.

Gemma's eyebrows lifted.

Jethro winced. "We have company."

Dana stood and wrapped her scarf around her neck before hurrying toward the mudroom.

Gemma looked at Jethro, paused, and then stood to follow her new friend. "Are you all right?"

Dana pulled on her heavy coat, then turned and smiled. "Yes. I'm fine, but I think I need to throw up for about an hour now, and I'd rather do that at home." She leaned in for an impulsive hug. "Thank you for worrying, but don't. I'm good."

Gemma returned the hug and leaned back, impressed by the woman. "You're so strong to realize exactly what you need." Maybe Gemma should take a page from Dana's book and really figure out what she needed and wanted.

Dana chuckled. "It's a slow process, but I'm happy. Very happy." She hooked her arm through Gemma's and returned to the living room to say hi to Jethro, greet twins Ian and Oliver, and head out the door.

Gemma watched as Jethro dumped Ian on one end of the cloud-soft sofa and Oliver dropped to the other side, both immediately pulling the levers for the built-in ottomans to roll out. From what she could tell, Ian had the broken leg and Oliver the broken wrist—black cast and blue cast. They were both beat to heck, with bruises, burns, and stitches evident wherever their skin was exposed.

Jethro handed Ian the remote control for the flat-screen on the opposite wall and then moved toward her. "Can we talk?"

"Sure." She paused before following him to the master bedroom. "Can I get either of you anything?"

Ian flipped on the television, turning to the sports channel as if he had a direct line to the right number. "Jethro is on it, I think. I hope."

Okay. Gemma followed Jethro into her bedroom and then turned as he shut the door.

He held up a hand. "I apologize for just bringing them here, but they're injured because of me, and I couldn't leave them out there alone and unprotected."

She blinked. "Of course you couldn't." Did he honestly think she'd expect him to forget his friends because of her? They obviously were very injured in the bombing. "I would've brought them here, too."

Jethro straightened to his full, impressive height, surprise glowing in his eyes. "Oh. Well, nobody is after them, so they actually bring protection rather than more danger to you and Trudy."

She held back a smile. He'd obviously come up with several good arguments to persuade her to allow the men to stay, but it wasn't even her house and she truly didn't have a right to say no. Which she wouldn't do anyway. "They need help and we're here, Jethro."

His shoulders visibly relaxed. "Oh. All right." He gave her that look, the one that warmed her inner thighs. "They can crash on the sofa."

Though the sofa was ultra comfortable for watching television, those men needed to heal. "They can have the master bedroom, Jethro," she said softly. "I can either stay in Trudy's room…or yours." She held her breath.

His smile was wicked. "Mine it is, then."

Her body tingled, head to toe.

One of his dark eyebrows rose. "I'd love to explore that blush you have going on, but I'm supposed to meet Angus Force at my apartment to survey the damage." His phone buzzed and he drew the device from his pocket, his gaze never leaving hers. "Hanson," he answered, pressing it to his ear. His expression didn't change, but the tension in the room did. "I understand. All right. Thanks, Raider."

Gemma took a step away. "What did Raider say?" she whispered.

Jethro placed a hand on her shoulder. "I'm not going to let anything happen to you or Trudy. Understand?"

Numbly, she nodded.

"Good. Apparently, Dr. Monty Cameron chartered a private plane earlier today and has flown out of Oregon. Brigid is tracking him now."

Chapter Thirty-One

Jethro hated leaving Gemma, but at least she was safe with the twins in the house and Wolfe across the road. In the midafternoon, with the weather still hating on him, he stared at the smoke billowing from the burned-out hollows of what he'd considered his safe haven. He carefully picked his way up the metal steps, avoiding the ones now hanging precariously.

Angus Force was already on the scene while Millie bustled around, thick goggles protecting her eyes and silver devices in her gloved hands.

Jethro looked at what used to be his fireplace. The metal had crumpled, revealing his burned-out pool table on the other side. It wasn't the first time he'd lost all his possessions, but this was more personal. The explosive device had destroyed the integrity of the apartment, and the ensuing fire had finished off the rest, including his art collection. "When did HDD clear the scene?"

"About an hour ago," Force said, kicking burned and now sopping-wet papers out of his way. "They took the remnants of the device, but Millie captured pictures and should have a few ideas to share with us when she's finished." The head of the Deep Ops unit looked pissed with the gaping hole in the ceiling above him.

Jethro looked at the now-mangled, gridded large window he'd spent hours staring through. "I liked this place." But it was only a space, and it had been lonely at times. Anger rippled down his chest and he let it flow out his fingertips as he'd been trained.

Force's jaw clenched. "It's okay to be pissed."

"I am angry," Jethro said, striding into what used to be his office. Less damage had occurred there, but all of his desk drawers were empty. "But giving in to anger dulls my edge, and I need to stay sharp to deal with

Fletcher." He stared at the open and now-empty cabinet in the corner. "The HDD scavenged my entire home?"

"They took it all," Force agreed, stepping into the doorway. "Under the guise of investigating this bombing, they secured everything they could. Don't forget, they're still looking at you for those three murders."

Jethro shoved his chilled hands in his jacket pockets. "I have not forgotten." It was only his connection to MI6, and possibly to Force's team, that was keeping him out of custody right now.

Force blew snow out of his eyes. "Was there anything here that could hurt you or that you're concerned about?"

"Of course not," Jethro said, eyeing the cracked cement floor. He'd really liked that floor. "We keep it all in our heads, mate." Paper trails and computer files couldn't be trusted.

Force tapped the doorframe and charred metal fell to the floor. "That makes your head both dangerous and valuable. How long before your agency yanks your ass back home?"

Jethro shook his head. "I don't know. Right now I'm in with the guy in charge, and he'll cover me as long as he can. But if another murder occurs, even if we all know it's Fletcher, I may be requisitioned home to keep me out of your federal custody." It wouldn't be a comfortable situation either. "I probably have a week at the most to find my brother and lock him down. After that…" He let his voice trail off.

"They never do let you completely out, do they?" Force mused, looking at the destruction.

"Not with what's in my head," Jethro agreed.

Millie popped into sight and tugged off the goggles. Her blue eyes were wide and ashes darkened her nose. "I caught a quick look as the bomb squad loaded up remnants, and the device was on a trigger."

Jethro stiffened. "Somebody detonated it?"

"Yes." She wiped at the smudge, looking like a wilted pixie. Today the streak in her hair was a deep green. "The timing was deliberate."

That meant Fletcher had been near enough to see Jethro and wait for the right second. "So he didn't want me dead."

"No, but if he knew the twins were in the apartment, he was more than fine with killing them," she said. "It was lucky for them they were both in the kitchen and somewhat protected by all the hard surfaces in there."

Jethro looked around at the apartment. "The bomb was in the fireplace."

"Yep," Millie said. "Any idea how he got in here?"

"No, but he's Fletcher and he's as well trained as am I," Jethro said. There had never been a mark he hadn't been able to infiltrate. "The bomb might've been there for days, too. He was excellent at masking explosives." Yet more evidence that nowhere was truly safe. The most surveillance cameras did was record the wrongdoings. "Have you dumped the cameras I have placed around the property?"

She rolled her eyes. "HDD got to them before I could."

He nodded. "I have backup and will give you remote access." The backup records went to an innocuous-looking laptop in his office at the school. "I can access them from the Web." He reached for his phone and started to scroll. "In fact, let's take a look right now."

"There's no need." Agent Rutherford stepped gingerly into the hollowed-out space, leading tactical officers loaded for bear.

Jethro sighed. "Don't tell me."

"Yep. You're on video planting a bomb right outside the door." Rutherford motioned to one of the guys wearing tactical gear and holding a Colt M4 Carbine.

Millie stepped in front of Jethro. "The bomb detonated inside the apartment, you dork."

Dork? Had she just said dork? It was completely inappropriate considering the situation, but Jethro smiled.

Rutherford's gaze flicked to her. "You're in enough trouble, Agent Frost. I suggest you step out of the way."

By the narrowing of Force's gaze, that was news to him. What kind of trouble was Millie in? That was a problem for another day. Jethro gently nudged her to the side and turned around to be cuffed. Again. "Force? Do me a solid and call my attorney, would you?"

Hopefully he could stay on this side of the Atlantic a little longer, but it was looking doubtful.

Then who would Fletcher start to hunt?

* * * *

Gemma fetched the empty dishes from the two males on the sofa, noting how much calmer they both seemed after taking some pain pills. Somehow, Nari had dropped some by during her lunch hour, which had been an hour earlier.

"Thanks," Ian said, his gaze on the football game playing on the screen.

Oliver smiled. "That's kind of you. You don't need to wait on us, Gemma. It's okay."

"It's no problem." She turned toward the kitchen, her heart hurting for them. From what she could see, there wasn't an unmarked spot on either man. So she dished up two bowls of ice cream she found in the freezer and delivered them. "Sugar always helps. Trust me." She waved away their happy thanks and returned to her work on the table.

Trudy emerged from the hallway, her eyes drowsy. "Where's Rot-co?"

At her question the dog jumped up from his spot beneath the kitchen table and wagged his tail.

Trudy tilted her head, her hair messy and her pajamas wrinkled, at the two men. "Who you?"

They both froze with their spoons almost to their mouths.

Oliver cleared his throat and smiled, obviously trying to look harmless and not like the wounded killer he appeared to be. "I'm Oliver and this is my brother, Ian."

Trudy studied them. "You're hurt."

Oliver nodded. "We were in an accident, but your mom and Jethro are helping us get better."

The toddler looked at Gemma, who nodded. Roscoe padded to her to be petted, and Trudy slung an arm over his furry neck.

"Rot-co is my best friend," she said, her tone expectant and firm.

Ian glanced at Oliver, who nodded.

Trudy seemed okay with the acceptance. "That's my mom."

"She's really nice," Oliver said while Ian remained silent. It appeared he was a man of very few words.

"She is nice," Trudy agreed, her shoulders relaxing. "Jet-ro is my dad."

Oliver's mouth dropped open.

"No, he isn't," Gemma said gently, focusing on her daughter. "Jethro is your friend and a nice person, but he is not your daddy."

Trudy frowned, her entire face scrunching up. "Tyler and Rose have a daddy. Why can't I have one?"

Gemma's heart took the hit and she barely kept from wincing. That was a fair question. "Honey, it's just you and me, but we have good friends like Jethro who love you." She sucked at this. What were the right words?

Trudy tilted her head again. "Tyler said his mommy and daddy sleep in the same bed. You and Jet-ro sleep in the same bed."

Oliver coughed. Ian looked like he was about to bust his stitches but kept from laughing.

Heat blew into Gemma's face. They'd only slept together one night, and yet apparently she hadn't hidden that fact from her daughter. "That doesn't make him your daddy," she said softly. "He's your friend and he's my friend and he loves you."

The girl lowered her chin. "Does he love you?"

Oliver's shoulders started to shake, but at least he laughed silently. He'd be lucky if he got any more ice cream from her.

"Jethro and I are friends, Trudy," Gemma said. More than friends, but they hadn't known each other for long. Though did time matter? She'd been with Monty for months and never truly knew him or what monsters lived inside him. With Jethro, she felt she did know him. More than enough to trust him, which she did.

Trudy's little lips pursed. "Huh." Then she turned and ran to the sofa, plopping herself between the two wounded warriors. "Canna have ice cream?" She settled her blanket over her legs and looked at first Oliver and then Ian. "They need blankies." She looked at her mother. "The purple one and the pink one. Please?"

Anything to get the girl to stop thinking about Gemma sleeping with Jethro. She hurried into Trudy's room, willing her face to stop burning with the embarrassing blush. She fetched the purple and pink throws that matched the Cinderella bedding and returned to the living room, tossing pink at Ian and purple at Oliver.

The men couldn't have looked more confused.

Trudy sighed. "Over your legs." She looked at her mother and rolled her eyes.

Gemma bit her lip. No doubt the two were as dangerous as Jethro, and based on the many scars she could see on their bodies, they'd seen their share of fights. Would they have any idea how to deal with a toddler? Maybe she should talk Trudy into watching television in the master bedroom for now; it was the only other room with a TV.

Ian flipped the pink knit blanket over his muscled legs, covering the hospital scrubs. "Like this?"

Trudy nodded and looked at Oliver, who followed suit. She then turned her full attention on Ian, staring pointedly at the remote control in his hand.

One of his dark eyebrows rose.

Trudy's chin lowered. "Larry the Tective Lizard is on after nap time."

"Detective," Gemma said, hiding her smile this time. Apparently Trudy had the situation well in hand. "It's Larry the Detective Lizard, and he's on channel twenty-three."

Ian looked at Oliver, then at Trudy, and then back to the television. Shrugging, he changed from the sports to the kids' channel.

Trudy reached over and patted his hand.

Roscoe surveyed the crew on the plush sofa, walked back and forth, and then leaped up between Trudy and Oliver, flopping his big head in her lap. She petted him, sighing with contentment.

Oliver pushed his tail out of the way. "Roscoe, knock it off."

Trudy turned toward him. "I wanna talk like you."

Oliver smiled and settled his head back on the wall above the sofa. "I like the way you talk now. It's perfect."

Trudy thought about it and then smiled. She reached over and patted his arm as she had Ian's. "Mama? Ice cream?"

Oliver's eyes flew back open. "Yeah. Ice cream sounds good." He grinned.

Ian eyed his empty bowl. "I could do with a bit more."

Oh, for goodness' sake.

Chapter Thirty-Two

Jethro found himself sitting once again in an HDD interrogation room with Scott on one side of him and Angus Force holding up the wall on the other.

Agents Rutherford and Fields sat across from him and, surprisingly enough, MP Detective Tate Bianchi sat to the side of the table.

"If I'd known we were having a party, I would've brought snacks," Jethro said, a rock wedged in his gut. "It's nice to see the US federal and local police working together, isn't it?"

Rutherford's smile wasn't pleasant, although he truly did have perfect teeth. "The only fight we'll have is who gets to fry your ass once I close this case, dickhead."

"You have a potty mouth," Jethro said dryly.

Rutherford patted a thick case file on the table. "I believe your government would allow us to put you in prison for life here, so long as we take the death penalty off the table. I could probably live with that."

How kind of him. "I'm fairly well-loved in the UK, gents." Not that well-loved. "Feel free to investigate me all you want. But as a British citizen, I have some extra rights that I could but won't employ." He wouldn't employ any of them, but he went with his instincts and prodded Rutherford in the right direction.

Rutherford pulled a still shot from the file folder that showed Jethro setting a box near his own front door. "This was several hours before the device detonated." Then he removed another shot that showed Jethro and Gemma in the truck, right before the blast. "This, of course, was taken one minute before you pressed the button."

Jethro frowned and pulled the picture across the table with one finger. He looked over at Force. "Judging by the angle, this is from a camera I do not have in place." His gaze flicked to Fields, partly for information and partly to piss off Rutherford. "Who gave you the footage?"

Fields pulled a cough drop from his pocket and slowly unwrapped it, today wearing a worn blue suit with a red-and-yellow-striped tie from the eighties. "We found all the cameras, which I take it were yours?" When Jethro didn't answer he continued speaking. "The cameras all fed into a control center beyond your kitchen, before the steps to the wine cellar, and we confiscated the records." He popped the cough drop into his mouth.

Interesting. Jethro hadn't used very strong encryptions on those because it wasn't necessary. It was nice to know Brigid wasn't the only computer expert in the HDD. "The camera that caught these shots also fed into my control center?"

Rutherford nodded. "Yeah."

Fletcher apparently hadn't lost any of his skills while serving jail time. Impressive really. A moment of sadness caught Jethro at the good his brother could've done with his brilliance. He pushed emotion away so he could get out of this without being shipped home. "Well, get your most-talented computer experts on this because I did not plant a bomb. The recordings are doctored, and I'm sure they're very well done, but they are fake."

Force remained stubbornly in place. "Let Brigid Banaghan study the videos. If anybody can find an alteration, it's her."

Rutherford regained control of the photograph and pushed it neatly back inside the case file. "Agent Banaghan is on your team, Force. That makes her compromised."

"I'm not on the Deep Ops team," Jethro countered.

"You really are," Rutherford said, his jaw so cleanly shaven it was a miracle he hadn't cut himself.

Scott drummed his fingers on the table. "As Jethro's attorney, I demand you turn over copies of those recordings."

"We will," Rutherford said. "Once we finish our investigation."

Wonderful. Just lovely. Jethro would be on the other side of the world by that time. He looked over at Tate. "Why are you here?" The time for niceties had ended.

Tate rubbed his bald head. The case file in front of him was beige-colored, unlike HDD's blue ones. "I followed your suggestion of feeling out who wanted my three victims dead. So far I have confessions in two cases. The stepson hired a hit man to kill the first woman, hoping to inherit her millions. The wife of the man shot in the head didn't care for the fact that he spent a lot of time at massage parlors getting happy endings, if you know what I mean." He sat back in the chair, a muscle ticking in his jaw. "Buckle and I haven't narrowed down the suspect list in the third murder. Yet."

"Great job," Jethro said, meaning it. Those types of cases were difficult to break, and Tate had nailed two of them. Even so, there would be no ties to Fletcher. "So you know I didn't commit either murder?" If Tate and Buckle were that good, they'd solve the third murder as well.

Tate ticked his shoulder. "There's the rub."

Oh, bloody hell. "Do tell," Jethro said.

Tate didn't look remotely amused. "Both of the confessed killers sent one hundred thousand dollars to a Swiss bank account held by a Dr. Jethro Hanson. A connection at the HS helped me to track down the owner. It's you, buddy." The detective didn't sound pleased by that fact.

Jethro sighed. "Too easy for you?"

"Yes," Tate said. "It was much too easy to track the murders to you." He crossed his arms.

"Maybe that was his intention," Rutherford said helpfully.

Jethro cut him a look.

Tate sighed. "Yeah, I thought of that, too."

Scott looked from Tate to Rutherford. "My client is here voluntarily, trying to assist you in solving three murders and a bombing. If you arrest him, according to the reciprocity agreement between governments, you will have to not only notify the Crown but immediately turn him over."

Rutherford frowned. "There's quite a long process in that and you know it. The Crown would have to go through many channels."

His attorney glanced his way, and Jethro thought through the repercussions before nodding. There didn't seem to be an alternative.

Scott smiled. "My client was MI6, gentlemen. That means he gets turned over immediately, as you know."

Rutherford lost the smug smile. Fields looked interested. Tate swore beneath his breath.

* * * *

Jethro entered the house right around supper time, and the delicious smell of casserole had his stomach growling. He kicked off his boots in the mudroom and emerged in the kitchen, going past it to find Ian, Trudy, and Oliver all sacked out on the sofa eating dinner while watching a movie about pixies.

Gemma looked up from her position at the table, where she'd spread out papers next to her plate. "That was a long day for you."

Jethro was too busy trying to get his mind around the fact that two of the deadliest operatives he'd ever worked with were munching supper and happily watching a movie with a toddler who had stickers all over her arms. A closer look confirmed that both Ian and Oliver also had stickers of unicorns, stars, and what looked like donkeys on their arms and necks.

A sense of homecoming hit him square in the chest. Oh, he'd liked his apartment, but it hadn't felt like home.

This did.

"Are you hungry?" Gemma asked, starting to stand.

"Yes, but I'll get it." He waved her down and tried not to stare.

The woman really was gorgeous. She'd caught all her thick, curly hair up in a band and tendrils fell to frame her heart-shaped face. The light blue sweater she wore over her ample chest turned her eyes an even darker blue, and her cheeks were a pretty peach color from the warmth of the room. He kept his thoughts to himself as he dished up his food and then joined her at the table.

She stacked her papers into a neat pile. "It doesn't look like the storm has let up any?"

"No," he said, reaching for a fork and feeling out of place and at home at the same time. Maybe Fletcher's campaign was working, and he was losing his damn mind.

"Where have you been?" she asked.

He relayed the news from his apartment, as well as his three hours in interrogation, diving into the delicious dinner. Chicken casserole was one of his favorites, and no doubt somebody had copied one of Pippa's recipes. Finally he wound down, more than a little aware that Ian and Oliver had listened raptly during his entire dissertation.

"I like the purple dress," Trudy said, stuffing a cracker into her mouth and pointing at the TV screen.

"Blue," Oliver said.

Ian cocked his head. "I like the pink one."

Life had gotten bizarre. Just plain and simply bizarre. Icy fingers clutched Jethro's chest, deep in his heart, at the thought of what he suddenly had to lose. Were Gemma and Trudy even his? Could he guarantee their safety? Right now he couldn't even guarantee his own, so what did he have to offer them?

"You okay?" Gemma asked softly.

"Yes." He kept eating, keeping his countenance calm while his blood boiled. So much for staying in control. None of this felt like control. He had to find his damn brother, and take care of him, and now. "Is there any additional news from Brigid and Raider?"

Gemma shook her head. "No. They're on a plane heading home now, after saying there's nothing else to do on the ground. I appreciate their help, but nothing they uncovered changes the law." She looked over her shoulder at Trudy, snuggled between the hulking men with Roscoe now on the floor by her swinging feet. "I just have to keep her safe until she's eighteen and he has no claim on her."

Jethro wasn't going to let that happen. His worries about his soul fled away. Perhaps he'd been a fool to try to become somebody other than who he'd always been. His mother's son.

His phone buzzed. "Excuse me." He tugged it from his pocket and stood, taking his plate to the sink. "Hanson."

"Hello, Brother," Fletcher said, his voice distorted by a device he'd probably made out of a paper clip and wrapping paper. "I heard you had some trouble at your flat and wanted to check on you as well as the twin poxy agents."

Jethro shut his eyes. So Fletcher had known Ian and Oliver were in the flat before he'd detonated the bomb. Even though his brother was a killer without a soul, they'd all worked for the same agency. He turned and leaned against the counter, opening his eyes to see both men watching him intently. "That wasn't very nice of you, Fletcher."

"No, it wasn't," Fletcher said, chuckling. "But they survived, according to the hospital records I managed to obtain. You know, those two have always been difficult to kill. Do you think it's a twin thing or a brother thing? Perhaps brothers? You and I are still standing."

Jethro took a moment to keep his voice level. "How about you stop playing games and just tell me what you want."

"I'm not playing games, little brother. I think you know that." A horn honked in the distance and Jethro stopped breathing to listen better.

"That's not true. The kills with the notes, the bombing at my place, the doctored videos all point to a game, which I would've thought to be beneath you," Jethro drawled. Had that been a vehicle horn? He listened for any other ambient noises.

Fletcher sighed, the sound creepy through the distortion. "Games promise winners and losers. That does not interest me. You should know that."

True. As a child, Fletcher had never been interested in playing games. He waged campaigns to see what he could do and what he could get. Or rather what he could get away with. “You know, it’s shocking you passed the psychological exams to join the SIS.”

His laughter increased. “Please. I’m smarter than anybody you’ve ever met.”

Probably true. But these days Jethro was surrounded by exceptionally brilliant people. “You’re free, Fletcher. Why don’t you take your ill-gotten gains and go retire on an island somewhere?”

Ian’s left eyebrow lifted at that.

Fletcher sighed. “Would you ever stop hunting me? Brother?”

No.

“I take it from your silence that you would not. It also appears that you’ve become attached to the people around you, which is new and rather surprising to me. I haven’t decided what to do about that situation.” Even through the distortion, he sounded thoughtful. “The bottom line is that you screwed up one of my very carefully thought out plans, Jethro. I can’t let that stand.”

The line went dead.

Chapter Thirty-Three

After a quiet weekend surveying Mother Nature and getting accustomed to having a lot more testosterone in her vicinity than usual, Gemma strode with Jethro across the parking lot at the university to fetch a couple more books so she could continue working remotely from the safe subdivision. While she could've stayed behind, she'd wanted a few moments out in the real world while Trudy was protected back at the house.

Jethro slipped his phone into his bag. The man looked deadly and smooth, even in professor mode. "I could've grabbed your books while I attended these student meetings I couldn't reschedule." His gaze swept the surrounding area as he took her gloved hand and started down the shoveled sidewalk.

"I know, but I wanted to get out of the house for a moment or two." She was feeling both safe and a little confined, which had to be a good sign of her mental health.

He sighed. "We have to come back tomorrow for the mandatory staff meeting, and I much prefer you safe under guard. But I get it."

She smiled. While she'd do anything to keep Trudy safe, she wasn't going to let fear of Monty or even Fletcher make her hide ever again. This was one simple trip to the university, with backups around them that she figured Jethro didn't even know she'd noticed. They'd get home safely by using his very cool spy techniques, and she liked the normalcy of some of that.

Besides. They were holding hands. Her heart did a happy little hop. She was holding hands with a British badass. They'd slept in the same bed all weekend while working on their cases, their classes, and their friends. Even so, holding his hand made their connection feel even more real. She fell into step beside him, wondering at the deep blue sky.

The storm had finally passed, leaving behind beauty. The sun sparkled off the snow. Had Gemma ever been this happy? She took a second to enjoy the feeling, despite the fact that the world was falling apart all around them. Was there a chance they could fix their problems and see if they had a chance together? He was everything and more than she could ever want. Smart, sexy, and kind. Plus, a total 007 badass with a mind for game theory. She'd learned years ago not to have big dreams like this, but right now she was with Jethro, and Trudy was safe. "Do you think you'll be forced to leave the country?"

"I think it's a good possibility," Jethro said, opening the door to their building. "I should know more soon." His jaw tensed.

Her stomach dropped. So much for her happy fantasies. She released his hand and walked toward her office. "See you in about an hour?"

"Yep. I have one student meeting and then will fetch you. Please stay in your office and the building until it's time to go. I have operatives covering the campus while we're here." He moved in the other direction after giving her a wink.

She twittered like one of those silly college freshmen. Shaking her head, she strode into her office and ditched her outerwear, loving the heavy coat Dana had left in the closet. She sat and booted up her computer, looking for the PowerPoint she wanted to tweak.

The new house in the cul-de-sac was feeling like home.

She was just finishing emailing everything she'd need to herself when a gust of wind tossed snow from the ground at her window. She started.

"Excuse me?" A twentysomething man with sunglasses and a brown parka poked his head in the door.

"Yes?"

He stepped inside, his brown hair long around his shoulders. "Ms. Falls?"

"Yes." She stood, reaching for her notebook to take it home. There was still time to add classes, so students would be popping by to change their schedules. That reminded her that she'd need to post online office hours for them. "What can I do for you?"

He handed her an envelope. "You've been served." He smiled and stepped back. "Have a nice night." Then he was gone.

The world froze. Her brain jerked. In slow motion, she turned and lifted the envelope, using her fingernail to rip it open.

"Gemma?" Jethro said from behind her. "I'm taking longer than I wanted and brought you a coffee."

She turned to face him.

He moved inside and set two mugs down on the desk. "What's wrong?"

She pulled out the papers but couldn't decipher the words. All the letters jumbled together on the page, so she handed them to Jethro. "I can't read them." Her voice trembled. "What do they say?"

He ducked his head to read and then lifted up, his eyes sizzling. "Monty is suing you for custody."

The crashing sound in her ears increased in force and the room tilted. Then the darkness edged in, and she fell.

* * * *

Fury felt clean in Jethro's veins. Powerful and clean. He sat next to Gemma behind her office desk while Scott shut the door and took the guest chair, finishing typing a text as he sat. The world had gone dark with night outside, and it felt as if danger was waiting patiently for them all.

Scott looked up, tucking his phone in his pocket. "All right. Let me see."

Jethro handed over the legal papers to Scott and then put his arm around Gemma. He'd grabbed her before she fainted all the way and had shoved her into her chair, holding on to her hands until she'd come back. She was shaking so hard right now she moved *his* arm. "Take a deep breath, Gemma. One and then two."

She did so, and the exhales were shaky.

"It'll be okay," he said. "No matter what, I'll make it okay." He'd lived a good portion of his life as a spy and could get her to safety, if that was what she really wanted. The pallor of her skin was an immediate concern, and he had to get her back into the moment. She was so accustomed to being alone that she hadn't realized she had an entire team behind her. "Say it." He put a snap into his words this time, needing her to concentrate.

"It'll be okay," she repeated, her voice a monotone.

Shit. She was going into shock.

He pinched her shoulder.

"Hey." She turned toward him. "Knock it off."

"Then stay with me." He held her tighter, noting a slight tinge of color finally coming back to her cheeks. She looked vulnerable and fragile, and right now she needed to be able to make some decisions. She hadn't given him the right to make those decisions for her, so he'd help her regain her focus. "Trudy is a nice name. I was thinking about it. Please tell me you didn't name your daughter after a famous female statistician."

Gemma frowned. "So what if I did?" There she was—back in full force. "Gertrude Cox was the founder of Experimental Statistics, Jethro. She's the perfect role model for a little girl."

He forced a smile for her benefit. "You're right." And an adorable dork, but right now wasn't the time to tease her. At least he'd gotten her out of her head so she could concentrate. "Now that you're thinking again, you can stay in control. Don't forget that. No matter what happens, you are in control and you are safe."

She blinked and then nodded.

Scott looked up. "Interesting. He's claiming paternity without a test and wants full custody because you, and I quote, 'robbed him of his chance to be a father and committed fraud by placing a fake name on the birth certificate.'"

"Is that illegal?" Jethro asked.

"No. Nor is it illegal not to tell a man he fathered a child," Scott said, folding up the papers. "However, Monty is willing to take and pay for a paternity test, and if you don't allow it, he'll seek a court order to obtain Trudy's DNA."

Gemma seemed to shake herself out of her trance, but her face was so pale little blue lines were visible along her temple. "Can he do that?"

"Yes," Scott said, his gaze sympathetic. "Especially because he's willing to pay for it. We've been documenting your history of abuse with him, and Brigid has found at least one other witness who will testify in trial, but you're going to have to face him."

"Trial," Gemma hissed, slapping her head. "This is crazy. Monty doesn't even want kids. He told me once during a fight that he'd never want a child."

Jethro tightened his hold. "I promise you, I won't let him get to Trudy."

Scott flipped the papers onto the desk. "I know the attorney on the other side, and he's a rat-faced bastard. Let me make a call." He stood and walked out into the hallway.

Jethro pulled Gemma around to face him. "Look at me."

She did so, the brown contacts hiding her natural color as well as some of her panic. "I was afraid this would happen. He doesn't want her, Jethro. He just wants to hurt me."

"Okay." Jethro brushed her jaw with his knuckles. "Just say the word and I'll have both of you out of the country."

Her eyes finally focused. "Seriously?"

"Yes." He let his words sink in for a minute. "I think you should stick around and fight him, but this is your decision."

She swallowed and her graceful neck moved. "I just can't handle this." Then she took a deep breath. "Wait a minute. You can't take off for another country with your brother out there framing you for murder."

"I can and I will if that's what you need. I mean it, Gemma." He was a man of his word, and he'd promised her he'd keep her safe. Nobody was going to harm Trudy or use her to hurt Gemma. "We could be in the air in an hour. Maybe two."

She clasped her hands together. "I don't know what to do," she whispered.

Scott returned. "Well, I spoke with Fred, and he says Monty just wants to talk to you."

"No," Jethro said.

Gemma looked at Scott.

Scott shrugged. "This is up to you. But we could meet at my office and you wouldn't be alone with him." He glanced at Jethro. "You might want to give this a chance before taking off for parts unknown. I mean, if you had that thought, which I don't know about because I'm an officer of the court."

In front of Jethro's eyes, Gemma's spine straightened. "I am so tired of running and being afraid. If he wants to meet, we'll meet." Her gaze focused fully on the attorney. "But I am not playing nice. He needs to know that right off the bat." Then she looked at Jethro. "I appreciate the offer, but let's try this first. Will you be there?"

"Of course," he said, his chest swelling at her courage. "You can do this."

"I know."

Chapter Thirty-Four

Gemma sat in her office as Scott left to set up the meeting, while Jethro returned to his office to finish packing up for the week since they'd both be teaching remotely. She'd thought about doing this for a while but had never gathered the courage. Maybe this was the chance she needed—it was as close as she'd ever get. It was too late to turn back now. So she turned to her laptop and made a video call, figuring he'd be at his desk for lunch. Some habits never changed.

"Hello?" Dr. Jack Cameron slowly took shape on the screen, a fork in his hand and a diet soda next to him.

Gemma's eyebrows rose even as bile swam around her stomach, threatening to make her puke. "You look a little the worse for wear, Jack."

His hair had gone mostly gray and his skin appeared sallow. Lines extended from his eyes and lips, and his face was much rounder than before. His mouth dropped open. "Gemma?"

"Yeah." She yanked off the irritating blond wig and tossed it behind her back. If she was going to be herself, she was going all the way with it. With one hand she removed the contacts and flicked them across the room.

He quickly looked behind himself at his diplomas and then to the side, where the office door was located. "What are you doing?" he hissed.

She stared dispassionately at him, digging deep for what she needed to say. This was her only chance to save her daughter and remain with all their friends, and she had to try. "You let me down."

His bushy eyebrows rose. "Why are you calling?" Panic rose in his voice.

She tilted her head, letting his panic feed her calm. "Do you even know where Monty is right now?"

Jack grimaced and threw out both large hands. Then he grabbed the hair above his ears as if he wanted to pull it out. "Yes. I heard that he found you and was on his way to DC. I'm so very sorry. I've been in a complete panic."

That was exactly what Gemma had been hoping to hear. Even so, her chest started to burn. Tears threatened to derail her, but she banished them, seeking bravery, or at least the ability to bluff. But her words poured out on their own. "Do you patch up his new fiancée like you did me? Do you help Monty hide the bruises and the cuts?"

Jack turned even paler. "What do you want?"

Yeah, that's what she'd figured. Some habits never died. "He's here, Jack. He's here in town and he wants access to my daughter. Your niece." Gemma leaned toward the screen, even her face on fire with anger now as she remembered all the pain Monty had caused her. "He doesn't want kids. He doesn't like kids. You know he's only here making a stink because he wants to hurt me."

Jack shoved what appeared to be a salad to the side. "I gave you money to leave. To get free and have that baby." He sounded more like a whiny toddler than a successful doctor.

"That baby is a beautiful little girl named Trudy," Gemma snapped. "You did give me money, but you should've done more. A lot more. You're a doctor, for God's sake." Now she threw up her hands.

Jack blanched. "I know. I'm so sorry. How did Monty find you?"

"Does it matter?" Gemma asked, trying to see anything good in the man. "You were a coward and you know it. You had a duty to report the abuse. Now, tell me if you're still going down that cowardly path and forgoing every oath you ever took. You're doing it again with another woman."

Jack looked down at his hands. "I've tried to get her to leave him, but she's too scared. She thinks she can save him. Maybe change him when they get married. I keep hoping."

Gemma flattened her hands on the desk to keep from punching the stupid screen. "He's going to kill her."

Jack shuddered. "You don't know that. It's possible he can change." But it didn't sound as if he was convinced of that. "I have tried to help her and have stitched her up a couple of times. He doesn't mean to lose his temper. But yes, he does hit her, and I have helped him to hide that fact."

Gemma wanted to throw up. "What if she has a child and doesn't get free? Are you going to patch that kid up and hide that abuse, too?"

"Of course not," Jack gasped.

Gemma shook her head. "You know, I think you would. You're lost. Why did you let him hit me?"

"I couldn't stop him. I'm so sorry." Jack's gaze lifted to the computer screen, his eyes stark. "Is that what you wanted to hear, Gemma? It's true. Does that satisfy you?"

"Almost," she said, the blood rushing through her head so quickly she could hear it. Jack didn't deserve to be a doctor. He was a cowardly man, aged before his time, living all alone without any real hope of saving his brother. It was pathetic. "Why didn't you get free of him? Find a life and make your own family?"

"I couldn't," Jack said. "He's all I've got. It's my fault I left him alone with those awful people."

A lot of people had crappy childhoods, but they didn't end up being monsters. "You've atoned for that," she said wearily, losing her anger. "But you've made mistakes since. How many women have you patched up to protect your brother? Is there something in this that you get off on? Do you like fixing what he breaks?"

Jack shook his head.

They were both silent for a couple of heartbeats.

Finally he spoke. "I have a niece?"

Gemma looked at one of the people who could've helped her and hadn't. "You'll never meet her, Jack." She ended the video call.

* * * *

Jethro sat next to Gemma with Scott on her other side so that the two men flanked her in front of the ostentatious conference table. It was after eight at night, but it was good they were getting this over with quickly.

He stared at the table. The thing was inlaid mahogany and probably cost more than a small country, and the artwork on the golden-hued walls was abstract and expensive. The plush leather seats were nice, though. The opposing attorney had said they could meet at his office this evening.

So here they sat in the enemy's camp. Jethro didn't like the other bloke having an advantage. Of course he could just snap the necks of anybody who bothered him, so there was that.

Scott looked over Gemma's head at him. "Whatever you're thinking, stop it. Let me be the lawyer here."

"Feel free," Jethro said, reaching for Gemma's hand beneath the table.

She clutched him, and he almost made the offer to break Monty's fingers one by one.

The door opened and Monty Cameron walked in beside his lawyer, a skinny man named Fred Counters. Monty's gaze instantly sought Gemma, and a flare of anger shone bright until he banked it. Even so, his cheeks turned crimson and his nostrils widened as he pulled out a chair to sit.

His lawyer followed suit.

Monty looked at Scott and then at Jethro. "I'd like to speak with Gemma alone."

"No," Jethro said.

Scott sighed.

The other attorney looked at Scott. "My client would like to have a private conversation. I can guarantee that he will be civil."

"You can't guarantee that fact," Scott said, a thread of pure steel in his tone. "Your client is a batterer who forced my client to go on the run to protect herself and her child. I am more than happy to litigate this, and frankly, I look forward to it." He shuffled a couple of papers. "We have two women prepared to go on record about abuse from your client."

Fred smiled, and the expression was a little lizard like. "Women scorned, no doubt. My client is a wealthy doctor and has often been the target of unscrupulous women." His gaze flicked to Gemma and back.

Jethro stiffened.

Her hold tightened on his hand.

Monty smiled. The guy was probably handsome to most, but Jethro could see beyond the veil. The guy had beefy hands. The idea that he'd used them on Gemma had Jethro's chin lowering. It would take very little effort for him to crack the doctor's hands and maybe just a couple of fingers.

Gemma elbowed him.

Monty watched the action and then turned his full attention on Jethro. "Who are you?"

"I'm the guy who's trying really hard not to break your neck," Jethro said, adding a smile at the end.

Gemma sighed and turned toward him. "What happened to my British professor who never lost his temper?"

He looked at her, seeing that her eyes were clear and determined. Her true blue eyes. "I'm trying. He's still breathing, right?" Then, miracle of all miracles, she chuckled, shook her head, and looked back across the table.

He'd done that. He'd made her laugh when facing a true monster. Finally his shoulders relaxed.

Monty frowned. "I would like a moment alone with the mother of my child."

"No," Gemma said before Jethro could jump in again. "You do not get a moment alone. In fact, you do not get anything. We're done." Her voice was strong, with more than a hint of anger in it.

Monty leaned forward. "I will take you to court and get partial custody at the very least. You know I will."

His attorney waved him back. "We'd like to make this as comfortable for the minor child as possible. The courts favor both parents being involved in a child's life, and my client is a successful doctor who is engaged to be married. His life is stable and we will have witnesses lining up to testify as to how wonderful a father he would be."

Scott tapped his fingers on the case file. "Your client is a woman beater who deserves to drown, and we'll line up witnesses to say so."

Monty turned his full focus on Gemma. "Is this what you want? A constant fight over a kid? Do you want me to have custody? I don't care how long it takes. They'll certainly give me supervised visitation, and someday you know I'll be granted partial custody. Unless..."

Scott kept control of the room. "Unless what?"

"You and me, Gemma," Monty said, his voice lowering. "Just one month together to see if we could work out."

Her burst of laughter lifted the tension choking the space. "You have got to be kidding me."

"No," Monty said, glowering.

Gemma chuckled. "You are batshit crazy, Monty Cameron. Aren't you engaged?"

"She's only a substitute for you," Monty said, his gaze freakishly intense.

Jethro sighed. "Now can I break his neck?"

Scott shot him an irritated look. "My client is joking to dispel the tension in the room. Please disregard that last statement."

"It was a question, not a statement," Gemma said primly.

Jethro grinned.

Monty glared at her.

Jethro lost the grin.

Gemma sighed. "Here's the deal. You are not going to be in our lives." She freed her hand, partially stood, and planted both hands on the table, facing him squarely. "As of an hour ago, I have your brother on video admitting that you've beaten women and he's patched them up on a regular basis without doing his legal duty to report the harm to the authorities."

Both Jethro and Scott swiveled to watch her. This was news.

She faced Monty head-on, and Jethro had never been more impressed. His body heated and his heart thumped.

"You're lying," Monty spat.

"No," she said, her voice deadly soft. "I'm not. He was just upset enough about your heading across the country to come for me that he confessed all without being as careful as he used to be. Who knows? Maybe his guilt weighs heavily on him these days."

Monty's skin flushed an ugly red.

His lawyer read him correctly and intervened before he could threaten her. "It sounds like you recorded somebody without their knowledge—I could keep that out of court."

Scott chuckled. "I could definitely get the video admitted in court, citing the best interest of the child. Try me."

Yeah, their lawyer was a warrior. His Marine training came through in his clipped, confident words. Jethro nodded.

Gemma continued. "Monty, you dick, you need to understand that I am more than prepared to file a complaint against both of you to the medical board. I will also immediately press charges against both of you, in addition to screaming to the press as loudly as I can." She turned toward the lawyer. "Tell your client he won't win this. I won't let him."

"Well, then." Jethro shoved back his chair and stood. "I guess she doesn't really need our help, Scott." He looked down at Monty and let the killer inside him show. "She kicked your ass, pal. Must suck to be you." Then he moved aside and let Gemma lead them from the room.

She was fucking amazing.

Chapter Thirty-Five

The house was peaceful when they returned to find Dana and Wolfe watching television in the living room. Well, Wolfe watched the TV while Dana was sound asleep against his chest.

He grinned as they discarded their coats and boots. "Trudy and the injured Brits are asleep and all is well." Then he smoothly stood and lifted Dana against his chest, cuddling her close. "See you tomorrow." The woman snuggled into his neck and remained sleeping.

Man, Gemma wanted that. That trust and protection and love.

She mouthed a thank-you, patted Jethro's arm, and went to check on a peacefully sleeping Trudy. The toddler had kicked off her covers, so Gemma gently lifted them back up, making sure Trudy's blanket was close to her hand. Love and a fierce protectiveness washed through her as she brushed back her daughter's hair.

As far as Gemma was concerned, she had one important job in this world that trumped all others. Keeping that girl safe. She leaned over and kissed her tiny forehead and then stood, stretching and backing out into the hallway.

The master bedroom door was open, so she peeked inside.

Oliver was sprawled across the bed, his covers also kicked off.

Ian lay on an air mattress on the floor, one arm beneath his head, his muscled chest visible above the blanket. "Everything okay?" he whispered, looking up.

"No. You need a bed," she whispered back. The guy had been blown up, for goodness' sake.

"Oliver has flashbacks and I'd hate to have to beat his ass in the middle of the night," Ian said smoothly. "This is more comfortable than I sleep most nights, so don't worry about it."

Oliver rolled over and groaned. "Flashbacks? You kick, dumbass."

Gemma shut the door on their argument, nearly running into Jethro.

He shook his head. "They might be some of the deadliest operators in the world, but they still argue like ten-year-old twins." He shrugged. "If it gets too bad, we'll dump water on them. They hate that."

Her mind was tired but her body wide awake.

"You were amazing earlier," Jethro said, an indefinable light in his eyes.

Desire shot right to her core. "I had phenomenal backup," she whispered, her throat going dry.

He moved, then. Quickly and gracefully, lifting her against him, his mouth taking hers.

She gasped in and then was taken over. Completely. His kiss was fierce and deep, and his hands settled at her butt. Somehow he navigated the hallway and managed to get them into his room, where he nudged the door closed quietly. Still holding her aloft with one hand, still destroying her mouth with his, he reached behind himself and engaged the lock.

The sound ripped through the silence.

Her breath deserted her.

He peppered hard kisses along her neck and beneath her jaw, removing her sweater in one smooth motion. Then she was on her back on the bed and her bra had somehow disappeared.

His mouth was instantly on her breasts, and she bit her lip to keep from crying out. Jethro Hanson was definitely a breast man.

There was something different about him this night. Something had been unleashed.

While he'd always been the very definition of still waters running deep, his power was more evident tonight. More real. More primal. More true to the animal Jethro could be.

She reveled in the moment.

This was for her and her alone. She could *feel* that.

He flicked one nipple and then the other, drawing the latter into his mouth as his hand boldly slid down her stomach to between her thighs. He gave a grunt of dissatisfaction, and his talented fingers snapped the sides of her panties so he could yank them away.

She gasped, arching against him.

The Brit wasn't the only one who wanted to play tonight. She trailed her hand along his flanks, feeling his rib cage and the strength to be found even there. Then she slid her palm over the ripped muscles of his abdomen and straight down, where she found him hard and throbbing.

His groan against her chest gave her confidence, and she closed her fingers over him, brushing her thumb over his tip.

He jerked against her.

Then he shoved her hand away and pushed two fingers inside her, sliding in easily. Yeah, she was more than ready.

"You're bloody perfect," he murmured, licking and kissing his way back up to her mouth, where he took her so deep she'd never get free. Then he leaned to the side, his hand fumbling in the drawer. A zip of paper crinkling and then he shifted, rolled the condom, and settled between her thighs.

She'd expected fast and her body craved it.

Instead, he settled his weight on his elbows on either side of her head and dropped his hands to cradle her face. "You're the strongest and most beautiful woman I've ever known," he murmured, his eyes blazing in the darkness.

Her heart swelled. Strong? She hadn't felt strong until lately, until he'd shown her parts of herself she had forgotten. "Jethro," she murmured.

"Yeah." He slowly penetrated her, his gaze pinning her as strongly as did his body. Inch by inch he brought them closer. It was more than physical.

She caught her breath at the exquisite sensation, teetering between pleasure and pain. Finally he planted himself deep inside her, joining them completely.

Her body trembled around him, becoming accustomed to and accepting his size. There was a lot to Jethro Hanson, and right now it was all hers. He was all hers. She smiled and scraped her nails down his flanks, feeling the masculine dimples above his butt and then exploring further. Even his butt was tightly muscled.

He tilted his hips and she gasped as electrical shocks jerked through her body. She writhed beneath him, wanting more. Needing more. All of him.

"Tell me what you want," he whispered, his breath heated against her mouth.

"You," she instantly moaned. "I want all of you."

He kissed her and pulled out to shove back inside her to the hilt. "You have me." His accent emerged thickly.

She arched against him, holding the moment tight. Desperate need coiled low inside her with a demand she'd never felt before. Her body swelled around him, softening and lighting up nerves she hadn't realized she had. His kiss grew more intense as he thrust his tongue inside her mouth, his tongue mating with her as frantically as the rest of his body.

He released her face and reached down to manacle one impossibly strong hand around her hip, squeezing as he pulled out and drove back into her, hammering wildly and somehow driving deeper with each thrust.

It was more than she could've imagined. More than she even realized she could have. Wild with pleasure, she rocked her hips, taking all of him. He gave her even more, thrusting harder and deeper until she was panting and scraping his butt with her nails. The entire world narrowed to Jethro and his incredible body, and what he was doing to her.

The pleasure was indescribable, and she needed more. She had to have more. "Jethro," she moaned. It was too much. "I–I can't..."

The hand on her hip slipped around and grasped the bottom of her thigh, opening her up even more to him. Then he looked at her, his masculine face brutally beautiful and determined.

"Look at me," he demanded.

She was. She never wanted to look away. His face was stark and so strong. So *male.*

"There you go," he whispered, changing his angle and holding her tight. "Come now, Gemma. Now."

Her body instantly obeyed and she blew right apart. Pleasure detonated inside her, live wires uncoiling and shooting sparks in every direction. He thrust even harder, prolonging the waves until the bliss nearly became too much. An erotic agony she hadn't realized even existed. Just as she began to come down, he let himself go. A drop of sweat fell from his forehead to her ear as he buried his face in her neck, spasms taking him over.

She held him tight, drowning in his pleasure. Feeling it as acutely as she had her own.

He stopped shuddering and levered himself up, smoothing her damp hair away from her head. Then he kissed her. Slow, deep, drugging...he took her over as easily as he did everything else, and she let him. Trusting Jethro was the easiest thing she'd ever done, and the riskiest. There was no question he could completely destroy her if he wanted, and she didn't care.

Because he wouldn't.

He released her mouth and kissed her nose, cheeks, and chin. "God, you're perfect."

"You are," she said as sleep drew near. Within seconds she was dreaming, safe in his muscled arms.

* * * *

After a night of bliss, Jethro couldn't sleep. He'd made love to Gemma twice more and now lay wrapped around her. She was small and trusting against him, and her dreams seemed peaceful.

Peace was an illusion at the moment.

Monty wasn't smart enough to go away, and Fletcher was surely planning further evil. In addition, Jethro had two wounded brothers in the other room who'd try to jump in front of the Fletcher freight train if they could. Not to mention Wolfe, who'd just blow up the train, even though he had a pregnant fiancée to worry about. In fact, Force's entire team was spending their precious time covering him right now.

He had to take care of his brother so he could create the life Gemma needed. A safe life.

She'd been right that he could control the violence inside him and the danger around them. He'd kept himself from getting close to any woman because he was so dangerous, but maybe a powerful man was actually what Gemma needed to feel safe. He could give her that.

The wind finally gave up the fight outside and the world stilled, caught in a frozen grip. His phone dinged near dawn, and he reached for it, gently setting Gemma to the side. A quick glance confirmed that he didn't know the number. So he slipped from the bed, padded into the adjoining washroom, and shut the door. "Hanson."

"Hello, Brother," Fletcher said, his tone cheerful. "I hope I did not awaken you."

Jethro scrubbed a hand through his hair. "I should've killed you after you murdered our mother."

Fletcher laughed. "You've never been as good at this as I, Jethro. You don't have it in you."

"You might be wrong about that," Jethro said. So long as Fletcher breathed, he was a threat. Jethro had been trained to negate threats, and now he had a lot to lose. "This is your only chance, Brother. Take your money and find an island. I won't waste my time hunting you." He could leave that to the various governments that wanted Fletcher gone even more than Jethro did. "Just go."

"I can't," Fletcher said.

Jethro sat on the edge of the luxurious spa tub. He wished he didn't understand Fletcher's refusal, but he did. "I've spent too much time trying to figure out whether it was nature or nurture that sent us wrong." Was there something in their DNA that made them killers, or had growing up in that cold house with the lovely façade destroyed them? "I think we went wrong on both fronts."

"Possibly, but who cares? Regardless, we're the same," Fletcher said. There were no ambient sounds to pinpoint his location.

"No." Jethro flexed his hand, which still ached where a falling beam had hit him when he'd carried Oliver out of the burning apartment. "We are not the same." Jethro was capable of love and maybe, just maybe, redemption. "You're beyond any hope, Fletcher. Your soul is truly damned." Mostly because Fletcher would never change.

Fletcher was quiet for a moment. "Then it's my job to damn you. I'd hate to spend eternity in hell alone." His tone was dark and his accent smooth. "This dream you have of that pretty blonde saving your soul is silly. It's too late."

The blonde was a stunning brunette who might've already saved his soul. Jethro sighed, his gut churning even as his brain focused in with laser precision. His brother no doubt was still taking contracts, so that was one way to track him. It was time to go on the offensive and stop worrying about defense. He had enough good people around him to cover Gemma and Trudy. "Why don't you and I just meet up and finish this?" he asked. "Unless you think you can't win?"

There was a small chance Fletcher would take the bait.

"Oh, we'll definitely have our moment together, Jethro. But now isn't the time. It has to be perfect, remember?" Fletcher clicked off.

Jethro perched his phone on the counter.

That's right.

Perfect.

Chapter Thirty-Six

Gemma finished dressing in black slacks, thick socks, and a wonderfully warm yellow sweater before heading out to face the day. Jethro had left the bed before she'd awakened, much later than usual. They didn't have to be to the university for the staff meeting until eleven, so perhaps he'd figured they should just sleep late. Right now, after the superb sex and excellent night's rest, she could easily see the wisdom in that plan.

She walked out to find Trudy in the center of the sofa, covered in her green blanket. Ian sat on her left and Oliver on her right, both covered in blankets, their legs stretched out on the ottomans.

"Morning," Ian said, reaching over to dump yellow star marshmallows from his bowl into Trudy's.

Trudy grinned. "Hi, Mama." She dutifully plucked the purple half-moons out of her bowl and put them into Ian's.

"Cool," Ian said, munching on his cereal.

Gemma's heart just turned over. "Don't you all want milk in your cereal?"

Oliver shook his head and handed over his yellow stars. "Then we couldn't trade. It'd be messy." The mottled bruises along his jaw had turned a brighter yellow than the day before.

Life had gotten bizarre.

Gemma glanced at her watch. "Trudy? How about we go get dressed for the day?"

"Okay." Trudy puffed up her cheeks. "Today is reading day so we get this week's goodies tomorrow." She patted Oliver's hand. "It's every week and different yummies each week. I'll bring my home tomorrow to give you some. It's good candy."

Gemma winced. “You’re staying here today, honey. I already called Barb and said you wouldn’t be in this week.” As her daughter scrunched up her face to protest, she held out a hand. “Barb said she’d leave this week’s candy and goodie bag in my office for you, and you can earn it today by reading to me and eat it tomorrow when your friends eat theirs at school.” A routine was crucial for them all.

Trudy grinned and snuggled back down between the twins. “Cool. I’ll share.”

“You bet you’ll share,” Ian said, his gaze on the television. “I like candy.”

Movement sounded from the other side of the kitchen right before Jethro came in through the mudroom with Wolfe and Dana on his heels. Dana was dressed in a thick green sweater and Wolfe had a coat tossed over his shoulder. He removed the coat to reveal a white cat with a mangled ear perched on his shoulder. A closer examination showed that the cat had one green eye and one blue one. His good ear twitched as he surveyed the room.

Oliver cocked his head. “Wolfe? Why do you have a cat on your shoulder?”

Wolfe gingerly placed the cat on the floor, where the animal stretched. “He doesn’t fit in my pocket any longer.”

Gemma almost laughed and then realized the man was serious. Hmm. Okay.

Jethro moved her way and kissed the top of her head. In front of everyone. Trudy’s smile extended from ear to ear and revealed a full mouth of marshmallow cereal.

Gemma’s face heated. “You eat all of the cereal and not just the marshmallows, young lady.”

Dana leaned down and scratched the cat’s ears before straightening and heading right for the coffeepot. “I thought I’d write my current article from your breakfast nook and keep an eye on the injured as well as Trudy. Plus, I thought we could color some new coloring books I found.”

Gemma inhaled. Everyone had put their lives on hold to help her. She swallowed.

Jethro tugged her into his side with one arm. “Get used to it,” he whispered, turning to kiss her temple.

Gemma looked around. “Where’s Roscoe?”

Jethro angled to look out the front window. “He’s outside, but I’m sure he’ll be scratching on the door at any moment.”

Was this what family really felt like? Gemma liked it, and apparently Trudy loved it.

Jethro’s phone buzzed, and he read from the screen. “It’s Brigid. She was up all night but managed to show that the videos of me carrying dead bodies and bombing my apartment were doctored. Unfortunately, she can't prove that it was Fletcher actually doing the deeds."

Well, that was something. Gemma smiled. "I assume she sent the proof to the folks at HDD?"

"Yes," Jethro said.

Relief even tasted good. Gemma leaned against Jethro's solid body. So at least the government would know that Jethro wasn't a killer. That had to give him a moment to breathe. "It's too bad Fletcher was able to hide himself from the cameras."

Jethro nodded. "That doesn't surprise me. I could fool a camera if I wanted as well."

"Ditto," Ian and Oliver said in unison.

"I'd just break it," Wolfe said helpfully.

Jethro turned toward her. "Why don't you call in sick for the staff meeting and I'll cover it?"

She shook her head. "If everything works out, I want to try and get a job at the university and want to look present and ready to work hard." Was that admitting too much? She shuffled her feet.

Jethro's eyebrow rose. "That's a wonderful idea."

She warmed. It was a great idea, and it'd be even better if his government let him stay right where he was and didn't force him to head off into parts unknown where she might not see him again. A chill clacked through her and she hid it. "Thanks." She kissed her baby goodbye and headed off to work.

Jethro was uncharacteristically silent on the drive to the university as he methodically backtracked and made it impossible to follow them. Well, except for the truck containing at least two of the Deep Ops team who were shadowing them. "You okay?" she asked.

"Not yet, but I will be," he said, taking her hand.

She shivered.

* * * *

Jethro hadn't liked Fletcher's glee earlier that morning. Oh, his brother had attempted to mask how much fun he was currently having, but his eyes had gleamed the same way they had after he'd beaten up a neighbor or two. It was the look he got when he was close to his idea of perfection. "Let's make this quick." He parked in front of their building instead of the day care because Trudy had stayed at home.

"No problem." Gemma stepped out of the truck and hurried through the chilly air to the front door.

Jethro followed, taking a look at the thick white clouds moving in. The wind speared him, but at least the storm had passed.

He followed Gemma inside the entryway, which was lined with posters of academics. A male student almost walked by and then stopped cold, turning to stare at them.

"Professor Falls?" the kid asked, his eyes wide beneath his yellow knit hat.

"Oh. Yeah. Hi, Trace." Gemma touched her curly brown hair. "It's a long story, but I was wearing a wig and decided to ditch it."

Trace did another double take. "You changed your eye color, too?"

She blushed. "Yes. These are my real eyes."

He smiled and blushed a little himself. "They're pretty. I mean, like really pretty."

Jethro stepped up. "Don't you have class, Trace?"

Trace's grin widened. "Hi, Doc. Yeah, I have class." The smart-ass physics major winked at him and then continued down the hall.

Jethro smiled. "I'm giving that kid a pop quiz when I get the chance." Oh, he wouldn't, but only because he liked the bloke.

"I need to grab a book I forgot yesterday and will meet you at your office before the meeting," Gemma said.

Barb bustled up, glitter in her hair. "Oh, good timing." Her eyes widened as she looked at Gemma.

Gemma sighed. "My real hair and eyes."

Barb shrugged. "Okay. I like this version of you." She grinned and handed over a book about a puppy and a couple of bags, one holding this week's goodies and the other with what looked like new markers. "Tell Trudy we miss her and can't wait until she comes back. This is the book you need to help her read so she can have the goodies and markers as a reward tomorrow. It's important you follow the schedule so she feels part of the group."

Gemma impulsively reached in for a hug. "Thank you."

"Sure." Barb winked at Jethro and then turned to hustle back down the hallway. "Give Trudy a hug for me," she called back.

Gemma tucked the items in her laptop bag. "I'll see you in a few, Jet."

"Sounds good," he said, scouting the hall for threats. Only students running late for class. "Have a nice day, *Professor*."

She waved a hand and made her way through running students to her doorway.

He settled his pack more securely over his shoulder and turned in the other direction, his mind already on how he'd get her to a safehouse he had in the Rockies.

Her scream ripped through his body faster than any blade. He pivoted and ran toward her, tossing a couple of male students out of the way. "Gemma?"

She stood in the entryway, looking into her office, her face stark white.

He drew her aside and took in the scene instantly.

"What's wrong?" A female student popped up behind Gemma.

"Nothing." Jethro shut the door. "Get to class."

Gemma turned her body into him and he held her, waiting until the students reluctantly dispersed.

Then he slowly opened the door, setting Gemma to the side, where she couldn't see into the office. "Stay here." He planted her back against the wall and stepped inside the office, slowly taking inventory of the gruesome scene.

Dr. Monty Cameron hanged from a rope secured above a damaged ceiling tile, his face purple and already bloated. His naked body showed several bruises and cuts, and one cut extended from his breastbone to his pelvis, which had allowed his entrails to fall out. The smell of death was all around.

Jethro's training superseded the emotions he felt as Gemma's lover and he moved right into seeking any evidence that could be used against him. There were no cameras in the room. "Gemma? Call the police and then get Angus Force on the line. In fact, let him call in the homicide detectives," he ordered.

She looked around the corner, her lips trembling. "Okay." Then she disappeared again.

Jethro conducted a cursory search of the office, looking for the murder weapon. This was no doubt Fletcher's doing, and somehow Jethro's prints would be on it. Damn it. No weapon. He moved closer to the body, avoiding the bloody mess on the floor. He scrutinized the skin, from top to bottom, but likewise didn't find any obvious DNA. However, just one hair from his head in the congealed mess would be enough to incriminate him.

Sirens blew through the quiet outside.

Jethro immediately stepped back into the hallway to find Gemma sitting on the cold wooden floor, huddled with her back to the wall. "It's going to be a rough day."

She looked up, her blue eyes wide with shock. "I don't understand."

There was no way to explain this. "It has to be Fletcher," Jethro said, shaking his head. So this was why Fletcher had been so damn cheerful just a few hours before.

Angus Force came through the door first, with Roscoe at his feet. He reached them just as more police vehicles skidded to a stop in the icy parking lot outside. "Is there evidence against you?" he hissed.

"Not in the office," Jethro said quietly. "At least none I could find. I'm sure it'll show up, though."

Angus breathed out. "Brigid is trying to get you cleared in the other three homicide cases, but with your background the brass isn't completely buying your innocence. Gemma said this guy was disemboweled, just like the other victims?" At Jethro's nod, Angus let loose a series of expletives that would've been impressive if the situation wasn't such a complete disaster. Finally he wound down. He looked toward Gemma, who was still hunched over. "Give Scott a call, would you? Jethro's going to spend the next several hours being interrogated, as are you, and we're going to need a lawyer."

"They don't have enough to charge either one of us," Jethro said, trying to reassure her.

She slowly stood and withdrew her phone from her pocket, her hands visibly shaking.

Angus nudged open the door and stared at the dead body, letting out a low whistle. "That is sick."

"That's Fletcher," Jethro said wearily.

Angus looked at him. "I don't want anybody near our homes, got it? If they want to interview you, we go downtown. None of this touches the haven we've created in that subdivision."

"That's more than fair," Jethro said. He didn't want murder or the authorities near their homes either. Plus, Trudy was safe out there, and he didn't want his problems to cause her even one nightmare.

From the look of Gemma, she'd be having bad dreams about this for quite some time.

HDD agents Rutherford and Fields burst through the door right before Detectives Bianchi and Buckle. It took less than a minute for the HDD to assert federal jurisdiction over the case, or at least attempt to.

Bianchi wasn't having it. This was a homicide in his territory, with no clear indication of federal jurisdiction.

Angus watched them argue. "This might give us a brief reprieve, but the feds will win eventually."

"I know," Jethro said, his shoulders feeling like he was carrying multiple boulders.

"They don't have enough to arrest you, but…" Angus said, watching as Tate stepped right up into Rutherford's face.

Crime tech analysts began pouring through the front door.

"But they'll have to notify the SIS," Jethro finished Angus's sentence. Which meant he was going home.

Chapter Thirty-Seven

Jethro allowed himself to be interrogated by both the feds and the local police for the rest of Tuesday and well into Wednesday morning, once Scott assured him that Gemma's interview had been concluded for the time being. She was now safe at home, so he sat and answered all the questions he could, denying any involvement in the deaths.

Finally, around dawn on Wednesday, Scott called an end to the questioning and walked him outside to his truck.

The winter chill swept along Jethro's skin, but it felt good to be outside.

Scott paused. "This is a reprieve until they finish with the tests on the body. Based on what you've told me, I'm surprised the murder weapon hasn't shown up as of yet."

Jethro looked at the quiet dark street fronting the police station. "As am I, but Fletcher always has a plan. Your efforts need to focus on Gemma first and me last." The two of them were providing alibis for each other, which wasn't great.

Scott nodded, his eyes weary. "I understand. For now let's both get some sleep. If you're correct and Fletcher managed to plant DNA on the body, or if the murder weapon is found with your fingerprints, you'll be arrested and charged very soon. We have to be ready to deal with that." The lawyer patted him on the shoulder and strode down the icy sidewalk, disappearing into the darkness.

Jethro jumped in his truck and took the long way back to the subdivision, backtracking several times to ensure he wasn't followed. Finally he made his way home.

Upon entering the quiet house he kicked off his boots and shucked his jacket, already feeling a presence in the other room. Remaining silent, he made his way into the living room, where Ian clicked on a lamp from his position on the sofa.

"Hi," Jethro said, his heart sinking.

"Hi," Ian said.

So this was how it would happen—how they'd drag him back home. Jethro rubbed a hand on his neck. "Where's Oliver?"

"Snoring away because he stole the whole bed," Ian said, irritation flashing in his bluish-green eyes.

Jethro inclined his head. "He's snoring and you're waiting up? I figured you would've gotten orders."

Ian's expression revealed nothing. "We don't work for SIS any longer."

Jethro rolled his eyes. "That doesn't mean anything. If they order you to bring me back, you're still under obligation. Did they?"

"Yep," Ian said.

Jethro couldn't get a bead on his friend. Ian wasn't a liar, and if he said Oliver was sleeping, the other man was snoozing right now. "Are you planning on waiting until light?" This wasn't making sense.

"No. We refused," Ian said easily. "Just thought you should know they have the word out to bring you in."

Jethro started. "You can't refuse."

"Just did." Ian threw off the pink blanket and stood on his good leg.

Jethro's breath heated. "They'll ruin you. Without question, your business licenses were just yanked." The twins had worked so hard on that business.

"No doubt," Ian agreed. "Guess we'll move to this side of the pond with you." He hopped forward, clapped Jethro on the shoulder, and then kept moving to his bedroom. "We're family, mate. That matters." He slipped inside and shut the door.

Jethro stood frozen for a moment, emotion bombarding him. Family. Yeah, he'd known that, but he hadn't expected the twins to sacrifice everything for him. He tried to regain his edge as he moved to the master bedroom, but exhaustion weighed him down.

Gemma sat up in bed, her eyes wide. "Are you all right?"

"Yes." He removed his clothing and slid inside, pulling her to face him. "I was worried about you."

She snuggled right into him, her knees between his, her small hand cupping his whiskered jaw. "I was more worried about you. We kept waiting to hear that the murder weapon had been found or something, but none of that happened. Your brother likes to draw out his games."

"No," Jethro said. "That's just it. He doesn't play games and nothing is drawn out. Each move he makes gets him closer to his ultimate goal, which at the moment seems to be framing me for murder." But that wasn't it. Not completely.

Gemma rubbed his jaw and down his neck. "I feel like I should be feeling something more about Monty being dead, especially murdered in such a horrific way." Her light sapphire eyes glowed in the darkness. "Maybe I'm in shock or just out of it, but I think I'm mostly numb." She frowned. "Shouldn't I be sad because he was Trudy's father, or even relieved because he's dead and I don't have to run anymore?" Her voice trembled slightly.

Jethro couldn't imagine what this was like for her. "Whatever you're feeling is what you should be feeling," he whispered, wanting to hold her tight and protect her from any more hurts. "This is fresh, and your feelings will come at you when you least expect it. It's all natural and right. You're the good guy here, and you've done your best to protect yourself and your daughter." He wouldn't let her blame herself for any of this, even for her own feelings. She had a right to be relieved that the asshole was dead. "It's okay, Gemma. All of it."

She swallowed.

He ran his knuckles along her delicate jaw. "Nari is an excellent psychologist, from what I understand. When things calm down a little bit, maybe you could talk to her?"

Gemma shook her head. "No. I want to be friends with Nari. But I will ask her for a recommendation for a therapist." She leaned into his touch.

He kissed her gently on her nose. There would be no more pain for this woman or her child—he'd make sure of it. "For now let's go to sleep, all right?"

She turned around, backing her sweet butt against him. "You sure you want to sleep?"

Perhaps not.

* * * *

After two rounds of wild lovemaking, Gemma could feel when Jethro finally fell asleep. It was nuts that she'd wanted to have sex after that nightmare of a day, but maybe she just wanted to forget for a few moments in his arms. And she had. She lay beside him for about another hour and then slid quietly from the bed, knowing Trudy would be up soon. She dressed in jeans and a sweater, having canceled her classes for the day. In fact, the school had canceled all classes in the math and philosophy building so the police could interview all witnesses and finish processing the crime scene. Her office, which was now a crime scene.

She walked quietly out into the kitchen to find both Oliver and Ian pounding away on laptops at the table. She smelled coffee and made a beeline for it, tossing them an inquisitive glance over her shoulder.

Neither looked up.

"We asked Brigid to bring us computers," Oliver announced, answering her unspoken question as he typed away. "Right now we're moving assets around because our business was just shut down."

Ian hit a button and then grinned. "Beat you."

Oliver rolled his eyes. "Whatever. Good. Handle the Bloc accounts now."

"Fine." Ian leaned toward the screen and began typing again.

Gemma poured a mug of coffee and leaned back against the counter, watching them work. It was as if she was suddenly surrounded by mercenaries and spies. Life was strange. "Jethro mentioned you guys gave up your business to protect him."

Ian just shrugged.

"Thank you," she said softly.

Oliver winked at her and kept typing the whole time.

Gemma caught sight of her cell phone charging on the counter and reached for it, surprised to find fifteen messages. She'd had her office calls forwarded to her cell phone, so she listened to them, noting most were from other professors and even students asking what was going on. The last message was from her mother, asking Gemma to call her. Monty must've told Fran where she was working.

She thought about it and then shrugged, dialing the number.

"Hello?" Fran answered.

"Hi, Fran," Gemma said.

Fran blew out air, no doubt full of cigarette smoke. "I'm glad you called. Please listen to me and listen to Monty. He has a right to know his daughter. How could you not tell me you had a child? I have a grandchild? You are the most selfish person in the entire world. I want to meet my grandchild."

Gemma took the barrage, remembering her mom yelling at neighbors like this. They'd moved around a lot, usually to states with great benefits that allowed Fran to stay home and drink constantly. Inevitably, Fran would get drunk and fight with the neighbors over anything from a misplaced newspaper to loud music. "Why? Why do you care to meet her?"

Fran sucked in air. "Because she's my granddaughter."

"So. You didn't care about being a mother," Gemma said, her ears ringing. "Come clean, Fran. Now."

Her mother coughed, and her lungs sounded phlegmy from her two packs a day. "Fine. Monty and I want us all to be a family. A girl needs a father—you're proof of that. If you'd had a father, maybe you wouldn't be in such a mess now."

Gemma didn't point out that it was Fran's fault that Gemma didn't have a father. "Right. So you're making Monty's case that we should be a family?" She sipped her coffee, somewhat surprised Fran's defection didn't hurt as much as she would've thought. Maybe she'd given up on Fran years ago and was just going through the motions every year when she called. Did that make her cold?

Or just a realist?

Maybe she was merely a survivor.

"Yes," Fran snapped. "We'll be a family. Monty said he'd build us all a nice big house by the river with a mother-in-law apartment for me. So I can get to know my granddaughter and not have to worry about myself as I get older."

So it was all about Fran. Good to know.

Gemma swallowed again. "I'm sorry to tell you, but Monty is dead."

Fran was silent.

Gemma let her process the news for at least a minute, trying not to feel sorry for her mother. Even so, she kind of did. Fran had always seen Monty as her ticket to a life of comfort and now he was gone. "Fran?"

"You're sure?" Fran asked.

"Yes. Definitely sure," Gemma said.

The flick of a match sounded over the line and then a deep inhale from Fran. "Did you kill him?" She'd lost the cajoling tone.

"No." Gemma took another drink, her stomach hurting all of a sudden.

"Well, shit. Where the hell does this leave me?"

Gemma drew back, surprised even though she shouldn't be. Fran wasn't even sorry that Trudy's father was gone. "It really is all about you, isn't it?"

"It's a lesson you should've learned very young," Fran snapped. "You have to take care of yourself."

Trudy trundled out of her room at that moment, and just as she reached the master bedroom, Jethro stepped out. To avoid running into her, he lifted her in the air and swung her around.

A delighted squeal emerged from the little girl.

He settled her at his hip and gently brushed her hair away from her face. "Good morning, Urchin."

Gemma's entire chest lifted. "You're wrong, Fran. You are so wrong, but I don't have the words to explain it to you." She turned away and moved into the mudroom, needing a moment of privacy. "We're done. Just so you know, you and I are finished." It was a difficult decision, but she couldn't let this woman anywhere near Trudy and their new family.

"Fine," Fran said. "I can't get anything from you now anyway." She ended the call.

Gemma sucked in air as if she'd been punched. Why? This wasn't a shock. Even so, she put the phone on the dryer and just stared at it. Unwanted tears filled her eyes. At least this call could definitely be considered closure.

Jethro appeared in the entryway, pulling her into his strong arms. "I heard the last part of that. I'm sorry."

She let a couple of tears fall against his T-shirt and then wiped them away, holding him around the waist. "It's silly to cry." She leaned back so she could look up at his rugged face.

He pressed a kiss to her nose. "It's never silly to cry." He looked toward the kitchen. "We're all regrouping today and making contingency plans. How about we have a big breakfast, build a snowman outside with Trudy, and then figure out how to make you safe?"

That was kind, but she needed him to be just as safe. Just as present. She cleared her throat. "I've lost so much time always running. I like you." What the heck was her mouth doing?

His dimple flashed. "I like you more." He kissed her again, taking her under. Then he let her breathe. "I wish I wasn't about to be yanked across the pond."

Her heart swelled and ached. "You think you'll have to go?" Would she be able to see him? Something told her probably not. While she didn't understand the spy world, she had a bad feeling that he wouldn't get to just go home and live out his years in a country estate. What would happen to him? "Jethro—"

"I know, but there's nothing we can do right now. So just trust me." He held her tighter. "But you have to understand that I might be extradited within the next couple of days."

Chapter Thirty-Eight

Thursday morning found Jethro's temporary home overrun with operatives. He leaned against the counter drinking an obscenely sweet latte provided by Wolfe.

Angus Force stood by the doorway, holding his latte and only taking a sip once Wolfe lifted an eyebrow. "Jethro's DNA was found on Monty's body in the congealed blood, but the murder weapon hasn't been found yet, oddly enough. The arrest warrant came in for Jethro early this morning. We need to find Fletcher before the HDD gets ahold of him."

Wolfe lifted an eyebrow. "How do you think he got your DNA and prints?"

Jethro shrugged. "Could've been several ways. I would've broken into the college office and taken them from there, but who knows? Fletcher is very good at what he does." Jethro had become aware of the warrant first thing, and he'd been expecting it, so the day was going as he'd thought it would.

Angus looked at his watch. "We have a full Deep Ops meeting in an hour in our offices with our superiors. I can cover for you, Jethro, but you need to stay here and off the radar."

Wolfe sat on the sofa next to Ian. "Dana isn't feeling well and is sticking close to home."

"That's good," Angus said. "We're about to disavow any knowledge of Jethro's location, so we have to act normal. Nari called and is taking a day off. She's already called in."

Gemma, her eyes wide, looked over at Nari. "Don't you have to attend the meeting at HDD?"

Nari shook her head. "I met with the brass earlier today and gave my psychological assessment of Jethro as well as his brother, so I'm not required." She winked at Trudy, who sat in Gemma's lap. "Plus, I should get some coloring time in as well after I finish up with some work at my house."

Trudy hopped once and clapped her hands. Her hair was a wild mess, and she looked young and innocent.

Jethro studied the group. Maybe he should just take Gemma and Trudy and run to an island where they couldn't be found. It wouldn't be a bad life. "You're about to destroy your own unit, Force." He couldn't let that happen.

"Not unless they know you're here, and they don't," Angus countered. "Our personnel records show all of us living in an apartment complex in Arlington, and the HDD is more than welcome to visit us at home. This property is owned by several dummy corporations that can't be traced to us."

Smart. Even so, it wasn't like the unit was loved within the HDD. It wasn't fair to ask Angus to stick his neck out like this.

Angus bent over and kissed Nari's head. "Everyone move out. Also, I had a camera hooked up in our main hub, so you can see what's going on, Jethro. If I say the words 'James Bond,' you three Brits need to take off. Fast."

Ian rolled his eyes. "Can't we use a different code?"

"Nope," Angus said, grinning.

The group dispersed.

Jethro grabbed Gemma in a hug, then kissed her forehead. "You look tired. Why don't you take it easy for a while?"

She looked up, her hands on his flanks. "I think I'll go give Trudy a bath." She looked at her daughter, who was munching happily on a chocolate. "She earned the treat yesterday, and I see she found this week's goody bag from Barb, although I believe she was supposed to wait until after lunch." Shaking her head and patted his arm. "One goal at a time, right?"

Their goal was to track down Fletcher and end him. Jethro would start hunting as soon as everyone left. He kissed her, trying to put all the things he couldn't say right now into the moment.

She kissed him back. "See you a bit later." Then she turned, lifted her daughter, and walked down the hallway and into the master bedroom.

Quiet descended.

Ian tossed a thumb drive across the sofa to his brother. "Study these to learn more about what Fletcher has been doing." He looked up at Jethro. "We have all the video from his time in prison and nothing to do for the next hour but watch it. We'll take these if you want to review your interviews with him."

Jethro couldn't believe all these friends were putting their careers and possibly their lives on the line for him. He didn't know how to thank them.

Oliver pointed at the laptop on the counter behind Jethro. "How about you get to work on this?" His eyes sobered as he must've read Jethro's expression. "You've saved our lives more times than I can count. You can't expect us not to do the same for you. Now, why don't you help out and get to work?"

Fair enough. He'd figure out a way to thank them later. Jethro took his latte around the counter and sat, opening up the laptop. Wow. Angus Force had managed to obtain all the interviews this time. Jethro had been watching one between a head SIS agent and Fletcher for about an hour when a ding sounded through his speakers.

He clicked the button and the dismal hub in the HDD basement office took shape on his screen. The camera had been positioned perfectly to capture the entire room. Angus and Wolfe sat at the hub in the center looking a little bored. Agents Rutherford and Fields faced the group, the camera angle capturing their expressions.

"Where is Jethro Hanson?" Rutherford asked.

"Haven't seen him," Angus replied negligently. "I can't believe you lost a Brit. Come on."

Wolfe snorted. "I know. He's probably having a martini or a mani-pedi somewhere in town. Can't you track his phone?"

Ian looked at Jethro. "Mani-pedi?"

Jethro pressed his volume up. "Remind me to punch Wolfe later."

Rutherford glowered, his anger easily visible through the camera. "You're hindering an active investigation, Force. Not only is that grounds for dismissal, it's a fucking federal crime."

Wolfe kicked his boots up on his desk. "Is a *fucking* federal crime different from a regular old federal crime?"

Angus crossed his arms. "I do believe it is, but I can't remember the statutory differences."

Rutherford kicked the nearest chair, which happened to be vacant. "Where is the rest of your team?"

Angus looked around. "Huh. Guess I hadn't realized I'd forgotten to call them in."

Agent Fields looked off camera. "Let's see. If I were going to fire you, the most likely candidates from your team who would want to continue working with the HDD are absent right now. I have to say that's a coincidence, isn't it?"

Jethro leaned back as the statement smacked him in the head. Angus had arranged exactly who would attend the meeting. Only he and Wolfe would get canned, but that would effectively end the entire team. "You have got to be kidding me."

Ian shot him a sympathetic glance. "They probably figured this might happen."

"It had better not happen," Jethro said, keeping his voice level. "Wolfe has a baby on the way, for bloody sakes."

Ian watched the interchange on the computer, no expression on his dangerous face. "Did Angus just call Rutherford a spineless dickhead?"

"I missed it," Oliver said, returning to his laptop.

Jethro watched the disaster unfolding on the screen as one of his oldest friends threw away his career. "This is crazy."

"Meh," Oliver said, shrugging. "It's not like they can just turn you over. You'd be in Great Britain and we'd be here trying to figure out what to do with your sociopathic brother. No offense."

"None taken," Jethro said, still overwhelmed.

Rutherford scowled at Angus back in the HDD office. "If I can prove you've broken laws, I'll take you down."

Wolfe flicked a chunk of fake wood off his desk. "We haven't broken laws, so I guess we'll still keep making those massive paychecks. That's good. I was hoping to buy an island off Scotland."

Rutherford's gray suit looked a little green through the camera, and his black tie was a washed out gray. "If I get an ounce of proof, I'll come after your fiancée, Wolfe. She'll never get another story in this town again."

Wolfe plunked his boots on the floor in a motion of pure menace.

"Uh-oh," Oliver said quietly.

"Tell me you didn't just threaten my pregnant fiancée," Wolfe said.

Angus looked at Wolfe, seemed to think for a moment, and then focused on Rutherford again. "If I were you, I'd clarify that last statement."

Rutherford lowered his chin. "You want to play, Angus? Nari is barely holding on to her job here, regardless of her family ties. Is the woman willing to go down with you? I can make sure she never works in this town again."

Jethro winced. "Do you think he's trying to get punched?"

Angus stood, looking more dangerous than Jethro had ever seen him.

Now Wolfe was rising so he stood shoulder to shoulder with Angus. "How about we just fight this out?" he suggested.

Rutherford looked ready.

Fields just shook his head. "Nah. I need my pension." He elbowed his partner. "We don't have the evidence we need to do any of that." He looked around at the sad office and then focused on Angus. "That should worry you, actually. It appears that you're successfully hiding a person of interest in several homicides. If we get the evidence, which something tells me we won't, your freedom is in jeopardy." Then he grabbed Rutherford's arm and yanked him toward the dysfunctional elevator.

Maybe they'd just crash.

When Fields and Rutherford disappeared from sight, Wolfe looked over at Angus, his image huge through the computer screen. "You good?"

"I'm good," Angus said, his expression still pissed. "I guess we're better at this than I thought. Is there really an island you want to buy?"

"Only if we all have to go in hiding with Jethro," Wolfe said.

Jethro groaned.

Chapter Thirty-Nine

Gemma was beyond frazzled by the time she finished throwing away all the paper plates from dinner. She and Nari had cooked pizzas, and the entire group had eaten at her house. Well, what she considered to be her house. Maybe Serena would sell her the home and build another. The woman did like a good project, and maybe she'd need one after her current job was finished.

She tried to push thoughts of Jethro being yanked back to MI6 out of her mind, but she kept failing.

Trudy had been uncharacteristically cranky all night. Maybe the tension emanating from all the adults was getting to her. Not even Roscoe could cheer her up, so Gemma had put her to bed early.

Jethro seemed to be just as grumpy as Trudy and was vocal in his objection to everyone putting their jobs in danger for him. But nobody listened, and soon the whole group had dispersed.

At the moment, Jethro was working with Angus Force. They'd taken over the mudroom to try to create a profile on Fletcher, and they didn't seem to be winding down anytime soon. Jethro had even mounted a corkboard he'd borrowed from somewhere to hang on the wall, and already tons of papers and lines were strewn all over it.

A spike at the back of Gemma's right eye promised a migraine to come, so she said good night and headed to bed. Hopefully the next day would be better.

She fell into an easy sleep almost immediately, barely registering when Jethro came to bed and wrapped his warm body around her. Her dreams were fractured and distorted, but she journeyed through them with little difficulty.

"Mama? I don't feel good," Trudy said from the doorway.

Before Gemma could register the words, Jethro had flipped on the lamp and rolled from the bed.

Gemma sat up groggily and shuffled from under the covers. "Trudy?"

Jethro picked her up and smoothed the hair back from her head. "She's warm."

Gemma reached for her cardigan to wrap around her body, then hurried toward her daughter.

Trudy coughed, reared back, and threw up all over Jethro's T-shirt. Then she started to cry.

Jethro patted her back and moved toward the bathroom. "It's okay, honey," he crooned, walking inside. Then he turned toward Gemma, the little girl held in his arms, panic in his eyes. *What do I do?* he mouthed.

Gemma reached for Trudy and took her, sitting them both on the bathroom mat. She felt the girl's head. "She does have a fever." She touched Trudy's cheeks. "Honey? Does your throat hurt?"

Trudy opened her eyes and nodded. "Everything hurts."

"We need a thermometer," Gemma said. "And some children's aspirin."

Trudy's body convulsed and Gemma turned her to the toilet, where the little girl threw up again. Gemma held her hair out of the way and moved to flush the toilet, pausing to glance in the bowl. Panic stilled her hand.

"What?" Jethro asked, pulling off his demolished shirt and throwing it in the bathtub.

Gemma looked up at him. "There's blood," she whispered. That was bad. Nobody should vomit blood. Panic sizzled through her body and landed in her chest. "Trudy? We're going to go see a nice doctor, okay?" She picked up her daughter and cradled her head, already moving for the bedroom. "We can find one on the way." She kept her voice as calm as possible, but her heart was racing. She could barely breathe.

"Got it." Jethro ran into the twins in the hall and explained the situation, telling them to hold tight and he'd call. Then he somehow managed to get coats and boots on them all, with Gemma still holding Trudy. Soon they were on the road, using their phones to find the closest emergency room.

Trudy threw up twice more on the way, and Gemma was grateful she'd grabbed the bathroom wastepaper basket as she'd hurried out the door.

"You'll be okay, Trudy," Jethro said, reaching out to rub his hand down the girl's back. "Tell us what hurts."

Trudy buried her head in her mother's neck and didn't reply. Her little body was tight with pain and her chest was convulsing.

Jethro sped up, following the navigational directions. "Does she have any health problems?"

"No," Gemma said, finding it difficult to even shove out words. What was wrong with her baby? The blood was terrifying. "She's had a couple of ear infections and a cold once, but that's all. Nothing like this."

"She'll be okay." Jethro sped up even more, and the lights of the hospital showed through the murk. He drove to the front door and ran around to help Gemma out. The night sky was black with faraway stars and the temperature below zero, but Gemma didn't feel any of it. She ran inside and up to the desk, and the kindly looking, gray-haired receptionist immediately had Trudy taken to an examination room.

A doctor instantly arrived to examine the girl while a nurse took notes about Trudy's medical history. The doctor was a young woman with kind brown eyes and efficient movements. Finally she settled Trudy in a bed with a drip. "We'll do tests, but I don't have a diagnosis yet," she admitted. "She's behaving as if she has ingested poison." She looked over at Gemma. "Is there anything in the house or where she's been that she could've taken?"

Gemma sagged against the wall. "Not that I know of, but we are staying in a newly built house. It's possible there's something under the sink?" God, she hadn't done her job as a mother. She hadn't even thought of childproofing the home, she'd been so caught up in running from Monty and then her fear of Fletcher.

Trudy was the most important person in her life.

"I just don't know," Gemma whispered.

Jethro dug his phone out of his pocket. "I'll call home and have the guys search the house." His rugged face was set in harsh lines of concern as he moved into the hallway to make the call.

The doctor checked out Trudy again. "Her blood pressure is too low. We'll have the tests back soon, and then we'll know how to help her." She cast a worried look at the nurse.

Gemma drew a chair up to the bed and held her daughter's hand. Trudy looked small and defenseless in the big bed, and her skin was so pale she looked barely alive. "Trudy?" The girl didn't move. Her eyes were open, but she didn't respond. "Honey? You're going to be okay." Gemma scooted even closer, resting her head next to Trudy's.

Trudy's breathing grew labored.

The girl struggled for a couple of hours, and Gemma stayed by her side with Jethro always near. Finally the doctor returned.

"All of the tests came back negative," the doctor said. "We need to do another round, and I want your friends to search your house again." The twins hadn't found anything. "She's negative for E. coli and salmonella, but I'm still waiting for other results." She patted Gemma's hand. "Hang in there. I'm going to call a couple of colleagues to consult." She quietly left the room.

Jethro set his hand on Gemma's shoulder. "She'll be all right." His voice was reassuring despite his obvious shock.

She nodded, her bladder protesting and her heart ready to scream out of her body. Trudy had settled a little. "I have to run to the restroom. Stay with her?"

"Of course. It's just around the corner." Jethro took her seat when she stood, his hand looking huge on Trudy's.

Gemma barely kept the tears in check until she hit the bathroom, where she grabbed the sink and held on tight. Okay. She could handle this. Trudy was strong, and the doctor seemed more than capable. Trudy would be okay.

Gemma nodded, used the facilities, and washed off her face, prepared to put on a brave front again.

The other stall opened and a man walked out.

Gemma started. She'd gone into the wrong restroom? Then his features took shape. She opened her lips to scream just as Fletcher covered her mouth with a rag held in his large hand.

"Hello, Gemma," he said as the world went dark.

* * * *

Jethro had never felt more helpless in his entire life. He was a fixer. When there was a problem, no matter how dangerous, he fixed it. As he gently kept his hand over Trudy's, he could barely breathe. He had to fix this.

His phone buzzed and he used his other hand to bring it to his ear. "Hanson." It hurt to even force out words.

"Hey, it's Ian. We searched the entire house again and couldn't find anything. We're headed your way now."

Jethro hung his head. "The food we had for dinner was mild and nobody else is sick."

"She didn't eat much at dinner," Ian said. "Maybe she was sick before?"

Jethro lifted his head. "Good point. Thanks. See you soon." He clicked off, made sure Trudy was still breathing, and then dialed Barb.

"Um, hello?" She sounded groggy and confused.

"Hi, it's Jethro." He explained what was going on and asked if Barb had any insight or if any of the other kids from the day care had fallen ill.

The woman sounded wide awake when he'd finished talking but had no idea what Trudy could've eaten. "I can't imagine anything, Jethro. Besides, Trudy hasn't been in daycare. Well, I did give her this week's goodies, but I gave that to all the kids, and it's normal stuff I usually make or buy. The kids ate them happily today at day care, and I assume Trudy had hers as well?"

The doctor skidded into the room on her tennis shoes. "We're getting reports of at least three other kids in emergency rooms right now with the same symptoms."

Jethro stood. "Barb? Call parents of the other kids to make sure this didn't originate at the day care." Maybe a bad flu was going around, but his instincts started to hum. "Call me back." If it wasn't salmonella or E. coli, what could it be? First he had to figure out where Trudy had been exposed, even if it was just the flu.

He needed his entire family on this, so he called Angus Force and explained the situation. With all of them on it, they'd help Trudy.

The doctor checked Trudy's vitals. "I'm brainstorming with the other doctors in a few minutes after we share information. Maybe we can figure out where the kids caught this or what they ate. The cases have to be related," she said.

Jethro's phone dinged and he answered it. "Hanson."

"Oh God, Jethro," Barb said, sounding as if she was hurrying through her house. "I talked to both Tyler and Jimmy's parents, and they're in emergency rooms right now as well. I'm running to the school to grab all the food and anything they could've eaten. One doctor called the CDC and they're sending techs to the day care to conduct a search. Maybe there's some bad chalk or something? I just don't know."

"Call me if you find anything out," Jethro said, clicking off to give the doctor a full report while his mind reeled. What in the world could those children have ingested?

She nodded. "Good. The more information we have, the better."

"Will she be all right?" he asked, for the first time in his entire life needing reassurance.

"Her vitals are stabilizing and she has stopped vomiting," the doctor said. "We need to find out what this is, but I'm hopeful right now."

Hopeful? He didn't want the doctor to be fucking hopeful. He wanted her damn-assed sure. "Thank you," he said, watching Trudy for any sign of new distress.

Female voices came from the hallway, and he recognized Nari's calm tone. Good. The unit was arriving. The more people around to support

Gemma, the better right now, and he wanted backup in every direction. No doubt Gemma was filling everyone in.

He couldn't think. He'd been captured before. He'd been brutally tortured before. Yet never in his entire life had he been so terrified.

Gemma's little girl had to get better. He'd give her a safe life. Already she'd slid herself right into his heart, as had her mother. He loved them both, and he'd protect them until the end of his days. "Just get better," he whispered, his voice ragged.

Nari strode into the room, her hair disheveled, as if she'd jumped from bed and headed right there. "How is she?"

"Hopefully a little better," Jethro said.

Nari looked around. "Where's Gemma?"

The world narrowed with a slash of sound. Jethro stilled. "I thought she was out in the hall speaking with you." He stood, gently releasing Trudy's hand.

"No. I was talking to the doctor," Nari said, her brow furrowing.

Angus Force strode inside the room, along with the doctor.

"What?" Jethro asked.

The doctor checked Trudy very quickly, her hands sure and her motions efficient. She listened to Trudy's heartbeat and then straightened, her stethoscope hanging from her neck. "I have a colleague over on the north side working on one of the cases. He lived in Utah about ten years ago and said this reminds him of a suicidal patient who ingested the pulp of a bunch of castor beans."

Jethro frowned. "Ricin? You're talking about ricin poisoning?" It was rare and impossible to detect. Castor beans? No way had the kids gotten their hands on castor beans.

The doctor shrugged. "It's a long shot and there are numerous other substances this could be. I just thought I'd mention it. Is there a chance any of these kids could be a target for somebody?"

Reality hit hard. Jethro slowly turned. "Gemma!" He ran out into the hall, careened off Wolfe, and barreled into the women's washroom. His heart stopped. The far window was open, with snow covering the sill. Wolfe emerged on his side, took in the open window, and hurriedly searched each stall. At the far one, he turned, shaking his head.

"He has her," Jethro said, the world halting. "Fletcher has Gemma."

Chapter Forty

Cold. She was so unbelievably cold.

Gemma's eyelids slowly opened and a hard cement floor came into view. She lay on her side, facing a metal wall. Where was she? Groggy, her head bursting with pain, she planted a palm on the cement and forced herself to sit up.

What was happening?

She turned around and put her back to the wall, shivering uncontrollably.

A man sat a few yards away, his back against the tire of a battered brown van; there was some sort of pack next to him. He was blurry, and she couldn't make out his features.

She tried to swallow, but her throat felt as if it was full of sand. Blinking several times, she looked around the space and tried to find reality. They were in some metal building, maybe a warehouse, a garage? The walls were damaged and the cement cracked, but the wind was kept outside. "Where am I?" she croaked. None of this was making sense.

He tilted his head.

Her heart started to beat faster. Finally. She lowered her head and stared at him until the blurriness disappeared. She recognized him. He was familiar. She knew him?

He just watched her.

Her mouth formed the words before her brain caught up. "Fletcher."

"Yes." No real expression lived on his face, but a hint of something glowed in his eyes. Curiosity? "Hello, Gemma."

Gemma. Yes, that was right. Her mind finally cleared. Then fear began to creep inside her, way too slowly. "What did you give me?" She was definitely drugged.

"A bit of chloroform. It might've been too much," he allowed.

Trudy. Oh God, Trudy. Gemma tried to stand, but her legs were rubber. "My daughter. What did you do?"

His smile showed that dimple he didn't deserve to have. "Yes, well. The only way I could get you alone, to throw Jethro off his game, was to cause a panic. She seemed to be the only tool I could use. I do apologize for that." There was not an ounce of sincerity in his tone.

Tears hung at Gemma's lashes and she wiped them away, her movements slow and clumsy. "You drugged my child just to get to me?" He had to have had at least an idea of where she'd been staying so he'd known which emergency facility to wait at. "What did you give her?"

He shrugged. "Ricin. It's surprisingly easy to obtain if you know where to look. I put a small amount—a very small amount—into some caramels I made and then added them to the goodie bags for this week." His tongue clicked, sounding creepy in the echoing space of the metal building. "The daycare woman is very organized and already had them lined up in her office. Slipping in one more treat was no problem."

Gemma's stomach revolted. She gagged.

Fletcher lifted his hand. "Don't vomit. Please. It grosses me out."

She stared at him, stunned. He looked like a normal guy. A good-looking one. "You attempted to kill a bunch of toddlers?" Not in a million years would she have thought anybody could be that sick.

"No. I put a minuscule amount in one candy. They'll all become ill, but hopefully nobody will die." He flicked the thought away with one unconcerned hand.

Fire slid through her veins, slowly awakening her nerves. "Hopefully?" she spat. "They're children. One of them could have a deadly reaction." Trudy was still in trouble. "You're fucking evil, asshole." She tried to scramble to her feet again and fell over. "Call the hospital right now and tell them what to do."

Fletcher shrugged. "There's no cure for ricin poisoning. Either they'll be okay or they won't."

Her mind reeled and her entire body ached for her baby. Trudy had to be all right. "I am going to kill you."

Fletcher scoffed. "That's cute."

Her ears felt too hot for her head. "How did you even know that Trudy would get the treat?" The guy almost seemed psychic.

He rolled his neck. "I hadn't realized you'd keep her out of daycare, but things worked out anyway." The man actually sounded proud.

"You're an ass," she muttered, trying to make the room stop spinning. "What about the hospital? How did you know which one I'd pick?"

"I knew from which direction you'd come and chose the best located hospital." He shrugged. "If I was wrong, I would've moved on to another hospital to find you because your daughter will be there for at least a night or two. If she survives."

Gemma's stomach lurched. "You are so going to die. Painfully." If she could only get to a weapon.

He sighed. "After everything I've done for you, I'd expect a modicum of appreciation at the very least."

Her chin dropped. Why wouldn't her legs work? How long did chloroform take to leave a body? "Appreciation? Are you nuts?" There had to be a weapon somewhere in that van.

"No. You're welcome for my disposal of Dr. Monty Cameron." Fletcher smacked his lips together. "Now there was a coward. He was fine beating on women, but the second he was in my care, he bawled like a baby." He sighed. "I normally require quite a substantial retainer to negate problems, so if you consider the situation, *you* owe *me*."

Owe him? "Oh, Jethro is going to cut out your heart and eat it, if I don't get to you first," she spat, wriggling her toes to bring back the feeling in them.

"Ah, my baby brother." Fletcher shook his head. "I have to admit, he has been a pain in my arse for much too long. I set him up so perfectly with our mother, and yet I ended up living in a cell instead of him. Not this time. I'll get it perfect."

She pulled up her knees and wrapped her arms around her legs, trying to force warmth into them. "Nobody will believe Jethro would kill me. You could stab me, leave his DNA, and have him on video, and our team will disprove it. No matter what you do."

"I realize that," Fletcher said easily. "However, he's caused enough trouble for the Crown that he'll be hauled back home, and chances aren't looking good for his longevity." He reached in the bag and pulled out a knife crusted with blood. "In addition, I've learned that prisons come in all sizes. The one he'll build for himself after failing you will be stronger than any I've ever faced. This will destroy him. That's prison enough."

"Then how is it perfect?" Finally feeling was coming back into her ankles.

Fletcher watched her feet. "My brother should never have turned against me. He hunted me and was closing in, so I had to kill our mother to teach him a lesson. Yet he got there earlier than I hoped and had a chance to say goodbye. I wanted him to see her die but not experience closure."

His eyes glowed across the distance. "Now I am going to get it right and not give him that last moment to say goodbye; he'll arrive just in time to watch you leave this world. I believe that will make this moment *perfect*, where it wasn't before."

"So you just want to hurt your brother? That's pathetic." Now that her body was awakening, so was the realization that Fletcher was a trained killer and she wasn't. Fear crowded into her rational thoughts and she had to squelch it. She was a mother and her child needed her. "Maybe there's no perfect. Have you thought of that?"

"I have but am willing to keep trying," he agreed. "Not only did Jethro betray me, he took our entire inheritance when I was incarcerated. It was a double insult, and that has to be repaid in full." He shook his head. "While I don't see his attraction to you, he's lost in a way he's never been before. Besides, who knows? Perhaps he'll get here sooner than expected and save you. He did it once, and I'm curious if he can do it again. I doubt it, though. This time I will get everything right, and you won't get that last goodbye."

The guy was sick. How could he speak so casually about death? "You really are batshit crazy," she said, testing her shoulders to make sure she could move quickly. Her body still felt numb. Drugged. Slow.

Fletcher tossed the knife up and caught it easily by the handle. "We're all a little crazy, don't you think? You see Jethro as a hero, and yet the things he's done in the name of duty chill even me. He's not who you think he is and he's going to show his true face when he finds you…just a mite too late. I'm happy to finally be able to answer his desperate questions about good and evil."

"What is your answer?" Gemma asked, trying to keep him talking. Her body wasn't ready to fight yet.

"That they don't exist," Fletcher said easily. "We are who we are and there is no question of good or evil. I'm a killer, as is my brother. It might be nature or nurture or a combination of the two. I'm not going to allow him to hide from the truth any longer."

Gemma could barely follow that reasoning. "So, the murder of your mother, all of these deaths, your poisoning children…are all to force your brother to…what? Be as dark as you?" The guy was crazy.

"No. Just acknowledge who he is," Fletcher said. "He's been under an illusion that he's the hero in our story. The truth is that everything he's done in the name of duty is just as bad as what I've done, and that in the end, he's a failure. He tried to make me fail, to show me as a criminal, and I can't let that stand. Plus, I didn't get it quite right last time. With Mother. I have to make it perfect."

He was talking about stabbing her. Gemma's stomach hitched. "Why wasn't it perfect last time?" She had to know what she was dealing with here.

"She had a chance to say goodbye," Fletcher said, his jaw tightening. "I wanted her alive, bleeding out but unable to speak with him. Somehow I got the timing wrong."

Oh, God. It was about timing?

He gracefully stood. "If Jethro's team is nearly as good as he believes, he should be able to get here before you die and see you take your last breath."

"Wait. Don't you at least want to make this a fair fight? I can't move my legs yet," she tried desperately.

"I care little about fairness." He strode toward her, the knife looking dull with the dried blood covering the blade. It was, no doubt, Monty's blood.

Gemma tried to scramble away from him, but she was already against the wall. "Please don't do this. My daughter needs me." The words poured out of her before she could stop them.

He crouched down, bringing a hint of warmth from his body. "I like it when they beg." His face cleared, as if he'd just realized something about himself. "Oh, I only kill for country or for money, but to be honest, I feel better right after a fresh kill." He smoothed her hair away from her face with his free hand, ignoring her flinch.

She was going to puke.

"Killing your ex gave me great pleasure," Fletcher admitted, apparently feeling free to confess since he was about to stab her. "I liked it when he sobbed. Did you know that he'd actually found you before I sent him the photo?"

She paused. "He had?"

"Affirmative," Fletcher said smugly. "He'd been messing with you. Something about a slashed tire, a broken window, and even breaking into some cottage through a basement window. The guy wouldn't stop confessing to me."

Her stomach lurched.

"It's like he wanted me to respect him or something." Fletcher shrugged. "Sometimes I think perhaps I would continue the killing even without financial gain."

"Yeah. You're crazy." Sucking in a breath, Gemma shoved him as hard as she could with both hands and swept out her feet, kicking beneath his knees and catching him by surprise.

He fell to the side.

She shoved to her feet, grabbing the knife and plunging it down into his thigh.

He bellowed and swung out, hitting her in the knee. She flew across the cement floor and scrambled up, running as fast as her shaking legs would allow. She hurried around the van, spotted the warehouse door, and ducked her head to run. If he caught her, she was dead.

She hit the door and shoved it open, barreling out into a silent morning. No wind, no snow, no storm. Only more metal buildings in an icy world. Wait a minute. She recognized this place. She turned to run and a sharp pain ripped through her head as he clamped his hand in her hair and twisted. She cried out, frantically trying to turn and fight him.

He dragged her back inside the garage and threw her against the van.

Her shoulder impacted the metal with a burst of pain and she fell. Before she could regain her feet, he manacled a hand around her throat and lifted her, shoving her around the van and then pushing her back against the wall where she'd sat.

Watching her, he opened the van and dug a silk men's tie out of a pack, quickly wrapping it around his bleeding thigh. Fury made his movements jerky.

She stood, her legs wobbling. Then she dove for the bloody knife on the ground.

He beat her to it, backhanding her almost casually. The force of the blow shot her back against the wall, and she hit her forehead, seeing stars. Then she fell and rolled over to a sitting position, facing him. Pain cascaded though her head and body. Fear chilled her and she blinked away tears.

He walked toward her, his hand on the bloody knife. "I'm going to enjoy this much more than I anticipated."

She screamed.

Chapter Forty-One

The neurons in Jethro's brain misfired. He paced the hallway, his movements frantic. "He got her. I let him get to her." He pulled on his ear, trying to regain that calm he always had.

Angus grabbed him by the arms and shoved him against the wall. "Nobody in their right mind would think Fletcher would poison a bunch of kids."

"I should have." Jethro pushed him away.

Angus snarled. "Take a fucking breath. Think. We talked about this asshole for hours last night. What does he want?" Fury and determination glowed bright in the man's deep green eyes. "You're the only one who knows him, Jethro. Now think. Why would Fletcher go to so much trouble to get Gemma?"

Jethro couldn't think. Right now the doctor was flushing Trudy's stomach with activated charcoal in the hope of counteracting the ricin poison. Would his brother have done such a thing?

Angus shook him. "Stop. Calm. Think."

The world narrowed, and Jethro let go of the professor inside him, drawing out the killer. He exhaled. Why would Fletcher take Gemma? "To hurt me."

"What else?" Angus asked grimly.

All right. He could figure this out. "Fletcher always needs to get things perfectly right. He can't stand failure." Jethro wiped a hand over his mouth. He couldn't think about what Fletcher would to do Gemma. He had to. "All right. He failed with our mother. I arrived before he thought I would, so that was a failure. I got to say goodbye, even though she was a witch until the end. He went to prison and I did not, so that was a failure. I won and he lost." Even if Fletcher would never admit, even to himself, that this was a game, there was still success and failure. "He'll kill Gemma the same way as our mother but do it right this time."

Angus released him.

Jethro set his stance. "He'll also want to make me pay. Oh, that's too petty for him to admit, but he'll want to make me pay for betraying him and turning him in. He won't be able to help himself."

"Where?" Angus asked. "Let's think. He killed your mother at her home?"

"Yes," Jethro said. "We need to cover all the bases."

Angus looked at the Deep Ops crew, who were all assembled in the hospital hallway. "This this is your op, Jethro. You call it."

He had to think. Jethro took everyone's skills and potential damage into account. He looked at the expectant and furious faces of the warriors around him, knowing that he'd need them all. "All right. Ian, Oliver, and Nari, I need you here covering Trudy. I don't trust my brother not to come for her. He's obviously willing to do anything."

The three nodded. Though the men were injured, they were highly trained and would protect Trudy with their lives. Nari was an exceptional fighter and would do the same.

"Wolfe, you check out the university because it's my second home, and Angus, you go to Serena's former apartment, where Gemma and Trudy were living." He shook out his hands and willed his frantic energy out of his body. It was entirely possible his brother would use any of those places.

He started toward the exit. "I'll hit my former apartment. Everyone remember that Fletcher is well trained and has no problem killing. If you have to kill him, do it."

They all ran out into the silent night after Nari promised everyone she'd text with updates on Trudy.

Jethro reached his truck, nodded at a serious Wolfe, and then barreled away from the hospital. How screwed up was his brother that he'd quite possibly poisoned several children just to force Jethro and Gemma into a vulnerable position? There would be no taking Fletcher in this time when Jethro found him.

He drove at frantic speeds across icy roads, sliding several times and nearly taking out more than one power pole. The closer he drew to his burned-out apartment, the more he felt his brother.

Would he be too late?

Jethro parked outside the chain-link fence and climbed over, approaching from behind the building. He angled around the side to avoid the debris from the fire, rapidly maneuvering toward the only accessible door.

A woman screamed.

His heart stopped.

Gemma. Falling back on training, he twisted the knob and stepped inside what used to be his garage. An old brown van had been parked sideways, and he let it cover him as he trod silently toward it, moving around the side just in time to see Fletcher plunge a knife into Gemma's side.

Roaring, Jethro rushed toward Fletcher, his hands already up.

Fletcher turned, surprise on his face, and slashed toward him with the bloody blade.

The knife cut into Jethro's arm, but he didn't feel a thing. Fury and something else, something *primal*, roared through him. He charged his brother, lifting him and bashing him against the metal wall. Fletcher grunted and brought the hilt of the knife down on Jethro's shoulder, fracturing his clavicle.

There was no pain.

Jethro dropped and punched Fletcher hard enough to hear his jaw crack. Fletcher hit back in a flurry of fists, adding his knees to maximize the damage. He got in several cuts with the knife, one into Jethro's hip. His brother had always loved a knife. Jethro grunted with the hits, acknowledged the pain, and sent it spiraling away. Then Fletcher caught him with a punch to the gut and Jethro bent over as Fletcher kicked him beneath the chin.

Jethro fell back, his shoulders on the cement, and barreled over to roll to his feet. He stopped Fletcher's advance with the weapon by kicking him in the nuts.

Fletcher backed away, his eyes wide and his cheeks puffed out.

Jethro tried to determine Gemma's status, but she lay on her side, blood seeping from her sweater to the ground. "Leave now, Fletcher. Let's do this another day."

Fletcher inched to the side, his body between Jethro and Gemma. "No. Maybe I had the wrong idea last time, and this is what makes it perfect. You weren't there. Perhaps you should've been there and we could've watched Mother die together." He tossed the knife to his other hand. "Yeah. Perfect."

Jethro's temper blew. He had to get to Gemma and cover that wound. "Leave now, Fletcher. Or I am going to bloody kill you." He edged to the side, trying to see her, but Fletcher kept pace with him, a maniacal smile on his familiar face. "Get out of my way," Jethro yelled, darting forward only to have Fletcher pivot with the knife and cut him across the arm.

Blood spurted from Jethro and he shook out his hand, making sure it still functioned. "What the bloody hell is wrong with you?" he bellowed, furious and shocked. The hurt still dug deep at his brother's betrayal, tormenting every nerve he had.

Fletcher chuckled and wiped blood off his face. "You're looking in a mirror, Brother." His knife hand stayed loose and ready to strike.

"No," Jethro said, not even realizing he'd kept a slight hope that he'd be able to save Fletcher. It was too late. He also couldn't let Fletcher drag this on any longer while Gemma bled out. "I'm sorry I couldn't help you."

Fletcher paused. "Oh, this is going to help me plenty." He glanced at blood on the cement near his foot. "She's going to die the way Mother should have, Jet."

Gemma stirred. "Jethro?"

"No," Fletcher screamed. "She needs to be out. To be silent!"

Jethro lunged just as Fletcher shot forward with the knife. Jethro dodged to the side, kicking at Fletcher's wrist. The knife flew up. In one smooth motion, Jethro regained his footing, snatched the blade out of the air, and flipped it around in his hand. Without pausing, he struck.

The blade slid into Fletcher's body as if it had been forged to do just that.

Jethro stabbed up beneath the breastbone several times, yanked the knife out, and shoved it full force through his brother's throat as he gasped his last breaths.

Fletcher hadn't hit the floor before Jethro was skidding on his knees across the bloody concrete to reach his woman.

"Gemma?" Jethro gingerly turned her over, his breath returning on a sharp gasp. "How bad?" Her white sweater was red on one side, fully saturated with blood.

Her head lolled on her shoulders.

Fuck. He pressed his hand against the wound and lifted her, sliding in the blood but continuing beyond the van to his truck. He'd take the van, but he didn't trust Fletcher not to have booby trapped it just in a case. "Hold on, baby. Just hold on." He left a trail of blood from them both on the ice as he careened through the open gate and ran down the fence line to his truck. "You're going to be all right." The words tumbled out of him, not making a lot of sense, as he jumped inside and settled her head in his lap, his hand pressed against her injury while he started the truck.

She mumbled something.

He pressed the gas pedal hard, steering with one hand. "What is it? Gemma?"

She stirred and then groaned, her hand moving to cover his over her cut. "Trudy."

"Trudy is fine. Her fever is gone and she's absolutely fine," he said, having no clue whether it was true or not. "She needs you, Gemma. Stay awake. Stay with me." He barreled around a snow berm in the middle of the road, searching for the lights of the city. They were so far away. "I love you. So much. Please don't leave me." The truck's tires spun up gravel as he neared an interstate on-ramp and took it too fast. Then he prayed to a God he'd forgotten, promising everything.

"Take care of Trudy," Gemma whispered, her face turned to the side and covered by her thick hair.

He couldn't release the wheel or her wound to brush the hair aside, so he just sped up. "You'll take care of Trudy. We all will. You have to hold on."

His phone buzzed and he hit a button on the steering wheel with his thumb.

"It's Wolfe. Nothing at the school and I'm driving back to the hospital."

"I've got her. Headed to the hospital. She's wounded, Wolfe." Jethro passed a minibus on two tires.

Wolfe was quiet for a moment. "I'll send out the word and we'll meet you there, Brother." The line went dead.

Gemma didn't move.

Jethro drove faster, found his exit, and drove through silent streets to the hospital. He careened to a stop at the front door. Wolfe was already running outside to help him carry her from the vehicle. "It's bad."

They made it inside and got her onto a gurney, where the doctors rushed her away for surgery.

Then silence. Jethro looked at Wolfe, who was watching the spot where the gurney had disappeared.

Wolfe turned and studied him, his eyes narrowing. "Holy shit. How bad are you hurt?" His face wavered in and out, like the image in a carnival mirror.

Jethro tilted his head. "Huh?"

Wolfe was already reaching for him before the ground came up and swallowed him whole.

Then…darkness.

Chapter Forty-Two

The world was nicely hazy. Gemma opened her eyes and white ceiling tiles came into view.

"Hey, there." The British accent was sexy and calm.

She slowly turned her head to see her Brit lounging in a chair, pretty much covered in bruises and bandages. "Jethro," she squawked.

"Yeah." He pressed a button and the head of her bed slowly rose. Something beeped behind her, and IVs poured liquid into her veins. "You scared me there, lady."

She shook her head to gain her bearings, and memories of the night came crashing back. She stiffened. "Trudy." Then she saw her daughter on his lap, cuddled beneath her green blankie. "What?" Why was the girl out of the hospital bed? What was happening?

Trudy jerked and then sat up, rubbing her eyes with her little fists. "Mama?"

Was she dreaming? Gemma swallowed, noting pain in her right side. It wasn't bad, but that could be because the entire world was fuzzy. "Trudy?"

Jethro leaned over and patted her hand. "She's okay. Perfectly fine really."

"In bed," Gemma said, lifting her hand as the room finally came into focus. "She should be in bed."

"Yeah," Trudy said, reaching for her mother.

Jethro lifted her. "Okay, but stay on this side and don't move too much." He lifted the white blanket and settled Trudy inside. "No moving."

"M'kay," Trudy said, curling her knees into Gemma's good side and patting her chin. "You were asleep for a long time."

Oh. That was why Trudy was out of bed. A closer look confirmed that the girl's cheeks were pink and her blue eyes bright. In addition, her hair was in neat braids, and it looked like there was sparkly marker on her nose. "How are you feeling?"

"Good," Trudy said. "Rot-co wants to come see you, but they won't let him." Her frown conveyed all that was wrong in her world.

Gemma slid her arm around her child and tugged her closer, into the part of her rib cage that wasn't awakening with pain. "How long have I been out?"

"Three days," Jethro said, lines of exhaustion extending from his eyes. "The longest three days of my life. You awoke earlier this afternoon and then went right back to sleep, but that was a good thing."

Trudy nodded. "We've been waitin' for you to wake up again. You slow."

"Hey. They have fresh cookies downstairs." Clarence Wolfe suddenly filled the entire doorway. He paused, his brows rising. "You're finally awake." His voice softened. "How are you feeling?"

She smoothed her baby's soft cheek. "A little groggy but grateful to be alive."

Wolfe grinned. "Yeah. The Brit has some moves."

Trudy sat up. "Canna go get cookies?"

Gemma wanted to hold her there forever, but it sounded like her daughter had been waiting all day for her to wake up. "Sure."

Wolfe strode over and deftly lifted Trudy from the bed, making her squeal with laughter. He settled her securely on his shoulders, where she held on to his chin as if she'd done so several times before. "I'm glad you're awake, Gemma. Now maybe we can get the professor to go home and get some sleep. The guy hasn't left your side." He turned and made sure Trudy ducked before they walked through the doorway.

Gemma turned her head. With his angled face and sharp jawline, Jethro Hanson had always been handsome. But with his fresh bruises and injuries, he looked like a badass operative. "Is Fletcher still after me?"

"No." Jethro scooted closer and settled the blankets more securely around her body. "He's not a problem any longer."

Her heart hurt for him. Even though it had been justified, having to kill his own brother must weigh on him. "I'm so sorry."

He leaned in and kissed her nose. "I'm not. He threatened what's mine."

Amusement tickled through her. "Yours?"

"Yeah." He set his chin on her good shoulder, his eyes a burning blue. "I can be polite and smooth, but we're beyond that. I'm making a claim, Gemma Falls."

Her entire body warmed and her lips curved right into a smile. Was it possible to love a man this much? Her heart all but swelled. "What exactly does your claim entitle you to?"

"Well, how about a future? You, Trudy, and me?" He smoothed her hair away from her eyes. "I already talked to Serena, and she's more than happy to build another house in the cul-de-sac and sell me the one we've been living in."

Gemma's breath hitched. "She's safe?"

"Seems to be, although she said she's not coming home for a while." Jethro's left eyebrow rose. "We're going after her next week just for a visual, to make sure she's okay. Although she did sound fine."

Gemma's head reeled. "You're buying us a house?"

"Yes, and I want everything that goes with it." He smiled, and that darn dimple winked at her. "I'm kind of a proper guy and will follow the proper protocol with ring, knee, and proposal, but I thought you should know that it's coming and you're going to say yes."

If she became any happier, she'd burst wide open. "Oh, I am, am I?"

"Yeah." He kissed her chin and then her cheek, his hand covering hers. "Trudy and I already have decided, so you might as well get on board now. Also, she wants two little brothers and a dog. I might have promised her that just to ease her fears during these last few days. With the three of us working on it, I'm sure our kids will be good ones." Even his wince was sexy.

"You can't guarantee two brothers," Gemma protested, trying not to laugh because her side was starting to hurt. "We might have all girls."

He shrugged. "I promised, so we'll just have to keep trying until we make it happen." He grinned. "I love you, Gemma. Thought I should say the words out loud."

She'd never realized she could be this happy. That she could feel this safe and loved. Her mouth opened and a doctor strode in.

He had thick gray hair and kind blue eyes. "Well, hello. Let's take a look at you, shall we?"

* * * *

Jethro left the doctor to make sure all was well with Gemma and walked into the waiting room, where the entire team had taken over. *His* team. Everyone had rushed to the hospital when the call had gone out. Trudy sat between Wolfe and Dana, happily munching a cookie and rubbing her now sock-covered foot over Roscoe's fur. "Roscoe?"

Over by the door, Angus Force shrugged. "Trudy said she wanted to see him."

Well, that explained everything.

"Well?" Ian asked, lounging across two chairs with his twin next to him.

"Gemma is awake and the doctor is with her now. She's going to be fine," Jethro said. He could actually feel the vibrations of relief that came from the group. "Thank you for everything you've done these last few days." Mere words weren't enough, but right now they were all he had.

"Sure," Raider said, hauling Brigid to her feet. His black hair had grown out during his last assignment, and he looked tougher than ever. "We'll head home and make sure the house is ready for when she gets out." The agent and his hacker looked tired but pleased.

"We'll come with you," Pippa said, reaching for Malcolm's hand. She'd made sure everyone had been fed the last few days, while Malcolm had worked with Angus Force on salvaging their Deep Ops team with the HDD brass. Taking down an international criminal like Fletcher couldn't hurt. "Come on, Millie. You can stay with us tonight."

Millie nodded and stretched to her feet.

Mal motioned toward the twins. "Why don't you two ride with us? We haven't finished our poker game, and I want my money back."

Jethro's body settled. It appeared Ian and Oliver had made friends while he'd been keeping vigil over Gemma.

Ian stood and reached for crutches he'd apparently obtained. "Trudy? You want to come with us?"

"I'm going with Wuf," Trudy said, still petting Roscoe.

"Okay." Ian gave her a high five and followed Oliver out the door.

Soon Dana and Nari began playing with Trudy in the corner while Angus and Wolfe finished off the cookies.

Angus tossed him a cookie, and for the first time in days, Jethro actually felt hungry. "You nearly gave up your careers. All of your jobs." Again, words weren't enough.

Wolfe shrugged. "If we do, we do. We're a team, and that's what matters."

Angus nodded. "We have a lot of options and would like to bring the twins in somehow but haven't figured out how to make it work yet."

Wolfe stretched his arms. "We have time. They're on the injured list for a while longer anyway."

The doctor emerged from Gemma's room, and Jethro turned to hurriedly stride his way. "Doc? How is she?"

The doctor smiled. "She's going to be fine. I'd like to keep her for a couple more days, and then you can take her home. But now that she's awake, Ms. Falls is out of the woods."

Jethro's knees went limp, so he just stood in place as the doctor patted his arm and then hurried off.

A tiny hand slipped inside his, and he looked down to see Trudy staring up at him. "Hi."

She grinned. "Hi. You gonna be my daddy now?"

"Yes."

"I figured." She lifted her arms. "Up."

He dutifully lifted her up and then carried her in to see her mother.

"Kisses," she demanded.

Jethro tipped her so she could lean over and kiss Gemma's face.

Gemma's gaze softened. "What are you two doing?"

"It's almost midnight, so Trudy is heading home with Dana and Wolfe, if that's okay?" Jethro asked.

Gemma smiled, looking beautiful and fragile in the hospital bed. "Definitely okay."

"Great. I'll be right back." Jethro carried the girl to Dana and kissed Trudy on the forehead. "I'm going to stay with your mom tonight. I'll see you tomorrow, Urchin."

She threw her arms around his neck and held tight. "Love you."

His heart just dropped—completely twisted around her little finger. He hugged her back. "Love you, too." Then he smiled at Dana and returned to Gemma's room.

After he'd sat she looked over at him, her pretty blue eyes clear. "You've been here the whole time."

"Of course." He took her hand, keeping his touch gentle. "How are you feeling?"

"Grateful," she whispered, her eyes glistening. "I love you, Jethro. Completely."

His breath hitched. He hadn't realized he'd needed to hear those words from her. Were his eyes tearing? "So much for my being a badass 007," he murmured.

Her chuckle eased the rest of his worry. "007 has nothing on you, Professor Badass."

He leaned in and kissed her, being gentle but thorough. 007 did not have Gemma and Trudy, and they were everything. "You're right," he said. "Now get some sleep. I'll be here when you awaken."

And he would be.

Forever.

Preview

Read on for an excerpt from Rebecca's newest Romantic Thriller!
First in a new series
YOU CAN RUN
A Laurel Snow Romantic Thriller
***New York Times* best-selling author**
Rebecca Zanetti

"I couldn't put it down!"
—*New York Times* best-selling author Lisa Jackson

"Rebecca Zanetti takes you on a thrill-ride, pitting characters you love against impossible odds."
—*New York Times* best-selling author Christine Feehan

Laurel Snow wouldn't call hunting a serial killer a vacation, but with a pile of dead bodies unearthed near her Genesis Valley, WA, hometown, she'll take what she can get. Yet something about this case stirs her in unexpected ways. Like the startling connection she feels to Dr. Abigail Caine, a fiercely intelligent witness with a disturbing knack for making Laurel feel like *she* has something on *her.* Then there's Laurel's attraction to Huck Rivers, the fish and wildlife officer guiding her to the crime scene—and into the wilderness . . .

A former soldier and a trained sniper, Huck seems to have his own secrets, not least of which are his whereabouts the night yet another woman disappears. And when the body is dumped where Laurel can't help but find it, she knows this cat-and-mouse game is deeply personal . . .

Once in the heart of darkness with Huck, Laurel must negotiate her conflicting feelings for him, her complex rapport with Abigail—and her mission to find a serial killer among a growing list of suspects and a danger that's far too close to home. So close, in fact, Laurel fears she will never find her way back to the woman she once was . . .

Chapter One

Laurel Snow swiped through the calendar on her phone while waiting for the flight to DC to board. The worn airport chairs at LAX were as uncomfortable as ever, and she tried to keep her posture straight to prevent the inevitable backache. Christmas music played through the speakers, and an oddly shaped tree took up a corner, its sad-looking branches decorated with what might've been strung popcorn. The upcoming week was already busy, and Laurel hoped there wouldn't be a new case. She stuck in her wireless earbuds to allow an upbeat rock playlist to pound through her ears as she rearranged a couple of meetings.

The phone dinged and she answered while continuing to organize the week. "Snow."

"Hi, Agent Snow. How did the symposium go?" asked her boss, George McCromby.

"As expected," she said, swiping a lunch meeting from Thursday to Friday. "I'm not a teacher, and half the time the audience looked confused. A young woman in the front row had serious daddy issues, and a young man behind her was facing a nervous breakdown. Other than that, one guy in the last row exhibited narcissistic tendencies."

"For Pete's sake. We just wanted you to talk about the FBI and help with recruitment. You're a good face," George muttered.

Laurel tapped her phone when the Wi-Fi struggled. "My face has nothing to do with my job. I'm not skilled at recruitment or teaching."

George sighed. "How many people have you seen today who wore red shoes?"

Yeah, she should change the computer update meeting from Tuesday to Wednesday. "Six," she said absently. "Ten if you include maroon-colored shoes."

George laughed. "How many people in the last month have worn yellow hats around you?"

"Just eight," she said.

George warmed to the subject. "Right now, where you are in the airport and without looking, who's the biggest threat?"

If she changed one more meeting, she could fit in a manicure on Friday. "Guy waiting in the adjacent area for a plane to Dallas. He's five nine, wiry, and has cauliflower ears. Moves with grace." Yes. She could fit in a manicure. "Another man to the north by the magazine rack in the bookstore is built like a logger and could throw a decent punch." Would there be time for a pedicure? Probably not.

"Why aren't you the biggest threat?" George asked.

She paused. "Because I'm currently performing parlor tricks for the deputy director of the FBI." She looked up to check her boarding time.

"I have a call on the other line. We'll talk about this when you get back." George clicked off.

Laurel didn't have anything else to say on the matter. Her phone buzzed and she glanced at the screen before answering the call. "Hi, Mom. Yes, I'm still returning home for Christmas." It had been three years and her mother's patience had ended. "I promise. In two weeks, I'll be there."

"Laurel, I need you now," Deidre said, her voice pitched high.

Laurel froze. "What's wrong?"

"It's your uncle Carl. The sheriff wants to arrest him for murder." Panic lifted Deidre's voice even higher. "You're in the FBI. They're saying he's a serial killer. You have to come help."

Uncle Carl was odd, but not a killer. "Serial killer? How many bodies have been found?"

"I don't know," Deidre cried out.

Okay. Her mother never became this flustered. "Is the Seattle FBI involved?" Laurel asked.

"I don't know. The local sheriff is the one who's harassing Carl. Please come help. Please." Her mother never asked for anything.

Laurel would have to change flights—and ask for a favor. "I'll text you my flight information, and I can rent a car at Sea-Tac." Murderers existed everywhere, but Uncle Carl wasn't one of them.

"No. I'll make sure you're picked up. Just text me what time you land." Her mother didn't drive or like to be inside vehicles.

"Okay. I have to run." Laurel clicked off and dialed George's private number with her left hand while reaching in her bag for a printout of her schedule. Being ambidextrous came in handy sometimes. Though she didn't have many friends at the FBI, for some reason George had become a mentor and was usually patient. Sometimes. Plus, she had just closed a serial killer case in Texas, and she had some juice, as George would say. For now. In her experience, juice dried up quickly.

The phone rang several times before George picked up. "I said we'd talk about it in DC."

"I need a favor," Laurel said. Her gaze caught on a younger man escorting an elderly woman through the terminal, both looking up at the flight information boards. "I don't have much information, but it appears there are at least a few suspicious deaths in Genesis Valley up in Washington State. I need to investigate the situation." There was something off about the guy with the older lady. He reached into the slouchy, beige-colored purse slung over the woman's shoulder and drew out a billfold, which he slipped into his backpack.

"Wait a minute. I'll make a call and find out what's going on," George said.

"Thank you." Laurel stood and strode toward the couple, reaching them quickly. "Is everything okay?"

The woman squinted up at her, cataracts visible in her cloudy blue eyes. "Oh my. Yes, I think so. This kind young man is showing me to my plane."

"Is that right?" Laurel tilted her head.

The man had to be in his early twenties, with sharp brown eyes and thick blond hair. His smile showed too many teeth. "Yes. I'm Fred. Just helping Eleanor, here, out. She was a little lost."

Eleanor clutched a plane ticket in one gnarled hand. Her white hair was tightly curled and her face powdered. "I was visiting my sister in Burbank and got confused after security in the airport."

Irritation ticked down Laurel's neck. "Return her wallet to her."

Eleanor gasped. "What?"

Fred shoved Eleanor and turned to run.

Laurel grabbed him by the backpack, kicked him in the popliteal fossa, and dropped him to the floor on his butt, where he fell flat. She set the square heel of her boot on the lateral femoral cutaneous nerve in his upper thigh. "You know, Fred? There's a nerve right here that can make a person . . . bark like a dog." She pressed down.

Fred yelped.

An airport police officer ran up, his hand on his harnessed weapon.

Laurel pulled her ID out of her jacket pocket and flipped it open. "FBI. I think this guy has a few wallets that might not be his." She shook out the backpack. Several billfolds, bottles of pills, and necklaces bounced off the tile floor.

"Hey." Eleanor leaned down and fetched her billfold and one container of pills. "You jerk." She swatted Fred with her purse.

He ducked and pushed the bag away. "Let me up, lady."

"Make him bark like a dog again," Eleanor burst out.

"Sure." Laurel pressed down on the nerve.

Fred groaned and pushed at her foot, pain wiping the color from his face. "Stop it."

The officer stuffed all the contraband back in the bag and then pulled Fred to his feet once Laurel moved her boot. He quickly cuffed Fred. "Thanks for this. I've got it from here." They moved away.

Laurel reached for Eleanor's ticket. "Let's see where you're supposed to be." A quick glance at the ticket showed that the woman was going to Indiana. "Your flight is over here at gate twenty-one. Let me grab my belongings and I'll take you there." She retrieved her oversize laptop bag and rolling carry-on before returning to slide her arm through Eleanor's. "The gate is just on the other side of those restaurants."

"Excuse me?" George barked through the earbuds. "Assistant Director of the FBI here with information for you."

"Please hold on another minute, sir," Laurel said, twisting through the throng while keeping Eleanor safe.

Eleanor looked up, leaning on Laurel. "How do you know my gate number? You didn't even look at the information board."

"I looked at it earlier," Laurel said, helping the elderly woman avoid three young boys dragging Disney-themed carry-ons.

Eleanor blinked. "You memorized all the flight information with one look?"

"I'm still here," George groused.

Laurel took Eleanor up to the counter, where a handsome man in his thirties typed into the computer. "This is Eleanor, and this is her plane. She's going to sit right over here, and she needs extra time to board." Without waiting for a reply, she helped Eleanor to the nearest seat. "Here you go. You should be boarding in just a few minutes."

Eleanor patted her hand. "You're a good girl."

Laurel crouched down. "Do you have anybody meeting you at the airport?"

Eleanor nodded. “Yes. My son is meeting me right outside baggage claim. Don’t you worry.” She pressed both gnarled hands against Laurel’s face. “You’re a special one, aren’t you?”

“Damn it, Snow,” George bellowed through the earbuds.

Laurel winced. “I am happy to help.”

Eleanor tightened her grip. “You have such lovely eyes. How lucky are you!”

Lucky? Laurel had rarely felt lucky to have heterochromia. “You’re very kind.”

“You’re beautiful. Such stunning colors, and so distinct. I’ve never seen such a green light in anyone’s eye, and your other eye is a beautiful dark shade of blue.” Eleanor squinted and leaned in closer. “You have a little green flare in the blue eye, don’t you?”

Laurel smiled and removed the woman’s hands from her face, careful of the arthritic bumps on her knuckles. “Yes. I have a heterochromia in the middle of heterochromatic eyes. It’s an adventure.”

Eleanor laughed. “You’re a pip, you are. Godspeed to you.”

Laurel stood. “Have a nice trip, Eleanor.” She turned to head back to her gate, her mind returning to her trip to Genesis Valley. She’d have to move all her appointments in DC to the first week in January, and her brain automatically flipped dates. If she juggled a Monday meeting that week, she would have time for a pedicure. Maybe she could skip her Wednesday lunch with the forensic accountants to discuss the recently developed tactical reasoning software. The accountants rarely escaped the computer lab, and when they did they always talked for too long. “Sorry about that, sir. What did you find out?”

George’s sigh was long-suffering. “Multiple body parts, including three skulls, were found this morning by kids four-wheeling on a mountain called . . .” Papers rustled. “Snowblood Peak.”

Laurel switched directions, her heart rate kicking up. “Just this morning? It’s a little early to be narrowing in on a suspect.” She’d spent some time snowmobiling that mountain as a child with her uncles before leaving for college at the age of eleven. “Could be an old graveyard or something like that. Might not be a case.”

“I know, and this is a local case and not federal, I think.”

She paused. “Actually, it depends where the bodies were found. The valley below Snowblood Peak is half owned by the federal government and half by the state. It’s beautiful country.”

“Huh. Well, okay. We could have jurisdiction if you feel like fighting with the state and the locals.” George didn’t sound encouraging.

She never felt like fighting. “Don’t we have an office in Seattle?”

“Yes, but it’s in flux right now. We were in the midst of creating a special unit out of there called the Pacific Northwest Violent Crimes Unit, but there was a political shake-up, a shooting, and a bunch of transfers. The office is restructuring now, and currently in place I have two agents dealing with a drug cartel.” Papers shuffled across the line.

“So I’m on my own with this case, if it turns out to be anything.” Which was normal for her actually. A flight from LAX to Seattle had been scheduled to depart out of gate thirteen, and a flight from LAX to Everett had been listed as gate seventeen. “Has my flight been changed?”

More papers rustled. “Jackie?” George bellowed. “Does Snow have a new flight?”

Laurel grimaced at the sudden pain in her ear.

George returned. “You’ve been switched to Flight 234, leaving in ten minutes. They’re holding the door open for you, but we could only get you a middle seat.”

At least the gate was close to her current location, and she’d be flying into Everett, which was a quicker drive to Genesis Valley than the drive from Sea-Tac. She loped into a jog, pulling her wheeled carry-on behind her. “I only have a weekend bag and my agency-issued Glock.” She hadn’t brought her personal weapon.

“I’m not expecting this to be anything. I’ll give you forty-eight hours to see if it’s a case we want or not, and don’t forget, you called in a favor,” George said.

Her temples ached. “Even so, you don’t want me being the face of the FBI. I don’t relate well to students or prospects.” At least two people had actually left during her presentation.

“Get good with people,” George countered.

She reached the gate and flashed her ID to the impatient-looking gate agent. The woman kept tapping her heel. “I’m boarding. If you get any more information on the skulls, please send it to my tablet so I’m not going in blind.” Her stomach cramped with instinct as well as from her knowledge of statistical probabilities. Three different skulls found on the peak?

There was a murderer close to her hometown.